SHORT & SASSY
VOL II

BY
ERICA THOMAS

Short & Sassy II

ISBN 978-0-578-52700-0

DEDICATION

WRITE THE VISION AND MAKE IT PLAIN UPON TABLES THAT HE MAY RUN THAT READETH IT. FOR THE VISION IS YET FOR AN APPOINTED TIME, BUT AT THE END IT SHALL SPEAK AND NOT LIE, THOUGH IT TARRY, WAIT FOR IT, BECAUSE IT WILL SURELY COME, IT WILL NOT TARRY. HABAKKUK 2:2-3. WHEN I WROTE THE FIRST STORY, I HAD NO IDEA I WAS GOING TO BE WRITING A BOOK. THE STORIES BECAME SO VISUAL AS I WROTE THEM, AND PROPHETIC. I PRAYED AS I WROTE THEM, EVERY STORY I WROTE, I FELT THERE WAS A DEFINING MOMENT, AND EACH READER WOULD GET SOMETHING FROM IT. I THANK YOU, LORD, FOR THE GIFT YOU GAVE ME, TO WRITE THE VISION. I DEDICATE THIS BOOK TO YOU, AND I THANK YOU FOR SENDING THE KEY TO UNLOCK THIS TREASURE WITHIN ME. I LOVE YOU, JESUS.

TABLE OF CONTENTS

Short & Sassy II

ACKNOWLEDGEMENTS

SPECIAL THANKS TO MARGARET DIEHL. AGAIN, SHE HAS DONE A PERFECTED JOB WITH *SHORT & SASSY VOL II*. I COULDN'T HAVE DONE IT WITHOUT HER. THE EASY PART WAS WRITING. SHE MADE THE JOB EASIER FOR ME WITH HER EXPERTISE OF EDITING. TO MAC WILLIAMS, WHERE DO I BEGIN, HE WAS MY AUDIENCE FROM THE VERY BEGINNING. EVERY STORY HE READ HE GAVE INSIGHT WITH NO CORRECTION, LETTING ME KNOW THAT I STILL CONTINUED TO HAVE THE SAME PASSION WITH WRITING AS I HAD FROM THE DEBUT BOOK. HE ALSO SAID, WHEN THE PASSION TO WRITE ENDS, PUT DOWN THE PEN. FOR THE BOOK COVER, I'D LIKE TO THANK TONY CLARK. MANY HOURS WERE SPENT TO PUT IT TOGETHER, BUT IT WAS SO WORTH IT. LAST BUT NOT LEAST, TO MY LOVERBOY, IF IT HAD NOT BEEN FOR YOU, THERE WOULD NOT HAVE BEEN A VOL I OR II.

FOREWARD

Sassy, what's the best way to describe this word? Usually, when someone describes someone else as "sassy," they mean it as a compliment. It means something lively and uninhibited. Amusingly, if someone instead uses the root word Sass, as in "Don't sass me!" they are saying something negative about the person they are talking about or to. This second, in a litany of many more books to come from this Extraordinary Author, embodies both definitions. This book is lively and uninhibited because it captures characters in their strongest and weakest moments and at any given time, it turns into a happy, and memorable endings. Some character's Sass, you'll see when they turn the tables on their antagonist. Both perspectives will keep you spellbound and keep you turning the pages wanting more. You may even think that the characters are your life partners, your neighbor or the person sitting next to you in church or school. You will easily connect with them and grow to love them.   So, turn the page and be prepared to be sassed.

Mac J Williams.

"In the thundering rain you stare into my eyes." As the song plays, Greg was staring into Genevieve's eyes. He traced his fingers around her lips; she opened her mouth and licked it. He kissed her softly, so wet and delicious. As they were kissing, he reached to unbutton her pants.

She said, "Let's not rush this. I really want to take our time with this. I love you so much, but I don't think this is a good way to start out. Let's focus on us, and then everything else will follow."

"You're the boss, G. I do want what we have, to last. I will be patient and wait; as much as I've missed you, I can wait until that time."

"You're not mad at me, are you?"

"Why would I be that way with you?"

"Because I know you want to make love to me, and I don't, at least not now."

"Sex isn't everything, but you are everything to me. I know what it feels like making love to you; that's no mystery to me. Do I miss it? Yes. Will I wait on it? Absolutely. We will work on strengthening our relationship as a couple, making no mistakes this time."

"I thank you for your understanding. It means a lot."

"I'm doing something different this time because now I know where my heart is, and I totally respect the woman I'm with. Whatever decision you make, we will work it out together."

"We are going to be just fine; I can see that already. We're communicating, and that's important."

"I didn't think it was important. I'd shut down and

wouldn't care. I was selfish, but then I started to ache when you were gone. That's when I knew how important communication was, and I knew if we ever rekindled our love again, that would be the main thing I would do with you, no matter what it was."

"I like what I'm hearing; you always turned a deaf ear to me."

"Your voice is music to my ears now. I love the way it sounds, and I need to hear more of it." She smiled. "I would like for you to stay the night with me, we can talk and catch up. I'm just not ready for you to leave yet."

"I think that would be fine. We have an understanding, so I don't see why I wouldn't."

"I'm glad you are; I have a t-shirt you can sleep in."

"Oh, how cute. Let me text Crystal and let her know that I'll be staying over." She texted Crystal who promptly texted back that she was waiting on her to let her know what was going on. Crystal said that she was happy for them, and she would talk with her later. Genevieve slipped on the t-shirt, took off her jeans, and lay in bed; he got in bed a few minutes later.

"Can I hold you in my arms?"

"I'd like that." She scooted over and relaxed in his arms.

He kissed her on the forehead and said, "You feel a little warm; you're not running a fever, are you?"

"I've been in and out of the rain; I may be coming down with a cold."

"Well, if you get sick, I'll nurse you back to health."

"That's good to know. So, tell me, after I left, what were you up to?"

"I searched for you. When you sent me the postcard, I

was happy to hear from you, but when we met at the restaurant and your husband came in, I was mad and disappointed. I was mad at myself and disappointed because you got married, but I knew it was all my fault. When you left to go back to New York, I was upset, but I still couldn't get mad at you. I said if I ever had another chance with you, I wasn't letting you go. In my heart, I knew I would see you again. My heart wouldn't give me peace. I had palpitations; I was going through separation anxiety. I knew you had to return. My heart needed you."

"Wow, I never heard you talk like that before."

"I never been in love before. All words are not to be given to everyone. Some words are just for a certain person. I'm not good at expressing myself, but with you, the words flow without stuttering. They spill off my tongue like they're already written on it, and all I needed to do is open my mouth. It's just that simple, but only for you."

"You make me feel special."

"You are special. So, where did this poetic side of you come from? You've never said anything about it before."

"When I was in New York, I went to this club that had poetry night. It opened something in me. I loved what I was feeling. I felt like my body was a pen that was dipped in a river of poetry, and when I started writing, it just spilled onto paper, and it never stopped. I had an overflow of passion to say in a poetic form; It was so beautiful, baby, I had never seen anything like that before. The song 'Kiss of Life,' was the fire I needed. My poem was the wick, and the song was the fire. It lit up my soul, and it exposed everything I was feeling. It exposed love, fear, and anger. Everything I felt for you it exposed all those emotions. I knew I loved you.

"I was angry because of what you did to me, and I feared that if I loved you again, you would hurt me, but I had to forgive you, and when I did, all that I was feeling left me. The only thing that stayed was my love for you. It was a perfected love for you. What I feared went away. I knew then that I could love you again, and not be afraid."

"Be my river; let your love flow into me. Let it run deep, quench every dry area, fill me up. I longed for this feeling. I couldn't get it from anyone else. They didn't know what I needed. They gave me what I wanted, not what I needed."

"But I did give it to you then, what you have now."

"Yes, but I didn't know I needed it until you were gone."

"I see. Can I ask you something?"

"Ask away."

"How did you know I was going to be at the bar?"

"Crystal told me. She told me you moved back to town. I knew you were here. She told me to give you time. Although she knew how I felt about you, you needed time to heal. She texted me that night, said that you would be there. I got there early. Carlos told me where to sit. He made it real dark so you wouldn't see me. When I saw you, my heart leaped, and I wanted to grab and kiss you, but I had to respect whatever you were feeling. I had to give you time. I didn't know how you felt about me, but I knew what I felt for you. I had to respect your boundaries. I couldn't cross them until you gave me permission."

"Crystal said something to me that night that made a lot of sense. She said to forgive you, and when I did, I was free. She told me to give you another chance, not to rush it, but make sure I was making the right choice whichever one I chose. So now here we are; I'm lying in your arms, having a heart to heart   conversation on my pillow. We never had this before; you would always turn over and go to sleep."

"That was then, this is now, and now you have my undivided attention. I will love you forever. Go to sleep, beautiful, I love you."

"I love you too, baby." He turned out the lights, and she slept in his arms. In the morning, he awoke to her vomiting in the bathroom. He ran to her and asked if she was okay.

"I'm fine, must've been something I ate last night, plus I've been in that rain. I could be coming down with a cold." He felt her forehead.

"You're still a little warm. Go back to bed; I'll fix you some breakfast and a cup of tea."

"Thank you, I appreciate that. She climbed back in bed, turned on the TV, and went back to sleep. He made her something light. Since she had a queasy stomach, he made her oatmeal and chamomile tea. When he returned to the bedroom, he saw she was sleep. He didn't disturb her; she needed her rest. He ran some errands, picked her up some soup and juice, and when he got home, she was still in bed, but woke up when he walked in. "How long have I'd been asleep?"

"A couple of hours. I'm making you some soup. I cut you up some oranges; you need that Vitamin C. I'll take care of you, just rest." She stretched and snuggled under the covers. He brought her food in on a tray, sat it on her lap, then sat beside her. He watched as she ate until he heard the tea kettle whistle. "Be right back." He went to make tea. When he returned, she had finished the soup and eaten her oranges. "Here, baby, drink this tea. I put lemon, honey, and ginger in it. Drink it slow; it's hot."

Sip, sip. "Oh, this is hot." He laughed.

"I told you. Let it cool." He felt her forehead. "You're still warm. Take a shower and just relax; I got you, baby." She got in the shower; he laid her clothes on the hamper and then went in the kitchen to start making dinner. When she got out of the shower, she wiped the steam off the mirror and looked at the beauty it reflected. She also noticed she had lost a few pounds. She had been working out but not consistently. She put on the clothes he laid out for her and walked in the kitchen where he was cooking.

"What's cooking, good-looking?"

He laughed. "Right now, it's just boiled water. Not sure what I want to fix yet. How are you feeling?" He felt her forehead. It was normal. "Well, you're not warm; how do you feel?

"I feel better; your TLC worked." He kissed her forehead.

"I promise to always take care of you."

"You promise? Once you say that you can't take it back."

"I've said a lot of things before that I couldn't keep, but with you, with all my heart, Genevieve, I promise to take care of you."

"That's comforting, and I know you sincerely mean it."

"I do, I really do."

"If you don't mind, I would like to stay the night again."

"You can stay forever if you'd like."

"Choose your words wisely, and don't say it unless you mean it."

"I know what I feel, and I would never say anything to you that I didn't mean." She smiled. "Well, I need to go home and get a change of clothes."

"You can always fill that closet up again."

"I know, but for now, I like the closet my clothes are in."

"Ok, boss lady."

"I am, aren't I?" They laughed. He turned off the pot, she put on her jeans, and they rode over to her apartment. She quickly packed an overnight bag, and they headed back over to his house.

"So, since I didn't start dinner yet, what are you in the mood to eat?"

"Let's get some Chinese."

"Is your stomach up for that?"

"My stomach is fine. I'm starving."

"Ok, Chinese it is." On the way, he phoned in the order. When they got to the restaurant, he went inside to pick it up. She got a text from Carlos.

He said, "When you get a chance, give me a call. I want to talk to you about something." She called him.

"Hey, what's going on, Carlos?"

"Hey, G, how's your weekend thus far?"

"So far, so good. What's up?"

"How would you like to perform Friday and Saturday night?"

"Are you serious?"

"People have been coming in here talking about you. They love you; they want an encore performance."

"I was just doing it for fun."

"Well, I'm here to tell you, fun or not, they are looking for you to perform on next Friday. So, what do you say?"

"I say let's do this."

"I'll get the word out; maybe we will get standing room only."

"Sounds like a plan. I'll tell Greg about it."

"Cool, I'll talk with you later." After they hung up, Greg got back in the car with the food.

"Guess what?"

"What, babe?"

"I just got off the phone with Carlos. He wants me to perform at the bar, Friday and Saturday nights. I didn't think it would be that serious, but it is. What do you think about it?"

"What you did the other night was inviting. I believe you will do just fine. You are my star, and you are going to be one at the bar. I'm so happy for you. Everything is turning out wonderfully; we are off to a great start."

"I love it, baby. It can only get better from here." They drove to his house, ate dinner, and she went to bed early since she had to go to work the next day. He watched TV in the living room. He didn't want to disturb her. He dozed off on the couch. He was awakened by her throwing up in the bathroom again, and he ran to her.

"Are you okay, baby?"

"I don't think I can keep anything down."

"I'm going to ask because I'm concerned—are you pregnant?"

"No, I haven't slept with my ex-husband in months. If I was, I'd be showing by now."

"I just thought I'd ask."

"It may be the food. Whatever it is, I can't keep anything down."

"Maybe you should make an appointment to see your doctor."

"I will. I feel fine; I just can't keep food in me."

"Make an appointment, or I'll make one for you."

"Yes, dear, I'll make one."

"Come on, baby, let me rock you back to sleep, lie in my arms." She lay in his arms and was asleep in a matter of minutes. In the morning, she got up to get ready for work, feeling energized.

"That was the best sleep I had in a long time."

"How do you feel?"

"I feel good. I'm going to pick up something to eat on the way to work and I'll text you later."

"Okay, have a good day. Will you be coming back here tonight?"

"Yes, I'm enjoying your company and all of this TLC."

"And I enjoy giving it to you." She kissed him and off to work she went. Genevieve was a tech support operator; she liked to work on computers. She took a lot of calls and had them off in two minutes; you would think she was right there in their home or office, the way she got it done so quickly. Many calls made the day go by. She called Greg to see what he was up to.

"I'm making dinner. As soon as you get home, it will be ready."

"Oh, as soon as I get home, that sounds good."

"It's an open invitation."

"I know, I know. I should be there in thirty minutes."

"I'll be here waiting." Click. She got on the train. She liked to take the train into work, avoiding traffic. Her stop was only four blocks from Greg's house, and she didn't mind walking. As she came up the stairs from the train, Greg was waiting.

"Oh, this is a surprise!"

"You didn't think I was going to let you walk to the house by yourself?"

"Well, I didn't know what to think but thank you for meeting me here."

"It's my pleasure."

As they were walking, she asked, "What's for dinner?"

"I made a roast cabbage, mashed potatoes and gravy, something light."

"That's not light, that's Sunday's dinner."

"Well, it's dinner, baby. No matter what day it is, we are eating good." She smiled, and he grabbed her hand and held it the remainder of the walk home. "Are you ready to eat?"

"Yes, I'm ready."

"Sit down. I'll make your plate." He served her a small portion and watched her eat. He was concerned about her not keeping down any food. She ate all of it. After they ate, he cleaned up the kitchen, and then they watched TV. Afterward, he grabbed her foot and massaged it. "Did you enjoy dinner?"

"Yes, it was really good. You always did know how to cook."

"It's my specialty; I enjoy doing it."

"Well, you do it well. I'm full and sleepy." She started coughing.

"You okay?"

"Yes, I'm fine, just a dry throat, I guess." She started coughing again.

"I'll get you some water." He went and got her a bottle of water. She drank it, but it didn't stop the coughing.

"I think I'm getting a cold. I need your TLC again."

"It's coming right up." He ran her milk foam bath, lit a candle, and put a bath pillow for her head to rest on. She got in, and he washed her back. He said, "Relax. if you need anything, call me." She relaxed until she fell asleep. He came in the bathroom, and she was sleep, so he woke her up. "Baby, you've been asleep about twenty minutes. Wash up, so I can put you to bed." She finished up in the bathroom and climbed in bed. She coughed through the night. He fixed her some tea, and she was running a fever again. He let her have the bed and stretched out on the couch. In the morning, he checked on her. she was asleep and was still warm. An hour later she woke up.

"I'm not feeling good today. I'm calling out sick." Another hoarse cough came out of her.

"Make an appointment at the doctor's?"

"It's just a cold. I'll be alright." But she couldn't shake the cold all week, and she stayed in bed most of the day. Friday night came. She was to perform at the bar.

"Are you up to doing this tonight?"

"I'm fine; I can do this."

"Well, get ready, and we'll leave about 9:30 pm." She didn't move as fast as usual; she really looked like she wanted to go back to bed. Finally, after an hour, and a cup of strong tea, she was dressed and ready to go. She texted Crystal that she would be there at 9:30. Crystal texted back and said she would see her there.

"You okay, baby? You sure you don't want to go back home?"

"I'm fine, baby, I'm fine." Her voice still sounded a little rough, he thought. They pulled up to the bar. He got out first. Genevieve moved slowly. He helped her out of the car, worried, and they walked in.

Carlos greeted them and said, "G, what's wrong? You

don't look so good."

"I have a cold, but I'm fine." Crystal walked in a few minutes later. She hugged Greg and was getting ready to hug Genevieve, but then stopped, peering closely at her friend.

"What's wrong, G? You look ashy and tired."

"I have a cold. I've been trying to shake it all week, but nothing. Eventually, I'll get over it."

"Well, whatever it is, you get over it quickly. I don't like the way you look, so you get better, fast."

"Yes, Mother, I will do just that." She started coughing more.

"Do you feel like performing tonight?" Carlos said. "You don't have to. I can find someone else to entertain them."

"No, they are looking for me"— cough, cough— "to perform"— cough, cough—"so I'm going to"— cough, cough—"give them what they're asking for."

"Ok, you're the boss. Let me go and introduce you. Ladies and gentlemen; welcome to Open Mic after Dark, I'm Carlos, and I'm here to bring you your entertainer for tonight. Let's welcome Ms. G to the stage." Everyone clapped. She walked up to the stage and grabbed the mic.

"Good—" She staggered for a minute. "I'm sorry, I'm fighting a cold, so bear with me. Good evening—" She stopped again, staggered again, and then fell forward. A man from the audience jumped up and caught her before her body hit the floor. Greg, Carlos, and Crystal came running.

"Please call an ambulance! Baby, baby, wake up, what's wrong, wake up! She was hot and sweating. "Somebody, call an ambulance!"

"We called them, Greg, they are on their way," Crystal said.

"Baby, wake up, please."

Her eyes opened. Looking confused, she said, "What happened?"

"You passed out; we are taking you to the hospital." The ambulance came with a stretcher. The paramedics put her on the stretcher and loaded her in. Greg rode in the ambulance with her, and Crystal and Carlos drove her car. In the ambulance, Greg was wiping her down with a cold rag. Her temperature was 108.05. He was very worried, desperate to find out what was wrong with her. He kept wiping her forehead. She started coughing again and tried to talk. "No, don't talk," he whispered. "We're almost there."

They pulled up to the hospital. The paramedics rolled her into the emergency room and soon she was taken back. Crystal and Carlos followed minutes later. They waited outside the cubicle. Greg was in there with her. Nurses and doctors were trying to get her temperature down. They started running tests and put an oxygen mask on her. Greg started freaking out.

"Why does she need that?

"Sir are you her husband?" the nurse asked.

"No, I'm her significant other."

"Well, significant other, you're going to have to calm down so we can find out what's going on with her. She's in good hands. We're just running tests. Her breathing level is low, so she needs some oxygen. We will take good care of her."

"Please do, she means everything to me."

"I promise. Now go back into the waiting room for now; we will come get you with an update on her."

"I can't leave her."

"For now, you must so that we can tend to her." Greg

walked out to Crystal and Carlos.

"What's going on with G? Is she okay?" Crystal asked.

"They don't know anything yet. They told me to come out here and wait, so that's what I will do." Greg started crying. "I was freaking out when they put this oxygen mask on her face. That's when they told me to leave, because I wasn't her husband." Crystal consoled Greg. "I promised her I would always be there for her, and at that moment I couldn't. She has to be in someone else's care."

"She knows that you will take care of her. She came back in your life at the right time so that you can be there for her. You are her foundation, and you need to be strong for her."

"I'm going to be that to her. I owe her that." An hour later, the nurse came out, she said

"You can go see her now." They all got up and headed into the room. She still had the mask on her face, but she could talk.

"Baby!" Greg turned away to wipe his tears. "How are you feeling?"

"I'm feeling okay. They ran some tests; I'm just waiting for the results."

"Okay." He turned around and walked out in the hallway, crying. Crystal approached her bed.

"Hey, love." She was sniffling from crying. "How are you?"

"I'm good, I just want to go home. I don't like hospitals."

"As soon as they tell us what's going on, we can take you home." Just as she said that, the doctor came in the room.

He said, "Is everyone in this room family?"

Crystal said, "No, but we are as close to her as family can get."

He looked at Genevieve and said, "Is it okay if I share your results with them in the room?" Genevieve nodded.

"We ran multiple tests, everything suggested by the symptoms you were having. We ran them twice for accuracy. They all came up negative but one. Genevieve, you are HIV positive. You have the flu now. If you had waited, it would have turned into pneumonia. Your fever was high so your body couldn't contain the temperature, that's why you passed out. The good news is, we can contain this, so it does not become full-blown AIDS. You came at the right time. We are going to make your immune system strong, so that your T cells don't drop.

"I will give you prescriptions for medications. You can start on them right away. We need to get your temperature down, and so we are going to keep you overnight. I will give you and your family some privacy." The doctor left and closed the door behind him. The whole room started crying. Greg faced the wall; Carlos sat in the chair, crying; Crystal stood by her bed, teary-eyed. Crystal hugged her while she was crying. Greg walked out of the room, and Carlos followed him.

"I can't believe what I just heard," Greg said.

"I can't believe it either, but we have to be there for her," Carlos replied.

"I told her that I would always be there for her; this doesn't change anything."

"That's good to hear; she needs that right now."
Meanwhile, in the room, Crystal was talking with Genevieve.

"I was so careful, Crystal. I don't sleep around. I was so careful."

"You can be careful, and this could still happen. Have you slept with Greg yet?"

"No, I told him that we would wait. I didn't want to rush it with him. You think he'd want to still be with me after this?"

"That's a crazy question, G; that man loves you."

"I know he does, but all these thoughts are going through my head…I need him more now than ever before, for support, if nothing else."

"I believe he will do just what he said he would." Just then Greg walked in and said he needed this time with Genevieve. Crystal agreed and left.

He walked up to her bed, reached out for her hand. She put hers in his, and he said, "When someone says they love you you'll know if they really do when their love is tested in a situation. The minute I heard you were HIV positive, I thought it was a bad dream. I could've walked out and never come back, but my love for you said stay, don't leave her. I said if you ever come back to me, I was not letting you go. I still mean that. My closet is full of empty hangers; I need you to fill them up. Come live with me. I want to take care of you, Genevieve; I want to be your strength while you go through this process. What do you say?"

"In my deepest thoughts, Greg, I didn't think you were coming back in the room. When I saw you walk out, I thought that was the last time I would see you. I wouldn't have blamed you if you left. If I knew I had it, I would have told you. OMG, what if we made love?" She began to cry. "I would have been devastated. OMG, Greg."

"It's okay; it's okay. We found out in time. I'm here for you, don't feel guilty; I know you wouldn't intentionally harm me. I know you better than that. Will you come stay with me?"

"I'd have to break my lease."

"Carlos will move in your place and pay the rent. We already talked about that. He's tired of staying with his mama anyway. So, what do you say, will you stay with me?"

"Yes, Greg, I'll stay with you."

"You made my heart happy. Now get some rest. I will come and pick you up tomorrow." Crystal and Carlos came in and said goodnight to her. Greg kissed her, and they left for the evening. The next morning, he came to pick her up. She was ready to go. She met him at the door.

"I'm ready to go; I got my prescriptions; they got my temperature down; they started me on my meds, and I'm feeling so much better."

"You look good too."

"I rested well; they took good care of me. It made me think of you. I'm ready to go home and be with you."

"Let's go then, my love." When they got home, he told her to relax, whatever she needed, to let him know.

She said, "I want to talk."

"Okay, let's talk."

"I know I got this from my ex-husband; he's the only man I slept with. I was negative last year. I get checked every six months. I don' t mess around like that."

"You don't have to explain anything to me, but I know you don't, G, and that's why I love you, because you respect your body; you don't just give it to anyone. I'm sorry that this happened to you, I fault myself."

"Why?"

"Because if I had done right at the beginning with you, you wouldn't have ever moved to New York."

"We are not perfect. We make choices, and whichever ones we choose, we learn, and we live with them no matter what they are. I'm not even mad. I was in love; I trusted someone with my body. I made a vow to God when I married him, and I was true to him. He wasn't true to me or his vows as I was to mine."

"I'll be true to my vows."

"What are you saying?"

"I want to have and to hold, for better or for worse, for richer, for poorer, in sickness and in health, to love and cherish until death do us part. I want that with you."

"What are you saying—you want to marry me?"

"With all my heart I do. Nothing has changed in my heart for you. My heart still beats for you. Just because you have this disease, that doesn't stop me from feeling the way I do, and it never will. It's an unconditional love I have for you. Your condition does not mean I have to love you differently. Nothing has changed, and nothing ever will."

"You don't think this is too soon?"

"Too soon for what, to know what I want?"

"Yes, after all that has happened."

"You're still thinking about being HIV positive, but I'm Positive this is what I want. Now, what's your answer?"

"Yes, Greg, I'll marry you. You've proven your love to me. My answer to you is yes."

"See, was that so hard?"

"You made it easier for me."

"I did, didn't I, now let's get you better so you can get back on stage, and poetically tranquilize your audience."

"Oh, yeah, I forgot about that, I love you, Greg."

"I love you too, G..."

TBC IN VOL. III

"Would you like to do the honors?" Dr. Johnson said to Dale. He nodded, walked over and cut the umbilical cord off his son. The doctor handed the baby to the nurse to get him cleaned up. Dale watched the nurse take care of his sons as Camille watched from a distance. When the nurse was done, she handed Dale one son and carried the other to Camille. Dale looked into the eyes of the infant, and his heart melted.

Camille said, "Dale, they look just like you. I wanted them to. Their ears are dark, so they will have your complexion."

"Baby, they are our blessings, so they will be amazing boys. We will raise them in a home of love, teach them to be respectful, not spare the rod, teach them how to earn, and raise the boys to be men."

"Baby, they are just eight minutes old; they are not graduating from college."

"I know. I'm just laying out the plan that I have for them. It's best I speak it over them now. I will speak a blessing over my sons, and not a curse."

"I love the way you think. You always speak with power, and everything you speak comes to pass. Now that you are speaking over our babies, what are you going to name them?"

"Oh, you don't want to be a part of this?"

"No. I said if we had a boy you would name him. Now we have two, so you get to name them both."

"Well, I already had Kevin picked for our son. Now that I have two of them, I'll name our other son Kavon, so Kevin and Kavon will be their names."

"Okay, so how will we tell them apart? They are

identical twins."

"Good question. Look at their ears again. One is dark, the other one light, so for now, the dark-eared son will be Kevin and the light-eared one Kavon."

"Sounds like chocolate and caramel." They laughed.

"Are you going to breastfeed them?"

"Would you like me to?"

"I want our babies to bond with you. As much as I can I will watch you nurse them; I don't want to miss that moment. I think it's so precious to watch a baby be nursed by his mother." Camille sat up and adjusted her breast so she could feed Kevin. He didn't take to her breast right away, but after a while, he began to receive the flow of her milk. Dale smiled as he watched this moment. He fed Kavon a bottle as he watched his wife feed their son. After she finished feeding him, she lay him on her chest, kissed his full head of hair, and gently massaged his back. Dale sat in a rocking chair next to her and cradled Kavon in his arms, singing him a lullaby. Camille watched Dale bond with their son. This was a perfect moment for her. She had a handsome husband, with two amazing blessings; she couldn't ask for anything more. Kevin was asleep and so was Kavon. Dale took Kavon over to the bassinet and carefully lay him down; he then went to get Kevin and lay him down too.

Dale said to Camille, "Get some rest, baby, I know you are tired. I will be right here when you wake up." He kissed Camille on the forehead, and she drifted off to sleep. Dale was tired too. He grabbed a cover, sat in the rocking chair and rocked himself to sleep. An hour later Dale was awakened by a cry. Camille was still asleep. He walked over to see it was Kevin crying. He picked him up and checked his diaper. It was a little wet, so he changed him. He looked into Kevin's eyes for the first time and saw a mixture of colors. Camille had Kevin first, so the only eyes he had seen were Kavon's.

As he looked into Kevin's eyes, he could see a split color in the irises. The right one was brown, the left hazel; he had never seen anything like that before. Dale's eyes were light in color, so he could understand why Kevin's eyes were like that. He hoped nothing was wrong with his eyesight because of the mixed colors. The nurse came in as Dale was inquiring in his mind about his son's eyes.

He said, "I see different colors in my son's eyes, and I was wondering if anything is wrong with his sight because of it."

"I've noticed them too, but your son is perfectly fine. If it was something wrong, we would've notified you. Your wife birthed two healthy boys. Kevin was the blessing—I mean they both are, but Kevin was hidden. Kavon came out first. Kevin was breech. It was a little complicated, but he came out, so he is special." At that moment Camille woke up, and Dale showed her Kevin's eyes.

She said, "When Kevin opened his eyes, I saw a beam of light. He opened and then shut them. I thought it was a glare from the room light, but it was his eyes."

"I can't wait until he gets older to see what they will actually look like."

The nurse said, "The same way you see them now is how they will remain. Camille, you had a successful delivery, with no complications. You can go home in a day or so." Camille was happy to hear that; she wanted to be at home with her newborns.

And a day later they were home with their twin boys. Dale stayed home with his family for a month so that Camille could adjust and get some rest. They took turns with the twins through midnight feeding, changing, lullabies, anything they could do so that the boys could sleep at the same time.

Camille loved to see how Dale was with their boys. He loved them so. She was blessed to have a man in her life who could be a husband, father, and a good provider. She didn't have to worry about anything; when he told her to rest, she did. He hired a nanny before he went back to work. He interrogated her because he loved his family and wanted them to be safe. She understood; she had family too, so she knew how much he wanted to protect them.

On the first day back to work, Dale kissed his sons told them to be good for their mother, then went to kiss Camille goodbye and said to call him if she needed him.

Camille said, "We all will be fine. Go enjoy your day at work. I do love you, Dale."

"I will love you always, Camille." He left out for work. Camille had her hands full, but she had help so she didn't feel overwhelmed. The babies were in the room with her, so she didn't have to go too far. She could hear their whimpers if they made any, and when they slept, she did too. When Dale left, the babies were still asleep. She slept for fifteen minutes, then woke and remembered that she had to pump the breast milk for the boys. She quickly got the breast pump, and pumped her breasts to fill the container, then went downstairs to make the bottles, brought them upstairs, and put them in the little refrigerator in her walk-in closet.

She walked back to her bed and was getting ready to lie down. She heard one of the babies make a sound. She went to check on him. It was Kavon. He had his eyes closed and a smile on his face; she grabbed her phone to take a pic and sent it to Dale; she didn't want him to miss moments like that. He texted back, "Thanks for sharing, baby, how are they doing?" She texted, "They are sleeping still." He texted, "Get some rest. I love you."

Camille sat in the rocking chair between the bassinets and watched them as they slept. They both looked like Dale. She was a pretty woman, but her heart was set on them looking like her husband. Kevin opened his eyes first and stared at his mother. The sun was shining on his face, and she saw the brown and hazel split-vision eye color; it was the most beautiful thing she had ever seen. Kevin kept his eyes open as though he knew she was staring at them. He didn't make a sound; he just stared at her.

She picked him up, and he made a gurgling sound. She smiled. While Kavon was still asleep, she was able to breastfeed Kevin, with his eyes open. She loved the eyes that looked back at her. She fed him for about four minutes until he didn't want anymore. She changed his diaper, and the minute she lay him down, Kavon started to cry. Perfect timing. She picked him up, sat in the rocking chair, and nursed him too.

After she fed him, she changed him, put the bassinets on automatic cradle rock, and let the music play.

Throughout the day, the boys kept Camille on her toes, although the nanny was there. Camille wanted the boys all to herself so by the end of the day she was worn out. Dale was working late hours, so he didn't come home until later that night. He tiptoed into the room and saw Camille getting ready to pump the milk for the midnight feed.

Dale said, "Hey, baby, how was the first day without me?" He walked over and kissed her lips and peeked over to see his boys asleep.

"I tried to be superwoman, doing it all by myself, so I am worn out. How was your day at work?"

"Work was good; it was productive. Let me take a shower and then I'll tell you all about it." Dale went to take a shower. While he was doing that, Camille finishing pumping and fell asleep. Dale finished his shower. As he came back into the room, he saw her sound asleep, with the pump still going. He finished pumping the milk until the container was filled. He removed it and covered her up and lay her head down on the pillow; he put the milk in the refrigerator. Then he checked on his boys and cuddled up with his wife.

Later, in the midnight hour, Camille woke up, turned over and put her head on her husband's chest. He stroked her cheek, and she kissed his hand. She grabbed his wedding ring finger and toyed with the ring, twisting as she spoke. "Dale, can I ask you something?"

"Sure, baby, what is it?"

"We've been married for a little over a year. Being married to you has been awesome. I love you for who you are and how you have shown your love for me. But I never asked you how you knew my name that night I came into the diner."

"Oh, you're right, I never did tell you that. We got so caught up in each other, I totally forgot how I knew you. You came to me in a dream. I saw you in a dream, Camille. I used to fantasize about the type of woman I wanted, and one day, I had this dream. I saw your face. I heard your voice. I liked the way your voice sounded, and you had the prettiest smile. I thought if I dream of her, that means I'm going to meet her one day. The diner where I met you in was in the dream also. I couldn't let you go; I constantly had you on my mind. When I went to sleep, you'd appear in my dream. That went on for a week. Once the dreams stopped, I went to that diner for a year, hoping that you'd walk through the door. I waited patiently for you. Seeing you in my dreams was so real, I knew I was going to find you one day. That evening when you came through that door, I said there goes my baby."

"You went to that diner for a whole year? You know how many times I passed that diner going home? I never stopped in there, but that day I did. I just didn't feel like driving in that traffic."

"When I walked you to your car that night, I reached for your hand. I knew you were real; we conversed that night, but I needed to touch you. When I touched your hand, I touched a dream; my dream was now my reality. That's why marrying you wasn't a hard thing for me. When you became pregnant it was the happiest day of my life, losing our first baby was devastating. I couldn't see myself losing you; I thought what if something happened to you while you were delivering our sons? I don't know if I could bare that pain. I love you so much, Camille; you are my world. You gave me a beautiful marriage, you gave me strong healthy boys, you say that I'm the best thing that ever happened to you. Baby, you're the best thing that ever happened to me." Dale looked into Camille's eyes and passionately kissed her.

After the kiss, Camille bit her lip and closed her eyes as Dale caressed her forehead. She whispered, "I kept thinking you were a dream. I appreciate you so very much, Dale."

"I wanted to meet my wife in a different way. I knew what I wanted. I'd had girlfriends, and I met them by blind dating or walking by them at work or wherever they were, but when I made up in my mind that I wanted a wife, that's when I had that dream, and I saw you. You, Camille, were destined to be in my dreams. I had to see you in them because if I had met you any other way, it probably wouldn't have been as promising as it is now."

"I'm just thankful it happened the way it did."

"You are my dream girl." They laughed. The babies started crying.

"Well, it's feeding time," Camille said. Dale picked up Kevin, Camille took Kavon. They sat in bed and fed them. After the feeding, they changed them. Dale and Camille lay down with the babies on their chests.

Dale said, "I love this."

"Love what, baby?"

"This moment; I get to see you as a mother and a wife. You do it so well."

"I'm enjoying seeing you interacting with our boys; I know you will take good care of them."

"No, baby, we will take good care of them; We are a team, and we will take care of them together."

"Yes, baby, that part."

Weeks later, Dale and Camille took the twins for their six-week checkup. The doctor said, "What are you feeding these boys? They are solid."

"Just breast milk, nothing else," Camille said.

"How is your diet, Camille?"

"I juice a lot of green vegetables."

"Well, it surely shows in your boys; they are rock solid. You have healthy boys. It's good that you take care of yourself while you are breastfeeding them. Kevin has heterochromia eyes."

Dale said with curiosity and concern in his voice, "What do you mean by that?"

"No need to be alarmed. Heterochromia means one eye color is different from the other; it's not normal that I see eyes like that, but his sight is normal, his vision is good, no sign of any unusual activity in his eyes. He's just blessed to have eyes like that; they almost glow, like he has a fire in his eyes. Kavon's eyes are brown, Kevin's are unique."

"Dale's eyes are like that; they glow. They almost change colors when his mood changes."

"Are you calling my eyes mood ring eyes?" They all laughed.

"No, dear, I just know when you are in a certain mood the color of your eyes changes; they just get a little lighter or a little darker. I've noticed things like that about you, Dale."

"Well, now that we know where Kevin gets his genetics from. They are healthy boys; let me give them their shots, and you can take them home." Dale watched as the doctor gave the boys their shots. He didn't like that they cried, but he knew they needed them. When the doctor was done, they took the twins home. The boys were asleep by the time they got home. They put them in the nursery so Dale and Camille can have time alone.

Dale said, "When did you notice my eyes changed colors?"

"The first night I met you at the diner. When you approached me, they had a fiery glow in them, like you were excited. Something sparked in you when you sat down; they were a warm soft hazel color. I've never seen you upset, so I don't know what color they would change to, but I did notice that. When you make love to me and look into my eyes, they light up like fire. So, yes, Kevin is not the only one with unique eyes; you have them too."

"Can I ask you something, Camille?"

"Sure, baby, what is it?"

"You think it will be like this forever, meaning the way we are right now? We're happy; we work together; we support each other; we love each other. Do you think it will be like this always? It just feels so right, like nothing can go wrong."

"Let me ask you this before I answer your question. I know you can't answer a question with a question, but just hear what I have to say, and then I'll answer your question. When you go to work, you work hard because you love your job. You work hard because it provides for your family and offers stability. You want to keep that job because it's a good foundation. Look at your family like you look at your job; are we worth working hard for, like you do at your job?

"You all are worth it and so much more."

"We will work together, Dale, because that's what families do. It feels so right now because it is new to the both of us. We will have trials and tribulations, but we work together, not against one another. We have boys who need to be raised in a house of unity. A house divided cannot stand. Who's to say that you will always feel the way you do now, or if I will feel the same way? Will we make it to fifty years of marriage? Are we going to be here until death do us part? We don't know the future, Dale, but we know the now, so let's take it one day at a time and love each other forever. Marriage is a ministry, so let's keep ours covered in prayer."

"Your words of comfort soothed my soul, and you let me know that our foundation is solid, and no weapon formed against it shall prosper." Dale grabbed Camille's hand and they walked into the nursery. Kevin and Kavon both smiled in their sleep. Dale said, "They have your smile, Camille."

"Yes, they do, and we have you, Dale."

"Camille, we have each other, forever and always."

Splash, splash. "Miguel, I can't find my rubber ducky." Miguel turned around as he was brushing his teeth.

"Chelsea boo, what did you do with it?"

"I don't know."

"Did you check in all those bubbles in the tub? It could be hiding from you?" Michael checked in the bubbles for the missing duck. It was at the end of the tub.

"I found it, Chelsea. It swam away from you."

"Come here, ducky, you are on punishment. Sit right there and don't move." She sat the duck on the edge of the tub. Michael looked at her and laughed.

"Are you ready to get out?"

"Yes, I ready, Miguel." He wrapped her up in her hoodie towel and got her into her jammies. He was ready to read her bedtime story. Promptly at 8:00 pm was her bedtime. Nothing had changed from the time he had Chelsea when she was six months old. Now, at the age of two, he still had her on the same schedule. As he was about to read to her. there was a knock at the door. Michael wasn't expecting company; he looked through the peephole and saw who it was. He went into Chelsea's room, turned on the TV and told her to watch it until he came back. He cracked the room door and answered the front door.

"Hello, Michael," she said.

"Hello, Samaya, how can I help you?"

Chelsea came out of the room and said, "Miguel, I got to go potty." She came to the door, Michael picked her up, and Chelsea reached for her mother. Michael pulled her back, and Chelsea started crying. Miguel gave her to Samaya. Chelsea hugged her neck, and Samaya squeezed her tight.

"Come in," Michael said. "I don't appreciate you coming by unannounced. You are to call when it is time for visitation, and this is not the night for it. Why are you here, and where is your son?"

"He's with my sister. I came over because I miss my daughter."

"Samaya, we talked about this when I got custody of Chelsea. You gave me all rights, and I gave you visitation rights for certain days. This is not one of them."

"I know and I understand fully what's going on. I know that you will be a good father to her; she needs you. I just don't want another woman to be her mother."

"I'm not dating anyone, Samaya."

"Not now you're not but who's to say later on."

"That's none of your concern. You had a good thing, and you messed that up, not me. You saw Chelsea, right?"

"Yes, I saw her."

"It's best that you go now."

"But—"

"Please go, Samaya. I have to get her ready for bed."

"Stay! Papa, let her stay." Miguel looked at Chelsea; she had a look of sadness. He picked her up.

Chelsea looked at Miguel and asked, "Can she stay?" Michael didn't want to tell her no. He didn't want to say yes either, but he loved Chelsea and he didn't want to disappoint her.

"Yes, she can stay a little while, Chelsea boo."

"Yay." She jumped down, grabbed her mother's hand and said, "Let me show you my room, Mommy." She pulled Samaya into her room. Michael stood by the door and saw her interact with her daughter. Chelsea was happy and that's all that mattered to him. Samaya grabbed the book that Michael was going to read to her. She read to Chelsea until she fell asleep on Samaya's lap, then she gently moved off the bed and put the child's head on her pillow. She kissed her on the cheek, turned her lamp off, and closed the door.

Michael was sitting on the couch when he saw Samaya coming out of the room. He got up and walked her to the door.

Samaya said, "Thank you for letting me see her."

"Not a problem. Next time, please call. I have her on a schedule, please don't break it."

"I will." Michael opened the door and watched her get into her car; he closed the door when she drove off. He had noticed the mark under her eye; it was a fresh bruise, but he didn't question it. Maybe Samaya wanted him to, but that was none of his concern. Whom he was concerned about was sleep in her bed. He opened the door to check on Chelsea; she was asleep. He cracked the door and went to his room. He watched TV until he fell asleep.

An hour later, he felt a tap on his cheek. He opened his eyes; it was Chelsea.

He said, "Why are you not asleep in your bed?"

"I want my mommy."

"Chelsea it's late. It's time for bed." She started to cry.

"I want my mommy! I want my mommy!" Michael picked up her up and said Shh.

"I promise you, Chelsea, if you go to bed now, I will take you to go see her tomorrow."

Sniffling, she said, "You promise?"

"I promise you, Chelsea, with all my heart. I will take you to go see her."

Michael put Chelsea in his bed and watched her go to sleep. He couldn't sleep, though; he was up most of the night thinking about why Samaya had come and turned his whole world around. Chelsea had been fine until she showed up. The last five months, Samaya hadn't come by, and now out of nowhere she shows up and upsets Chelsea. He didn't like that.

Saturday morning, Chelsea was already up. She went in her room, picked out her clothes, put them on, and woke up Michael. He opened one eye and looked at her, then he sat up and laughed.

"What's funny?"

"You have your clothes on backward and your shoes on the wrong feet."

"So? I'm dressed."

"Yes, dressed funny."

"But I'm dressed."

"Yes, you are, Chelsea boo, let's have breakfast. I'll find you something to wear, and then we'll go see your mother."

"Yay, I'm going to see mommy, yay." Michael was glad to see her smile; it made his heart happy, and he would do anything just to see her that way. He found her something to wear, fed her her favorite cereal, washed her face, brushed her teeth, and they were out for their trip to visit Samaya. Michael had moved an hour away from her. His job had moved, and he needed to be closer to his employment; plus, he knew she wouldn't drive an hour every day to see them.

On the drive, Michael put on a movie Chelsea could see in the headrest; he put her headsets on so she could hear the movie while he listened to his music. She was enjoying the musical so much she was kicking the back of his chair. He just laughed. As long as she was happy, it didn't matter how hard she kicked it. There was no need to call Samaya to let her know they were on the way. If she showed up unexpectedly at his place, he could return the favor. They pulled up to the apartment complex. Michael got out and unfastened Chelsea from the car seat. She jumped out energized and ready to go.

Walking up the stairs, they heard arguing. When they reached the door, the door opened, and a man threw Samaya out of her apartment. Chelsea saw the man getting ready to hit her mother.

She kicked the man and said, "Leave my mother alone." The man was getting ready to hit Chelsea, and Michael punched him.

"That's one girl you will not hit." Michael and the man got into a fight; Samaya picked Chelsea up, ran downstairs and called the police. Michael twisted the man's arm and slammed him up against the wall. The police showed up shortly, asked questions about the incident, and then asked Samaya did she want to press charges. Samaya said no.

Michael looked crazy in the face; he picked Chelsea up, went to the car, fastened her in, put on her headphones, and headed back home. Thirty minutes into the drive home, his phone rang; it was Samaya. He ignored it. She called again; he almost answered it. The Bluetooth came on in the car, and he hit the end button. She kept calling until he answered. "What do you want. Samaya?

"I killed him!"

"You did what?"

"I killed him. They are getting ready to take me to jail. Please go and get my son." Michael was already thirty minutes into the drive back home; he quickly turned around and headed back to the apartment. He sped down the street; there were several police cars and ambulances outside when he pulled up. His old neighbor, Ms. Eloise, was standing outside,

He said, "What's going on here?"

"I was in my kitchen, and I heard a scream and then a gunshot. I called the police, and now here we are waiting to see what happened."

"Can you take Chelsea in your house and watch her until I find out what's going on?"

"It's a crime scene. It's taped off. I don't think you can go up."

"Well, I'll stand out here and wait till I can find out

something. Chelsea, go with Ms. Eloise while Daddy waits for your mommy to come down."

"Okay, Papa."

"Come on, Ms. Chelsea, I have some cookies and milk for you."

"Yummy," Chelsea said. Michael stood outside and watched the police go in and out of the apartment. Meanwhile, the police were questioning Samaya. Samaya was sitting on the couch with a bloody nose, talking to the police.

She said, "It was self-defense. He came at me and hit me, slammed me up against the wall. You can see the dent in the wall. I ran in the room and tried to lock the door. He kicked in the door. I grabbed my gun and shot him. I couldn't take the abuse anymore; I feared for my life."

The officer said, "Are there any other bruises on you, besides your eye and nose?"

"There are some on my back." The officer asked the lady officer to take Samaya to the bedroom and take pictures of her back. An officer came downstairs and asked if there were any witnesses. Did anyone hear anything?

The officer saw Michael and asked, "Do you know the young lady?"

"Yes, I know her."

"Are you related to her?"

"No, we use to date a while ago."

"She has a lot of bruises on her. Have you ever noticed her being abused before?"

"I've noticed a black eye when I would come and pick up her daughter."

"Oh, she has a child?"

"She has children."

"We didn't see them in the apartment. Would you happen to know where they are?"

"I have custody of her daughter, and her sister has her son."

"Are you the child's biological father?"

"No, but I have custody papers. If you want to ask any other questions concerning my daughter, you can ask Samaya. I just came to make sure she was fine and see whether she is going to jail." While the officer was asking questions, the coroner came with a black body bag and stretcher. Michael couldn't believe someone was killed in the apartment he used to live in. This was a twilight zone; he just couldn't believe it. Fifteen minutes later, they brought the body down. Michael was glad Chelsea wasn't around to see this.

Meanwhile, Samaya and the lady officer came out of the room. The officer handed the other officer pictures of her back, face and arms. The officer looked at the pictures and looked at Samaya.

He said, "For now, we will not arrest you, but I would like for you to come down to the station so we can ask more questions in detail. Most likely you will not be charged for this. He had a restraining order against him as well as a trespassing warrant. We won't handcuff you. If you are ready, we can head on out." Samaya grabbed her jacket. Michael saw Samaya coming down.

He saw how bruised she was, and he asked the officer, "Are you arresting her?"

"No, we are just taking her down for questioning." He waited until they put her in the car and drove off. He didn't want Chelsea to see her mother getting into the police car. He knocked on Ms. Eloise's door.

She opened it and invited him in. Chelsea was sitting at the table drinking milk and eating cookies.

Michael said to Ms. Eloise, "I need you to watch Chelsea for a little while longer. Something tragic has happened, and I need to go down to the police station."

"Of course, of course, not a problem. Do you know how long it's going to be?"

"No, I don't, but I will keep you informed."

"Chelsea will be just fine. If she needs to stay over, I have jammies for her from the last time I watched her."

"I appreciate it so much, Ms. Eloise. I will pay you for watching her."

"You keep your money. I watched her many times before. She will be fine; you go and take care of business." Chelsea got down from the table and ran to Michael.

"Papa Miguel, we go home now?"

"I have to take care of some business, Chelsea boo, but I promise when I'm done, I'm coming back and taking you home."

"Pinkie promise me." She put out her pinkie and he wrapped his pinkie around hers.

"I pinkie promise you, Chelsea." She wrapped her arms around his neck, and he kissed her on the cheek, said goodbye and left. On the ride down to the station, he called Charles, his lawyer, gave details about what was going on and asked if he was available to represent her.

"Sure, not a problem. I owe you a favor anyway," Charles said.

"That's good to know. I'm on my way downtown. I will see you then."

"I'm leaving now. I will be there in twenty minutes," Charles said.

"See you then." Michael hung up the phone with Charles. He found a parking spot and headed into the station. Since Samaya wasn't being arrested, they didn't have her in the interrogation room. She was sitting at a desk. She hadn't answered any questions yet. When she saw Michael walk in, she smiled.

Michael walked up to her and asked, "How are you doing?"

"I don't know. When I woke up this morning this was not on my agenda, so I'm in a daze. Where's Chelsea?"

"She's with Ms. Eloise."

"Oh, she's in good hands. I called my sister. She is going to keep my son tonight. If they let me go tonight, I'll go by and pick him up."

"What happened, Samaya, what led up to this?" Just then Charles walked in. Michael met him and shook his hand and brought him over to Samaya. Michael introduced Charles to Samaya.

Charles asked, "Have they questioned you yet?"

"They asked me questions at my apartment, but not here yet."

"Are they charging you for the murder?"

"No, they are not; at least, that's what they said at my apartment."

"Was it self-defense?"

"Yes. It wasn't premeditated. I feared for my life."

"Then they can't charge you."

Just then the questioning officer sat down and said, "There were records of calls that were placed from your address for domestic violence, and there was a restraining and trespass warrant against him, so for now, we will not charge you for this. I see it as self-defense. You are free to go right now, but we will be in touch." Samaya thanked the officer and walked out of the station. They walked to Michael's car and got in. She still had the dazed look on her face.

Michael said to Charles, "We'll keep in touch. I will let you know if anything changes." Charles agreed, they shook hands, and he went on his way. Michael didn't know what to say to Samaya, so the drive was quiet. Then he said, "You can't stay in that apartment; it's still a crime scene. We'll go by a store and pick you up some clothes, and you can stay with us tonight."

"You sure it's okay?"

"Yes, we have Room for one more. Chelsea would be happy to have you over." Samaya smiled. They went by a local store. She picked up some outfits and toiletries, Michael paid for her items, then they headed to the complex to pick up Chelsea. When he picked her up, he thanked Eloise for keeping her. Chelsea had already had a bath and had her jammies on. He picked her up and carried her to the car. When he opened the door, and Chelsea saw her mother, Chelsea screamed.

"Mommy!"

"Hello, Chelsea, how are you?"

"Fine, Mommy."

Michael said, "Mommy is going to stay the night with us. Would you like that?"

"Yes, Papa Miguel, I would."

He strapped her down in her seat and said, "Wonderful. Well, then let's go home." Michael put on her headphones, turned on her movie, and they headed home. Samaya stared out the window. Michael didn't converse with her; he didn't want to bother her until she wanted to talk. Michael looked in his rear-view mirror. Chelsea was sound asleep. It was 7:45 pm so it was almost her bedtime. She had her bath already, so she was on schedule. They pulled up in his driveway, he picked Chelsea up and carried her into the house, took her into her room and put her to bed. He cracked the door.

Samaya asked, "Can I please take a shower?"

"Sure, let me grab you a towel and washcloth." He went in the closet, grabbed the items and handed them to her. She went into the bathroom and took her shower. Michael put on some water for some chamomile tea, something to soothe Samaya so she could sleep tonight. She finished her ten-minute shower, came into the kitchen and sat on the bar stool. Michael handed her a cup of tea.

Samaya said, "Can I talk to you?"

"Sure, you can."

"So many things to say about today, I don't know where to start."

"Wherever you feel comfortable, that's where you start."

"I've known Marcus longer than I've known you."

"Who is Marcus?"

"The man I shot in the apartment today."

"I thought his name was Mark?"

"Chelsea couldn't say Marcus, so she called him Marks or Mark."

"Continue."

"I dated him years ago, before Chelsea was born. He wasn't as abusive as he was now, but I tolerated what he did do."

"Samaya, why would you date someone like that?"

"Because that's what I thought I deserved. Michael, you were too good for me. I didn't deserve you, and that's why I went back to him. You were good to me, and I didn't think I deserved that."

"Samaya, you're so beautiful, why wouldn't you think you deserved better?"

"Beauty has nothing to do with self-esteem. Just because

I'm beautiful doesn't mean I'm secure. How you see me is not how I see myself. I have shortcomings. I may not like the way I look or other things about myself. I am a beauty in a body filled with insecurity."

"No matter how I showed you love, how concerned I was for Chelsea, you still thought you deserved less than what I was showing you?"

"Correct."

"Continue."

"When we started dating, everything was fine for the first six months. Then when I wanted to hang out with my friends, he thought I was out cheating because I didn't answer my phone. The night I came home from hanging, I went inside the house. It was pitch black. Before I could turn on the lights, I felt this slap across my face, and I fell on the floor. The only lights I saw were stars. He turned on the light, picked me up off the floor, and called me all names but the one my mother gave me. I told him I was out with my friends, and he said I was lying because I didn't answer my phone. I told him my phone was on silent, and he slapped me again. He said, 'When I call, you answer. I don't care who's around, you answer when I call.' I stopped hanging out with them after that.

"As long as I was around him, he was fine with that. I was isolated and alone, but he was happy and content. Although he saw my misery, it was pleasurable to him." Michael couldn't believe what he was hearing. He just looked at Samaya with a look of disbelief on his face.

He said, "How long were you dating him before you met me?"

"Two years."

"Was it the last two years?"

"Yes."

"Was he the only one you were dating?"

"Yes."

"I really don't want to ask this question."

"Yes, he is Chelsea's father."

Michael sighed. "Did he know he was the father?"

"No."

"Were you going to tell him?"

"No."

"Can I ask why?"

"Before I got pregnant, I was planning on leaving him. I had lost my job, my car broke down, and I didn't have finances to move anywhere, so I was in limbo for a few months. I was in a deep depression because I wanted to leave; I had had enough. One night he fixed me dinner and apologized about his abusive ways. He said he wouldn't do it again. I accepted that, and we moved on from there. Later that night, we were in bed, and he wanted to make love to me. I wasn't in the mood, and I told him that. I said goodnight to him, rolled over and was going to go to sleep. Suddenly I felt this punch in my back that almost took my breath away. He rolled me on my back and told me that when he asks for it, I'm to give it to him. I lay there while he aggressively had sex with me. After he was finished, he apologized over and again. I just lay there with this throbbing pain in my back, numb from what he just did. I turned over and went to sleep. He never bothered me after that."

Michael said, "I can't believe what I'm hearing. When I saw you for the first time you didn't look like you'd been through something like that."

"I have scars. You just don't see them."

"But I've seen your body before, I didn't see any."

"My scars are internal."

"This is a lot to take in; I am in disbelief. I don't know if I can take any more of this tonight."

"I need to finish because if I don't, I will be up all night tossing and turning. I need to release this."

"Let me put on a pot of coffee and check on Chelsea." Michael put the coffee maker on and then peeped in the room to check on Chelsea. She was still asleep. He closed the door and went back into the kitchen and sat at the counter. "Are you hungry?"

"No, I'll just have a cup of coffee." The coffee was almost finished brewing.

Michael said, "You want me to fix your cup?"

"No, I'll fix it." Samaya got up to fix her coffee. She walked past Michael and just broke down, started crying, and fell on the floor. Michael got on the floor with her and held her in his arms. He turned his head; he didn't want her to see his tears. He held her in his arms and let her release all the pain she had stored up. He held her like that for an hour. She was drained, tired, traumatized. She cried herself to sleep, and he picked her up and put her in his bed, covered her up, then grabbed a pillow and blanket and made up his sleeping quarters on the couch.

Michael couldn't sleep. He made a cup of coffee and sat at the counter. He was trying to wrap his head around what Samaya shared with him. It blew his mind. He was glad he had custody of Chelsea; it would've crushed him if something happened to her. She was his heart, and he was her protector. A tear dropped in his coffee. He put his face in his hands and cried for about a minute, then he felt a yanking on his shirt. It was Chelsea.

She said, "Papa, why are you crying?" Michael picked Chelsea up and hugged her and cried some more.

He said, "I love you, Chelsea boo, so much."

"I love you too, Papa."

"Why are you not in your bed?"

"I have to potty."

"Well, let's go then."

"Where's Mommy, Papa?"

"She's asleep. Let's not bother her right now."

"Yes, Papa." Chelsea used the potty, and then Michael took her back to bed and stayed in the room until she fell back to sleep. He cracked the door and lay on the couch. He slept for about two hours, then was disturbed by the toilet flushing. He woke up and thought it was Chelsea, but it was Samaya. She came out of the bathroom and walked past Michael.

He said, "There's a bathroom in my room. Why didn't you use that one?"

"I wanted to check on Chelsea. That's why I came here that night unexpectedly. I wanted to see her because I knew what I was going to be doing the next day."

"What do you mean? You knew what?" Samaya walked back into Michael's room and got back in bed.

He walked into his room and sat on the bed and said, "What were you going to do the next day?"

Samaya sat up in the bed, closed her eyes and took a deep breath and said, "I was meditating about that day for some time."

"Meditating on what?"

"His death."

"You mean premeditated."

"Yes."

"You mean you planned to kill him?"

"See, I'm trying to make sense of it. Did I plan it, or was it out of self-defense?"

"What led up to that day?"

"When I found out I was pregnant with Chelsea, I was devastated. I had gone to the doctor's because I missed my cycle. I was eight going on nine weeks. I didn't want anything from Marcus, not even a baby, but I was protective of what I was carrying. If he hurt me, he would hurt the baby. I knew I was going to keep her because of how I was protecting her in my womb. I had to keep her. I had no money for an abortion; I had no money at all. One day we were sitting down having a conversation, and my phone rang. I glanced over at my phone, and then I looked at him, and he punched me in my face. He got up and pulled me across the table and started choking me. He said your phone is more important than me, is it, is it? I said no, no it's not. He finally took his hand off my neck. I was coughing so hard I started vomiting.

"I ran in the bathroom and locked the door. He came knocking on the door, saying he was sorry, but I wouldn't unlock the door. I stayed in there for about a half hour. I heard the front door close. I opened the bathroom door and crept out to see if he was out there; he wasn't, so I packed a duffle bag of clothes and left. I went over to my girlfriend's house and stayed the night. In the morning she took me to a shelter in a different city where she had connections. It was a shelter for abused women, and because I was pregnant, they took me right in.

"The police were called when I got to the shelter. They took pictures of my neck so they would have probable cause to arrest him. While he was in custody, I went back to the house with the police to gather the rest of my belongings. Although he was in jail, I still didn't feel safe, so I changed my name. I went by my middle name, which is Samaya, and changed my last name to my father's last name."

"So, what's your first name?"

"Frances."

"I like Samaya better."

"Thank you."

"You're welcome. Please continue."

"So, I stayed at the shelter through my pregnancy. They had a prenatal clinic next door, so we didn't have to travel far for care. While I was in my trimesters, I was taking some training in the medical field. It was a one-year course. I started in my third month. I was determined to be about something. I knew I was going to raise my daughter by myself and I was in no shape to be in a relationship. I didn't want to be. I went on the computer diligently every day taking the course. They were all free, so I didn't have to worry about loans. I had six months of training, and then Chelsea was born.

"After she was born, I had six months to find somewhere to stay. They only allow you a year and some months to stay, to help you get on your feet. I didn't have a car, so it was kind of hard trying to find somewhere to stay and someone to watch Chelsea while I was still trying to finish my course. My girlfriend called me up one day and told me that a co-worker had room for me until I could get on my feet, and that's when I met you."

"Very interesting. I was told that you had been evicted and were staying at a shelter, when it was vice versa."

"She said it was just a general conversation. She may have just said it wrong."

"No worries. I'm listening."

"While we were staying with you, you were so kind. I wasn't used to someone treating me the way you did. I wasn't used to someone beating on me either, but you were too good for me, and I didn't think I deserved it. Marcus was released from jail a few months before Chelsea turned a year old. I ran into him coming home from work one day. I was catching the train and he was on it. I was scared stiff. He said hello and kept walking.

"I did some research. He was on probation, so that was my protection. I saw him a few more times. He looked pitiful, and I felt sorry for him. He looked like a bum. He was in jail for two years; he lost the apartment and everything in it. I knew it was my fault. When he saw me again, he apologized about what he did, said he deserved to go to jail and that being in there made him think about what he had done. He was sorry, and again, me being so forgiving, I accepted his apology. We started talking quite frequently. He told me his experience in jail, how he appreciated his freedom, and that he never wanted to go back there. Since you and I weren't dating yet, I thought it was okay for me to rekindle that relationship. I took Chelsea over to his sister's house a couple of times. She has a photogenic memory; she doesn't forget anything.

"He asked me who Chelsea was. I told him she was my sister's daughter. I didn't want him to know I had a child; he would have known it was his. Until I knew he was going to stay true to his word, she was my sister's child, not his. I started hanging out with him more, gaining his trust, and everything was good. We became intimate again; it was okay, and then we happened."

"What about us?"

"You and I started dating and then I had to choose who I wanted to be with. I chose the both of you. Please forgive me, Michael."

"You know you could have jeopardized my health. You know the type of diseases that are out there; what were you thinking?"

"I wasn't. I'm sorry. I'm so, so sorry."

"I don't sleep sloppy, Samaya. I thought we had an understanding."

"I'm sorry, Michael."

"When I found out you were sleeping with someone else, I got tested quickly, and six months after that too. I don't play with my health, Samaya. You might not care about yours, but I care about mine." Michael got up and left the room. Samaya got dressed, headed for the door and opened it.

Michael ran to the door and said, "Where do you think you're going?"

"I don't belong here. I made a mess of everything."

"Where are you going to go?"

"Back to the apartment. They have finished the investigation. I can go home and clean up."

"Go back to bed, I didn't mean to raise my voice at you; I was a little upset. I'm sorry; please go back to bed. Chelsea will be upset if she doesn't see you in the morning, and there have been enough tears in this house for one night. She's the last person I want to see crying, so go back to bed, Samaya."

"I'm not tired."

"Then watch TV with me."

"Not in the mood for that either. I just want some coffee."

"Then let's go get some." They proceeded to the kitchen. Michael made a fresh pot. Samaya looked in the fridge and pulled out eggs, cheese, sausage, tomatoes, green peppers. She set them on the counter and looked for a skillet and bowl.

"I'm in the mood for an omelet you want one?"

"Sure, it's almost four in the morning, we could have an early breakfast."

While she was cutting up the ingredients for the omelet, she said, "I was going to leave you."

"When?"

"When Marcus and I were dating."

"Why didn't you?"

"You left me before I could. That's the night you gave me the pregnancy test, so you pretty much made it easy for me."

"You were going to leave me, Samaya." Sigh.

"I didn't do right by you, Michael. You deserved better than me. I wasn't honest with you, and I should have been."

"I've forgiven you for that. Can we move on from there?"

"I told him I was pregnant. That's when you saw that text, 'I hope the baby is mine.'"

"By the way, what's your son's name?"

"His name is Christopher."

"After you moved out, Marcus moved in. Everything was okay because he was still on probation, but after the baby was born and he was off probation, the beating started again. He had this repressed anger in him because I had been dating you. When he saw you at the mall, you told him that you were Chelsea's father and you were also my man. He held that anger in until after I had the baby. I didn't want Chelsea to see me get hurt; that's why I gave you custody of her. I don't think I'm a good mother, but you are a good father to her, and she needed you. I knew you would keep her out of harms' way, I knew she would be in good hands

"Chelsea is my heart. I love that little girl. I love my son too, don't get me wrong, but it's something about her; she has me wrapped around her finger. "Did she ever see him hit you?"

"No, she just heard the noises." Michael sighed and looked away.

Samaya said, "What's wrong?""

Still with his head turned, he said in a broken voice, "Nothing. Continue."

She turned around, started making the omelets and said, "I filed for a restraining order against Marcus. Something had to happen. I got tired of the abuse and covering up the marks were getting harder to do. We hadn't been to court yet; I had a temporary one served, and it went to his sister's house. They didn't know he was staying with me. I set it up like that."

"Set it up like what?"

"When he got released from jail, I had the papers served at her house. That was his last known address, and she was out of town, so they couldn't serve him papers. He stayed at my house that night. The next day when you came over, we got into an argument about my son. He wanted to see him, and I told him no because we needed to talk. He got mad because I told him no, and he started beating on me. I couldn't run to the bedroom where the gun was, so I ran outside. That's when I ran out of the apartment and ran into the two of you."

"Where did you get the gun?"

"I bought it a year ago and had it in a safe in my car. I didn't want it in the house. I didn't want him to know I had one."

"How did it get in the house?"

"After I left your house, I took it inside because no children were in the apartment."

"I'm going to ask you this question, and I want you to be honest with me."

"Okay."

"Did you provoke him to hit you?"

"No, I didn't. I was tired of the abuse."

"Then it wasn't premeditated, Samaya, it was self-defense. Although you had the gun in your possession, it was self-defense."

"I think it was premeditated."

"Why do you think that?"

"I could've had the papers served at the apartment, but I didn't. I didn't want him to know he had papers served, that's why I sent them to his sisters'. She lives in a different county. I think I wanted him to come to the apartment. I knew he was going to be abusive; I knew what I was going to do if he was. We both had a plan."

"But you didn't provoke him."

"No, I didn't, but I knew what I would do if he touched me."

"Samaya, that's self-defense."

"I guess. So, after the altercation that you had with him, and the police were called, I knew then this was it. I'd had enough. When the police left, he closed the door, I went to go in the bedroom and before I could get in the room, he grabbed me by my hair and slammed me up against the wall. I spit in his face, he punched me in mine. I broke loose from him and ran in the bedroom., I tried to lock the door, but he was able to get in before I could lock it. I reached under my pillow, and then let the rounds loose from the chamber. He looked like the matrix falling backward. I only shot two rounds; if it was more than that, they would have known. It would have been a crime of passion. I shot in self-defense, although it may have been premeditated."

"Samaya, this is crazy. I can't believe you put yourself through that. You can't go back to that apartment. Stay here with us; I have room for one more."

"And what about my son?

"We have room for him too. He can stay in the room with Chelsea."

"You've come to my rescue again."

"The way I feel, I think I always will."

"That's comforting." Samaya fixed the omelets. They sat down and ate. It was almost six in the morning by the time they finished eating.

Michael said, "With all the evidence against him, I don't think you'll be arrested for shooting him. If they were going to, you'd be there right now instead of here."

"I know. I'm just glad it's over."

"Never, ever put yourself in a situation like that. This could have been the other way around; you could've been the one toe-tagged in the morgue."

"Yes, I know. I'm getting sleepy. I'll clean up the kitchen later."

"You go get some rest. I got the kitchen."

"Thank you, Michael, for everything."

"No worries, Samaya, no worries." She headed back to bed.

Michael cleaned up the kitchen and then relaxed on the couch. Hours later, there was a knock on the door. Michael got up to answer it; it was the police. "Can I help you?"

"We are looking for Frances Jones."

"Give me one second." Michael closed the door and went to wake Samaya up.

He said, "The police are at the door asking for you."

"What do they want?"

"I don't know. You need to find out." They knocked on the door again. This time it woke up Chelsea; she came out of the room rubbing her eyes.

Michael and Samaya went to the door.

Samaya opened it and said, "I'm Michelle Jones. Can I help you?"

"We have a warrant for your arrest."

Chelsea ran to Samaya crying, "Mommy, mommy!"

"Please don't handcuff me in front of my daughter."

They agreed.

Samaya turned and hugged Chelsea. She said, "I love you, then looked at Michael. You have Room for One More?"

"Yes."

"Please go and get my son."

TBC IN VOL. III

I AM YOUR CELLO

Silence speaks volumes, and that's all Gabriella heard. It broke her heart, cut it in two. Because his love language was different from hers—he didn't have one at all—he didn't notice hers. She leaped into a heart that wasn't ready for her; she didn't ask if he wanted to be loved by her. She didn't case the heart out to see if it was ready to receive what she had to offer. She just leaped into it.

What kind of fool had she'd become, she thought, sitting on the beach, waves would come pay her a visit, wash away the sand from her feet; she constantly dug in the sand, thinking about the mistakes she had made. After the last wave came in, washing the sand off, she got up and walked back to her car, turned on something easy to listen to and drove home.

She had purposely left her phone on the beach; the waves came and took possession of it. Leaving the phone was the best thing she could do. Although he would call, it did nothing for her; she would open up to him, and he wouldn't understand what she was saying. Did he purposely do that to her? Did he want to see her suffer like that? So many things went through her mind, which made the pain even worse. Because he didn't respond to her, she felt like he was a dead end. There was nowhere else to go with him. No matter how she tried to find a way, she couldn't get through to him.

She was burnt out. To revive herself, she slowly, day by day, released him, released her thoughts of him, released her pain, released the lies he told her that she believed. She released everything she held onto of him. Like a bunch of balloons, she released it all into the atmosphere. She wasn't running after it, wasn't jumping to grab it; she let it go and didn't turn back. Relaxing in a hot bubble bath, lights off and candles lit, she listened to her instrumental music. She loved to hear the cello play. She was a cellist herself; she recorded herself playing, and she listened to the sound of her heart on the instrument. The cello was soothing to her; every pitch of sound was medicine to her soul. She'd orchestrate her own music; she was gifted that way. She didn't go to school to learn how to play; what she felt in her soul, she played on the cello. She just picked it up one day. Her heart was the sheet of music; her soul played the cello. Every pain she felt made the pitch high and rapid; she was ranting and raving, desperately crying out how she felt.

She always played with her eyes closed. That was her way of concentrating on what she was playing. All her thoughts were in the dark; it was like a blank canvas. She could write everything on it. When she was almost finished, she would lean her face against the strings and open her eyes; tears would run down them. She had just released her pain on the strings. She'd wipe the strings down because she didn't want them to rust, and she'd take rosin oil and wipe the bow, then carefully put the cello and bow away in the case and slide it under her bed.

After soaking for a while, she got out, slipped into something comfortable, and headed out on the town to meet up with some friends for dinner. She didn't worry about them calling her on her cell; the plans were already made. If there were any changes, they knew how to get in touch with her. She arrived right on time, as did her friends; they were waiting for her at the reserved table. She walked over. "Hey, ladies," Gabriella said.

"Hey, Gabby, what's going on?" Janay said. Janay was her childhood friend; they had been best friends since first grade. Gabriella gave her a hug.

"Hello," Gabriella said softly to Rita and Miranda.

Janay got up, grabbed Gabriella by the hand, and said, "Excuse me for a minute, ladies, I need to talk with Gabby." She took her in the ladies' room and said, "Spill it."

"Spill what?"

"What's bothering you? I've known you all my life and when you whisper, something is wrong, so spill it. Was it a pain on the strings moment tonight?"

"Yes, it was."

"Close your eyes, Gabby."

"Do we have to do that here?"

"This is the best time to release it. Whatever pain you released on the strings, release it to me now. Close your eyes, Gabby, place your hand on your heart, inhale, and release your pain."

"No matter what I say or do, he never listens to me. I feel like I'm talking to a wall. He talks around what I say. It's like I'm talking a different language. It's my love language, and he doesn't understand it. Why did he even come into my life? Why did he string me along, why did he play with my heart, why did he even bother to say hello to me, why did he make love to me, why did he tell me he loved me, why did he say I am his forever, why did I believe his lies, why didn't I listen to what he said, why did I, why did I, why did I?"

Janay hugged Gabriella and whispered in her ear, "What did he say?"

"One day we were just having a general conversation, and he said he and co-workers would look at different women that worked for the company. They would go into a room, lock the door and pull up pictures on the computer. I didn't pay it any attention, but he said my name would come up all the time. They would look at my picture.

"I only did head shots, never full body pictures. They were hoping they would find one. I felt if they were all looking at my picture, not just him, married and single men. I felt like they were trying to see who would date me. I know it sounds childish, but that's what I felt afterward, after we went out and we made love. He was different; the phone calls and conversation weren't the same. I reached out to his friend, who is also a friend of mine, and told him how I felt. He said, 'Share what you're feeling with him. If he cares about you, he will listen and give you an answer; if he doesn't respond, then you have your answer.'"

"Did you ask him?"

"He doesn't know how I felt about our conversation, but I did ask him, what we are doing, what do we have?"

"What did he say?"

"He said I was his lady, but, Janay, I don't feel like that. I feel he played a game with me. he told me what I wanted to hear. He knew I loved him. I don't think this was his first time doing this; he may have done it to other women, but why me? I'm so innocent. I never want to hurt anyone. I didn't have any motives, Janay; I told him what I wanted from the beginning. Why did he want to do this to me? I should've listened. He didn't tell me this until after we slept together. I think he was telling me it was a game and he won. I wonder how much the bet was."

"You think there was one?"

"I don't know what to think. Then I had a dream that he looked at me, smiled and walked away, and I never saw him again. My heart broke in two; I cried for days. I don't think he cares for me."

"Gabby look at me, beautiful; you are a sight for sore eyes. Whatever his intentions were, good or bad, he will reap the reward of that. No deed ever goes unpunished. Even if he knew what your heart wanted, he disrespected your desires. You didn't go in blind; he came at you guarded with intent—an intent to hurt you by any means necessary.

"I know you, Gabby, and I know what you have to offer. One day a man will crown you as his queen because you present yourself as one. Tiaras are for little girls. That's what Mateo gave you because he is a little boy that doesn't know how to handle a woman, so he only gave you what he thought of you, not what you're worth. You need someone who's going to enhance what you are, bring out the best in you, not the worst. Real men wipe away your tears, not make you cry them. Do you feel better now?"

"I really do, thank you so much. You're the only one who knows me like this."

"And the man who's going to love you wholeheartedly will know you just like I do. He will be able to tell when something is wrong with you by the tone of your voice and by your body language. See, Gabby, men study who they want to be with; they take their time knowing the very person that you are. A man who's interested in you doesn't want to bed you; he wants to know the soul part of you. You know when you have that man, he's going to do something different with you. He'll stand out; his words will be different; he'll say things to you no man has never said before because they are preserved just for you. You won't have to beg him to be with you; he'll always be there for you. Wait for him, Gabby; he'll be glad you did. "

"I was so faithful to him. I never dated anyone else, wasn't interested in anyone—just him."

"Just because you were faithful to him may not mean he's the one you were supposed to be faithful to.

"You will be rewarded for the heart that you have. I hear the pain in your voice. I can't even imagine what your heart is feeling, but in time you will heal. This is just the aftermath of your hurricane. You will recover from this and start anew with a solid foundation that will stand any test, but the man who will be placed in your life won't tear up your structure; he will guard and protect it.

"This is the last time we will have a conversation like this. The next time I hear you whisper, it better be you're getting married and I'm your matron of honor. Let's go and eat; I'm starving."

Gabriella and Janay went back to the table.

Rita said, "I was getting ready to come in and drag you'll out of there; I'm starving, but while you were in there, guess who's here with his friends?"

"I'm not in the mood to know, so don't say a word," Gabriella said. Janay looked at Rita with a, 'you better not say nothing' look. Rita looked at the menu instead. Gabby looked up and saw Mateo leave. She didn't budge because Janay stared her down.

She whispered in Gabby's ear, "If he wants you, let him come to you." They ordered their food and ate, chitchatted for the rest of the evening. Then they hugged and said goodnight, and Gabriella went home. Pulling up in the driveway, she saw someone sitting on her step. It was dark, so she couldn't see who it was; then a cat ran past her step, and the motion light came on. It was Mateo. Gabriella exited her car and walked to her house.

"Are you lost?"

"No, why do you say that?"

"You never come here."

"I was driving home, and I detoured. I called you and you didn't answer. I know you go to dinner with your friends at the same restaurant on Fridays, so I went to see if you were there. I saw Rita and Miranda, but I didn't see you. I waited about thirty minutes to see if you would show. When you didn't walk through the door, I started to leave. I glanced over again to see if you were there, and you were, but I didn't want to interrupt your dinner, so I waited here, hoping you would come home."

"What do you want, Mateo?"

"I don't understand a lot of things; I was hoping you could teach me."

"Teach you what?"

"Teach me how to love you. Please, Gabriella, if you lead, I will follow you."

"Why now?"

"When a fool sees the folly that he has done and the error of his ways, he corrects his mistakes and hopes it's not too late to make his wrong right."

Gabriella sat down next to him and said, "I tried talking to you in a language that was meant for you and I—I knew it was just for you, but you were not ready to receive it."

"I wasn't ready to receive a lot of things from you. I worry I'm not capable of it."

"Everyone is capable of love, Mateo."

"You're right. Everyone is capable of love—to love me, yes, but for me to love you, no."

"You've been in love before, haven't you?"

"Yes, but no one like you."

"What's makes me any different from someone else?"

"You stand out, Gabriella. You make love sound innocent and pure, make it feel like sheets hanging on the clothesline with fabric softener on a sunny day while the summer breeze whips through them...the smell of that is mesmerizing. That's how you make love feel. It's clean and fresh. You want to be clean before you lie on them. That's how you are, Gabriella. I can't just come at you any kind of way. I don't know how to love you, how to talk love to you. I can't approach you any kind of way."

"That's very different. I never heard anything like that before. If you noticed me like that, why are you scared to love someone like me?"

"Not only am I scared to love you, I'm scarred to love you."

"But you want to love someone?"

"I want to love you."

Gabriella walked up to Mateo and looked into his eyes and said, "Speak to me."

"I don't know how to."

"Talk to me."

"I have no words to say."

"Open up your mouth."

"I am speechless."

"Don't be afraid."

"I am."

"Speak from your heart."

Mateo closed his eyes and said, "I felt the love by the touch of your hand. You swiped my brow like a soft wind across my face. You tenderly caressed my ego, knowing it had been bruised; you delicately removed the bandages around my wounded heart and carefully inspected it as though it came out of surgery. My heart had been bruised from different wars; it battled day and night pouring out love, only to be defeated with the lack of them giving me back what I gave.

"I've been wounded and scarred, broken and battered. My heart was shipwrecked; it was floating in pieces, and you were my lifeline, that one piece I was floating on just when I was about to sink and give up. I saw a beam of light in my darkest hour, Gabriella. You saved me. Even when I was afraid, I trusted you. I understand the Love Language now. It kept pulling me in. I couldn't decode it until I understood it, and you were tapping at the doors of my heart. I was afraid to open them to you.

"My heart was a mess. It was like a tsunami. My heart was strewn everywhere; I felt disconnected, and I couldn't communicate on any level. I felt lost, Gabriella. Although I was wounded, you came and took the bandages off my heart. Although I was still wounded and guarded, you were patient enough to stand by and delicately take them off. You saw pain. You saw scars; although my heart was battered, you still saw love in it. Rejection was my defense. I didn't want anyone getting close to me, so no matter how you tried, I'd put up my defense and reject everything you wanted to give to me.

"Hurt people hurt people, and you were too good for that. I had to change me to keep you."

"Why change for me? Why not change for yourself so that you wouldn't hurt anyone?"

"I'm selfish. I didn't care who I hurt. I wanted everyone to feel my pain. Although they didn't cause it, I wanted them to feel it."

"Why should I think you've changed, Mateo? Why should I think you even want a relationship? Why should I think you've healed, that you're not playing some sick game—why should I think—" Mateo kissed her as she was getting ready to form another word. The very word she was getting ready to say was the right form to kiss her lips.

After the kiss, Mateo said, "You're the only woman who made me shed tears. I know men don't cry, but real men do, and I'm not afraid to tell you that. Gabriella, I was afraid to love you, but not afraid to tell you what made me want to. I hurt a lot of women, I did, and I know one day I will reap the seed I sowed for my intentional deeds, but I don't want to hurt you anymore. Knowing when you hurt, I hurt myself, and I don't like the pain I feel. Now I know how you felt."

"Do you really, Mateo?"

"I promise you I do."

"So, where do we go from here?"

"Let's start all over."

"And begin where?" Gabriella said.

"The first time you loved me."

"That's not fair."

"Why isn't it?"

"Because when I first loved you, you rejected it. Although you rejected me, rejected my love, I still remember how that love felt. It was the best feeling in the world, Mateo; it was a love I never knew before. I was floating and flowing at the same time. I was floating on a cloud, and my love was pouring out of me, flowing on a current to you. I felt this energy like an electrical charge."

"Stay right there, Gabriella."

"Stay where?"

"In that flow. Don't think about the pain, think about that moment when you first felt that love for me, and I promise I will hop on that same current with you. I want to feel what you felt. I want to be where you were, where you are, where you will remain."

"Remain sounds like a long time, sounds like forever, sounds   like eternity."

"You know why I say remain?"

"Why?"

"Because you never changed. You're genuine, soft, kind, and beautiful, no matter how I treated you, you stayed the same. Your love never changed for me. You don't lust for me, you love me. You could have easily walked away, but you stayed and waited for me to change, and I'm so glad you did."

"I waited patiently and impatiently at the same time, if that makes sense."

"Explain."

"Deep in my heart, I knew you would be mine, although it looked like it was turning for the worse. I knew in my heart that you were mine, although you weren't spending time with me, not calling, not making reservations to be with me. Even so, I reserved you in my heart. I had to give you time for whatever it was, whatever you needed, I had to give it to you. I backed off so far away that even if you said something to me, I wouldn't react to it.

"I was in the process of guarding my heart and blocking you. I got tired of waiting for you; it would not be fair to love someone who wouldn't love me back. As faithful as I was to you, I thought, the man I'm being faithful to may not be the one I'm being faithful for."

"Were you looking for someone else?"

"No. I was looking to be found by someone else."

"Do you want someone else?"

"That's a good question."

"Do you have an answer?"

"Before I answer that, I want you to hear something."

Gabriella went in the house to grab the CD she recorded playing the cello. She came back and handed it to Mateo. She said, "Listen to this CD, and if you give me the answer I am looking for, then I'll answer your question. If you are into me, then you'll understand what's on that CD and you will say the right thing."

"But for now, good night, Mateo. I expect to hear from you tomorrow with the answer. If you don't have the answer by tomorrow, then you are not on the same current as me, and what you said tonight was all a lie."

"Why so blunt? You don't believe me?"

"I believed your lies before; I can't go through that again. I'm telling you now, you will not take my heart through that pain again. Listen to the CD and then call me tomorrow. Good night, Mateo." Gabriella went into the house, not looking back. Mateo understood why she felt that way. He was at fault. He knew he couldn't change how she felt, but if listening to what was on that CD would, he was going to do everything he could to make that happen.

He watched her go in the house, then he went to his car. He put the CD in, but he didn't drive home. He sat in front of her house and listened to it. As the music plays, he touched his heart. He felt her pain at the beginning; he dissected every sound; he listened with his heart, not his ears. He felt her anger and frustration; he felt her arguing with him. Every high- pitched note he heard was like she was screaming. Then he noticed the calm pitch. It sounded like she was tired and ready to give up. He heard a different tune, like a sharp squeal at the end. What made that sound? Mateo knew cellos—he'd introduced Gabriella to the cello.

He loved how she grabbed hold of the instrument. He listened to that CD for an hour. He sat in front of her house and listened to it again and again until he knew exactly what she wanted to hear. He called her. The call went straight to voicemail. He called her again, same thing. He got out of his car and went to knock on the door. She opened it.

She said, "I see you couldn't leave, so I watched you from my window. What did you hear, Mateo?

"Do you want to hear it in my language, or the love language?"

"Do you know how to speak in a love language?"

"I will try."

"You've never done it before."

"I'm learning. Will you let me try?" In a frustrated exhale, Gabriella said go ahead. She sat on her step to listen.

"When I heard you playing, you were thinking, thinking, do I want to let him go? You thought about how much you loved me. You were reminiscing; it was a soft, settled moment, then you started to vent your frustration. It was the calm before the storm. You were crying out to me, and I didn't listen to you. And then I heard a certain sound that I never heard in all my playing of the instrument. I never heard this sound before. I know how oil sounds on the strings, so smooth. This is my first-time hearing tears on it. The sound was rusty, like something was breaking."

"It was my heart. I'd had enough."

"I want to try and make it better. At times I can be naïve. It's not because I don't want to do something; it's just that I don't know how to. I'm a novice at a lot of things. All my life I wanted to be the teacher because I thought I knew everything; now I want to be the student. Teach me how to love you, Gabriella. I never wanted something so bad. Will you teach me?"

"Study me, and you will learn how to love me. Look at me as you do your cello, how you sit it between your legs." Gabriella got up and Mateo sat down. She sat between his legs. "Hold me like you do the cello." He pulled her back into his chest. "Now stroke me like you do the cello." He caressed her face and arms. "When you play, how does the music sound in your ears? That's how my voice should sound to you, music to your ears. How you delicately stroke the bow over the strings, that's how you should be with my heart, stroking it delicately.

"Take your time with me as you do to play the music that soothes your soul."

"You make it sound so easy, Gabriella."

"Let me ask you, when you started to play the cello, was it easy for you?"

"I didn't understand it. I couldn't read the notes; it was complicated, but I had a love for the instrument. Although I couldn't read the music, I loved the way the instrument looked, and I loved how it felt in my arms."

"I am your cello, Mateo. My heart is your music. It has strings on it, and you have pulled on them many times before, but it's not complicated. You want to study me because you want to know me, the deeper part of me, the way I sound when you touch me, so you keep playing on that note until you finish the song. I am your melody, from the beginning of the song to the very end. Let's make music together, create a melody from our hearts, a sound only we can recognize. Let's do something we've never done before."

Mateo whispered, "OMG, I love the way that sounds."

"That's what I wanted to do with you from the very beginning."

"Can we start over? I want to take my time with you. Yes, Gabriella, you are my cello; I am your cellist, and I will create a melody that will forever be tattooed on your heart."

"Mateo, you're speaking love language."

"It feels so good too. You made me dig a little deeper inside myself. I was like an oil well; it took a little digging. Eventually you hit the right spot, and words started to come out of me like gushing oil, and I wanted to spill all that into you."

"Talk to me."

"There was a reservoir in me that had never been touched. It was hidden behind the pain, the hurt, the bandages. I trusted you enough to handle my heart. You stitched it together. You helped removed the pain, as I was healing, I promised myself I would never let someone hurt me again, but I knew I could trust you with everything I have, and I knew if I could trust you, I could love you.

"How do you feel now, Mateo?"

"That I could love you forever, Gabriella."

"Is that what you want?"

"Only if it's with you."

"Your words make me feel so warm it comforts me."

"Can I hold you? I need to."

"Yes, Mateo, please."

I changed my mind. I don't want to hold you." Gabriella frowned. "I want to kiss the lips that spoke the words that healed my soul."

"I did all that?"

"You did that and so much more, that I couldn't do for myself, my situation was a revolving door; I didn't know how to get out. I had women who thought sex, gifts, and a good home cooked meal could solve it. None of that worked; I needed healing. I needed you. You reached the abyss of my soul. You did that when I first met you, and I ran away like a scared little boy, but it felt so good to me, so, so good." He traced her lips with his finger, she closed her eyes, and he kissed her softly.

She said, "Why does this kiss feel so different?"

"Because the inside of me is different. Instead of a forced kiss, I wanted to take my time with it. I wanted to feel everything from the moment I touched your lips to the moisture of your tongue that you so delicately placed in my mouth to the panting of your breath. I wanted to feel your heartbeat against mine. I wanted to feel everything in slow motion. I wanted to feel it all."

"OMG, Mateo."

"I said the same thing, Briella."

"Oh, I love that name."

"That is my name for you, because I love you."

"Say it again."

"I love you."

"No, Mateo, say it like you love me."

"I love you, Briella."

She whispered, "Yes, baby, just like that."

"And I will always say it like that. You turned me onto something new, and I know it is just for you and no one else."

"How do you know you won't?"

"Because I flow with you, Briella. You're the water that flows down my bank. We create a river that will always flow. I love the way you feel on me, through me, you cover me, you glide. You filled me up in places where I was empty, and I will forever be thankful for that."

"So where do we go from here?"

"Down the aisle if you want."

"You mean marriage?"

"No, the Isle of Capri in Italy."

"Oh, what's in Italy?"

"Us on our honeymoon if you will marry me."

"You want to marry me?

"I feel I already am."

"You feel that too?"

"I felt that, and I got scared, but I knew I had to face my fears. Although we didn't talk for a while, you chased me down and didn't even know it."

"How so?"

"You were always in my thoughts, everywhere I went, you were there, so in facing my fears, I knew you were not going to hurt me. I let my guard down so I could love you."

"I will marry you, Mateo. I see a different side of you I have not seen before. You needed that part of you to be revealed, and it only came out after you were healed. It was covered in layers of pain, but now you're free, and that's the Mateo I want to marry."

"Then let's start making plans. Get some sleep, my love, I'll call you tomorrow."

"Oh, I have to get a new phone. By the time we get to Italy, my old one should be there."

"What do you mean?"

"Oh nothing. I'll call you when I get a new phone." Mateo kissed her on the cheek, then got in his car and went home.

A week later Gabriella was on her way to meet up with her girlfriends for dinner. Janay had been texting her, asking what was so important she had to tell her in person. She finally arrived at the restaurant.

Janay said, "Oh, don't you look different, you're glowing and smiling. So, what is so important you couldn't tell me over the phone?"

Gabriella walked up to Janay and whispered in her ear,

"I'M GETTING MARRIED."

TBC IN VOL. III

IS SHE YOUR PRIORITY?

"Can I get a scotch on the rocks?" Danny asked the bartender as he slumped in the chair like he was having a bad day.

"Scotch on the rocks coming up. Here you are, sir." The bartender laid a napkin on the counter and put the glass on it. "Why the long face?"

"Today is my birthday."

"Well Happy Birthday; this drink is on me."

"Thank you. I think this will be the only gift I'll get today."

"Is that what the long face is for?"

"No, not really."

"Then what's wrong?"

"It's my girl."

"What about her?"

"She called me about an hour ago to wish me Happy Birthday. It's going on six o'clock now."

"What's wrong with that?"

"I expected to hear her voice first thing this morning. Instead of her, I heard from my friends and exes."

"I see." The bartender turned around to wash some glasses, then he turned back around with a towel drying a glass.

"What is that supposed to mean?"

"What is what supposed to mean?"

"I see?"

"Is she your priority?"

"What does that mean?"

"It means if she's the last person on your mind when you go to sleep, she'll be the first thing on your mind when you wake up. If she's not, then she's not your priority; she's not important to you. Are you upset because she didn't call you first or upset because she waited until later to call you?"

"Probably both."

"A woman knows her place in a man's life by the attention he gives her. What you give is what you receive. Let me ask you this: what did you do for her birthday? Did she have a birthday yet?"

"Yes, hers is a few months before mine."

"What did you do for her birthday?"

"I called her and gave her greetings."

"What else?"

"That was it."

"You didn't buy her anything?

"I said I would."

"Did you?"

"No."

"And you didn't take her out, send flowers or anything?"

"No, I didn't."

"So, you made her feel like a friend?"

"No, she's my lady."

"I understand what you're saying, but do you know how she felt?"

"No, I don't know how she felt." Sigh.

"Do you ever ask?"

"I assumed everything was okay if she didn't say anything."

"Bottom line, you made her feel like a friend, and still you want her to act like she's your lady. Before today, what was your relationship like with her?"

"I know she loves me."

"I didn't ask you how she felt about you, I'm asking how your relationship was; what do you two do together. Do you spend time together?"

"Not as much as I should, but I do call her sometimes."

"She doesn't sound like a sometime woman; how often do you call her?"

"About twice a week."

"What do you talk about, and please don't say the weather."

"Jobs, news, events?"

"So, you don't talk about her."

"Not really."

"Who controls the conversation when you call?"

"She does."

"You know why she controls it?"

"Why?"

"Because you're not interested in her. A man who's interested in a woman likes to take control of the conversation because he wants to know more about her."

"I did that at the beginning of the relationship."

"Somewhere along the way, you lost interest in her. A man in love wants to dig inside the mind of a woman to see how she thinks and reacts; he wants to peek inside of that soul of hers to see where it's going. Her mind likes to be stimulated. If you don't know how to, you will turn her off. How long have you been dating?"

"A year."

"Have you talked about your future together?''

"She does."

"But you don't?"

"No, not really."

"Then she's not your priority, and that's why you got the phone call later today instead of this morning. You don't value her. If you are not going to build a future with her or spend time with her, don't waste her time."

"Is she your only lady?"

"Yes, she is."

"Well, you keep treating her like this and you won't have one. You don't make her feel like she's the one, so she is going to treat you like you treat her. Although you say she loves you, if you are not feeding that love, she is going to burn out."

"If she says she loves me, why didn't she call me this morning?"

"See, now you're being selfish. Although you treat her like a friend, you expect her to respond to you like she's your lady. Maybe you need to ask her why she didn't call you this morning. I hate to ask this question, but do you love her?"

"I don't know."

"Trust me; you don't. She probably shows you more love than you show her. I suggest you pick up that long face and revaluate yourself. She's not at fault for calling you late; you are. You need to communicate more because if you don't, you are going to lose her and any other female that comes along.

"I was just like you, selfish. I wanted all the attention. I didn't really care about how she felt. She burned out quicker than tires on a race car. Losing her made me realize, there are many women out there, but there's only one of her. You don't get many women like her. She's no little girl, but I treated her like one, and she showed me quick she wasn't. She was my wife, and I took advantage of her, just because I was married to her. I assumed that I didn't have to work hard to keep her; she was already mine on paper. Irreconcilable differences were the reason we separated. We were different in so many ways. When, they say it's cheaper to keep her, that's the honest-to-goodness truth.

"She didn't want alimony, didn't want to split the assets. What cost me was my sanity; I had to go to therapy. I matured quickly, and I put away my boyish ways. she made me grow up quick. What I thought I was, she made me see I wasn't. I was grown, but not mature. I was the age of a man but a little boy in my behavior. I wanted to play-house while she was creating the reality of one. She put me in a world I've never been in, and now I wish I was more mature to see that. It's true when they say women are more mature than men.

"Do you still talk to her?"

"Every day. Every chance I get, I give her a call. My day is never too busy that I can't call her. If I don't call, I'll text her, but she will hear from me one way or another. I make her my priority because she's important to me. See, what I didn't do before, I make it my business to do now."

"Do you think she'll give you another chance?"

"We are talking about it. I let her know where I messed up. I love her because she's forgiving and understanding."

"Do you think you'll remarry?"

"We talk about that too. We are the best of friends, and I am always going to support her, so when she is going through something, I am all ears for her. We didn't become enemies once we divorced. I'm glad of that. I lost the marriage, and I didn't want to lose the friendship. She will always be my best friend. I still buy her gifts for her birthday. This year I brought her a diamond tennis bracelet."

"Yeah, my lady said she wanted one of those when I first met her. I told her it was too soon for jewelry. I promised I'd get her one later, but I haven't seen her for about four months, so I don't think about buying her anything."

"Whose fault is that?"

"Whose fault is what?"

"Whose fault is it as to why you'll haven't seen each other?"

"It's mine."

"So were you ever going to make plans to see her."

"Eventually."

"Do you think she was going to wait around until you found time to be with her?"

"She's understanding."

"She probably is, probably is. Would you like another drink?"

"Sure, I'll take another one."

"Oh, by the way, my name is Jorge."

"Nice to meet you. I've never had a Spanish bartender before."

"First time for everything." Jorge poured him another scotch.

"So, what are you going to do for your birthday?"

"I texted her to see if she wanted to hang out with me. She texted back and said she had plans."

"I see. Do you think she's moved on?"

"She doesn't sound like it when I talk to her."

"I think she's moved on. There's no way she could stay and not see you for that length of time. I call that a friendship, not a relationship."

"But she says she's been faithful to me."

"And she probably has been, but just because she's been faithful to you doesn't mean she is being faithful for you."

"I don't understand."

"When a woman loves, she loves only you. She's into you, and you're the only one she wants in her life. She sounds like a woman who doesn't sleep around, sounds committed. When I first met my wife, it had been two years since she was intimate with someone. I knew by the way she felt when I made love to her. She felt preserved; she felt like she had never been touched before. She was saving herself. She always said she would save herself for her husband, and when we divorced, I knew she was going to preserve herself again. I believe what she says. I can bank on that. I know her to be a committed and faithful woman. Those are the ones you keep. I was faithful to her I just wasn't attentive to her needs. Were you stringing her along?"

"I could have been."

"You didn't care about how she felt?"

"Maybe not. Maybe I wasn't ready for her."

"Whether you were or not, it's good to let her know what you're doing in your relationship. You either want to be with her or you don't. Let her know, that's the mature way of doing it. If not communicating with her is your way of breaking up with her, then you have boyish ways that need developing. Little boys do things like that; men confront and talk about it. They give reasons why it's not working."

"Who said I was breaking up with her?"

"Your inconsistencies say so. You're not consistent with her. You may not be breaking up with her, but how you are making her feel? She can and will move on secretly without you knowing it. If you're not consistent with her, she will find someone else that will be."

"How do you know how she feels?"

"Because I've been in that position. I know now, wished I'd knew then. I'd still be married to her. So, yes, I think she's moved on."

"I don't think so. She loves me."

"There you go with that L word again. What does love have to do with anything? Just because she loves you doesn't mean she won't leave you. My wife loved me and divorced me; what makes you think she won't leave you?"

"Dang, so you think she's moved on? Hold that thought. I must use the restroom." As he left, a young lady walked in the door and greeted Jorge with a smile. He gave her one back. She grabbed an apron and went behind the bar. She gave Jorge a kiss on the cheek, knelt and started checking the inventory to see how much alcohol needed to be ordered.

Danny returned from the restroom and said, "Okay, where were we? Oh yes, do you think she's moved on?"

"Why don't you ask her yourself?"

"One day I will."

"Why put off tomorrow." Jorge tapped the lady on her shoulder, and said, "Sam, someone wants to ask you a question?" The lady stood up and Danny's mouth gaped open with a surprise.

She said, "Hello, Danny, how are you?"

"I'm doing fine, Samantha, and, how are you?"

"I'm doing well."

"Oh, Danny, I would like for you to meet my ex-wife, Samantha. I call her Sam for short."

"This is your ex-wife?"

"Yes, she is."

"She told me she was married before, but she said his

name was George."

"The way my name is spelled it looks like it could be George, so that's what she calls me, but my name is Jorge. The J and G sound like an H."

"Sam, my love, I was having a conversation with this gentleman, and he would like to ask you a question."

"What would you like to ask me?"

"I'm confused."

"About what?"

"How long have you been back with your ex-husband?"

"Who said I was back with him? We run a business together. This is our bar. Is there something you want to ask me?"

"Can we talk in private?"

"If that what makes you happy." She came out from behind the bar and found a table. They sat down.

Danny said, "I thought you had plans tonight?"

"I do. I'm helping my ex-husband run the bar. I don't have to tell you exactly what I'm doing; you made that clear to me."

"How so?"

"I haven't seen you in months, so I didn't feel I had to tell you my comings and goings. I don't owe you anything. What did you want to ask me?"

"I want to know have you moved on."

"Yes, I have. Are you surprised?"

"I shouldn't be, but I am."

"What makes you think that I would stay with you? You don't call; we don't make plans to see each other; we don't talk about our future. I'm tired of carrying a conversation that gets no feedback. I'd have to figure out what to say to you, and that gets old. After a while it gets boring, and so did the relationship. Since you weren't calling, there was no need to tell you I was moving on. I'm not dating someone else; I'm just not dating you. I can move on and still be single."

"So, it's over for us."

"It's been over. I'm not a priority to you. The back burner is not a position for me. If I don't put myself second, I won't let anyone else do that to me either. You better ask my ex-husband.

"Can we be friends?"

"Sure, we can be friends, with no future."

"Meaning?"

"We can be friends, but that's all. I don't want to have a relationship with you. You made it clear that you don't want one, and I'm making it clear there won't be one. See, you men think you're slick; you try this 'can we be friends' to see if you can build a relationship, see how far you can get. If you don't value our relationship now, you won't later."

He looked at her tennis bracelet and said, "That's a nice bracelet. It looks like it cost a pretty penny."

"I don't know how much it cost; it was a birthday gift. I don't look at cost; I look at the thought. Are we finished with this conversation? I really need to take care of the inventory."

"Yes, we are finished. I see there is nothing left to say."

"No, Danny, there really isn't. I wish you well." Samantha got up and went back to the bar to finish up. Danny got up and walked over to the bar, put his glass on the bar.

"I'm sorry I was negligent of your feelings. I wish you the best, too. Here's a birthday gift for you; I owe you that." He left a nice tip and walked out. Samantha lifted the glass and there was two hundred dollars.

Looking surprised, Sam asked Jorge, "What all did you tell him?"

"Enough to make him think about how he shouldn't have taken advantage of a good thing."

"But you did, Jorge."

"And, Sam, I suffer for it every day. I didn't understand me, but you taught me in ways, selectively, how to be a better me. I want to try again and see what happens."

We can work on it. I never like to go backward. Once you show me who you are, that's the way I see you, but I think you're worth a second go around."

"I promise you I will make it up to you. You're a good thing in so many ways. I can't afford to let you go again; my therapist will charge me double if I mess up again." They laughed.

"I love what we have right now. We have a good business relationship. The only thing I want to mix right now is drinks, not business with pleasure."

"As long as I have that, I'll have you."

"You'll always be my best friend, Jorge."

"I couldn't ask for anything more." Jorge grabbed two shot glasses and poured a shot of Patron in each one.

He handed her a glass and said, "To our Business, Friendship and Us."

"Cheers." (*CLANK*)

NO, NOT HER!

"Man, let's hit the showers. I have something to show you afterward," Terry said to Dante. They had just finished playing basketball at the indoor court at the fitness club.

"You can't show me now?

"Do you see me with my phone?"

"No."

"Well then, I can't show you now. My phone is in the locker. I'll show you after we shower."

"You should've said you had something to show me when you had the phone with you. You know I'm impatient."

"Well, guess what, my friend, today is the day when you are going to learn to have some. Go and wash the funk off you and meet me back here in ten minutes." They showered and met up by the lockers. Terry went in his locker, grabbed his bag, and got dressed. Dante was already dressed and waiting on the bench.

Terry said, "Did you even take a shower?"

"It doesn't take me long to get funk free like you. What do you have to show me?"

Terry pulled out his phone and went to a dating website. He showed Dante.

"Oh, the catfished website," Dante said.

"It doesn't say catfish. The website is called Seek and Find Love."

"Catfished means people will say and show something different about themselves than the truth. They'll put up a picture of this pretty woman, and when you meet her in person, she looks like—sorry I left my phone in the car I'll be back—and you speed off. I don't trust dating websites. People are just not honest these days.

"I put my real picture up."

"But that doesn't mean someone is going to be as honest with you as you are with them."

"Well, let me show you some of the women that hit me up." Terry scrolled through the pictures. Dante looked. They were okay. Then he saw a picture that piqued his interest.

"So, are you going to go out with all of them?" he asked.

"You know me."

"Yeah, that's why I asked. What if they want to get into a serious relationship; are you going to tell them that you're just a benefits man?"

"They don't have to know my business."

"But they'll tell you theirs."

"Why are you so concerned about their feelings?"

"Because I use to be you; that's why I'm concerned about their feelings."

"Well, you won't be with me when I date them, so they won't know."

"What if you decide to settle down and the very woman you give your heart to does the same thing to you?"

"I'm not settling, so it won't happen."

"Let me see those pictures again." Terry scrolled through them again. Terry pointed and said, "I like this one." Terry picked the one that piqued Dante's interest.

Dante said, "No, not her."

"Why not?"

"I saw that picture on another website. I met up with her, and she is not what she looks like in that picture, trust me."

"I thought you didn't do dating websites?"

"I don't anymore. That's the same picture she had up five years ago. She catfished me. I'd hate to see her do that to my boy."

"Dang, bro, thanks for looking out."

"Yeah, no problem, so what's on your agenda today?"

"Going by my mom's house, take her shopping, and then go see my daughter. What's up with you?"

"I have papers to grade, so I'm going to spend my day doing that."

"Hit me up later. We'll grab a beer or something."

"Bet, we'll do that." They walked to their cars and headed to their destinations. When Dante got home, he immediately went to his laptop and went on the website. He registered and created a fake profile and email address just to see her picture. He knew that face. He didn't see her online five years ago; he saw her face to face twenty years ago. It was the real thing and so was her name. Dante knew her from high school. Her eyes were just as hazel as ever. She had been serious about him, he hadn't been about her, but he often thought about her. He wasn't going to catfish her either; he just wanted to know what she was up to.

He pulled out his yearbook and turned to the page where she kissed and signed his book. He saran wrapped her kiss so it wouldn't smear the other pages. He liked the color lipstick she wore; gold lipstick made her lips pop. He had noticed in her current picture that she still wore the same color. Never once did he kiss her lips; she was that futuristic kind of girl. He thought if he'd ever kiss her, he'd be in the twenty-first century somewhere; yeah, she was that back to the future kind of girl, but he wasn't mature enough at the time to receive it. She said certain things to Dante. Maybe it would be something he'd walk into later, but what she felt for him at that time, he couldn't and wouldn't grasp or accept. Now he was in a different mindset, a different decade. If he were going to settle down, it would be with someone like her.

Jada Martin was her name. He was excited about that. She had the same name in high school, but that didn't mean she wasn't married. He wondered about her life now. He still remembered where her mother had lived, and he wondered if she still lived there. It had been a while since he'd been in the neighborhood. After he'd graded the papers, he was going to take a drive down to that familiar area. He started grading the seniors' final papers. He'd been teaching seniors for the past five years. Every year after they'd graduated, he'd throw them a barbeque at his house. All the kids from previous years came to the cookout. He still had a close relationship with them.

An hour after grading the papers, he took another shower, casually got dressed and headed to her mother's house to get answers to his questions. An hour's drive was worth everything. It got him out of the house, and he had time to get his questions together. He wanted to ask the right ones, not seem desperate. He just wanted to know what was in her past and her future.

Fifteen minutes before arrival, he stopped by the gas station to fill up so he wouldn't have to on the way back home. He pumped the gas and then went inside to get something to drink. Walking up to the register, he overheard a conversation. A voice said, "It's a shame what happened to Ms. Martin; she was the neighborhood mom to all the kids." Dante paid for his drink and walked towards the conversation.

Dante said, "I couldn't help overhearing your conversation. You said something about Ms. Martin, Jada Martin's mom?"

"That's right."

"What happened?"

"Her house caught on fire last week; her mother didn't make it out. Jada was staying with her mom, taking care of her. She had become ill some years ago. Jada went to run errands. She only left her for an hour. Somehow the house caught on fire. When she returned, the fire truck and ambulances had the street lit up like Christmas. The funeral's next week; they're waiting on family from out of town."

"Do you know where the funeral will be at?"

"Sure." The gentleman gave Dante the information. He thanked him and headed to his car. He got in and sat there. He didn't start it up, just sat there, figuring out if he wanted to take the fifteen-minute drive and see the reality of the news he'd just heard. Now the trip was no longer about what Jada was doing with her life, it was how she was coping with the loss of her mother. He started his car but kept it in park; he just sat there. He was numb. He started seeing the memories of his childhood. Ms. Martin was his babysitter in his younger days. His mother and her were the best of friends, so they watched each other's child when needed.

He shed tears in the car. It was better he shed them now. He didn't want to do it in front of anyone from the neighborhood. He started driving out of the gas station. He slowly crept down the street. There were no cars behind him, so he wasn't in a hurry. He knew he was getting closer. He saw familiar stores that was some still open for business, and some new ones. The light was getting ready to change to red, but he still wasn't in a hurry. He slowly rolled up to the light until it turned red.

Green the light turned; he was still sitting there as if it was red. He noticed and drove on. He turned into the neighborhood and parked his car. He got out and stood in front of the house. The windows were busted, the house as black as the charcoal on the grill. He got back in his car and drove home. He had all the information he needed as far as the funeral. He didn't ask where Jada was; she had her family coming in, and he knew they would comfort her. The drive home was longer than an hour—or so it felt to him. Terry called him as soon as he walked through the door.

"What's up, man, what are you doing? Come meet me for drinks."

"I just stepped in the door from a long drive. I'm really not in the mood for drinks."

"The way you sound, you need one. Plus, in your words, I just got catfished from a date, so I need to hang with someone I know that looks like they say they do."

"Give me twenty minutes and I'll see you then." Dante laughed about Terry getting stood wrong instead of up; he needed that laugh. He would thank Terry for it later. He turned on some lights in the house, washed his face and headed to the bar. Laughter was his company during the ride; he kept thinking about Terry getting catfished. He couldn't wait to see what he had to say.

Dante walked in the bar and said. "So, Mr. Fisherman, you got catfished. What did she look like?" Terry looked at him and rolled his eyes like a ticked-off female.

"I won't say what she looked like. I just need to drink until I can get the way she looked out of my head."

"Was it that bad?"

"Man, she wasn't an accident; she was a catastrophe, catastrophic." Dante started cracking up. "It's not that funny."

"Let me laugh because I need to; I need to laugh so that I won't cry."

He started crying, and Terry consoled him. "What's wrong, man? You can talk to me."

"I have to be honest with you before I tell you what's wrong."

"Spill it."

"That picture you showed me earlier on that website, that lady named Jada."

"Yeah, what about her?"

"That's an accurate picture of her."

"She's that pretty for real?"

"Yes, she is."

"So why did you say it wasn't?"

"Because I know her. I grew up with her; we went to school together."

"And what else did you do together?"

"Nothing. We are friends, not the best of, but we are friends."

"Now that I know that she is who she is, I'll ask her out."

"No, not her."

"Why not? You want her?"

"It's not that I want her."

"Then what is it?"

"She just lost her mom." Dante started crying again.

"Aw, man, I'm sorry to hear that."

"When you showed me her picture, I went into protective mode. I didn't want you to dog her out. I know you, Terry. You could do that to any other woman—you shouldn't, but she's special to me, and I couldn't let you do that to her."

"Did you know her mom passed away when you saw her picture?"

"I didn't know anything. I just knew who she was."

"How did you know her mom passed?"

"I took a trip over there today to find out how Jada was doing. I haven't seen her since high school. I knew where her mother lived at and on the way there, I found out about her passing. That's where I was coming from when you called me."

"Wow, man, Dante, I'm sorry."

"Yeah, I am too. I'm going to her funeral next weekend to give my support."

"I'll support you; you know that. If you want, I'll go with you."

"I would appreciate that."

"From college, I had your back, and nothing has changed since then."

"I know you have. Thank you for being there for me then and now."

"No problem. Order what you want; it's on me." They ordered drinks and talked the rest of the evening. Dante had to turn in early; he had class in the morning, so he had his last drink and headed home. It was a month before graduation, so there was planning to do for the barbeque a week after graduation, then the cookout. He already had planned the menu; all he had to do was order the meat. Each student would bring a covered dish.

Monday morning, in class, he noticed a few students missing. He didn't question it; after all, they had finished their finals. At the end of the semester, this was normal. He handed out their papers. For the rest of the week, he didn't teach; he asked each student what they were going to be doing after they graduated, were they going to college, the service, etc. He wanted to make sure they were going to be doing something to make their future better. The week slowly crept by. He wasn't in a rush to see the weekend. Dante knew he had to come face to face seeing Ms. Martin lying there. He didn't go to the wake; he didn't want to mourn twice, so he waited to go on Saturday.

Terry called him in the morning. "You want me to swing by and pick you up or you want to meet me there?"

"You can come by and get me." Next thing he heard a horn blowing. He looked outside. Terry was in the driveway. Dante locked up the house and got in the car. "How long have you been in the driveway?"

"I just pulled up when I called you. I figured you needed a chauffeur today. I don't know how you will feel after the funeral, but I'm here to support you in every way."

"Thanks, Terry, that means a lot. You know I owe you."

"No, you don't."

"Let me be the judge of that one." They drove to the church. The parking lot was full, so full they had to park two blocks down from the church. The church was almost standing room only. The usher handed them a program, and they found a seat. Dante looked at the casket. He got there in enough time to view the body, but the casket was closed. There was a big picture next to the casket. He remembered her beautiful smile. "I'll be back," he told Terry. Dante walked up to the ivory and gold casket and put his hand on it. He looked at Ms. Martin's picture and swiped the picture with the back of his hand. That's how she swiped his cheek when he cried, because his mother had to leave him with her. He returned the gesture. He put his hand on the casket one more time and wiped his tears before heading back to his seat.

By the time he reached his seat, the preacher asked everyone to stand as the family proceeded into the church. He saw Jada coming in first. She looked beautiful as ever. He also saw the student who had been absent from class holding her hand, walking next to her. Could she be related to Jada? Jada stood in front of her mother's casket and touched it, crying uncontrollably. The lady who was holding her hand consoled her while the rest of the family looked at her picture and then went to their seats. Jada finally found her composure enough to take her hand off the casket. She walked by her mother's picture and kissed her on the cheek, then proceeded to her seat.

The funeral flowed with all good things said about Ms. Martin. She was everyone's mother in the neighborhood; she was loved by many, and before she was too ill to come to Sunday service, she was a devoted church member. She was the oldest member of the church. The preacher made that very clear how faithful she was. He read her eulogy, then preached a good sermon. The choir sang a few selections, and within two hours the funeral was over. The family walked behind the casket as it was being rolled out to the car. Jada noticed Dante, and she smiled at him. He returned the smile. The family went to their vehicles to drive to the cemetery. Dante and Terry waited in the fellowship hall for the family to return.

Terry said to Dante, "Are you okay?"

"Yeah, man, I'm fine, still in a little shock, but I'm

fine."

"Well, you were right about one thing."

"What's that?"

"Jada does look like her picture on the website. She's beautiful."

"I told you she would be, but I hope you still not trying to go after her?"

"No, man, I wouldn't. She's out of my league."

"I'm glad you see that. Let's find a table before the family gets back; it's starting to fill up quickly in here." They found a table, and an hour later, the family returned. The family was fed first, and then the others were served. Terry and Dante went to go get their food. They passed the table where Jada sat and she smiled at them. On the way back, they passed the table and didn't see her there. Jada was sitting at their table. Dante put his plate down and went to go hug her.

She said, "It's so good to see you, Dante. It's been some years, but I was hoping I would see you here today. I know how much you loved my mother."

"It was so crazy how I found out. I was on my way to her house to ask about you, and I overheard a conversation. That's how I found out that she had passed. Can I ask why her casket was closed? I really wanted to see her."

"She was badly burned in the fire and I didn't want anyone to see what I saw. I had a picture blown up so they can remember her beauty, her silky gray hair and the porcelain skin she always took care of. It was no more, and I couldn't let anyone see that. I love and respect my mother; I couldn't shame her like that."

"I understand."

"I know you do. I was with you at your mother's funeral, and I remember us picking out her clothes. You dressed her the way she liked to be dressed."

"Yes, I did. That was a hard moment for me. I'm glad you were there for me."

"As kids, we said we would always be there for each other. Remember, I used to fight them boys who would pick on you all the time?"

"Yeah, you were the tomboy back then."

"I still am."

"As fine as you are, you still got that in you?"

"Yeah, some things just don't change."

"You hide it very well."

"You don't expose everything about yourself. Just enough to keep them wanting more."

"Oh, how rude of me—Jada, let me introduce my friend. This is—"

"I know this is Terry."

Terry looked surprised. "How do you know who I am?"

"I've seen your picture on that dating website; it's in my favorites." Dante had a look of disappointment, but Terry smiled. "You look just like your picture. I didn't reach out to you; I didn't want to get catfished, but it's good to see that your picture matches who you are." As they were talking, the young lady who had been holding Jada's hand earlier approached their table.

Dante said, "Well, it's nice to see you, Raina; I've missed you in class. I hope all is well."

She said, "Sorry I was out for a few days, but I had to be here for my family."

"Oh, you are related to the Martin family?"

"Yes, I am." She turned to Jada and said, "Mommy, they want to see you in the kitchen to ask if you want to take any food home. There's a lot of food that was donated, and people have already

88

packed up plates to go."

"I'll be there in a few." Raina went back to her seat to be with the family.

Dante said, "Raina is your daughter?"

"Yes, she is she's my one and only, and no, Dante, you are not the father."

"Well, I know that we never got that far. I hope you're not one of those women who don't know who the father is?"

"Oh, trust me, I know who the father is; you're looking right at him."

"Who?"

"It's Terry. Terry is her father."

Dante stood up and said.

"NO, NOT HIM!"

TBC IN VOL. III

DADDY, HEAR MY CRY

The pillowcases were stained with memories. Kimmie removed them to do laundry. Streaks of foundation, eyeliner, and lipstick were all smeared into the satin cases, looking like a wild night of romance, long ago. It was wild, but last night was a night filled with tears of pain. She grabbed her sheets and the rest of her laundry and headed downstairs to do her wash. She started the machine and began adding items to the sudsy water. She took her time. She wasn't in a rush. The last item to put in was Omar's shirt, filled with the oils of his skin and Creed, a two-hundred-dollar bottle of cologne she had bought him for his birthday, that was still sitting on her dresser. He left it for the nights he would stay over. That was three months ago, and he had never returned to claim it.

She was undecided whether she wanted to wash the shirt—wash away the scent of his skin mixed with the cologne. It was the only shirt of his she had. Or should she wash it and erase that memory forever? She stood there in deep thought until the water stopped, then she dropped the shirt, closed the lid on the machine, and went upstairs. She sat down on her bed, reached into the laundry basket, grabbed the shirt, inhaled the cologne, and burst into tears. She was not ready to let go. She lay on her bed with the shirt beside her. She cried aloud. She heard a voice saying, "I am here," but she blocked the voice out and wept more. As much as she loved him, in her mind she had moved on, but in her heart, she couldn't.

On and off again, up and down it was, back and forth, that was the course of their relationship. Steady, never; one minute it was on, the next minute it wasn't. A year at that pace, and after a while, she said enough is enough. She canceled her subscriptions to "I've been a fool for you" and the lies he told, and she believed, and started a new one, "Be true to yourself." She got tired of the promises, the petty games only children played. She wanted freedom, free from the heartache and pain, from the tainted love that sounded so true but was disguised like the wolf in sheep's clothing. Everything that he said was disguised as something else; he was never true to her. But how can someone who has been hurt hurt someone who has been true to them? It was an insane thought that made no sense to her. She had questions to ask, had her questionnaire already to interrogate Omar, but she knew she wouldn't get the truth out of him.

Kimmie promised herself, the minute she healed, she would never let anyone in to damage her again. She felt he had purposely hurt her. He knew the damage he was doing to her; she felt he didn't care. He was more concerned about his feelings not getting hurt than hers, so since she knew it was a dead end, she stopped right where she was and began to take care of herself. She hung the shirt up in the closet, went downstairs to put the softener in for the rinse cycle, got a text from Renee, who said that she would see her after five this evening. Renee was Kimmie's sister, who spent every weekend with her. Renee's husband was in the military; she worked during the week and on the weekend. Instead of being at home alone, she stayed with Kimmie.

Kimmie replied, "Okay, see you then. What would you like for dinner?"

"Let's go out, my treat."

"Okay, I will be ready when you get here." She looked for something to wear, then put the laundry in the dryer. She went in the living room and lay on the couch until the clothes were finished drying. She started deleting old messages from her phone, messages that took up too much space. She came across Omar's. She wasn't ready to delete those. Every time she deleted messages, she made sure his wasn't one of them. She deleted fifty messages; all that remained were Renee's and Omar's.

Kimmie glanced through their text messages. They were warm, soft. They never argued; it was just general conversation, but fun and friendly. Rereading, she still couldn't understand what was wrong with him. She found herself getting emotional. She felt like she was on a merry-go-round, hearing the same music, seeing the same scenery. She put the phone down. It was four- thirty. She took a shower, got dressed, and by that time the dryer had stopped. She put the laundry in the basket and made up the bed, ready for her guest tonight. Renee texted that she was outside. Kimmie grabbed her bag and headed to the car.

"Hey, Nay Nay."

"Hey, Kimmie, how are you?"

"I'm here."

"Well, I can see that. You're sitting in my car."

"I mean I'm managing."

"You talk to him?"

"No, and I think it's best I don't."

"Oh, look at you, Ms. Therapist."

"Well, if I can dish it out, I think I can swallow a little of my own medicine. People don't realize that just because I hear their problems and straighten some out, doesn't mean I don't have any of my own."

"Any sessions today?"

"I had one client whose problems were similar, to what I'm going through. She had some good information; I wanted her to sit in my seat while I lay on the sofa." Renee laughed. Kimmie sighed.

"During your relationship with Omar, any therapy sessions with him?"

"No, he doesn't think he needs therapy."

"Why not?"

"I guess nothing bothers him."

"Do you think you could help him if he'd ask?"

"I don't know. I'm in love with him. I don't know if I could separate the two."

"What do you mean?"

"I don't know if I could sit there and be his therapist and have these feelings for him, and not be able to mix personal with what he needs therapy for. I don't know if I could handle what he would say that would trigger certain emotions in me."

"You have to think about the person's well-being to help them in their situation. We need to put our feelings aside to deal with whatever is bothering them; we should never get personal when it's about business. He ever talked to you about anything?"

"His pain, him being hurt, not trusting anyone."

"Then that's what you help him with if he ever needs your advice. Don't mix them together. He has to heal from one to be good at another."

"I know that."

"Do you?"

"Sigh, I do."

"Sometimes you have to give things time. Some people don't heal as fast as others. What may take you a month to get over will take someone else a year."

"Oh, so you're my therapist now?"

"Isn't that what we went to school for?"

"Do I have to pay you for this session?"

"You can take me to dinner."

"Oh no, Missy, you say you're treating; it's your dollar tonight."

"Girl, you know I got you."

"I know."

"Can I ask you a question?"

"I'm listening."

"When was the last time you talked to Daddy?"

"It's been a little while. You?"

"Yesterday. He's waiting to hear from you."

"I know."

"I talk about you all the time."

"I know that as well."

"When you're not too busy, or even if you are, find time for him."

"I will."

"Come on, let's go eat." They both loved sushi, so they ate at the sushi bar, and had a delightful conversation. Stuffed on raw fish and rice, they headed back to Kimmie's house for movie night.

As they were changing into their nightwear, Kimmie said to Renee, "You pick the movie for tonight; I picked the last one."

"What are you in the mood for?"

"Nothing about love or mushy stuff."

"How about 'Alien'?"

"Sci-fi, sure I'm up for acid for blood any day." Renee put the DVD in; they grab the cover and lounged on the couch.

Kimmie asked, "How's Jerome?"

"Oh, he's fine/ I just got a letter from him yesterday. He sends his love."

"It feels good to communicate, doesn't it?"

"As much as we can, it sure does."

"I envy you guys."

"Don't. It hasn't always been this way. You have to work at it, but we have an understanding now."

"What you guys have, I wanted for Omar and me."

"But did he want the same thing you wanted?"

"Does it matter?"

"Girl don't make me hurt you. You can't be one-sided in a relationship. If you don't want the same thing, it will never work. You must build it together, have the same architectural plan. For instance, if you're building a house, that's what you're building. But if he wants a mansion, and you just want a house, if you start building your side, and he's building the other, after you finish building, one is going to look different from the other.

"You didn't agree on the layout, so you'll be living in two separate houses. Because you built what you wanted, instead of coming together, you'll be separated, with miscommunication, disagreement, stubbornness, or a lack of concern of the other's feelings making a big wall between you. You can't be selfish in a relationship. If you are, it's better to be alone. You can't force someone to want the same thing you desire. If it's not their choice, then they are not the one for you to have, no matter how much you want them."

"I don't think we wanted the same thing."

"Well then, don't beat yourself up about it. You know, you grow. I'm going to start charging you for my information."

"Girl, I'll buy you a Birkin's' bag."

"With shoes to match?"

"Don't push it, Nay Nay."

"We talked through most of the movie. Here comes my part. I love it when Ripley says this. 'Get away from her, you B....!'"

"I love how she fights that alien."

"Yeah, she's a real trooper. What do you want to do in the morning?"

"Go to the flea market maybe."

"Sounds like fun. Ready for bed?"

"Sure." Kimmie turned off the TV, and they headed to bed.

Renee slid between the sheets, saying, "Oh, you got the romantic sheets."

"They are easy to sleep on."

"When was the last time the cases were stained?"

"Last night."

"How long did you cry?"

"About an hour."

"Talk to Daddy."

"I will. Goodnight, Nay Nay."

"Goodnight, Kimmie." Renee went off to sleep. Kimmie lay there in silence. She knew she needed to talk to her father; he would have the right thing to say; he knew his daughter better than anyone. She decided she would do it when she was alone; she needed that time for just him and her. She went to sleep. In the morning after their run and smoothies, the sisters went onto the flea market, bought veggies for their salads, picked up a few more items, stopped by a couple of more vendors, and headed to the gas station to get gas. Kimmie sat in the car while Renee pumped gas.

Renee then hurried back into the car and said, "When we pull out of this gas station, look at me."

"Why?"

"Do you trust me?"

"I do."

"When we leave, you look my way; you got it?"

"Yes, I got it." Renee drove and Kimmie looked at her but noticed movement in her peripheral vision. Without thinking, she turned her head as Renee yelled. "Kimmie, no!" She saw Omar in his car kissing a woman.

She stared, then turned back to Renee and said, "Let's go home." On the way home, Renee thought Kimmie was going to be quiet, but she quietly said, "My healing has begun."

"What do you mean?"

"I didn't react to what I saw. My heart is healing from the pain he caused."

"That's a good thing, isn't it?"

"It's better than good." Kimmie said nothing else after that. They went home, ate dinner, watched TV and then went to bed. In the morning they went for their run, ate breakfast, chatted a little more, then Renee packed up her things and was heading home.

Before leaving, she said, "Kimmie, I am always, always here if you need me. I am a phone call away and a thirty-minute drive from you. You need me, you pick up that phone and call me, you hear me, Kimmie?"

"Yes, Nay Nay, I hear you. I do love you, sis."

"I love you so much more. I'll call you when I get home." They hugged one another. She watched Renee get in the car and drive off. She closed the door and went upstairs to her bedroom, stood in the middle of the room with outstretched arms and her eyes turned up to the ceiling. She cried out, "Daddy, please hear my cry."

"I am here."

She fell to her knees crying, saying, "I saw Omar yesterday. I thought I was over him. The very thing I thought was what I saw. I thought he couldn't hurt me anymore; I thought I was strong enough to go through; I thought I could fight this battle with my own strength. I am weak; I am hurting; I am insecure; I am lonely; I am angry; I am afraid; I am in love; I want him to want me like I want him; I want him to love me like I love him. He doesn't care; he doesn't share; he's selfish; he's thoughtless; he's abandoned me."

"Kimmie, I call you by name because you are mine. Before you were born into this world, I knew you. I am here to quiet the voice of your tears. I have heard them many times in the midnight hour. I've seen your tears, and I know your fears. I am your strength in your time of weakness, Kimmie. What does my word say? You talk to me, tell me what I have already told you." She was still on her knees, head to the floor with her arms stretched. She lay like that for a minute or so.

She then said, "You will never leave me nor forsake me. You have plans for me, plans to prosper and not harm me, plans for hope and a future. If I delight myself in you, you will give me the desires of my heart. Your promises are yea and in you, amen, but those who hope in the LORD will renew their strength. They will soar on wings like eagles; they will run and not grow weary; they will walk and not be faint. Your rod and staff they comfort me. My steps are ordered by you. I can't do anything without you. You have not given me the spirit of fear; you shall cover me with your feathers, and under your wings I shall find refuge. I am not to be afraid of the terror by night, nor of the arrow that flies by day. You are my strong tower; you will revive me. Your right hand will save me because I'm seeking you, Daddy, and you hear me.

"You said you will deliver me from all my fears. You said that you would give me a peace, not like the world, a peace that passes all understanding, if I seek ye first, and the kingdom, all these things will be added to me."

"And you praise me?"

"Because I am fearfully and wonderfully made."

"I've missed our intimate moments. We used to talk all the time. I am always here for you, Kimmie."

"Daddy, I would always see myself sitting on your lap and sharing moments with you."

"It has never changed. I have not changed. Whatever way you feel comfortable talking to me, whether on your knees, at my feet, or on my lap, I just want you to spend time with me. That's why I created you. You will become stronger. Remember my promises; remember my word; remember I do love you."

"Thank you so much for listening to my heart."

"I created it. I know. I knew what you needed before you said anything; I just wanted to hear it from you."

"I love you, Daddy."

"I love you too, Kimmie." After she finished, she got up off her knees, went in the bathroom to wash her face, and looked at herself. She felt revived, strong, victorious. She went downstairs to make a cup of tea. Her phone rang and it was Omar. She let it go to voicemail. She was in the process of healing and didn't need any distractions. She grabbed a box, went upstairs, put the shirt and cologne in it, taped it up, addressed the box, and put it by the door so she could mail it tomorrow. Her phone rang again, and it was Renee.

"Hey, love, did you make it home?"

"Yes, I did. Oh, you sound so different; what's been going in the last hour since I left you?"

"I talked to Daddy."

"Oh, you did, Kimmie! Aw, it was refreshing, wasn't it?"

"It was more than that. I feel so much stronger now. I feel my healing coming. Then Omar called."

"You didn't answer it, did you?"

"No."

"That's a distraction. If he wants you, he will have to step up his game. You are a woman with standards. Never lower them for any man. If you do, then you are settling, and you will not get what you really want."

"Girl, when do you want your bag, because you are preaching something."

"Kimmie, sometimes we already know the answers. It's good when you hear it from someone else, but I will send you a picture of the one I want." They laughed.

"You know it almost feels like he never existed."

"It may take that feeling to help you heal. Maybe you-all weren't ready for each other. Maybe he came in your life to grow, maybe for a reason and season. Someone else may be in your life for a lifetime."

"I do want a lifetime love."

"You need a man of action."

"I sure do, after you tell me what that is."

"I will next weekend. Get some rest, I love you. Have a good night."

"Good night, Nay Nay."

CLICK.

To Be Continued

A MAN OF ACTION

Monday morning on her way to work, Kimmie stopped by the post office to mail the package. The night before she had deleted messages, pictures, and erased the voicemail that he left. She wanted to move on, and she wanted to be sure it wouldn't be with regrets. She had made up in her mind this was it. She parked her car in the post office lot. As she started to go in, she noticed Omar's car parked three cars up. She slowly walked up to the car. The window was down, but he wasn't in it. She thought why waste postage? She put it in his car through the open window and proceeded at a fast pace back to her car.

She heard her name being called. She knew the voice and didn't want to turn around. She got in her car and was about to start it up when Omar knocked on the window. She looked at him with eyes of hurt and pain. She was strong, but it was a daily process to would build up that strength.

She rolled down the window and said, "Hello, Omar."

"Hey, Kimmie, how are you?"

"I'm fine. How can I help you?"

"I want to know what you put in my car. I don't want to open it, and the car explodes with me in it."

"I'm not devious like that. It's the items you left at my house."

"Oh, so it's a Dear John in the box?"

"If that's what you want to call it. Is there anything else? I have to get to work."

"So, it's over for us—that's what you're saying?"

"It was over when you never came back. Can I go now?"

"Do you want to know why I didn't come back?"

"Not really, I have to go to work, and the way I saw you kissing that lady yesterday, that was enough information to let me know why."

"You saw me yesterday?"

"At the gas station, up close and personal. I saw everything. Yes, you told me months ago you would be out of town. I wanted to do something special with you, and you were right here in town. I saw you. So I can't even trust you. Everything you say always comes up a lie. I need to go. There's not a bomb in your car, but if you don't move, you will have flattened toes from my tires." Kimmie backed up, Omar moved out of the way, and she drove off. She wasn't shedding tears; she was healing, and it felt good. When she got to work, she called Renee before her first client showed up.

Renee answered, "Good morning, Sunshine, how are you?"

"I had an encounter with Omar this morning."

"What happened?"

"I was going to mail his items back to him, and I saw his car with the window down. I put the package in his car. He wanted to know what was in it; the fool thought it might be a bomb. I told him what it was, and he asked me was it over. I told him yes. He was trying to explain why I hadn't seen him, and I told him I saw him yesterday locking lips with a lady."

"What did he say?"

"He was surprised I saw him. He was supposed to be out of town."

"Oh yeah, that flea market is near where he lives."

"It doesn't matter. Things can't be hidden from me. I don't go searching for them, but if it's for me to find out, they will be delivered to me on a silver platter."

"You have a point there. So how did you feel when you were talking to him?"

"Like he was a distant stranger, someone I used to know a while ago."

"Any palpitations or flutters?"

"None."

"Well, your mind is made up. You are moving on."

"I am, and it feels good." Kimmie heard the door shut. "Nay, my client just walked in. I'll call you back around lunch."

"Okay, have a good session."

"You as well."

She hung up with Renee, turned around, and to her surprise it was Omar.

"What are you doing here? I have a nine-forty-five appointment; you have to go."

"I am your 9:45 appointment."

"You can't be. This session is two hundred dollars an hour, and it's a two-hour session." Omar reached in his pocket and put on her desk five one-hundred-dollar bills.

"The session is four hundred."

"I need an extra hour."

"Why didn't you pick another therapist?"

"Because you know me. I know I can get the truth from you."

"Have a seat."

"I can't lie down on the couch?"

"Oh, you want therapy, therapy? Is it that serious?"

"It might be."

"Well, whatever makes you comfortable." Omar lay on the leather couch, and Kimmie sat in her chair. She slid her glasses on, grabbed her note pad and pen, synchronized the timer to her watch, and began the session. "What is your full name?"

"Omar Lamont Kennedy."

"Age."

"Forty-four."

"What brings you into my office today?"

"I can't seem to love the right person."

"Do you know what love is?"

"Never been in it, so I don't know what it feels like."

"In your forty-four years of you living on this earth, you've never experienced love?"

"I have not."

"Do you have a heart?"

"Of course, I do; I'm breathing."

"So you've never had strong feelings for someone?"

"I thought I did."

"How did you feel about this person?"

"I couldn't stop thinking about her. She was the first person that ever did that to me."

"What did she do to you?"

"She smiled. It was the most beautiful smile I had ever seen in my life. She didn't know I saw it; she was looking at her phone. I was sitting at a table across the room from her, and she looked at her phone, and she smiled. I thought if her smile is that beautiful, everything else about her will be perfect."

"So, you just noticed that and nothing else?"

"That's the only thing that had my attention."

"Did it matter to you that it may have been her significant other that made her smile like that?"

"The way she smiled that day, I wanted to make her smile like that forever."

"Did you make contact with her?"

"No, I didn't."

"Why not?"

"I didn't think I could have someone like her."

"But you didn't know her."

"Exactly, but the way she looked she wouldn't be interested in me."

"So, you judged your end before the beginning."

"What does that mean?"

"I'm not good enough for her, and she's too good for me."

"I thought that."

"What are you afraid of?"

"Rejection."

"Have you been?"

"Plenty of times."

"How do you feel after you've been rejected?"

"I shut down and build a wall around me."

"You guard and protect yourself so no one can enter in."

"I do."

"How long have you done that?"

"For years."

"So, you've been hurt?"

"Yes."

"So, you answer rejection with pain and build the wall?"

"Yes."

"When was the first time you were rejected?"

"I was fifteen. I was going through puberty, I had acne and

braces. I liked this girl; I thought she was cute. I approached her and said I thought she was cute. She said no one would like me; my head was too big. She called me a wart face with a metal mouth; I was hurt."

"Sounds like insecurity."

"I was at that time."

"Are you insecure about the way you look or because of who you are inside?"

"It used to be about how I looked. I never called myself handsome; I always went by what other people said about me. It took me a while for me to find my own identity. I lived my life through other people's eyes; I did what they thought I should do, so what people said about me on the outside affected me more on the inside."

"Would you like to take a break, get a glass of water or something?"

"No, I'm fine."

"Okay, let's continue. Have you ever talked to anyone about this before?"

"I don't share my heart with everyone. It's not that I will feel they would look at me different; I just choose not to do it."

"Are you afraid to love, afraid to be rejected if you choose to go that way? I believe rejection triggers you wanting to love. You have fears, and fears keep you from living, face them, or you will miss out on living. You're not living now; you're existing. You're missing out on what love can give you. Have women ever told you they love you?

"Plenty."

"Did you feel their love for you?"

"Kimmie, how can I feel something when I don't even know what it is?"

"Let me ask you this—why do you choose to be with a woman? Is it for companionship, just sex, to have fun? Give me a reason why you choose to be with a woman."

"I love sex, but that's not all I want. I do want to be with someone, but not just anyone. She has to be like the lady I saw with that beautiful smile, different."

"Maybe you'll see her again one day."

"Sigh, maybe."

"Okay, you have fifteen minutes left in your session. What do you like about yourself?"

"I like that I'm successful. I had a vision, and I spent years building my company. I'm glad I didn't waste time doing it. I like that I'm in my forties and I don't have children. It's not that I don't want any; I just was never with someone I wanted to have them with, so I'm glad I'm not dealing with that."

"What do you dislike about yourself?"

"That I could've love and chose not to."

"So, you were almost there?"

"As close as this couch is to your chair." Kimmie looked up from her notepad and saw Omar looking into her eyes.

"Okay, your fifteen minutes is up. How do you feel?"

"Like I need another session."

"I'm booked for the rest of the week. We can schedule for next Monday."

"That will be fine."

"Same time as today?"

"Perfect."

"Okay. I will see you next Monday at 9:45 am."

"Looking forward to it." Kimmie got up to open the door to let him out.

He walked by and kissed her on the cheek and said, "Thank you, Kimmie."

"For what?"

"For not kicking me out of your office, for this session, and for not running over my feet."

Kimmie smiled. "You're welcome. I will see you next Monday."

"I cannot wait." He proceeded to his car. Kimmie waved as he drove off, then went back in her office and lay on the couch.

Quickly, she sat up and yelled. "WHAT JUST HAPPENED!" She called Renee.

"Give me ten minutes and I'll call you back. I'm finishing up with a client."

"Okay." She got a text from Omar. She didn't answer it; she waited to hear back from her Renee, who called her back twenty minutes later.

"Hey, Renee, you want to catch lunch?"

"I hear urgency in your voice. Are you okay?"

"I don't know. Something just happened, and I can't grasp it."

"Let's grab lunch and we can talk." Kimmie grabbed her purse and walked to her car; Renee came out five minutes later and jumped in the car with Kimmie.

Renee said, "What's the urgency in your voice? That's not normal."

"My nine-forty-five appointment today!"

"Yes, what about it?"

"You won't believe who walked in my office."

"The way you're sounding and the excitement in your voice, it can only be one person. Omar?"

"Yes. I couldn't believe it. He used another name just to have an appointment with me."

"Hmm, I knew it was him. I saw his car parked outside when I pulled up for my 10:00 am appointment. I didn't want to text you. I knew you had a session going on. So how was it?"

"It was an eye opener, for him and for me."

"Is he coming back for another one?"

"Next Monday."

"Why did he pick you to be his therapist?"

"He said because I will tell him the truth."

"You think he's reaching out to you?"

"I don't know, but whatever he needs therapy for I will help him with it."

"Sounds like a person that's not ready to let go."

"It's just therapy, Nay Nay."

"It's more than that. He just may be your Man of Action."

"What is that?"

"A man of action is like Daddy; he is a man who is more than his words can say. He's a man of integrity, a man of purpose, a man of structure. Whatever he says, he does. He moves on what proceeds out of his mouth. He's a doer and not just on what he says; a man of action knows what you need. He studies what he's interested in; he's attentive to your needs. You don't have to whine and beg. He won't let you do that. If he's into you, he will make sure you are well taken care of, but at the same time, for him to be that to you, you have to be the same way to him."

"Oh, I like that. Well, I know that I can be that to him, I mean the man of action."

"I know you can, Kimmie, so wait on him."

"I will do just that. Okay, since we didn't go anywhere for lunch, you want to order something?"

"Well, I'm done for today; I'm going to head on home."

"I have one more appointment at two, and then that's it for me."

"Can I say something?"

"I'm listening."

"Omar is your man of action. He just needs a tune-up."

"I knew you were going to say that."

"Give it time. Give him time."

"Just hearing him talk relaxes me because I can hear his heart and understand why he is the way he is. I don't want him to heal for me; I want him to do that for him so he can think clearly and make better decisions for himself."

"Your love for him is there. You will steer him in the right direction. That's why he said you will tell him the truth, and he relies on you to give it to him."

"You think so?"

"I know so."

"I don't want to open the door I'm trying to shut. I don't want to be misled again."

"You can slowly shut the door to your heart for him and still be his therapist. Just don't ask him any questions that will open wounds for him and for you. Let him open up to you on his own. Don't ask a question you already know the answer to; don't add insult to the injury."

"Okay, so what do you want to do this weekend?"

"Nothing. I'm going to let you have this weekend to yourself, pouring out your heart to Daddy. This past weekend was what you needed. This weekend, I think, will be a totally different prayer. Last weekend you were in a storm; the ravaging waves were in your midst; you had to clear your mind. This weekend, you will be at peace. We can do lunch tomorrow; I will talk with you this evening. Concentrate this weekend on your session with him for Monday, pray that it will be a successful one. This is about him, not about you. Help him find the answers he is searching for."

"I think my prayer will be different from now on. I vented a lot of my pain, but now I pray with compassion, pray with understanding. It is a big difference from the day I saw him kiss that woman until today when I saw him again."

"Because there is a change in you, there may also be a change in him, but wait for it."

"I will."

"Let me go, Jerome is going to be on Skype tonight; I don't want to miss that. I will be talking with you later."

"Okay, Love, looking forward to it." Renee got out of the car and walked a few cars down to get in hers. Kimmie got out and waved to her as she drove by. Kimmie went in for her 2:00 pm appointment that lasted an hour. Afterward, she locked up the office and headed home. As she was walking up to her door, she saw a box on her step.

The note read, "When you are ready to totally let me go, you can mail this package to me." Signed, "Omar." She picked up the box, unlocked her door, kicked off her heels, and sat the box by the door, the same spot where she had it earlier that morning. Whether she was totally ready to let him go or not, she didn't want to go through that confused state of if they were together or not. She heated up some leftovers in the microwave, heard a ding on her phone, and checked it.

It was a text message from Omar. It said, "Did you get my package?"

"Yes."

"Did you open it?"

"I know what's in the box."

"Open the box, Kimmie." Kimmie opened the box, and just like she said, it was what was in there before.

She texted back, "Only the same things I packed earlier."

"I know. Here's what I want you to do with those items. I left my shirt and cologne there for a reason. I was coming back. If you would please hang the shirt up, and put the cologne on the dresser, I will come and retrieve them from you."

"What if I don't want you to come to my house?"

"Kimmie, remember who you are talking to. I know how you feel about me."

"And so, I'm supposed to feel a certain way about you, and you take advantage of it."

"Be patient with me; I am changing for the better."

"What is that supposed to mean?"

"Give me time, and I will show you. Have a good night."

"Good night, Omar." In a frustrated exhale—she just wasn't up for games, she'd been through that with him for the past two months—she put the box back by the door, ate her food, took a shower and turned on the TV. She then cut it off and said, "Daddy?"

"I am here."

"I don't know what to think now. Omar came into my office today for therapy and I felt love for him again. I'm not over him, but I don't want to be hurt again either."

"Be still, guard your heart. You have control over your feelings. Be honest with them as well. What is your desire, Kimmie?"

"Honestly, Daddy?"

"Yes."

"I want Omar to open up his heart and be real about who he is and what he wants."

"Then let that be your prayer. Pray with compassion and understanding. The very thing you desire that is what you pray for. A double-minded man is unstable in all his ways. Pray knowing that's what you want, and never diverge from it."

"Thank you, Daddy." Kimmie went to sleep after her prayer. In the morning, she got up and went for her morning run, fixed her smoothie, and headed to work. She knew the week wouldn't rush by. She couldn't wait for Monday. She had only two appointments per day, so days went by slowly. In between her appointments, she looked at some of his text messages she didn't delete. They still made her feel warm and in love. He knew what to say—she just couldn't understand how he could say the very thing about love and not be in love.

Her next appointment lasted fifteen minutes. The client had an emergency, so Kimmie rescheduled that appointment and headed home. The rest of the week flowed as usual, then the weekend was here, and she had two more days until she'd see Omar in her office. She didn't reach out to him; she waited on him to do that. She was guarding her heart; whatever he was up to, he was not entrapping her in it again.

Saturday, she did laundry, cleaned up the house, and just relaxed. It was a weekend she needed to herself. She got a lot accomplished. It was a nice summer night, so she poured herself a cup of lemonade and sat on her step. The summer breeze was beautiful, the sun was getting ready to set, and she was just enjoying that moment. Then she got a text from Omar.

"Are you enjoying the summer breeze with that beautiful sunset?"

"It's funny you should say that. I am doing just that."

"Can I come and join you?"

"Sure, that will be fine." Omar always said he was coming over and never showed up, so it wouldn't be a surprise if he didn't. Within ten minutes, he had pulled up in her driveway. He got out and kissed her on the cheek.

He asked, "How was your week at work?"

"It was good."

"You mind if I sit on the steps with you?"

"No, not at all." She scooted over, and he sat down.

"Would you like a glass of lemonade?"

"I would like that." Kimmie got up to get him a glass. She came back, handed it to him and sat back down. The breeze was romantic, warm and soft.

"Would you like to go for a stroll on this beautiful night?" Omar said.

"It is a nice night for a walk, sure." He finished up his drink, as she did. She grabbed her keys and locked her door, and they started their walk down the block. Kids were playing in the street, the sprinkler system was on, and the kids were having fun getting wet and playing games.

"Oh, how I miss the days of my youth when we had fun times like these kids," Omar said.

"It is a joy to see them outside and not in the house playing video games. A lot of the parents on my block keep it old school; they have their children out here running around having fun, not missing out on the best things in life. It's a pass it down from generation to generation."

"That's a good way of doing that. They can share it with their children."

"I know." The ice cream truck was coming down the street.

Omar asked, "Would you like an ice cream cone or something?"

"I'll have an ice cream cone if you don't mind."

"Not at all." He waved at the driver to stop. He got a vanilla and chocolate ice cream cone. "Do you want sprinkles on yours?"

"Sure." Omar paid for the ice cream and handed Kimmie hers, and they continued their walk. The sun had almost set. They started walking back to her house.

When they got to her step, he said, "Thank you for this moment. I will see you on Monday."

"Have a good night, Omar."

"You as well, Kimmie." He waited for her to go into the house, then he got in his car and went home. Kimmie felt the flutters again. What was Omar doing? He was so gentle and kind, different than he had been before. Why the sudden change? Was it a distraction, was it a game he was playing again because he knew how she felt about him? She was tired just thinking about it. She went upstairs, lay across her bed and went to sleep, waking an hour later. She sat up in her bed, grabbed her book, and began to journal how things had changed in a matter of days. After her conversation with her daddy, she was calmer, not afraid to be herself, bold, but at the same time compassionate.

She still wanted to take her time with this as she should have from the beginning. She knew what she saw in her dream with Omar, and it was confirmed in her spirit. What was confirmed in her spirit was not to be said until the time of fruition. She had foreseen a future with him, but it was just for her, not for anyone else to know, so she understood now. Saying things prematurely will abort the promise. She knew now that the promise was to be kept secret until the right time to share. She shared some things with Omar, but not enough for him to panic, just something for him to think about.

Early Sunday morning, Kimmie got a text from Renee to see if she would be coming to church. She texted back that she would be. She picked out something cute, took a shower and got ready, made her smoothie and headed to church. The service started at 10:00 am. Kimmie was there at 9:50 am. She believed in punctuality, no matter where she had to be. She parked and headed in. She saw Renee in the pulpit, and her sister came down to greet her.

She said, "I'm so glad you came today."

"I wouldn't miss this for anything." Today Renee was being ordained as a minister. Kimmie fell under the prophetic side, but she didn't want to play with her gift until she was fully committed to her calling and the ministry. Kimmie took her seat in the front row. People were coming in, so the seats were filling quick. Someone sat next to her; she didn't look to see who because she was reading the program.

the gentle voice said, "Good morning, Kimmie." She glanced over to see it was Omar.

"Good morning. What are you doing here?"

"A couple of months ago you told me about the service for your sister. I knew how important it was to you. If it was important to you, I knew I had to be here to support you."

"That's so nice of you, but you didn't have to."

"Yes, I did." The service was about to begin. Renee received her license and preached her first sermon, rightly dividing the word. She preached the people to their feet. Omar enjoyed the sermon as well. Kimmie was seeing a difference in him. After the service, Kimmie went to Renee and hugged her tightly.

"I'm so proud of you, I enjoyed every minute of it."

"Thank you, Kimmie. I see we have a guest with us today."

"Hello, Renee, your message touched me. I'm glad I came."

"Glad you enjoyed it. Please don't make this your last time attending."

"I will be back. Would you ladies care to get something to eat? It's my treat."

Renee looked at Kimmie and said, "MOA, Kimmie." She knew exactly what Renee was talking about.

"Sure, that would be fine." Omar escorted the ladies to his car and opened the door for them. They went on to dinner, short but sweet, with general conversation, good food and a good time. Then he took them back to their cars, kissed Kimmie on the cheek, and headed home.

Renee said, "Enjoy this moment."

"I know, the best is yet to come."

"The best is already here, Kimmie." They hugged and went home. When Kimmie got home, she looked at the box by the door, items still in it. She picked it up and hung the shirt back in the closet, and put the cologne on the dresser, then she sat on her bed and said, "Daddy?"

"I am here. I am not the author of confusion; I see your heart, and I'm healing the wounds of your past. Be still, Kimmie, be still. He is your husband, wait on him."

"I had already seen it in my dreams, and you have confirmed it in my spirit, and you spoke the very thing I needed to hear. Thank you, Daddy."

"Blessings always to you." She wrote in her journal, had a cup of tea, and prepared herself for tomorrow's session. In the morning she went for her daily run, made an egg white omelet, and headed to work. She got to the office at 9:15 am. She saw Renee parking her car. They had gone into business together right after college. Renee's office was upstairs.

She stopped by Kimmie's office and said, "Good morning. Are you ready for your session with Omar?"

"Yes, I'm excited. Daddy confirmed some things last night, and I believe his report."

"Soon I'll be sitting in the congregation watching you get your license for ministry."

"You know I am a woman of order."

"And you'll do it decently."

"That's the only way to."

"Let me get to my office; we'll chat later."

"Okay." Renee headed upstairs. Five minutes later Omar came in.

"Good morning Omar. You are fifteen minutes early."

"I know. I need to cut my session short today. I have an

appointment somewhere else today, so can we make it an hour instead of two?"

"Sure. Would you like to lie on the couch or sit?"

"I would like to sit this time."

"Have a seat then. What would you like to talk about today?"

"I'd like to talk about that smile I saw on her face."

"Okay, let's talk about it."

His phone beeped; he looked at it and said, "My appointment got moved back. I have to go right now. Can we continue this another day?"

With disappointment in her voice, she said, "Sure, that's fine."

"Better yet, my appointment won't take that long. I can meet you for breakfast."

"But I already ate."

"Well, meet me for coffee."

"Okay, where?"

He gave her the address and said, "Meet me there in thirty minutes."

"I'll be there." Omar put four hundred dollars on her desk and left. Kimmie texted Renee and said she'll be going out for a few. Kimmie grabbed her keys, locked her office and headed to the diner. When she walked in, the diner was crowded so she found a seat by the window, where the sun was shining in. She sat there and pulled out her phone.

Ten minutes later, she got a text from Omar saying, "I love you so much, Kimmie." She looked at the text and smiled. Then she heard his voice.

"That's the same smile I saw a year ago."

Kimmie looked up. "What do you mean, a year ago?"

"I was sitting at a restaurant one evening, and I saw you. You were sitting like you are now, looking at your phone. Your poise and everything are still the same. Nothing has changed about you, Kimmie. When I saw you smile that day, I melted just like your ice cream did going down on your cone on Saturday."

"My ice cream melted because I wasn't in a rush to eat it. I just had lemonade."

"And I didn't want to rush things with you. Your smile did something to me that no other woman could have done. It changed me. It took me a while to talk to you because I didn't think you were interested in me."

"Why would you think that?"

"You have a certain power in you; you changed me with your smile. I don't have anything to give you like that."

"So, I can't love you for who you are?"

"Yes, you can, but—"

"Omar, this is not a competition of who can and who can't. Don't try to do more with me; just be who you are. When you try to do something other than that, you are not being you, and you will wear yourself out. I loved you from the beginning because of you. Please, don't you fake it with me, Omar. Please don't."

"When you saw me kissing that lady…she was a woman I dated a while ago. I wanted to see if she could make me feel the way you did. She didn't and neither did the others. I knew then that there was only one woman for me and that was you, Kimmie."

"What are you saying. Omar?"

"I'm saying I'm ready to commit to you."

"I see. Oh, did you make it to your appointment?"

"You were my appointment."

"I don't understand."

"I made reservations at this diner. I had them save that seat for you so that I could see that smile again. You made me melt all over again, and I want to make you smile like that forever."

"Remember when I told you if you ever see her again, don't be scared to approach her?"

"Yes, I remember you saying that."

"Well, let's start over then."

"I would like that. Good morning my name is Omar."

"Good morning to you, Omar. My name is Kimmie."

TBC IN VOL. III

SILENT PRAYER

"Meet me for lunch!"

"Where?"

"You decide."

"Why me?"

"Because you pick the best spots."

"Who's buying?"

"If I say meet me for lunch, that means I'm buying."

"When do you want to meet?"

"In about an hour." "I'll text you the address."

"Bet."

Vaughn and Sonya were coaches for the Junior Varsity Basketball team. They supported one another. When her girls weren't playing, she went to his games, and he returned the favor. They always talked about the games afterward. If they lost, they went over the plays of how it could have been better; if they won, they went out and celebrated. They clicked on the court, never off it; it was always about the game, nothing more. They both were in a relationship, and they never talked about their private lives.

Sonya was wondering for two reasons why he wanted to meet up with her for lunch. One, it was a Saturday, and two, school was out for the summer. She texted him the location and got dressed to meet up with him. She got to the restaurant early, so she picked out a spot for them to sit. He arrived ten minutes later.

He said, "Coach Sonya, so nice to see you again."

"Coach!" She laughed. "I'm only the coach when I'm on the court at the games, and since school is out for the summer, you can call me Sonya."

"I just always see you as the coach, but maybe I need to see you in a different way."

"It sounds like you have something on your mind. This is different; we don't have any games going on. Why did you need to meet up with me?"

"I just needed to see a familiar face. My girl, she doesn't know about sports; she doesn't know about a lot of things. It's like stale bread with her, nothing appetizing."

"So, am I your appetizer?"

"You're not stale bread if that's what you mean. I just needed to get out of the house. I didn't want to hang with the boys, but I thought about you, and here we are."

"So how has your summer been?"

"It's been good spending time with my mom and dad. I did some fishing on the boat, so it's been enjoyable. How about yours?"

"I just came back from visiting my sister. She just had a baby, so I spent some time with her. Other than that, it's just been normal."

"Normal, sounds boring."

"You have stale bread in your life; I have rotten eggs in mine. I'm thinking about breaking it off. There's no life in it. It's routine, nothing intriguing about it. The one good thing is we don't live together, so the break-up shouldn't be hard."

"I hear you on that. I try to take her fishing with me, but she doesn't want to mess up her nails, she doesn't want to smell like fish, so I go alone or sometimes with my dad. It's a good bonding moment with him. What we catch, we take home and have a fish fry, invite friends over."

"It sounds like a good time."

"It always is with friends and family. You like fishing?"

"I never tried it."

"It's fun, very relaxing. You ought to try it one time."

"Maybe I will."

"Tonight, Dad and I are going. You should come."

"Night fishing? Can you catch fish at night?"

"Fish bite all day. The time of day doesn't change their appetite. They see bait; they're biting. We fish on the bridge. I'll teach you how to throw a line out and reel it in when you feel a tug on your line."

"I have no plans tonight; this ought to be fun."

"I guarantee, you will have a good time."

"Okay, then fishing tonight it is."

"I'll come pick you up about 6:00 pm."

"Sounds like sunset. That's a good time."

"That's the best time. Let's order, I'm starving." They ordered their food, he paid for their lunch, and they said their goodbyes. When Sonya got home, she finished her laundry, found a pair of shorts and a t-shirt to wear, something comfortable to catch fish in, and found a pair of old sneaks. If anything was going to be fishy, she didn't want to be something new. She tied her hair up in a bun, then got a text from Vaughn saying he would be there in a few. She waited outside for him, and he drove up minutes later.

He said, "Oh, I see you're dressed for the occasion."

"Well, it didn't sound like a black-tie event; who goes fishing in stilettos?"

"You know, I've never seen you in heels. You're always in sneaks and loafers."

"I've never had an occasion to wear them around you."

"Maybe I should create one."

"You're funny. So where is your dad?"

"He stayed to the house with Mom. They had an event to go

to. He canceled on me, so it's just you and me."

"Are you going to be okay without him?"

"Sure, he's my hanging partner. Maybe if you get the hang of it, you can become my new fishing side chick."

"Whew, glad you said fishing side chick and not your side chick."

"I would never ever put you in that category, and my apologies, you are not a side chick at all. You're my friend, so you will never hear me call you that again."

"I know you meant well. No need to apologize."

"Sonya, when I say let me apologize, please let me do it so I can clear my conscience."

"Okay, Vaughn, I accept your apology."

"Thank you."

"You are so very welcome."

"I like how you said that."

"It's just words."

"It's not what you said, it's how you said it."

"Well, how did I say it?"

"Softly, like you care."

"Oh!"

"That's it, that's all you have to say?"

"For now, yes."

"Oh!"

"Really, Vaughn?"

"Well!"

"And!" They started laughing.

He said, "We sound like an old married couple."

"Hope we don't start finishing each other's sentences." They laughed some more. When they reached the fishing pier, he took out the tackle box and rods, and they walked over to his favorite spot.

She said, "Look at that sunset; it is absolutely beautiful."

"Yes, I like to come around this time to see it set. It puts me in a different mood."

"What kind?"

"Just being grateful, being thankful. If I see the sunset, I pray I will see it rise again."

"'And when it shall rise, I will open my eyes and say thank you Lord for another day.'" They looked at each other in surprise. Instead of finishing each other's sentence, they said the same thing at the same time.

She said, "How did you know I was going to say that?"

"I didn't, like you didn't know I was; it just happened." They both looked puzzled for a couple of minutes. He took the poles and baited the hooks. He threw the lines out and handed her a pole. "Watch out, the fish may eat your bait. If you feel a tug on your line, start reeling it in."

"Okay, I feel something tugging."

"On your line?"

"No, in my spirit."

"You care to share?"

"Not right now. In due time."

"Okay, I will wait." She then felt a tug on her line. She started slowly reeling her line in. It kept tugging and she kept reeling. She reeled in a mullet, a nice size at that. Vaughn unhooked the fish and put it in the cooler. "Good job. Let's see you catch another one."

He baited her line and threw it out. Not two minutes later, she felt a tug on her line and reeled in another mullet. He baited, she caught, bait, catch, bait catch. He pulled his line in and watched her catch all the fish. Two minutes after he baited, she pulled them in. Within one hour, she had caught fifteen fish. He looked at her with amazement. "You said you've never been fishing before?"

"That is correct."

"When my dad and I come out here, it takes us about fifteen minutes to catch one, and here you come out here and catch them in two."

"I'm on a good start?"

"You're blowing my mind. I didn't catch anything, and our rods are right next to each other."

"I guess I was a fish magnet today."

"I totally agree. Are you ready to go?'

"Yes, this was fun. I'd like to do this again."

"I'll let you know when. I want to drop some of this fish off to my parents' house; do you mind riding over there with me?"

"Not at all; I don't have anything to do." They packed up the car and headed over to the house.

When he saw his dad's car in the driveway, he said, "That's strange. They were supposed to be going out."

"Maybe they changed their mind."

"Maybe. Would you like to take some fish home? We can cut it up here and I can bag it for you."

"I'd like that." He grabbed the cooler, and they headed into the house.

His dad was sitting on the couch. Vaughn said, "Dad, I thought you guys were going out?"

"The couple we were meeting up with had a change of plans, so we stayed home."

"Okay, well, this is my friend Sonya; Sonya, my dad, Benjamin."

"Nice to meet you, Sonya."

"You too, Daddy Benjamin."

"She's a keeper, Vaughn."

"Don't start, Daddy." Vaughn's mother heard them from the kitchen and came out. Vaughn saw his mother and was getting ready to introduce them.

"Mommy, this is—" Before he could get another word out, she walked up to Sonya, put both of her hands on her face, and they both closed their eyes. Vaughn and his dad looked on with curiosity. Then Vaughn's mother removed her hands from Sonya's face, grabbed her hand and took her in the kitchen.

She said to Sonya, "My son is your assignment. You keep praying for him. You asked for him. You cover him in prayer as you have been doing."

"You were tugging on my spirit."

"I was. I wanted to meet you."

"How long have you known I've been praying for him?"

"For some time. When I saw you at his games, I knew it."

"Why didn't you tell me then?"

"You weren't ready to let go of what you had. When you were sincerely ready to receive what you desired, you held onto what made your flesh happy until you realized you needed more than that. When you made that decision, and the prayer you prayed was answered, you began to cover him in your prayers."

"What are you saying?"

"What did you desire?"

"I desired to be married to a man who would love me the way God does, who would take care of me, and I prayed that I would be the wife he desired."

"Have you ever prayed for anyone like that before?"

"Like who?"

"Vaughn. Have you ever prayed for someone like you prayed for him?"

"No, ma'am, I haven't."

"He is your desired husband to be."

"He can't be."

"Is something wrong with my son?"

"No, ma'am, I didn't mean it like that. I meant I don't look at him like that."

"When you're not looking, that's when you'll find him. You have a powerful ministry in you. You may not see it now, but it is there. Men and women will be drawn to you because of the anointing that's in you. You started to pray for him because you always wanted to cover your husband in prayer. You are rehearsing now what will take place in your marriage. You pray for him day and night, for his health, wealth, and protection. The day of your wedding, you will anoint his feet and pray over them. That is what you desire. He is teachable; he will respect the anointing that is on your life. You will minister to him and he to you. You both are covering each other now in prayer."

"You mean he is praying for me?"

"Ask him and you shall receive your answer. I call you daughter now. I pray over your marriage; I pray over your womb that you will birth a generation that will listen to the sound of your voice and obey. I break every generational curse, from your side and his side; I tear down everything that will come against you. I pray the angels encamp around your dwelling; I bind up sickness, and loose healing. I wrap you and my son in the secret place of the Most-High God. You both shall abide under the shadow of the Almighty. My son is a man of integrity; he is the Psalm 1. As you prepared yourself for him, he has prepared himself for you. Go now, daughter, and prepare yourself for that day." They hugged each other in accord at what had just been said. Sonya went back in the living room, where Vaughn and his Dad await her return.

Vaughn said, "What was that all about?"

"Can I talk to you privately?"

"Sure. Dad, can you cut up the fish for me?"

"Sure, son, not a problem."

Vaughn and Sonya walked outside and sat on the steps. She said, "When I desired to be married, there were so many things I wanted to do for my husband. I wanted to anoint his feet will oil as Mary did at Jesus' feet. I thought it was so intimate. I wanted intimate moments with my husband: we minister to one another, pray over one another, study the bible together. I desired that more than anything. When I was sincere about my prayer, a man dropped in my spirit and I began to pray for him. No man has ever dropped in my spirit like that before. It was a silent prayer; I prayed from my spirit. God knew exactly what I wanted. He heard every moan and cry. I cried out to him for the man that he was going to place in my life. I never prayed for a man like that before, but if he was put in my spirit, I knew, at the appointed time, he would be what I desired."

Vaughn said, "I knew when you were sick before you even told me you were. I knew then what we would be. You were in my silent prayer in the midnight hours. Days that you had headaches, I would anoint my head with oil and pray for you that they would cease. I saw you in the spirit before I would see you in the gym. The feeling was so strong to pray, I had to stop what I was doing, go in the locker room, and intercede for you. I wanted to be able to pray you through sickness and whatever else you were going through. I prayed for you before I prayed for myself. The day of my wedding, I too want to anoint my wife's feet so that she will be able to stand with me through every trial and tribulation, that she may never leave my side when times get hard, be a stronger vessel when I become weak, that we will have a love so strong that it can't be broken. That's when you dropped in my spirit, and I knew then that you were what I desired. Vaughn grabbed Sonya's hand.

She said, "So, what does this mean?"

"It means I'm going to finally see you in a pair of heels. On our wedding day."

TBC IN VOL. III

"I like this tree, James, I think it would look great in the den."

"Is that where you want to put it?"

"I like the bay windows, so it would look good there."

"We have this big living room and you want to put it in the den?"

"Well, let's get two trees."

"And who's going to decorate the both of them, Tracy?"

"We'll have a contest. Whoever's tree is the best-looking one, the loser has to shovel the snow outside for a week."

"So, you are really going to shovel the snow for a week?" Tracy threw a snowball, hit James in the back of the head, and then ran. James ran after her and tackled her in the snow.

"Win or lose, I would never have you shoveling snow. That's my job, amongst other things," he said.

"And what is that?"

"Would you like for me to show you now?"

"Oh, you're so mannish."

"But you like it."

"Oh, baby, I love it."

"Let's find these trees so I can show you what I'm working with."

"Oh, baby, yes."

"Oh, I was talking about decorating the tree."

"Oh, I knew that."

"No, you didn't." They both laughed. James and Tracy had been going six months strong since their trip back from Aruba. They found love afterward and had been together since. Now they were planning their first Christmas party with friends and were out looking for a Christmas tree. The event was three weeks away, invitations had been sent out a month prior, RSVPs a must, and much time had been given to respond. They found two trees, put them in James' pickup truck and headed home. On the way, James called his friend Eric and asked if he could meet him at his house to help take the trees in the house. Eric agreed.

"While you are putting the trees up, I'm going to run to the airport and pick up my niece. Her plane should be coming in soon."

"Oh, I forgot she was coming in today."

"Yes, and I want to be there when she comes in. I don't want her waiting there for me."

"Is your car gassed up?"

"Yes, love, it is."

"Be careful and hurry up back to me." He kissed her. She left for the airport. Minutes later Eric showed up. "Good timing; we just got home."

"I wasn't that far when you called. Where's Tracy?"

"She's on her way to go pick up her niece."

"Is she pretty?"

"I never met her. Besides, you have a girlfriend."

"I have a friend. Big difference."

"Oh yeah, one of those. I keep forgetting you're not the committed type."

"I'm committed, just not to women."

"Man, whatever, help me with these trees."

"Why did you all get two of them?"

"We are having a contest of who can decorate their tree the

best."

"These are some big trees. You have enough decorations for them?"

"We have plenty."

"So, I see you and Tracy are going strong. You ever think about asking her to marry you?"

"Every day I think about it. She is different from any other woman. I know in my heart she's the one."

"Yeah, you knew in your heart Michelle was the one too."

"Yeah, I know." Sigh. "And I don't want to end up like I was before, left at the altar and broken."

"Do you think she would do that to you?"

"I know she wouldn't, but I still have my doubts."

"She's not Michelle."

"I know, but I'm cautious. I do love her, that I know. I just don't want to go down that same road and be disappointed."

"Just talk to her. Tell her how you feel, and maybe that will ease your doubts."

"For a man who won't commit, you sure sound like one who would."

"My talk game is on point; I got skills. When I'm ready, I'll do that C thing, but for now, I'm loving life."

"Yeah, whatever that is."

"You got your thing going, and I got mine."

"Man, whatever, grab the end of this tree."

Tracy pulled up to the airport and saw her niece. She beeped the horn and walked down to the car. Tracy got out and hugged her.

She said, "Shelbi, you look so good."

"You know we have good genes in our family."

"The way you look, it looks like you took them all."

"Auntie, you are still a clown."

"Nothing doesn't change with me. How was your flight?"

"It was good. We left and landed on time."

"That's good. I wanted to get here at the right time so you wouldn't be waiting."

"It would be okay if you were a little late. I'm not in no rush to get anywhere. So, tell me what's been up with you and James since you got back from Aruba? I know we have some catching up to do. I was ecstatic about the news you told me; you sounded so happy. Are you still the same way?"

"I'm that way and then some. He makes all the other men look like little boys. He's really into me, and I appreciate that. He's in tune with my thoughts and emotions. He really understands me."

"Those are the best ones. When you find one, you keep him."

"I think we found each other."

"That's even better. When you unexpectedly find each other, it was meant to be."

"The trip was planned. Falling in love with him wasn't."

"The trip to Aruba?"

"Now that was definitely unexpected, but I knew he needed a friend there, and I was right there for him."

"And that's why he loves you like he does."

"I wonder sometimes why he's in my life."

"You're in his life because the wrong one was. She didn't appreciate him, but he needed someone who would."

"I do appreciate him very much."

"Do you think he will ask you to marry him?"

"It's too soon to tell. I know he's been hurt. I know he doesn't want to be embarrassed again."

"You're not the type of person who would hurt him."

"No, I wouldn't dare hurt him on purpose. I see him as I see myself, genuine and caring."

"Well, wait on him. Don't rush it; don't talk about it. Wait on him."

"I will. So, who's in your life?"

"No one. Men don't know what they want these days, and I don't feel like waiting around until they find out."

"That's why I waited to be found, and by the right one."

"Yeah, I think I'll be fifty when he finds me. By that time, all the games they've been playing, they'll be tired and want to settle down. What I'm going to say is, 'You done played out your best years as a player and now you want to give me the retired portion of your life? Nope, I'm good.'"

"Girl, you are silly."

"No, Auntie, I'm real. I'm not icing no knees, rolling him around in a wheelchair with his retired jersey on because he doesn't have any strength left in him. Do I look like a nurse who works for hospice? I don't think so."

"Shelbi, you are a clown for days."

"Just giving you the facts. So where are we staying?"

"We're staying at my place."

"You mean you haven't moved in with James yet?"

"I like my independence. We're not rushing to move in together."

"I hear you, Auntie. Take your time with this one. He

knows when it's the right time."

"Yes, and I'll wait on it. As long as we are enjoying each other that's what matters."

"That's what counts."

Back at the house, James and Eric finished setting up the trees. James said, "You want a beer or something?"

"Brandy if you have some."

"Sure, I have some." James went behind the bar, poured two glasses and handed Eric one.

Eric said, "Man, this house is huge. I love what you did with your artwork; you have a mini-museum in here."

"I know. I'm thinking about turning this house into a museum and buying another house. It's hard moving artwork from one place to the other. People love my art, and they buy it, but the ones they don't buy I have to bring back here."

"For the price you put on your art, you can buy another place in no time. And your work is exquisite."

"Thanks, man, I appreciate that."

"You're my boy; I give props on everything you do." Eric finished his drink and said, "I'm getting ready to go. I got a hot date."

"Man, you're getting ready to pull out."

"Quicker than a man that don't want to get a woman pregnant."

"Boy, you are stupid."

"No, bro, I'm smart. and that's why I don't have no kids." James shook his head, then shook Eric's hand, gave him a hug and walked him to his car. Tracy and Shelbi drove up, got out of the car and walked toward the men. Tracy kissed James, then introduced Shelbi to James.

"Shelbi, this is my significant other, James. James this is my niece, Shelbi."

"It's nice to meet you, Shelbi. Tracy has said so many good things about you."

"Thank you, James, as she has said the same about you." Eric looked on with an expression, 'and what about me?"

"Oh, Shelbi, this is Eric. Eric, Shelbi."

"Nice to meet you, Eric."

"Likewise, Shelbi." Shelbi and Tracy headed towards the house while Eric stared after Shelbi.

Tracy turned around and said, "Bye, player, don't even try it."

James laughed and said, "Your card has been pulled. You can't hide your game face; she exposed you."

"Man, whatever. I'll holler at you later."

"Later, man." James waited until Eric pulled out of the driveway, and then went in the house. Tracy and Shelbi were in the kitchen making some hot chocolate.

James walked in the kitchen and said, "The trees are up. When do you want to start decorating them?"

"We can do them in the morning. I'm too tired to do them now. We can get the decorations out tonight so we can get a fresh start on them in the morning."

"Sounds like a plan. While you ladies are warming up, I'll go get the decorations."

"You don't need any help?" Tracy said.

"No, my love, you have company. Entertain her. I can do this." James headed out to the garage.

"He really cares for you, Auntie."

"I know. I still think do I deserve him. When you think of how good a person is to you, it makes you wonder what you did to have someone like him."

"We are all deserving of something. Don't sell yourself short. Be thankful that he's in your arms of gratitude rather than in someone else's arms with a different attitude."

"I am very grateful for him."

"And that's why you have him. He needed someone to be that."

"Thank you, Shelbi."

"You're welcome, Auntie."

James came in with the decorations. With two more trips, all the decorations were in the living room. Tracy and Shelbi went in the living room, and James turns on the fireplace.

"It's going to be cold tonight. I'll gather some wood out in the back to add to the fire to make it real cozy for you ladies." He left.

Shelbi said, "Are we staying here tonight?

"We can. I wanted to start on the tree first thing tomorrow morning."

"Okay. Can you show me where I will be sleeping? I want you guys to spend some time together. I have phone calls to make."

"Oh, you don't want to hang with your Auntie?"

"I respect your relationship, and I don't want to take time away from it."

"You wouldn't be; he's understanding."

"I understand that, but don't take that for granted." Shelbi went and hugged Tracy. Tracy showed her to her room, and Shelbi got situated. Tracy headed back downstairs. James came in and put more wood on the fire.

He said, "Where is Shelbi?"

"She's in the guest room. She wanted us to have some quality time together."

"That was very nice of her, but she's your niece and I know you wanted to spend time with her. I would have understood."

"I said that you would, but she was adamant about it. She told me not to take it for granted."

"Take what for granted?"

"Your understanding." James put the wood in the fireplace, went in the kitchen, poured two glasses of wine, then turned off the lights in the living room. The light from the fireplace lit up the room just enough for him to see Tracy and her glowing face. He escorted her to the fire. He sat down, and she lay her head in his lap.

He said, "Ever since I've known you, Tracy, you have not asked me for anything. You're always considerate of me. I don't think you know how to take things for granted because you always put others first."

"That's the only way I know how to be, James. I don't know no other way to be."

"You were beautifully and wonderfully created. Every bit of your being was intricately put together, and you were made beautiful from the inside. I believe God took his time making you. You were designed just right."

"I've never heard any0ne say that before; that is so beautiful."

"And that you are, inside and out. You're just beautiful all over, Tracy."

"You're going to make me blush. I love you, James."

"I love you more, baby." They kissed and then headed to bed. Later in the night, Shelbi came down and saw the fire still going in the fireplace. It was dying down, but it was still nice and cozy in the room. She looked at the tree, got some water and poured it in the tree holder. The aroma from the tree filled up the room like a pine forest. While they were asleep, she decided to decorate the trees. All the decorations were neatly packed and looked very expensive, so she took her time sorting them out. There were so many bulbs, garlands, stars, tinsels, and lights.

She started with the tree in the living room, stringing the lights first. She grabbed a stepping stool to put the lights all the way up to the top, then she picked up the garlands and strung them around along with the tinsel. She then took the bulbs and placed them in the right places, one by one, to make the tree look festive and well-balanced. She did the same with the other tree in the den. She put the tree skirts around the bottom of the trees. Altogether it took her three hours to decorate them. Lastly, she took the twelve poinsettias and set six of them around the trees. She turned on the lights. She'd outdone herself this time. She had decorated trees many times before, but this time, she saw her creativity taken to the next level.

She was about to put the rest of the decorations leftover back in the bag when she saw a box that hadn't been opened. She looked in it, and there were the mistletoes. She thought about where to hang them and found the perfect spots. She hung them up. After all that work, she was tired. She doused the fire, left the lights on the tree lit, and headed up to bed. Tracy was awake, so she saw under the door when Shelbi walked past the room. She turned and watched as James slept. She thought maybe one day he could be her husband. She would make a fine wife, and he a good husband. She looked at her ring finger and thought what kind of ring would look good on it. She smiled. She couldn't sleep so she got up and went to see what Shelbi was up to.

She knocked on her door. In a faint voice, Shelbi said, "Come in."

"Hey sleepy head, wake up."

"Auntie, I'm tired."

"You went to bed before I did, how could you be tired?"

"You'll see." She went to sleep without another word. Tracy smiled and closed the door. She went back into the room and saw James was awake.

He said, "You're up early. You want to start on the tree?"

"Sure, let me put on a pot of coffee."

"Let me grab my robe and I'll head down with you." Tracy waited on James, and then they headed down into the kitchen.

She said, "You smell that pine from the tree? It smells so good."

"The odor fills the house. I smelled it coming downstairs."

"While the coffee is brewing, let's look at the trees and see what we have to tackle." They walked towards the living room and saw the tree lit up. It was the most beautiful tree they had ever seen.

James said, "I see why you were up so early. You started before me."

"Baby, I never came downstairs. I checked on Shelbi and then came back in the room."

"Do you think the other tree in the den is done too?"

"There's only one way to find out." They walked into the den. The tree looked exactly like the one in the living room.

"Oh my! I wonder how long it took her to do this?"

"Three hours, Auntie," Shelbi said.

They turned around. Tracy said, "You did a beautiful job on the trees. You didn't have to."

"I know, but I'm creative, so I put my gifts to good use. I was hoping you would like them."

"We love them. I don't think I could have done a better job. You made it look like a wonderland; it's absolutely beautiful."

"Thank you, Auntie. Well, I'm going back to bed. Wake me up when breakfast is ready."

"I sure will." Shelbi went back to bed, and James and Tracy went back in the kitchen to get their cups of coffee. James went all the way into the kitchen, but Tracy stopped in the doorway.

"What's wrong?" asked James.

"Should we keep the lights burning or turn them off?"

"OMG."

"What?"

"You're standing there."

"Standing where?"

"Under the mistletoe."

Tracy looked up, saw the mistletoe, smiled, and said, "You know what that means."

"It means more than what you think, but you tell me your version and then I'll tell you what it really is."

"It means whoever is standing under the mistletoe you should kiss them, am I right?"

"That's the customary version, yes."

"Is there another one?"

"My own."

"Are you going to tell me?"

Sipping his coffee with a twinkle in his eye, the same twinkle he had in Aruba, he said, "Years ago around the holiday everyone made a big thing about kissing the person under the mistletoe. I never put myself in the position to be caught under one because I don't kiss everyone. I bought some and made a promise to myself that the one that would be caught under it would be my wife. I had branches with different colors on them; one with a red bow and one with white." Tracy looked up again and saw that it was red.

She said, "What does the red bow mean?"

"That she is in my heart."

"And what does the white one mean?"

"That she is pure."

"When would you have known to put the mistletoe up?"

"When I felt I knew that I found the right woman. But I didn't put them up, Shelbi did, and there is no way she could have known my thoughts and plan; you didn't even know."

"Even if I did, I wouldn't have said anything. I didn't know she was going to put up the decorations."

"Do you think she put up the white one?"

"Does it matter?"

"I guess it doesn't."

"It does matter, Tracy, step back and looked up." Tracy stepped back and looked up on the other side of the kitchen doorway and there was the mistletoe with the white bow.

"What does this mean?"

"It means I want you to tell me what's in your heart." James walked up to Tracy, looked her in the eyes and said, "Talk to me."

"I know you've been through something."

"This is not about me, Tracy. What do you feel?"

"I feel close to you, knitted soul to soul. I feel compatible with you. I feel complete. I feel safe with you. I feel your presence everywhere I go. I feel you in my sleep. I feel you surround me. I feel that you cover me in prayer. You're my protector. I feel you in my heart, James; you're written there."

"Tracy."

"Yes, baby."

"You said, whatever it takes you will be there for me."

"I said that, and I promised."

"Can I tell you what you did?"

With her eyes closed, she whispered, "Please tell me."

"You made me happy. You made me smile. You are powerful, Tracy; you have strength unknown, but your strength has made me stronger. You supported me like pillars. You're amazing, and that's what I wanted a woman to be, the woman I would marry. I didn't look for you; you were already there. You made me feel so good, and I can't let you go."

"What are you saying, James?"

"I need you in my life, eternally."

"So, what are you saying?"

"Be my wife, Tracy."

"Is this what you want?"

"Since we left Aruba."

"Six months later and you're only telling me now?"

"I needed time. I didn't want to rush it; I didn't want you to think you were a rebound or anything."

"Do you love me, James?"

"I really do, Tracy."

"What makes me different from Michelle? You loved her too. You were going to marry her six months ago; what's the difference?"

"You make my heart skip a beat. She didn't."

"I want to marry you, James. I really do."

"So, is that a yes?"

"How can you propose without a ring?"

James took the stepping stool and reached up to grab the mistletoe with the white bow. He unraveled the white bow, and the ring slid off the ribbon. He got on one knee and said, "Mi Amor, the woman that I see dancing in my dreams every night, will you marry me?"

"I thought about this just the other night, about being your wife."

"Is that a yes?"

"Yes, James. Yes. I will marry you, but I don't want it to be an expense for you. I saw how much you spent on the wedding before."

"And that's why I want to marry you. You are so considerate. That's why I want to give you everything; you're so thoughtful. And that's why you are my everything, and I am going to take care of you." James put passion in his kiss, and Tracy returned it.

"The ring is beautiful. It's bigger than the one she had."

"I took my time picking this one out. This time I let my heart pick it out. I thought of you when I saw it, and my heart agreed this one was for you."

"You always think with your heart?"

"I didn't before, but I am making the right choice with it now."

"I'm glad you are. When do we make the announcement?"

"At the Christmas party."

"I think that would be perfect. Let me ask you, why didn't you wait to ask me at the party?"

"Because if someone else had stood under the mistletoe, I would have been disappointed. The ring was for the first person who stood under it."

"Then I should be your wife. I stood under it first." Shelbi said.

They turned around and looked and laughed. Shelbi walked up to James and kissed him.

To be continued.

After a gentle kiss on James' cheek, Shelbi said to him, "Welcome to the family." She turned to Tracy. "Congratulations, Auntie, I'm so happy for you."

"Thank you, love. I thought you were going to bed?"

"The coffee smelled so good, I started sleepwalking, and that's when I heard your conversation. I was joking about being your wife; I know my aunt is the right one for you, James."

"She really is. I couldn't have picked anyone better."

"I don't think there is anyone else other than her for you," Shelbi said. James nodded in agreement. "What are we having for breakfast? I'm starving."

"Let's go out and get something to eat," Tracy said. "We can do some shopping while we're out."

"You girls go and get something to eat. I have some painting to do."

"You sure you don't want to join us?"

"I'm positive. Take the money that's on the dresser and have a good time out, no rush back."

"Okay. Shelbi, go and get ready, and we'll leave in about an hour."

"I'll be ready in thirty."

"I need an hour," Tracy said.

"What do you need the extra thirty minutes for? Oh, cuddling time?"

"No, girl, now go get ready."

Shelbi went upstairs. Tracy grabbed James' hand and ran upstairs to the room and shut the door. James lay down, and Tracy lay on top of him and kissed him like he was just released from prison. She said, "I want to make love to you so bad. I know we haven't been that way yet, and I don't want to do anything until that night, but I feel so attached to you, like we are one body."

"I feel that way too, and I respect you for not wanting that yet. You don't rush anything, Tracy. Although I'm a man, and I love the way a woman's body feels, I will wait for that time."

"I'm glad we are so understanding."

"That's the only way to be."

"Let me get dressed." She pulled on some sweats, grabbed the money off the dresser, and said, "Oh, baby, there's five hundred here."

"I know."

"But I have my own money."

"I know that too. Just a little bit more to add on to what you have."

"Can I ask you something?"

"Was I the same way with Michelle, so giving?"

"Yes, that's what I was going to ask."

"Yes, I was. I told you I was always a giver, but with you, I want to give so much more of me. I trust you with everything I have. That's not easy for me, but I can do it with you without a second thought."

"I am in a good position right now."

"You're the only one that can be in your position. Now go and shop till you drop."

"I won't be out long."

"Take your time. I'll be here when you get back." Tracy headed downstairs. Shelbi was in the kitchen finishing her coffee.

"You ready, Auntie?"

"Yes, dear, whenever you are." Shelbi finished her coffee, and they went out.

In the car, Shelbi said, "So how does it feel to be engaged?"

"I've been engaged before."

"Let me rephrase that. How does it feel to be engaged to James?"

"Like a dream and I don't want to wake up."

"You want me to pinch you so that you know you're not?"

"No, crab, I don't need to feel your pincers." They laughed. "James makes everything so real; I just can't understand how Michelle could mess up something like this."

"Women are just like men, Auntie; they don't know it's a good thing until they lose it. The way I see him, you don't mess around on that one. He could walk around hurt and vengeful because of what someone did to him, but he's soft-hearted. He forgives quickly and moves on swiftly."

"That's a good way of looking at it. I know I would never hurt him."

"And that's why you're wearing the ring." Tracy looked at it and smiled.

"It is beautiful."

"Just like the person wearing it."

"Thank you, Shelbi, thank you for your honesty."

"That's the only way to be. I don't sugarcoat anything. I see it, I speak it. You taught me well."

"I taught you to be true to yourself and others."

"And I will never forget it." They drove up to the restaurant, went inside, found a table and looked at the menu. "Did you guys set a date yet?"

"A date for what?" A voice asked. Tracy and Shelbi look around to see where the voice came from. Eric walked up to the table. He repeated, "Setting a date for what?"

"To buy another house," Tracy said. She hid her hand so he wouldn't see her ring.

"Oh, at first I thought you all were engaged or something." Tracy gave Shelbi a look like, don't say anything. "Well, you ladies enjoy your breakfast." He walked on to his table.

"Why didn't you say you were engaged?"

"First off, we were saving the announcement for the Christmas party. Second, he's not my friend, he's James'. If he wants Eric to know, I'll leave it up to him to tell him."

"You have a good point there. Mum's the word. I don't know anyone in this area, so I won't say anything."

"Thank you. What do you want to order?"

"The omelet looks good. I think I'll order that."

"Yes, I want something light as well. I want mine with egg whites." The waitress came and took their orders. Tracy texted James to see if he wanted something to eat. He didn't text back; maybe he was painting and busy, she thought. The waitress brought their food.

Tracy got a text from James saying, "Sorry, baby, I was painting and left my phone in the room. I ate something, so no need to bring me anything. Thanks for thinking about me."

"You are welcome, love," Tracy said.

"Every time I look up from eating my food this woman keeps looking at us," said Shelbi.

"What woman?"

"That one over there." Tracy turned around. As she turned so did the woman, so her face was hidden.

"That's Michelle."

"James' ex?"

"Yes."

"Why does she keep looking over here?"

"I don't know, Shelbi."

"Would you like for me to go and ask her?"

"No, I don't need extra attention today."

"Well, it looks like I don't have to. Here she comes." Tracy didn't turn around; she waited until Michelle approached her table, but Michelle walked right by them and sat with Eric.

Tracy said, "Oh, she was probably looking at Eric, that's why she was looking over here."

"No, Auntie, the last time I got my vision checked it was 20/20, and I know she was looking at you."

"Let's finish eating and get the shopping out the way."

Ten minutes later, Michelle and Eric were leaving left. They walked by Tracy and Shelbi. Eric walked by first, then Michelle. Tracy noticed she'd gained some pounds since she last saw her.

Michelle stopped and said, "Oh, hey, Tracy, I didn't know that was you." Shelbi looked at her and rolled her eyes.

Tracy straight-faced her and said, "Hey, I didn't notice you here either. How are you?"

"I'm well and yourself?"

"I'm perfectly fine."

"I hear James is having a Christmas party."

"Yes, by invitation only. Did you get one?"

"No, I didn't."

Shelbi said, "Then, You're Uninvited."

"Well, according to James this morning, I am." Shelbi was about to get up. Tracy looked at her with a 'no' expression, and she sat back down.

"Well, if he invited you, I guess we will see you at the party."

"I guess you will." Michelle walked off.

Shelbi said, "Auntie?"

"Let's finish our breakfast and go."

"You're not going to question James about this?"

"If he invited her it must be a good reason."

"If I was you—"

"But you're not, Shelbi. Insecure women question their men. I'm secure in myself and the man I'm with. I don't think he would keep secrets from me."

"You said 'think,' Auntie."

"Yes, I did."

"So, it's still questionable. See if you said, 'you know,' then there's nothing to worry about, but you said 'think'; that means you will be questioning him later. I hope he's in the mood for interrogation." Tracy was unsure. She trusted James, but this relationship was still new. Although she was wearing the ring, that did not mean he was committed. Shelbi was right; she did have some questions for him, and she would get the answers she knew all along. They finished breakfast and headed out to shop. The encounter with Michelle, she put a damper on Tracy's mood; she wasn't as joyful as she was earlier.

The expression on her face made Shelbi ask, "She pulled you off your square, didn't she?"

"What does that mean?"

"A person has the power to change your mood."

"I was fine until she said she talked to him this morning."

"She didn't say she talked. She just said according to him this morning. It could've been a text or Eric could've told her about it, and she said James did just to see your reaction."

"I didn't give her one."

"You're not supposed to. You're wearing the ring. Where is your ring?" Tracy pulled it out of her pocket and put it back on.

"I took it off when Eric came by. I didn't want him announcing to the world before James and I did. Yes, I'm wearing the ring—and so was Michelle."

"Yes, but you have the ring around his heart. Your love is secured, and nothing can penetrate that."

"How do you know these things?"

"By the way he looks at you. He has that twinkle in his eye for you; I hope you noticed that."

"I've noticed that in Aruba, and when he looks at me, it still does that."

"A twinkle in the eye is just like butterflies. Any woman can give a man an erection, but only one can give him butterflies. Ask him did you give him that."

"Which one?"

"The butterflies, Auntie, the butterflies. Did you get them with him?"

"When I first met him, I was going through my divorce. I got them the night I met him at his art exhibit."

"Did you tell him that?"

"No, I didn't. He was dating Michelle at the time. I thought I was just nervous, but they never went away."

"In your conversation tonight, you need to bring that up. I don't know what you've been talking about for the past six months, but if you are going to be getting married, it's time to have a heart-to-heart conversation."

"Are you some kind of therapist that I don't know about?"

"No, just gifted. I have a spiritual degree in love; I didn't have to go to school for it, it's in my DNA.

"I should've known. I've seen it in the years of you growing."

"Yes, Auntie, of all people you should know." Tracy smiled. "After we are done shopping, drop me off at your apartment. You'll need this time alone."

"Yes, we do need to talk."

"I think it's the right time to." Tracy cut the shopping short, dropped Shelbi off at the apartment, and then headed to James' house. James was in the studio painting when Tracy arrived. She walked in the studio.

He said, "Hey, baby, you're back early, were the stores crowded?"

"Too crowded, so crowded it changed my mood and I just wanted to come home." James noticed how she felt, and it wasn't normal. He wasn't going to ignore how she was feeling, so he stopped painting and pulled her into him and said, "Talk to me."

"I ran into Michelle."

"Did you? Is that what changed your mood?"

"Seeing her was fine, it's what she said."

"What did she say?"

"She knew about the Christmas party, and you invited her."

"Is that all she said?"

"Yes."

"And did you believe her?"

"I don't know what to believe right now."

"What does that mean?"

"Everything has happened so fast. You were going to marry her six months ago, and now we are engaged."

"Tracy, I need to know do you trust me." She turned her head. "Look at me, please, I need to know that you trust me."

With a teardrop and closed eyes, she said, "With all my heart I do, James. All my heart, baby, I do trust you."

"I will forever be honest with you, and believe me when I say this, I have not talked to Michelle since that day we were at the movies. That's the last time I talked to her. I don't know where she got that information from, but she didn't get it from me. I am in love with you. I would never jeopardize my relationship with you."

"She sounded so convincing when she said that she talked to you."

"Come here, baby, let me wrap my arms around you, like you have your heart wrapped around mine." He wrapped them around her waist so tight. "How does that feel?"

"Like if you hug me any tighter, we'd be one body."

"And that's what I am with you, one; I will always be that with you, Tracy. I can be me with you; I can be free, and still be me, and you let me be who I am, not changing anything. That's why I love you; that's why I want to marry you. Michelle gave me something you didn't."

"What is that?"

"She gave me her body. She gave me something I wanted; you gave me your heart, which was something I needed. When you gave your heart, it made me want to share mine with you freely. You shared your desires, your dreams, you helped me find me. I didn't know what I really wanted until I came back from Aruba. I found me because of you. I'm a grown man but still finding myself. I was undecided about what I needed in my life. Every door I needed opened in me, you unlocked, just by you being you, sharing you.

"When I met you, something broke in me. The words I spoke to you, I had not said before. The flow of them came out of my mouth without hesitation; they were deeper than I could imagine. I didn't know I could speak like that, until I met you.

"Before you ever said a word to me, I heard you; I looked at you like I never looked at a woman before. I didn't undress you with my eyes; I covered you with my love. I think I've always loved you, Tracy, but at the time you were going through your divorce, and I didn't want to spring that on you. I settled for less."

"I'm listening."

"I settled for what pleased me sexually, not soulfully."

"Talk to me."

"Michelle pleased my body in ways I couldn't imagine, but you calmed the savage beast and soothed my soul. I loved how she made me feel, but I was still searching for someone. I was satisfied and dissatisfied at the same time. I needed more, and she couldn't give it to me."

"Did you tell her that?"

"I did, but she didn't know what I meant. I didn't know what I needed. She just kept giving me what pleased me—that's all she knew how to do—but you came with a different conversation, and my soul was satisfied. No other woman did that to me, Tracy, that's why I know you are my wife. I'm glad Michelle didn't show up at the wedding. My wife was already there.

"Every man needs what you have in you, Tracy. You're so powerful; there's a brilliance about you. You sparkle; you shine your light in dark places. You exposed the savage beast in me, tamed it into a cub, and I've been purring after you ever since. But every man won't have you because you belong to me. That's why you stood under the mistletoe; you're so pure and genuine. I knew there was a certain type of woman for me; I just didn't know it was going to be you. It's been you all the time, and I've been craving you ever since the day I met you."

"OMG, James!"

"And that's what I said the first time I saw you."

"Why didn't you say anything then?"

"You needed time to heal. When I met you, I didn't know you were going through a divorce, but as we got to know each other, the more you shared with me, the more I adored you."

"Why did it take us so long to have this kind of a conversation? It is very much needed."

"I think we were still in the wooing stage of our relationship. Michelle came and put a damper on your mood."

"She's no threat to me. I just want to make sure we have an understanding."

"We will always have that."

"I wonder how she found out about the party?"

"I didn't tell her, so she didn't get it from me."

"She walked over and sat at the table with Eric before she approached our table."

"Oh, did she?"

"Do you think she knows about us?"

"It's a possibility, but she's no threat to you or no match for you. I know what I want so if she does show up, I will handle it."

"I know you will, so let's start working on the menu. Did you get all the RSVPs?"

"Yes, they all responded. All that's left to do is decide on the menu and order liquor for the open bar, and we will have everything done."

"Okay so I'll leave you to your painting and I'll think of something for the menu."

"I'm done painting for now. Let's go do some shopping, get you back into that mood you were in before you had breakfast."

"You do care about my feelings."

"I care about everything when it comes to you." He put up his paint and supplies, slipped on some clothes and they headed out to shop. Tracy called Shelbi and checked on her. She let her know she was going shopping and she would be by the apartment afterwards. While out, they talked about the menu and decided on prime rib, mashed potatoes and gravy, sautéed green beans in butter and garlic, and creamed spinach, all served with a Cabernet Sauvignon. The menu was set, now onto shopping. The traffic was jammed and so were the stores. They hit the malls, got a bite to eat. Most of their purchases were made at home online; they were just doing last-minute shopping. On the way home, James got a text from his best man and friend from the wedding, Sean.

"My date for the night canceled on me, so I will be solo for the night. Wanted to let you know early for the head count."

James texted back. "Thanks. You'll have a good time and maybe you'll meet someone there."

"Oh, you have someone in mind?"

"Are you looking?"

"No, not really, but I do want to have a good time."

"Bring your charismatic personality and see what happens."

"Bet, I'll see you then."

James said to Tracy, "Sean's date canceled. Maybe Shelbi can be his date that night."

"She's picky, plus she's from out of town, so it wouldn't work."

"I'm not trying to marry them, Tracy, just a companion for the night."

"Oh, well in that case, fine. I will introduce them that night."

"Sounds good to me." In the three weeks before the event, they called the caterer, cleaned, shopped, painted, visited the sick, worked, and played. The weeks flew by. A week before the event, they had the lights on the house and bushes lit up on the outside. Everything was coming together. Tt was a casual-dress event with friends and family, so no need to pull out the tux and gown; it was going to be a night of joy and laughter. Tracy made an appointment for Shelbi and her to get their hair done that early morning. Tracy knew how to cut hair, so she would be cutting James' hair that afternoon.

Open bar from 6:00 pm to 7:00 pm, dinner served at 7:00 pm. Tracy was looking at the invitation, white with gold trim. She loved how James put her in charge of the celebration. She did the invitations, picked out the dinner and silverware. He was making sure she was a part of his life; he included her in everything. Friday night, the eve of the dinner, Tracy was in the kitchen tidying up. James came up behind her and kissed her on the cheek.

She turned around, and he said, "You're the best thing that has ever happened to me. No one could've made me any happier than you."

"We belong together, and nothing can stop that. I love you, baby."

"I love you more. Let's get some sleep; we have a long day ahead of us." Tracy and James went to bed. She set the alarm for early morning so she could pick Shelbi up and then head to the salon. She then went to sleep. Later she woke up crying. James woke up and quickly comforted Tracy, asking, "What's wrong? What's the matter?"

"I had this dream that Michelle had a leash around your neck like a dog, and she kept pulling on you. You couldn't go anywhere. She had this control over you. Everywhere she went, she had you on a leash just pulling you; there was no way for you to escape. I couldn't reach you; I couldn't help you; I was crying and couldn't help you. It was so real, James. I was right there and couldn't help you!"

James said, "It was just a dream, baby, just a dream."

"It was a nightmare. It seemed so real."

"It's over now. Let me hold you. I'm right here. Go to sleep, baby, it's okay."

"I want to stay up. I don't want her taking you from me."

"She can't do anything to me or us. I am not going anywhere. Trust me, I will hold you so you'll know I'm here."

"I'm not a person who hates people, I'm really not, but that dream put a different taste in my mouth about her. I don't want to say it, but that word sure is forming to announce it."

"Go to sleep, Tracy. I know you could never say anything like that."

"Hmph." She took a deep breath and slowly drifted to sleep. James watched her, and at the same time, he thought about what she dreamt about. What could that dream have meant? He stayed awake for about an hour thinking about it, with no clue how to decode the nightmare. He went to sleep, and two hours later her alarm went off. She got up, took a shower, got dressed, kissed James on the cheek and headed out to pick up Shelbi.

She texted her that she was on the way. Fifteen minutes later she honked the horn, and Shelbi came out.

"Good morning, Auntie. You look like you need some more sleep."

"I do, but I have so much to do today."

"I don't like the sound in your voice. What's the matter?"

"I had a bad dream last night, and I woke up crying."

"You want to talk about it?"

"No, I don't want to repeat the way I was feeling afterward."

"Must've been some dream."

"Yes, one I don't want to dream of again. Changing the subject, what are you wearing tonight?"

"Something cute like me."

"Of course, you are. With that petite shape, you could wear a onesie and still be cute."

"With some heels, heck, yeah." They pulled up to the salon and walked in. Their stylists were ready for them.

Tracy got a text from James. "Are you okay?"

"I'm fine."

"No, you're not. I can feel you. Be truthful with me."

"I can't get that dream out of my head."

"Do you have anything else to do after you get your hair done?"

"No, not really."

"Come home to me and relax."

"I will. I love you."

"I will love you always." Their hair was done in two hours. Tracy wasted no time. She hurried back home to James and went into the bedroom where he was waiting for her. He undressed her and lay her on the bed. He poured hot massage oil in his hands and gave her a sensual massage. He rubbed and massaged every area of her body; he pleased her body as she pleased his soul. It was nothing erotic, just soothing. She quietly went to sleep. He lay there and watched her. He wanted to carry her burdens; he was feeling every bit of her pain and anger. He didn't want her to worry; he was the man who was going to fight her battles and protect her, so he lay and watched her take every breath in her peaceful sleep.

Two hours later, she woke up to his eyes looking at hers.

He said, "Did you sleep well?"

"I did, thank you so much. I needed that."

"No problem. Are you ready to cut my hair?"

"I am. Let me get the clippers." James got the chair and cape. He sat down. She put the cape around him and started cutting his hair.

James loved the attention she would give him doing it. She would softly blow the hair off his ears. But this time when she was cutting the front, she straddled him and edged the front in a seductive way. James swallowed as she moved her body on his. He was aroused.

After she finished and was about to get up, James said, "Please don't get up."

"What's wrong?"

"Nothing. I just like the way this feels."

"I do too."

"I know you would feel so good to me, Tracy. I can feel me inside of you, but I will wait until we say our vows. I love you enough to wait. That's something that I haven't done before, but I will wait for you."

"It will be well worth it."

"I know."

"Can I get up now?"

"Sigh, yes."

"We have things to do. It's 1:00 in the afternoon, the caterers will be here at 3:00." Tracy looked outside; it was starting to snow.

"Looks like we have a visitor." James came to see what she was looking at.

He saw the snow and said, "If it sticks, I'll make sure to shovel it. Don't want no one slipping and falling tonight."

"From the looks of it, you better start early. I heard we are getting about two to three feet tonight."

"Let me get the salt and start putting it down." Tracy went downstairs and started setting the table. She turned on some music to set the mood. The snow was coming down hard now. She turned on the Christmas tree lights. The house was filled with the aroma of pine from the tree, and the spirit of the holiday was everywhere in the house. Tracy was in a better mood. She walked up to the window in the den and saw James putting the salt on the driveway and sidewalk. She smiled in her heart, and it showed on her face. She got a text from the caterers that they would be arriving in the next half-hour. She made sure their space was set up and ready.

Minutes later, Shelbi pulled up, and soon after, the caterers. James showed them where to park and where to set up. Shelbi went upstairs to get ready. James got a text from Sean to see if he could come early due to the snow. James texted back sure. Everything was starting to come together. The house felt warm with the fireplaces burning. James prepared the liquor for the open bar. Time was closing in with one hour to spare. The doorbell rang; it was Sean.

"Hey, man, what's going on, come on in." James took his coat and hung it in the closet. "I see you still came dateless."

"Yeah, she was a last-minute date, nothing serious, just someone to accompany me. The house looks beautiful; you sure know how to decorate."

"Oh, this is none of my doing. Tracy's niece did all the decorating."

"Well, she's got my vote. I love it. I'd like to see what else she can do." Just as he said that, Shelbi came walking down the stairs. Sean looked at her like she was a girl coming down the stairs for her prom. "And who is this?"

"This is Tracy's niece, Shelbi."

"She can dress too." As she got to the bottom of the stairs, James introduced them.

"Sean, this is Shelbi; Shelbi, Sean."

"Pleased to meet you, Sean."

"The pleasure is all mine, Shelbi. You're absolutely beautiful."

"Why thank you, you're stunning yourself."

"Would you two care to have a drink?"

"Sure," they replied. James made them a drink, then left them to mingle while he went to dress. Tracy was almost ready when he entered the room.

"I think we have a match downstairs."

"Who?"

"Sean and Shelbi."

"No, for real."

"Yep."

"Oh, this I have to see."

"Give them some time to converse, you can interrogate her later, detective."

"Ha ha, you're so funny. Go and get dressed, love. The guests will be showing up momentarily."

"Okay." A half hour later the doorbell rang. James ran down, and Tracy walked down after him. He opened the door; it was his mom and dad. Other cars were pulling in the driveway. He hugged his mother and shook his dad's hand. Tracy gave his mom and dad a hug. Non-stop the doorbell rang. The guests were showing up promptly at 6:00 pm. James went behind the bar and started making drinks for the guests. the smell of the prime rib filled the room. Music was playing; there was lots of laughter; the atmosphere couldn't get any better. The doorbell rang. It was Eric, the last guest to show up.

"Well, I'm glad you made it. Usually, you're the first to come."

"I know, man, I got tied up in something."

"I don't even want to know."

"Oh, not like that. I have to tell you something."

"Give me a minute. I have an announcement to make." James walked away, Eric tried to grab his arm, but James moved swiftly. James hit his glass.

"Good evening, everyone. I have an announcement to make. First, I want to say I'm glad that you all are here to celebrate my first Christmas dinner at my home. Those whom I have chosen to be here are very dear to me, and I thank you for taking time out of your busy schedule to be here. Although I sent the invitations out a month ago, you still chose to be here tonight with me." He walked over and grabbed Tracy's hand. The doorbell rang and Eric went to answer it.

He opened the door and said, "I thought I told you to wait in the car."

"It's cold out there, and you're taking too long to come back and get me."

"Don't go in there. He's making an announcement."

"Okay, I'll wait in the hallway." Eric walked back into the living room to hear what James' big news was.

James said, "Tracy has been in my life for quite some time. She started out as my best friend, and after that, she became so much more. I love this woman with all my heart, and I want to spend the rest of my life with her. We got engaged a couple of weeks ago, but I wanted to share the news with you all tonight. She said yes to me."

"And I'll say it again in front of family and friends, yes, James, I will marry you." Everyone said 'aw' and clapped their hands. After everyone stopped clapping, they heard a clap from the hallway. A woman came into the living room.

Shelbi said, "I told you before and I'll tell you again, you're uninvited."

"I know I am, but I just wanted to congratulate James. He's not only going to be a husband; he's going to be a father."

James looked at Tracy then looked at Michelle and said, "Tracy's not pregnant."

"No, she's not, but I am." Michelle took off her coat and showed off her protruding stomach.

Tracy, James and Shelbi said, "What the hell?"

Tracy looked at James with tears in her eyes, she said.

"She just put that leash around your neck.

TBC IN VOL. III

NOW YOU'RE SPEAKING MY LANGUAGE

Friday night, everyone was getting ready for the storm. Six to ten inches of snow was in the forecast for tonight, and since Kendall didn't have to work this weekend, he went to the store to pick up some food. He got to the cashier, paid for the items, and headed to his car. He saw a lady at the corner getting ready to cross the street. A car was coming. He heard the car horn blow, but the lady didn't seem to notice it. He screamed to her, but she didn't answer. He dropped his groceries, ran in the road and grabbed her. They fell to the ground, tumbling, while the car drove by with the horn blaring. She looked startled and scared and fought him. He helped her up.

Kendall said, "Didn't you see the car? Didn't you hear the horn blowing?" She looked at him, still wanting to fight, then she started moving her hands. He didn't understand what she was doing.

He said again, "Didn't you hear the horn blowing?" She started moving her hands again, and he still didn't know what she was doing. A lady passing by noticed the conversation and entered in, using her hands.

Then the lady said to Kendall, "You scared her. Why did you push her out of the road?"

"There was a car coming, and she didn't hear the horn—or me—so I pushed her. I didn't want her to get hit." The second lady told the first lady what Kendall said.

Then the second lady said to Kendall, "She says, 'Thank you for saving me. I appreciate that. I will be more careful the next time.'"

"You're welcome. What are you two doing with your hands?"

"We are using sign language; she is deaf. That's why she didn't hear you or the car."

"Oh, I see. Ask her if she is alright."

The lady asked, and the first lady replied, "I am and thank you very much."

"Ask her if she needs a ride. It's starting to snow and it's getting cold."

The second lady signed to the first lady, then told Kendall, "No, she doesn't have far to walk."

"But it's snowing hard. Is she sure she doesn't need a ride?"

She said, "No, she's fine, and thank you again."

"You're welcome." The ladies started walking. Kendall had forgotten that his groceries were on the ground. Now he ran across the street to get them. They were covered in snow, and he almost didn't see them. He put his packages in the car and headed home. The deaf lady was walking in the same direction. He drove slowly for two reasons: it was snowing, and he wanted to make sure wherever she was going she would get there safely.

She was headed into Kendall's apartment building. Kendall smiled. He was glad he didn't have to drive any further; he didn't want her to think he was a stalker. He was concerned that she couldn't hear and almost got hit. He parked his car, grabbed his groceries and headed in. She pressed the buttons for entry and the door unlocked. She went in. By the time Kendall got to the door, it had closed. He put his code in and went in. He saw her going to her apartment. He walked to the elevator and watched her as she fumbled through her purse while he waited for the elevator. The doors opened. When he reached his apartment, the first thing that hit his nose was the garbage he forgot to take out.

He put his bags on the counter and grabbed the trash to take to the chute. It had a "chute is filled to capacity" sign on it, so he went downstairs to put it in the other dumpster. When he got off the elevator, he saw the lady sitting by her door, crying. He walked up to her and asked what was wrong. Her mouth and hands were moving at the same time. Kendall doesn't know what she was saying. He held up one finger, reached for his phone, pointed to his phone, and then pointed at her, asking if she had a phone. She pulled her cell phone out of her purse. He said slowly so she could read his lips, "What's your phone number?" She took his phone and entered her phone number. He then sent her a text message.

"What's the matter?"

"I can't find my key."

"Where did you last have it?"

"I think I lost them when you pushed me out of the way. I had my keys in my pocket or hand; I can't remember."

"Would you like to go look for them? I will help you find them."

"Yes, but I have to use the restroom."

"Come with me, you can use mine." Kendall took her to his apartment, and she used the restroom.

She then texted him, "Thank you."

"You're welcome. You want to go look for your keys now?"

"Yes, we can." They walked outside. Snow had covered the streets; there was already four inches. She sighed and texted, "There's a lot of snow. I don't know if we will find it."

"Let's try."

"Okay." They walked four blocks down and proceeded to look for the keys. It was night, dark, and the snow had covered everything, so without a shovel, it was hard to look. They looked for about twenty-minutes without a sign of her keys.

He texted her, "It's getting cold. Let's head back to the apartment."

"I need to find my keys."

"We'll look for them tomorrow. Let's go." They headed back. When they got in the hallway. Kendall texted, "Do you have any family you can stay with?"

"No."

"Well, I can't leave you sitting outside of your apartment. If you don't mind, you can stay with me tonight, and then I can help you look for your keys tomorrow.

"I don't know you. I can't stay with someone I don't know."

"Technically, I'm not a stranger. I just saved your life." She looked at him and smiled.

"Okay, just for tonight, and we will look for my keys in the morning."

"Okay, let's get you settled in." They went back upstairs; his apartment was a little cold, so he turned on the heat. He went into his room and pulled out some pajamas and a shirt. He held them up to her; she nodded her head and smiled. He handed them to her, and she went into the bathroom to change. While she was changing, he pulled out the sofa bed and put on some clean sheets and a pillow. She came out of the bathroom and sat on the sofa bed with her legs folded.

Kendall pointed at her and then rubbed his stomach. She nodded yes. He made her a salad and gave her a bottle of water, while he cooked a pot of spaghetti. She sat on the bar stool and ate her salad while she watched him cook. While the noodles were boiling, he texted her and asked what her name was.

"Adriana."

"My name is Kendall." She looked up and smiled. "How do you say your name in sign language?" She showed him slowly with her hand how to say it. He tried to but got it wrong. She laughed, and so did he. She grabbed his hand and formed his fingers to make the gestures. She did it a couple of times until he got it right. When he did it on his own, she clapped her hands, smiling, and pointed at him, as if to say you got it. Kendall was glad that he made her smile.

"How old are you?"

"Twenty-four." She formed her lips and pointed at him. "And you?"

"I'm thirty."

"Okay, where do you work?" she texted him.

"I'm a security guard. How about you?"

"I'm a fifth-grade teacher. This is my first-year teaching. I teach deaf students, and I love it."

"That's awesome. Is life complicated not being able to hear?"

"I don't know. Is your life complicated being able to?"

"Good point. I don't know how it is not to hear, and you don't know how it is to hear."

"My life is just like yours. I live it. Being deaf is not a handicap nor challenging for me; I am normal like any other person."

"Do you have a lot of friends who are deaf?"

"I have some friends that can hear and some who are deaf."

"That's awesome."

"I think so."

"Are you ready to eat?"

"Yes." He fixed their plates, and she started eating. She pointed down to her plate and gave him two thumbs up.

"Thank you," she signed.

"You're welcome." She finished her plate.

"Are you full?" he said slowly.

"I'm full." She understood him.

"You can read lips very well?"

She formed her lips slowly. "Yes, I have to learn what people are saying. I can read lips whether they are talking fast or slow. When I respond, I form my lips slowly so they can understand."

"Isn't that frustrating?"

"It can be at times, for me and for them, because they can't speak my language, so I go to places where I can have a regular conversation and that's with my friends that know how to speak the language."

"Sign language looks complicated to learn."

"Just like any other language, Spanish, French, Italian, it all takes time. I know Spanish sign language. Since I had to learn English, why not Spanish?"

"I like Spanish. It's a very sensual language, a love language."

"Yes, it is, but with Spanish, you have to have the tongue for it. You can't just say words and not sound Spanish."

"Do you have to do the same thing with sign language, sound Spanish?"

She laughed. "Sign language doesn't have sound. What matters is they know what I'm saying in Spanish, that's all." Kendall looked at his watch.

"It's 10:00 pm," he said. "Are you ready to go to sleep?"

"Not really, I like the conversation I'm having with you."

"Okay, let me take a shower and I'll pull out a game or something we can play."

"I would like that."

Kendall was getting ready to clean up the kitchen when Adriana tapped him on the shoulder. "I'll do the dishes."

"You sure?"

"Yes."

"Okay, you clean up while I clean up." She smiled. She ran the dishwasher, and Kendall went to take a shower. She put the food in a container and washed the dishes. By the time she was finished, he was. She turned off the kitchen light, walked to the window. The snow falling looked beautiful. The entire street and cars were covered. She didn't hear Kendall coming into the room. He tapped her on her shoulder, and she turned around and smiled. He held up a Connect-Four game, and she nodded her head yes. They sat at the table and played a few games. Adriana was very competitive; every game they played she won. It was midnight when they stopped playing.

Kendall said, "Get some sleep. In the morning, we will look for your keys." Adriana had a look of disappointment on her face. "What's wrong?"

"Nothing."

"Something is wrong by the look on your face. What's the matter?" She started moving her hands, and then stopped and sighed. She looked for her phone and texted.

"No one has never paid me any attention because of my disability. And now I have yours, and now you're stopping."

"Oh, I'm not stopping it; I'm just tired. We can do this tomorrow. I can be your best friend if you want. I think you're a cool girl to hang with, so let this be the first night of a good friendship. We can shake on it." Kendall held out his hand, she shook it and smiled. "Good night and get some rest."

She signed, "Good night." She got under the covers and turned on the TV. Kendall went to bed but didn't sleep; he thought about Adriana. He had a desire to protect her. He felt like a big brother, and if she didn't have one he was going to be that to her. He knew he couldn't be with her all the time, but moments he could be, he would be. Finally, he went to sleep. In the morning, he awakened to an unusual smell. He got up and went into the living room. He didn't see Adriana, so he went into the kitchen. His girlfriend Mika was there.

"Good morning, Mika, why didn't you tell me you were coming over?"

"I wanted to surprise you. I see why you didn't want me to come over last night; you had company."

"And where is my company?"

"She left."

"And went where?"

"I don't know. She put on her clothes and left after I came in."

172

Kendall hurried and put on his clothes to look for Adriana.

"Where are you going?"

"To look for her."

"Who is she?"

"That's none of your concern."

"Don't you want any breakfast?"

"You can't cook. Throw it away and leave my key on your way out." He slammed the door and went looking for Adriana. He ran downstairs and didn't see her in front of her door, so he ran a few blocks to where she would be looking for her keys. There he found her. He went up to her, speaking slowly. "Good morning."

She signed, "Good morning."

"Why did you leave?

She started moving her hands and trying to talk. She looked angry, then she stopped, and started looking for her keys again. He stepped in front of her and said, "Talk to me. Why did you leave?" She started moving her hands again. "So, you're not going to tell me."

"No." A car started to move and when it did, Adriana noticed her keys; they were under the car. She ran to get them, smiling in relief. She started walking back to the apartment, Kendall right behind her. he didn't say anything to her. Whatever it was, he was going to let her cool off. She keyed in the code, the door unlocked, and they both went in. Kendall stood there until she got into her apartment. She went in and slammed her door. He went to his apartment, hoping Mika was still there. She was.

"What did you say to her?"

"I asked her what she was doing here."

"You couldn't have asked her that, she's deaf."

"Oh, I know sign language. We had an interesting conversation."

"What did you tell her?"

"That I was your woman, and you weren't interested in her, although she said you were."

"You told her what? We're not together."

"What do you mean we're not together?"

"I haven't called you in a while; I don't ask you to come over. Shouldn't that tell you anything?"

"I just assumed you needed your space."

"If I don't text you back or don't call you, that should tell you something."

"I wasn't ready to let you go."

"But I was. When I asked you for my key, that should've told you that it was over, but I see you had a spare made."

"I wanted to know who was taking my place."

"You, insecure woman you! Okay, you can keep that key. I'll have my locks changed by the time the door hits your behind. You had no right telling her anything about me; there is no us. It's over, and it's been over. Please leave, Mika, don't ever step foot near me or her again."

"She means that much to you."

"She means enough for me to tell you what I just told you. Please leave now." Mika looked at him, rolled her eyes as she was leaving, threw the key at him, and shut the door. Kendall texted Adriana. She did not respond. He went downstairs to knock on her door, and she didn't answer. He waited at her door for fifteen minutes; she did not open it. He went back upstairs and sat on the couch, texting her again. No response. Kendall was furious. He didn't think of her as his girlfriend, but he did care enough to think about her feelings. He walked over to the window. It had started to snow again. He saw a moving van pull up to the apartment building. He texted her one more time, still no response. He sat back down on the couch, turned on the TV and watched it, falling asleep. He woke up two and a half hours later.

He looked at his phone and saw a response from Adriana. He was anxious to see what it said. "Thank you for everything. Goodbye." That wasn't what he was expecting.

He texted back, "What do you mean, goodbye?" He waited for a reply, but there was none. He went downstairs to knock on her door.

The next-door neighbor was coming out of his apartment. He said, "She's gone. She moved out about an hour or so ago. I helped her move."

"Where did she go?"

"I don't know. I just helped her move the items on the truck." Kendall remembered seeing a van pull up, but people were always moving in and out. She must have left while he was sleep. Kendall exhaled a heavy sigh and went to his apartment. He didn't have any other information on Adriana; he didn't know her last name, where she worked, nothing. All he had was her phone number, and she wasn't responding to his messages. He felt like he had just lost his best friend. He had just made a promise to her that she was that—could she have felt something for him that he didn't feel for her?

He wished he knew what she was saying. He wished he understood so their communication would have been better. Although they were talking, it wasn't in her language. The night came, and the next morning, and she still did not respond to his messages. He was worried about her. Where did she go? Was she okay? Was it something he'd done or something Mika said? Had Mika told him everything she said to Adriana? He was starting to feel more than just her best friend, more than her big brother; he felt a connection with her. He wanted to learn more about her, but he didn't know where to start since he didn't know where she was.

Kendall remembered some sign language. He knew how to sign good night and good morning; he knew how to say her name. He went online to see what else he could learn. He sat at the computer for five hours, learning sign language. He was driven, excited; he wanted to learn more. He signed up for classes after work. Two hours a day he spent learning that language. When he was done with class, he would go home and be on the computer for three more hours. He was determined to know and speak sign language fluently.

On his breaks at work, he was reading the book. He would stand in front of the mirror and sign. He wanted to make sure he looked right doing it. Learning the language became his passion and took all his free time. He didn't have a social life anymore. In one year, he learned to sign, took the test and passed it. He didn't know if he would ever see Adriana again, but if he did, he would understand what she was saying. From time to time, he looked at the text messages he had sent her and that she had sent him; he never erased them. A year had passed, and she had never responded to his messages. He knew if she hadn't done it by now, she wouldn't.

One Sunday night, he didn't want to be at home, so he went to the bar to watch football. It was the playoffs, Philadelphia Eagles against the Chicago Bears. He wasn't a fan of either, but he was a football fanatic. He sat down, ordered a beer, and watched the game. A gentleman sat at the bar next to him and asked for a beer. The bartender didn't know what he said. Kendall said, "This gentleman would like a Bud Light."

The man looked at him and signed, "You know sign language?"

"Yes, I understood what you said."

"Thank you."

"You're welcome." Kendall went back to watching the game. He was watching, but he wasn't; he kept looking at his phone, thinking of Adriana. Maybe one day she would text him back. It had been a year, but he was hopeful. By the time he paid attention to the game the score was 16-15, Eagles leading by a point. With ten seconds, it was 3rd down, and the Bears were close enough to make a field goal. If they scored, the Eagles would be out of the playoffs. The kicker was in position. Before he kicked the ball, the Eagles coach called a time out. He kicked the ball. Although it was a good field goal the time out saved the Eagles. It was their last time out. The kicker had to kick the ball again. In position, the kicker kicked. The ball hit the post and fell in front of the post instead of behind it. The Eagles won, by a point. It was the best game of the season. Although Kendall wasn't a fan, he joined the uproar.

He signed to the guy next to him that the next beer was on him. The man signed back, thank you. Kendall said you're welcome, paid the tab and headed home. Leaving the bar, he saw people reacting to the game, how happy they were, couples hugging and kissing, friends just having a good time. All he wanted was his Adriana. On the way home, he got a text.

He didn't notice the number. The text said, "I am a friend of Adriana's. She has been talking about you, and she misses you. I snuck her phone to get your phone number to text you. We are at this restaurant having dinner. If you hurry you can catch us and surprise her.

Kendall texted back, "I'm on the way."

He got in his car and drove to the address. He walked in and looked around. He didn't see her. Was this a set-up? He walked around the corner and there she was. She was having a conversation, so she didn't see him until he walked up to the table. She saw him, and she stopped moving her hands. Kendall signed, "Hello, Adriana."

With a tear falling down her face, she signed back, "Hello, Kendall." She got up and hugged him so tight. He gripped her like he was never going to let her go. She kissed him, and he didn't stop her, then she abruptly stopped.

She said, "Are you married now?"

Kendall looked surprised. He signed, "Married to who?"

Adriana looked surprised because he knew her language. She signed, "To your girlfriend. She told me you all were getting married."

"No, I wasn't marrying her. She's not my girlfriend anymore." She started kissing him again, and her friend started clapping and laughing.

"How did you know I was here?"

"Someone knew you wanted to see me, and they reached out to me." She turned around and looked at Sheena and smiled.

Sheena signed, "I knew you missed him. I had to do something."

Adriana went over to Sheena and kissed her on the cheek and signed, "Thank you, my friend."

"You are so welcome."

Kendall sat down with them and they began conversing. He knew exactly what they were saying, so he joined the conversation.

Adriana looked at him with amazement. She signed, "Now you're speaking my language, I like that."

He looked at her with love in his eyes and signed, "I want to communicate with you, it's important to me and so are you." She smiled. She started to sign and then stopped. She gasped, grabbed hold of his shirt and gasped again.

"What's wrong?!"

She grabbed her chest, gasping for air. Kendall shouted. "Call 911."

To Be Continued...

Sheena moved Kendall out of the way. She reached into Adriana's purse and got her inhaler. She opened her mouth and pumped the inhaler. "Inhale, breathe, Adriana, breathe." She pumped it again. "Inhale, breathe, come on, breathe."

Kendall said again, "Someone call 911."

Sheena signed to him, "No, she is fine."

"How do you know?"

"Wait." Sheena pumped the inhaler again. Adriana began to breathe normally. Kendall stood there with a frantic look on his face. Adriana looked at Kendall with sorrowful eyes. He went over to her and sat down next to her. She lay her head on his chest and began to cry. He comforted her, not knowing what was going on. Sheena signed to everyone, "I think it's time to go."

"What is going on? Go where? I just got here; I'm not ready for her to go yet."

"Adriana is sick. She needs to go home."

"Sick? What do you mean, sick?" He looked at her and signed. "What's wrong? You can tell me. I promise I'll understand."

"I have lupus and asthma." Adriana grabbed her purse. She was getting ready to leave.

Kendall got up and signed, "Where are you going? Please don't leave me."

Sheena tapped him on the shoulder. "She needs to go home."

"Well, can I come over? I don't want her to leave me right now."

"She needs to rest."

"I promise I won't bother her. I just don't want to leave her right now."

Adriana signed to Sheena, "I need him. Let him come over."

"Are you sure?"

"Yes, I am." Sheena told Kendall it was okay that he come over. They left the restaurant. Adriana wanted to ride with Kendall. Sheena agreed and gave her the pump.

"Use it if you need it. Don't wait too long. The minute you can't breathe, you pump this inhaler." Adriana nodded. Kendall opened the door. She got in, then he got in. She leaned over and lay her head on his shoulder. He wrapped his arm around her and followed Sheena to their home. Adriana fell asleep. He didn't bother her but glanced at her face now and then as he drove. She looked different a year ago, now, tired and frail. He was concerned. He missed her. This time he wasn't letting her get away from him.

They reached their home. Sheena parked the car in the driveway. Kendall parked behind her. She got out of her car and rushed to get Adriana, who woke up confused. Sheena opened the door, grabbed Adriana's hand and helped her out of the car. Kendall turned his head and wiped his tears. He followed them in the house.

Sheena signed to him, "Have a seat in the living room, I will be back." He sat down on the couch and watched them go upstairs. He waited patiently for Adriana to come back down. Twenty minutes later, Sheena came down without her. She signed to Kendall, "You can come upstairs now." Kendall followed her upstairs and into her bedroom. Adriana was lying in bed with a mask over her face, almost sleep. He stood there about to break down into tears. Sheena signed to him, "I wanted her to rest, but she wanted to see you. Please let her rest." She left the room and closed the door.

Kendall didn't know what to do. She blinked her eyes, so he sat on the bed. She put her head in his lap, and he burst into tears. What happened? A year ago, she was so vibrant, full of life and energy. She reached up and wiped his tears. He kissed her hand and cried uncontrollably. She lay there looking at him, breathing with short breaths, wiping his tears.

He signed, "I don't know how much time I have with you, but

I will spend every moment with you." She smiled and went to sleep. He caressed her face as she slept. Sheena checked on her. Kendall signed, "Can I stay with her tonight?"

"That will be fine. If there are any changes with her breathing, please let me know."

"I will." She came over and kissed Adriana on the cheek, said goodnight to Kendall and went to bed. Kendall watched Adriana through the night. He slept, but when she moved, he woke up and her eyes met his. She took the mask off and sat up.

"Thank you for staying. I was hoping I'd see you when I woke up."

"I'm not leaving you."

"You have to go to work."

"I know, but I do want to come over here afterward. Are you still working?"

"No, I'm on disability, that's why I had to come stay with Sheena. I couldn't stay in my apartment after I got sick, that's why I needed my keys. I was moving the next day, and since your girlfriend told me you all were getting married, there was no sense in me contacting you, but I did keep your number."

"I was so worried about you. I didn't know where you went, and now that I found you, I'm not leaving you."

"I thank you so much."

"You are welcome, very much so. How long do you have to do the breathing treatment?"

"Every day. My lungs are deteriorating." She started coughing. Kendall took the mask and put it on her face. As he did so, she held his hands. He closed his eyes. He was emotionally attached to her, and his tears showed her that. She touched his face, and he opened his eyes. "Please don't cry, share my days with me with joy and laughter." He knew then she was not going to be with him long.

"I promise I will." She leaned against his chest and went to sleep. In the morning, Sheena came in to check up on her. Kendall lay her on the bed; she was still asleep. He signed to Sheena, "I have to go to work. I want to come back here when I get off if that's okay."

"She would appreciate that."

"I would like to stay here with her."

"I was hoping you would. She needs you right now."

"I need her. Call me if there are any changes with her."

"I will."

"Who's going to be here with her all day?"

"I will; she can't be left alone."

Kendall turned his head, crying. "I have to go." He left the house, got in his car, and cried like a baby. What did this woman do to him? He had never showed emotion like that before. He was making decisions as he drove home to get ready for work. When he got home, he packed some clothes, called into his job to say he wouldn't be coming in; he needed some time off. He had been with the company for some time, so he had vacation, along with money in his 401k.

He texted Sheena and said that he was coming back this morning. She said okay. He went by the bank to transfer some money into his checking account, paid his rent and bills for two months, picked up some groceries, and headed back over to their house. He knocked on the door. To his surprise, Adriana opened the door. He smiled and so did she. She kissed him on the cheek. He headed toward the kitchen and she followed him.

"Sheena told me you were coming back this morning. I wanted to meet you at the door when you came back."

"I'm glad you did; how are you feeling?"

"I feel okay as long as I take my medication and do the breathing treatments. I'm okay."

"Have you eaten breakfast yet?"

"I was hoping to have it with you."

He smiled. "What can you eat?"

"Everything." They laughed.

"Pancakes and sausage?"

"I would like that."

"Where is Sheena?"

"Upstairs resting. She stays up through the night checking on me, so when she has a chance to get some rest, she does."

"I see. This house is beautiful."

"It's her parents' home. They live in another state. When they found out I was sick and needed twenty-four-hour care, they opened their home to us, so she could care for me."

"That was very nice of them."

"I thought so too. Sheena was with me when I first got sick. She was a stranger to me before she became my best friend."

"Stranger? How so? You seem like you've known each other for a while."

"Remember that night when you saved me from getting hit by that car, and you didn't know I was deaf? And a lady came by and translated for us?"

"Yes, I remember that night."

"That was Sheena. When you saw me that night, I was moving the next day to go stay with some friends and be closer to my job. One night I went out to eat. I went to the restroom and had trouble breathing. A lady came in and saw me holding onto my chest. I remembered her face from that night when she was assisting me. I didn't know what was happening; I just knew I couldn't breathe. The color in my face changed. She called the paramedics, and that's when I found out I had lupus. She gave me her phone number and said if I needed anything to call her. I began to get weaker from then on."

"How did she go from being a stranger to your best friend?"

"I was in the hospital for a couple of days; my immune system was low. I texted her and thanked her for being my hero. She asked me how I was. I told her I was still in the hospital, and she asked me if I needed anything. I told her I needed a friend, and she's been there ever since."

"What happened to the friends you moved in with?"

"Oh, they're still around, but she's my best friend. She was to me what they weren't. They gave me a house to live in, but she gave me a home. She showed me warmth and compassion; she cared for me; she went out of her way to make sure I was going to be fine. I told my friends that I couldn't work and couldn't help with the rent. They said they were fine with it, but I felt the tension. I told Sheena about it, she talked with her parents, and now here I am.

"That's so awesome. For as long as she allows me to be here, I will be here with you."

"I know that, and I know she will appreciate it."

"Are you ready to eat?"

"Yes." He fixed her plate and just watched her eat. Sheena came down.

"I smelled something good. Is there anymore?"

"Sure is." Kendall fixed her a plate. He made more and then ate with them.

"I need to go run some errands. Kendall, can you look after our patient until I get back?"

"I want to get out too."

"You can't be away from oxygen long, so you have to stay put. You saw what happened last night. You can't be doing a lot of walking either, so you stay put, missy. You have good company now; I know he will keep you entertained." Adriana pouted her lip and folded her arms like a spoiled child. "Give me love." Adriana hugged Sheena, and they kissed each on the cheek. She looked at Kendall, and said, "Take care of her, she means a lot to me, and I know by the way you've been shedding tears, she means something to you."

"She's special to me. Thank you for allowing me to be here with her."

"I wouldn't have it any other way." Sheena went upstairs to get ready. Kendall washed the dishes, and they went and sat in the living room.

Adriana signed, "What made you want to learn my language?"

"I wanted to know what you were saying without you being frustrated. I know it would have been easier to talk to me if I understood what you were saying. Day and night; I studied, I felt I needed to."

"You studied very well. I am very impressed."

"I didn't think I could do it. It was complicated at first, but the more I thought of you, the more I wanted to learn."

"Welcome to my world."

"I don't want to be just in your world of language, but in your life."

"With open arms, I welcome you to both." She hugged Kendall, then she lay down in his lap. He stroked her hair as she fell asleep. Minutes later, he did the same. Sheena came downstairs about to leave. She looked for them and found them in the living room. She grabbed a blanket from the chair and lay it over Adriana, then she left to run her errands.

After a long nap, Adriana got up. She woke Kendall.

"I have to use the restroom. My breathing is not good; I need my oxygen, but I'm too weak to walk up the stairs." He picked her up and carried her upstairs to use the restroom. When she was finished, he carried her to her room, put the mask on her face, and lay in bed with her. Kendall never left her. Every appointment, he went with her. He cooked for her, bathed her, played games, painted her toes. He carried her, gave her piggyback rides, took her to the park. Everywhere they went, he took the oxygen with them. He didn't want her to just be in the house, but he didn't let her walk anywhere; he carried her everywhere. Although she was taking her meds and wasn't doing much walking, she was sleeping more, not really moving around. Kendall knew then she wasn't going to be around much longer.

As she slept, he went to go talk with Sheena. He said, "Superbowl is coming up in two weeks. How about we throw a big party. Let's celebrate everything that she might not be able to see again." Sheena began to cry.

"I know we don't have much longer with her. That would be a good idea; I will get in touch with her friends."

"That will be perfect." They planned it quickly. People responded. Adriana stayed in her room every day, and Kendall brought her food to her. Sometimes she ate; sometimes she didn't. She was drinking liquids, not eating solid food, so he made her soup. The weekend of the Superbowl, Kendall and Sheena, with other friends, were cooking and decorating. The plan was coming together, and since Adriana was confined to her room, it made the surprise even better. It took four hours to put everything together. The night had come to an end, and everything was ready for Superbowl Sunday. Sheena said goodnight to her friends, and Kendall went upstairs to check on Adriana.

She was sitting up writing in a book.

Kendall signed, "What are you doing?"

"Just writing. Something smells good. What did you cook?"

"Sunday's dinner. Wanted to get it out of the way."

"I want some Sunday dinner."

"You want it now?"

"I can wait. It does smell good."

186

"You'll like it, I promise you. How are you feeling?

"I'm okay. My breathing is getting shorter. Even when I'm using the oxygen, I still feel shortness of breath."

"You want to put the mask on now?"

"No, I'm fine. Will you hold me tonight?"

"I will hold you every night."

"I know you would, but for tonight, hold me."

"Yes, Adriana, I will hold you. Are you ready to go to sleep now?"

"I'm ready to take a nap. I'll sleep tomorrow." Kendall didn't understand what she meant by that. She turned off her lamp, and he lay down. She lay on his chest and he held her all night. He didn't move. She was relaxed, and he wanted to make it as comfortable for her as he could. Although he was uncomfortable, he sacrificed everything for her that night. Sunday morning, Adriana got up and put her mask on. Kendall was still asleep. She took her oxygen with her and went to the restroom, then ran her bath water. She lay comfortably in her bubble bath. As she relaxed, Kendall woke up to find her gone. He didn't panic, but he didn't want her to go downstairs either, so he got up and walked to the bathroom. He opened the door and saw her there relaxed.

He signed, "Good morning, Beautiful."

"Good morning, Handsome. I didn't put you in a panic, I hope."

"No, I just wanted to make sure you were okay."

"Oh, I'm fine. I feel pretty good today. I feel stronger; I feel my independence."

"That's good to hear. You want me to wash your back?"

"Please." He washed and rinsed her back. After he was done, he kissed her on her forehead.

"You ready to get out?"

"Yes." She got out he towel-dried her and helped put on her clothes. He wanted to carry her back to the room. "No, I can walk back to the room."

He was glad to see she was doing much better. When she walked back to the room without her oxygen, she sat on the bed. Her breathing was okay, not normal, but it wasn't short.

Kendall signed, "Are you okay?"

"I'm fine. I'm hungry."

"What would you like to eat?"

"Surprise me."

"I can do that." He went to fix her breakfast. Sheena was in the kitchen already cooking breakfast when he got there. "Good morning."

"Good morning. How is she?"

"To my surprise, she is doing much better this morning than I've seen in a month. She seems much stronger today." Sheena looked away to finish cooking breakfast. He thought it was odd that she didn't say anything about his good news. She finished the breakfast, fixed a plate, put it on the tray, and signed.

"Can you take this up to her?"

"Sure, I can do that." He took her breakfast to her.

When she saw him come back so soon, she signed, "Oh, that was quick, did you microwave it?" He laughed.

"No, Sheena beat me to it."

"She remembered my favorite breakfast. Omelet with spinach, mushrooms, onions, green and red peppers, cheese, turkey bacon." She ate breakfast like it was her last meal and was finished in no time.

"You have a good appetite."

"Yes, I know. I can't wait to eat Sunday dinner."

"Oh, you have that kind of appetite."

"I do."

"Well, I'll be sure to pack your plate with everything." She got up and walked over to the window. Surprisingly, it was snowing. She loved the snow.

She turned around and signed, "It's snowing outside. I want to go out later."

"I'll take you wherever you want to go."

"Thank you. I'm going to take a nap. Will you lie down with me?"

"It would be my pleasure. Let me take the tray downstairs."

"Don't leave me." He saw the desperation in her eyes, and he put the try on the floor and lay in bed with her. She snuggled in his arms. He loved the way he was feeling at that moment. Even if it were just for the moment, he would cherish it forever. Hours went by. There was a knock at the door. Kendall woke up and he saw Sheena standing there, gesturing him to come to the door. He slowly got up to see what she wanted and closed the door.

She signed, "Company is downstairs waiting for her."

"She's still sleeping." The door opened, and they turned around.

Kendall signed, "What's wrong; are you okay?"

"Yes, I have to use the restroom." She went and used the restroom,

Sheena said, "It's three hours before the Superbowl game begins. I think we should start the celebration now."

"That will be fine. She wants to go outside in the snow. Do you think that's a good idea?"

"Let's give her what she wants. We'll just watch her carefully."

Adriana came out of the bathroom. "What are you guys talking about?"

"I was telling Sheena that you wanted to go out in the snow. Do you still want to go out?"

"Yes, yes, I do, I do. She ran into her room and changed her clothes. She was ready in ten minutes. She closed her bedroom door and signed. "Let's go." She ran downstairs, and just as she was about to go out the door, there was a shout and a lot of signing.

"*SURPRISE, ADRIANA.*" The house was filled with friends and her students with their parents. The children ran up to her and hugged her. She fell to her knees and hugged and kissed them. Tears of joy ran down her face. She was so happy to see her students; she hadn't taught them since she'd been sick. She missed them so much. Her friends came and hugged her, and then walked her into the living room. The whole place was decorated. There was a Christmas tree in one corner, with presents under it, Valentine balloons next to it, a Happy Birthday banner on the wall. For every occasion of the year, there was a decoration.

Kendall and Sheena came in the room. Adriana went to them and hugged them.

"Thank you, thank you! I missed them, and you brought them to me. It means so much to me, thank you, thank you, so much." Tears were still streaming down her face, and they knew she appreciated what they'd done. Adriana took off her coat and sat down next to her students. She had a conversation with them for about twenty minutes, then they bought her presents from under the tree. She opened every one of them. She enjoyed the gifts of love. She had boxes of chocolate, roses, every occasion, she got a gift for it. She was overwhelmed, but she was enjoying the love they were showing.

Adriana signed, "How about we go outside and have a snowball fight?" The kids were excited; Kendall was concerned. Sheena looked at him as to say, give her what she wants. Everybody in the house put on their coats and went outside. It was still snowing, and the streets were filled with it. It looked like cotton on the streets, pure and white, like it hadn't been touched. Adriana ran in the snow and fell. Kendall ran after her, but she fell on purpose to make an angel. He stopped and watched her enjoying the snow. The children came and made one with her. She got up and so did the kids, and they looked at their angels. It was beautiful, her big angel surrounded by her little ones. Sheena came and took a picture of it.

Adriana started the snowball fight, and everyone joined in. She ran and laughed. Kendall and Sheena watched her closely; she was having the best time of her life. They played for an hour and then went in the house. Adriana sat on the couch while they warmed up the dinner. Her breathing was starting to get shorter, but she didn't tell anyone. Kendall came in the living room and said, "Dinner is served."

Everyone headed towards the dining room. The table was covered with all types of food, turkey, ham, collard greens, sweet potatoes, green beans, cranberry sauce, mac and cheese—every food they could think of was part of the feast. Kendall sat Adriana at the head of the table, then he put a tiara on her head.

"You made me feel like a king being with you. You are my queen, and I want you to know that."

"I haven't done anything special."

"Spending time with me was all I needed." He kissed her, and everyone said aww. "Okay let's eat; the game will be on soon." Everyone fixed their plates. The children had a little table to sit at. Adriana enjoyed everyone having a good time. She ate all her food. Kendall watched her; he knew her breathing was getting shorter, but he didn't want to ruin the good time she was having. Everyone's belly was filled, and they moved from the dining to the living room. The kids sat on the floor, and everyone grabbed a seat. Kendall and Adriana sat on the couch. It was almost kick-off time, New England Patriots playing Los Angeles Rams. No one was a fan of either team, it was just the Superbowl game, so they watched it.

An hour into the game, the guests started to get bored and tired. It could've been the food that was making them sleepy, but there was no commotion in the house. The children were already asleep, so the parents wanted to get them home. Slowly people started to leave. Adriana walked them to the door until it was just her,

Kendall and Sheena.

Adriana signed, "I thank you so much for doing this for me. I so appreciate it. You made me feel so special, and I will always, always remember this." She hugged them. Sheena went into the kitchen to start cleaning up. Kendall and Adriana went back in the living room to finish watching the game. She lay on Kendall's lap looking up at him. She reached up and touched his face. He looked down at her.

She signed, "Thank you for being a part of my world. You've made my days so enjoyable."

"What are you saying?"

"I'm saying I'm ready to go to sleep now."

"What does that mean, Adriana? What does that mean?"

She moved her lips, saying, "I love you." A blank stare looked back at him. Her arm slowly fell from his face. He knew then she was gone. He called 911 and went into the kitchen.

Sheena signed, "Is that boring game over?" He grabbed her hand and took her into the living room. He walked her slowly to Adriana. She looked at Kendall, then looked at the still form on the couch. She dropped to her knees and cried, holding her and crying. Kendall stood there, letting her have her moment with her friend. He shed tears as well. He couldn't believe she was gone just like that, in a matter of minutes. She professed her love for him and then she was gone. He didn't even get a chance to tell her how he felt. He didn't expect her to say it; he wasn't expecting her to leave him. Sheena wasn't ready to let her go either. She just held her and cried.

A knock came at the door, and Kendall let the paramedics in. They worked on Adriana, but she was already gone. They put her on the stretcher and covered her face. Sheena hugged Kendall and cried. They consoled each other. Sheena had to make phone calls, so Kendall went upstairs to Adriana's room. When he opened the door, there was an envelope on the pillow where he lay his head every night. On the envelope was written

KENDALL. He sat on the bed and opened it.

I am asleep now because you are reading this letter. Every day I was with you I cherished them. I knew my days would be short, and I thank you for everything you sacrificed to share those days with me. I know you loved me; although you didn't say it, your actions proved it, I knew by the way you took care of me. I know if I was well enough, I would've married you and given you beautiful children, but this body was not meant to birth; it had to leave this earth. I know I will always be in your memory. I thank you for your time. I do love you Kendall, never forget that.

He lay in her bed and grabbed her pillow that had her scent on it and hugged it as if it were her. Sheena walked in and around the room, just looking trying to process that Adriana was gone. She walked out of her room and closed the door, so Kendall could grieve. He stayed there until morning.

Later that morning, he went downstairs. Sheena was in the living room.

"Good morning."

"Good morning, Kendall."

"I'm going to head on home now if you don't need me. Are you going to be okay?"

"I'll be fine. I have some friends coming over soon. I do thank you for staying here with her; she needed that."

"I needed that. She showed me love in an intimate way, and I will always remember that."

"I knew she was leaving us yesterday."

"How?"

"I had a dream the night before. It was so odd, though. She said when I had a dream that she would no longer be with me, she would be gone the next day. That's why whatever she wanted to do yesterday, I let her do. She had enough strength in her to enjoy her last moments here. I didn't want to share it with you then; I wanted you to enjoy her without sorrow. You smiled the whole time with her, and that's what she wanted."

"She left here the way she wanted, not the way we wanted. We would have told her don't do this or that, but she wanted freedom, and we gave it to her. Please let me know when the funeral is; I don't want to miss it."

"Her parents want her body flown home so she will be leaving on Wednesday."

"So yesterday was my last time seeing her?"

"I'm afraid so."

"I had my moment with her. I will grieve at my home. If I can have a couple of her pictures? I would like to take her pillow as well."

"Take whatever you like."

"What are you going to do about the decorations?"

"I'll leave them up until I'm done grieving. I like the memory we shared with her; I'm not ready to take it down yet."

"If you ever need me, you have my number."

"Thank you. That means a lot." Kendall hugged Sheena, then he went upstairs and packed his bag, grabbed some pictures from her room and the pillow, and headed home. He cried on the way home. She touched him in so many ways; he wouldn't feel that again, but he wouldn't forget it. The next day, he went back to work. He didn't want to, but if he stayed home, he would just cry all the time. He needed to keep his mind occupied. During his shift, he got a text from Sheena. It was the picture she took of Adriana's snow angel with her students. He looked at the picture and shed tears, then sent a thank you.

He sent the picture to a photo shop. After work, he went to pick up the picture, along with a frame. When he got home, he put the poster-sized picture in the frame and hung it on his bedroom wall. He stepped back saying.

"Adriana, my Angel, I miss you and I love you so much, you

made these wings on earth, now you have them in heaven.

The End......

"It's time to start looking; we don't have much time," Rhonda said.

"I'm not in any hurry," William replied.

"But I am."

"Why the rush?"

"We agreed that you would start looking the minute we found out the results." He was looking out the window. He turned around, walked over and lay next to her in bed.

"I'll start looking tomorrow."

"Nothing is promised. Tomorrow may never come."

"I pray every night it does."

"Well, I would look for you."

"I'd like to see you try it." She tried to get out of the bed and lay back down.

"I thought you were going to look?"

"You know I can't move. I'm surprised you let me get that far."

"You're stubborn. I was not going to interrupt you."

"You always let me be myself. I love that about you."

"I married you for your brains."

"Oh, so you don't think I'm beautiful?"

"Rhonda, please baby, I've always told you, you were beautiful, but you knew that."

"I know, but it is nice to hear it."

"I tell you that every day. I tell you before you go to sleep. I whisper it in your ear when you do sleep, and when the sun rises, those are the first words out of my mouth to you. I like you to hear my voice when you're sleeping, so you have beautiful dreams."

"And I do have them. I dream about the day I first met you."

"That was a wonderful time."

"All of our years were wonderful. You gave me what I asked for, and I thank you for that." He looked away. "Look at me, love." He turned to her. "You need to start looking soon."

"I love you so much. You have given me twenty-five years of a beautiful marriage. There is no one who could take your place. I don't feel there is anyone out there for me. If there were, I wouldn't have married you."

"I understand what you're saying, but we agreed."

He stood up and cried out, "I don't care about an agreement! I just want my wife to live." He lay his head on her chest. She caressed his head and cried with him.

"I don't have much time. I want to see who will be taking my place."

"I don't want to do this."

"Do you want me to be happy?"

"More than anything in this world."

"Then do this for me. You have sixth months to find her."

"Only because you asked me to, but I will always love you, always."

"I know you will. I have a little appetite. Can you run down to the diner and get me some clam chowder?"

"For you I will do anything."

"Thank you." He kissed her and drove down to the diner. Their favorite waitress was there, and he sat at the counter.

She said, "Hey, good looking, what brings you in here?"

"Rhonda wanted some soup, so I came down to get her a bowl."

"How is she doing?"

"Not good, Lena."

"I miss seeing her; she hasn't been in here for a while."

"Her strength is not what it used to be."

"How long?"

"They say six months."

"How do you feel about it?"

"I've been married to her for twenty-five years; I can't imagine being without her. She is my life partner, my best friend, companion and confidant. We had children together, raised pets. We started a garden together; we did everything together. I don't know how it is to be separated from her."

"It seems to have taken a toll on you."

"Daily I think about it, but every day that she's with me I am thankful."

"Here's your soup. It's on me. I put some crackers in there. You tell her I said hello, and that I send my love."

"I'm not ready to go yet; I just need to vent right now."

"Well, I get off in twenty minutes. We can have a cup of coffee, and you can tell me what's on your mind."

"Thank you, I would like that." She put the soup on the warmer, finished up her shift. William found a booth for privacy. Lena came minutes later with coffee.

"Penny for your thoughts?"

"We made this agreement that if the cancer returned, and it metastasized, I would—" He looked away.

"You would what?"

"Rhonda always made me happy; she did a wonderful job as a wife. She held that position and did it perfectly."

"I'm listening."

"She wants me to remarry. She doesn't want me to be alone when she's gone. I have six months to find her."

"What if you don't find her by that time?"

"I don't know. I know she won't be here, but at least she can see that I tried."

"What does your heart say?"

"It says love my wife forever, never let her go."

"You are true to her. You're a man of dedication; she honors you for that."

"I know, Lena."

"Give her what she asked for."

"I don't know where to begin to look."

"You probably won't have to."

"I've never cheated on my wife before."

"Your desire is to be faithful to her, and her desire is for you to be happy. I wouldn't call it cheating. Fulfill her desire, William."

"You make it sound so easy."

"She loves you enough to share you. Knowing that you will be taken care of is all she's concerned about." William got up to check her back.

"What are you looking for?"

"Wings."

"What kind?'

"Fly wings, because everything you said, we said in the room, and I think you were the fly on the wall listening to our conversation."

"Now, that's funny."

"Thank you for the conversation; I needed it."

"My pleasure. Give my love to Rhonda. Tell her I miss that smile."

"I sure will." Lena grabbed the soup, gave it to him, and he headed back home. He went into their bedroom. She was sitting up in the bed.

"Was Lena there?"

"Yes, she misses you and sends her love. The soup is on the house."

"She's so thoughtful."

"Yes, she is."

"Do you like her?"

"That's an odd question to ask."

"It's not a trick question, Bill. Do you like her?"

"I never gave it much thought."

"Start thinking."

"Aggressive, aren't we?"

"If you could only see what my heart feels, you would know why I feel the way I do."

"Talk to me."

"The day we got married, not only did you become my husband you became my teacher. I was always naïve about a lot of things. Whether you noticed it or not, you never once complained about anything. You'd ask for a screwdriver, I'd give you a hammer. I was a novice until you made me an apprentice. You were patient with me; you made me a better person. My better is coming to an end, and I want you to be taken care of. I want to know that you will be in the best care when I am no longer here."

"You have given me the best days on my worse ones. I don't think we've ever looked at each other differently. We tried to be perfect with everything; when we made mistakes, we apologized. We made spills, we wiped them up. We break things, we replace them. We tried to do things unnoticed, but noticeably we showed our love for one another. We couldn't hide that, and everyone knew it. Everyone felt it when we walked into a room. It was like a fine perfume; it filled the air. Public intimacy we showed everywhere. I was never ashamed to show you how much I cared for you. I can't do that with anyone else; can't you see that, baby? We complement each other when we're together. I don't think anyone else can be that with me. You're irreplaceable."

"That is so beautiful. It is so good to hear that, and I know you mean that with all your heart. That's what you gave me all these years. You were never selfish. If you had two hearts, you'd give me them both, but at this moment, time is not on our side. We don't have much of it. Invite Lena over. I would like to see her."

"Are we playing matchmaking?"

"No, you said she misses me, so I would like her to come see me."

"You're up to something."

"Think what you want, dear. Now can you hand me my soup, so I can eat?"

"Certainly, my love." He heated up the soup, grabbed a tray and watched her eat. "What time would you like Lena to come over?"

"When her shift is over."

"Would you like me to cook dinner?"

"Yes, she'll be staying for a while."

"How do you know that?"

"Because she wants you, and I approve of it. No more questions, baby, save them for tomorrow. I'm tired now. I've taken my medication, and I want to go to sleep." He removed the tray and turned out the light. She went to sleep, and he went into the living room, gathering his thoughts. What questions could she possibly ask? It looked like she was in charge, and he was not about to interfere with her plans. Lena was a lady of stature, long legs, a beauty defined as elegant, a smile that would brighten anyone's day. She didn't have to say anything; her gifted personality filled the room. A whiff of her presence started a conversation. A woman who minded her business became someone else's.

He had never given Lena much thought; she was just a nice person to have a conversation with. He was leaving it up to Rhonda. Whatever she was going to do he was not going to interfere. Morning arrived, and he checked in on her. She was still asleep. He took a shower and headed down to the diner. Lena was there having a conversation with customers. When it wasn't busy, she'd sit with them. They enjoyed her company so much that her tips were enough to pay her rent in two days. People would pile in from the morning until it was time for her shift to end.

William came to the diner early enough to let her know about Rhonda's invitation, so she would have time to reschedule or attend. He sat in a booth, and she saw him when he came in. She excused herself from the table, grabbed a pot of coffee and a cup, and headed to serve him.

"Good morning, William. What are we having for breakfast today?"

"Just coffee for now."

"Do you need a menu?"

"No, but I do have a message for you. Last night I told Rhonda what you said, and she would like to know if you would come by this evening after work."

"I have no plans. I would love to."

"So, we'll expect you by 6:00 pm?"

"That's a good time."

"I will let her know."

"Okay, see you guys later." He left ten dollars on the table, though the coffee was just a dollar. He tipped her well even if it was just a cup of coffee. Her presence was like a full course meal, very satisfying. While he was gone, Rhonda woke up; she was making breakfast when he came home.

"Good morning, love." He went to kiss her. "I have a response to your invitation. Lena said she would come see you this evening."

"I was hoping she would. Can I ask you something?"

"Sure, you can."

"When you talk to Lena, do you feel relaxed?"

"I feel I can let my hair down, although I'm bald. I feel I can open up to her. I trust her with what I have to say, knowing that what I've shared with her, she won't share with anyone else, if that's what you're asking."

"Do you trust her?"

"Yes, I do."

"She's a very pretty lady."

"That she is."

"I give a compliment when it is well-deserved, and she deserves one. She has beauty like none other. She has hidden treasures within her."

"How do you know all this?"

"I don't." She finished her breakfast and went out on the patio, sitting in the sun, he followed her and sat next to her.

"The sun feels so good against my skin. I love this feeling. I just want to drench in this moment right now, take in everything I can get, the fresh air, the sun. Things I took for granted, I now appreciate."

"We all have been granted certain things we never appreciate until they're gone or almost. I never took you for granted; I knew when I first met you, you were mine forever. My forever lasted twenty-five years, and I'd give anything to have twenty-five more."

"Live the twenty-five more with Lena."

"Somehow, I knew you were going to say that. Why her?"

"I trust her like you do. We've known her for about five years, and her service to us never changed no matter how busy it got. She always served us with the same smile, same courtesy, nothing about her ever changed. She'd sit down and talk with us, and her presence was just magnifying. I noticed every time she waited on us it brought a smile to your face."

"She's our favorite waitress. I knew she'd take care of us."

"The smile on your face for her was different from the smile on your face for me."

"So, what are you saying, I don't love you?"

"It has nothing to do with love. Your smile for me says, I adore my wife. Your smile for her is a thankful one. Your lips move a certain way when you smile. When I married you, I didn't just marry you to be my partner; I married you so that I could learn you. When I did, I knew you. You were like a frog in biology class; I wanted to open you up and know everything about you. You allowed me, and that's when we became one. You let me enter in, holding nothing back."

"I'm an open book to you."

"Be that way to Lena, and she will be that way to you."

"You are making this easy for me."

"As your wife, I always made our life together that way. You didn't have to struggle to love me; I gave you me. You never had to fight to find out what was wrong with me, you knew."

"And as your husband, I've always worked so that you didn't have to. Life was good for us."

"Yes, it was. Well, that's enough sun for me. Let me go lie down so I can have enough strength for our company this evening."

"You need any help?"

"No, my love, I'm a big girl; I can manage." Rhonda went to bed. William went into the kitchen to prepare the meal for the evening. As he was preparing, the doorbell rang. It was Lena.

"Oh, you are earlier than expected."

"Yes, I feel that I'm needed here." He was surprised and wanted to know how she knew that.

"Well, I was just starting to cook dinner."

"You mind if I help?"

"Not at all." Lena grabbed an apron and started cutting up the onions and green peppers while he prepared the steaks.

"Where's Rhonda?"

"She went to go take a nap."

"Let me go peek in on her."

"Sure, go ahead, I can handle the kitchen." She walked by him and touched his hand. He closed his eyes; he felt like he was touched by an angel. Her hand felt like fire, and a soothing feeling came over him. She walked towards the bedroom and poked her head in. Rhonda was lying on her side. She saw her back and assumed she was asleep.

"Come in, Lena."

"Oh, I didn't know you were up."

"I heard you when you came in."

"How are you feeling?" Lena sat on the bed.

"I'm feeling as expected."

"You need me?"

"I do."

"How can I help?"

"My cancer has metastasized."

"Bill told me."

"What else has he said?"

"That you don't want him to be alone when you're gone. He said he had six months to find someone. Is that how long you have?"

"It is."

"How can I help?"

"Are you dating anyone?"

"Not at the moment."

"Is there a particular person you would like to date?"

"I don't think he's out there."

"Define him."

"Someone. Like me. I always wanted a mirrored relationship, where you can see yourself in your mate. I can learn from that. I can see myself and the error of my ways and do better. For instance, when I eat, you can tell that I am, and it's annoying to some people. If I hear my mate do the same thing, and it's annoying to me, I fully understand how my bad habit can be disturbing, and I work at it."

"Love will make you change."

"I believe that wholeheartedly."

"You have to sacrifice and compromise."

"I believe that as well."

"Is that why you are single?"

"I'm single by choice. I don't want to force someone to understand me. People don't take time out to know you; they are so in a hurry. I'm not in no rush, and if you can't respect what I want, then you're wasting my time."

"Do you want a companion or a husband?"

"What's the difference?"

"Do you want just a relationship or marriage, no ring or a ring?"

"You can have a ring and no marriage, but I do want the whole kit and caboodle. I want the ring, the commitment, trust, communication, honesty, faithfulness. I want it all because if I'm going to give it, why can't I have what I give?"

"I know someone like that."

"Where is he? I'd like to meet him."

"You already met him; he's my husband."

"What are you saying?"

"I would love for you to be his companion. I think you're a perfect match for him."

"What size shoe do you wear, Rhonda?"

"A size eight."

"I wear a size nine. There's no way I can fit into your shoes. I can't give him what you gave him."

"I'm not asking you to duplicate what I gave him; I'm asking you to give him you, give him Lena, not Rhonda."

"Why me? You could've picked someone else, why me?"

"The years that I've known you, I've never seen you out of character. You're genuinely pure, untouched, you have a virgin way about you."

"That's a first! But you've only seen me on the clock. You don't know who I am off it."

"Well, that's how I see you. How are you off the clock?"

"The same." She laughed. "Does he know that you chose me?"

"Yes, he knows."

"What was his reaction?"

"Why don't you ask him yourself?"

"I don't know if I would feel comfortable doing that."

"How do you get to know someone?"

"By having a conversation with them."

"But this is different."

"How so?"

"He's your husband. It's the difference between having a conversation with him as a customer and having a personal one."

"You've had a personal conversation with him before. The only difference is, it was about him and me. Make this conversation about you and him. You're a smart girl; you'll figure it out."

"I guess I will. Would you like anything to eat or drink?"

"No, I'm not hungry right now, but what I would like for you to do is spend a weekend with us so we can get to know you on a personal level."

"I'd like that."

"Perfect. I'm going to lie down for a bit. Have Bill show you where the guest bedroom is."

"I will do that. Rest well." Lena went back in the kitchen to help finish cooking."

"Did you get lost?"

"No, I didn't, but I did run into an interesting conversation with Rhonda."

"She dropped the bomb on you?"

"Nuclear. It almost wiped me out.

"How do you feel about it?"

"I was going to ask you the same question."

"I never thought about another woman other than my wife, never made room in my heart for any other woman but her. She feels that once she's gone, there will be space for someone else. It doesn't work that way."

"Let me be your friend. That's what I can be to you. As I told her,

I can never replace her, but she feels comfortable with me, so whatever she desires, I will be that for her."

"That's good to know. Well, dinner is almost done."

"She's taking a nap right now. I'll give it about an hour or so, then I'll check on her."

"What would you like to do now?"

"She said that you could show me the guest bedroom. She would like me to spend the weekend with you two, get to know you better."

"Sure, I can show you that." He turned down the heat under the pots and showed her the bedroom.

"It's nice and spacious."

"When we had the house built, we wanted two master bedrooms so if we ever had an argument, we could give each other some space with the same size room to cool down in. She didn't believe in sleeping on the couch. Sleep in the same luxury we do. I never once slept in this room, and neither did she."

"That says a lot."

"We don't argue on purpose to make up. She's one woman you don't pick a fight with." Lena walked to the window and saw the garden.

"Beautiful garden. It looks like you took some time with it."

"We did. We started that one years ago. It needs some love; we haven't been out there in a while, but I enjoyed that time with her."

"There are certain things you would still like to do with your wife. You miss the intimate times with her, and gardening was one of them. Don't be surprised if she beats you to the garden. Cherish the times you will have with her. Create moments with her that will be lasting ones.

"I will."

"Show me the rest of the house." He gave her a tour, which ended back in the kitchen.

"I'll help as much as I can, but you're the one that has to create the memory, and make it a lasting one, for you."

"My memories with her are unforgettable."

"Make these the same way. Give her life; make the next two years like the first day you met her."

"She has six months."

"She has whatever will be given to her."

Bill had a puzzled look on his face. "You're an angel, Lena."

"I am a messenger, just doing my job."

"What is your job?"

"To make people smile. I've been doing that all my life. Smile to make them happy, to change the mood they're in. It's like I feel what they are going through just by their expressions. Sometimes, I just feel something isn't right, and I don't leave them until I know they are fine. It's a gift, and I'm thankful for it."

"You are gifted. I felt it when you touched my hand, it felt like fire."

"My hands have always been that way. What may seem normal to me is exciting for someone else."

"No, you don't understand; your hands felt like the sun. I've never felt a touch like that before."

"It's nothing."

"No, it's something."

"Excuse me for a minute. I have to use the restroom." Lena walked past Bill. She didn't touch him, but he felt that warmth again, not as hot as her touch, but enough to warm the cooled area. While she was using the restroom, Bill went to check on Rhonda. Walking past the bathroom, he saw this bright light shining under the door. It lit up the floor in the hallway. He was scared to walk past the door, so he stood there in awe. Then the door opened.

He said, "I saw the light."

"So, did I; the sun is beautiful out today." She walked back into the kitchen. He didn't know what to make of what had just happened. He looked in the bathroom; it wasn't as bright as it was when she was in there. He checked on his wife, still asleep. He went back in the kitchen. Lena was setting the table for dinner. He stood there with this wondering look on his face. Who was this woman? He wasn't scared of her, just curious.

She said, "Hope you don't mind me setting the table?"

"No, it's fine."

"I'll finish up here. Can you go wake Rhonda up so she can eat with us?"

"She hasn't had much of an appetite lately, so she may not be hungry."

"Can you go see for me?"

"As you wish." He went back into the bedroom where Rhonda was wide awake.

"The aroma in the house gave me an appetite. Is dinner done?"

"It is." He helped her out of bed and held her as she walked slowly to the table.

"How was your nap?" Lena asked.

"It was relaxing."

"That's good to know. Are you ready to eat?"

"Yes, I am." Lena fixed their plates. They sat and enjoyed the meal along with a delightful conversation. After dinner, Lena cleaned up the kitchen. Bill and Rhonda went to their bedroom, and Lena went to the guestroom. All lights were out; the house was pitch black. Later that night, Rhonda got up to go to the kitchen. She held on to the wall to keep her balance. Lena came out of the room to use the restroom. As she was coming out, she saw Rhonda as she lost her balance, about to fall. Lena caught her by her hands. The hallway lit up like the sun. Fire went through Rhonda's body like an electric charge, and then the light went away. Rhonda stood up and started walking, not holding on to the wall. She walked faster than she had in the last three months. She looked for Lena. She looked in the guestroom, but she wasn't there. She looked through the house and couldn't find her. Walking into the kitchen, she saw a note on the counter. She read it, got something to drink, and then went to bed.

In the morning when Bill woke up, he woke up to an empty bed. He went to look for Rhonda. She was in the garden, sipping coffee.

He said, "Good morning, my love, it's nice to see you out here. You look absolutely beautiful today." She stood up, and he reached for her to help.

She said, "I'm fine." She walked over to the roses. He couldn't believe his eyes. She didn't need his help; she was walking like nothing was wrong with her. "Would you like to get our hands dirty today?"

"I would love that, baby, I would love that."

"Let me go tell Lena what my eyes have just witnessed."

"Oh, I have a message for you, from her." She grabbed the note that was left on the counter and handed it to him.

It said, "Cherish these Moments with her. I will see you soon."

TBC IN VOL. III

RED DOOR

Meeting at 2:00 pm. That was the first thing Erin saw in her email when she logged into work. It didn't say what the meeting was about. She asked her co-workers did they get an email for a meeting, and they said no. She thought it strange that she was the only one going to the meeting. She worked until her lunch break. She took her hour lunch, still wondering what this meeting could be about. She didn't rush her lunch; she had an eerie feeling about the meeting, so to slow the hour until it was time, she watched the clock. She didn't eat; she just watched the clock. She had a lot on her mind. Her roommate had moved out two months prior and she was already behind in her rent. She didn't need this meeting to tip the iceberg.

She thought about her friend Darryl. She flirted with him a lot on the media. They would inbox messages; there were flirtatious moments but not enough to go out on a date. Erin had dreams, and she shared them with him. She asked once, 'If we built a house together, what would it look like?' Now, they were building a house together by messages. One day Erin sent him a link of a house and said I think this is the house we built. Darryl agreed. They messaged each other a few more times, but after a week, the conversation died down. She didn't reach out to him as much; she saw that he was online, but she wouldn't message him.

She sighed, and as soon as she did, she looked at the clock. It was 2:00 pm. she hurried back to her desk to clock back in and went to the conference room. When she walked into the room, she saw her manager and a person from human resources. Nervously sitting down, she folded her hands. Twenty minutes later, in a daze, she was carrying her items in a box to her car. People were looking, but she didn't notice. Although it was raining, she wasn't in a hurry to get to her car. It had been raining all day. All she heard echoing in her ears as she put the box in her car, was 'you're fired, fired, fired.' She didn't know what to do. She was behind on her bills and rent. She started the car and headed home.

When she pulled up in her driveway, she noticed her furniture on the side of the road. She jumped out quickly and ran to her belongings. Her clothes were scattered on the ground like someone had been rummaging through them; her shoes were soaking wet. She looked around for her dog. All she wanted right now was her dog. She saw her on the couch, shivering from the rain. When Pebbles saw her, she jumped into her arms. Erin cried, hugging her. She put Pebbles in the car, then salvaged as much as she could of her clothes and shoes. When she got in her car, she cried while she called her grandmother to tell her what had just happened. Her grandmother told her to come to her house. Pebbles jumped in Erin's lap; she was still wet and shivering. Erin turned on the heat so she could warm up. Pebbles licked her face. Erin was glad nothing had happened to her; she didn't know how long she had been in the rain, but she was glad she wasn't harmed. She pulled out of the driveway and looked at all she had owned—flat screen TVs, bedroom set, wardrobe, all destroyed. All she had now was a few items and Pebbles. She didn't know what she was going to do, but she needed to do something quick, or the next thing that would be gone was her car.

She drove to her grandmother's house tearfully. When she arrived, her grandmother was waiting at the door with towels. Pebbles jumped out of the car and ran into the house, shook off the water and found a warm spot on the floor. Erin grabbed the things she salvaged from the curb and followed the dog in the house. She laid out her things on the floor. Her grandmother wrapped Erin up in her towel and then said, "Wash your clothes; you don't want them to mold."

"Yes, Nana, I will."

"Take you a nice hot shower. Dinner is almost ready."

"Yes, ma'am." Erin started the wash and then took her shower. She had some clothes there already from when she spent the weekend, so she put on a t-shirt and shorts and snuggled up on the couch. Pebbles jumped on the couch, looking at her with sorrowful, blinking puppy eyes. She couldn't help but cry. Pebbles licked her tears. Erin hugged Pebbles.

As she continued to cry, her grandmother came in the living room and said, "Do you want to talk about what happened today?"

"Nana, it happened so fast I don't know where to begin."

"At the beginning."

"I went into work today and got an email that I was having a meeting at 2:00 pm. Next thing I was walking out with a box of my belongings to my car."

"Did they say why they fired you?"

"They said I mismanaged money."

"They said you were stealing money?"

"That's what is sounds like, but I don't steal, Nana; I have no reason to steal."

"Why did they wait until 2:00 pm to fire you? Why didn't they do that as soon as you came in?"

"Had something to do with Human Resources. They had to have all the documents, proof and what they were firing me for so I wouldn't sue them for wrongful termination."

"Did they have proof?"

"They had it, but it didn't look right, Nana. Every night I would count my drawer in front of the manager; we would both sign off on the amount, and she would put it in the safe."

"Oh, the manager, that was your friend who skipped out on you two months ago."

"Yes, ma'am, Elaine. She quit her job and moved out the same day, which is kind of strange, and now here it is, she's gone, and I'm out of a job."

"You think—no, she couldn't have done that."

"I already thought it. I think she stole money from my drawer, and I had to take the fall."

"Yes, that's what I was thinking. Do you think you can prove that it happened that way?"

"Nana, it doesn't matter now. I need to move on from that. If that's the dirt she's done, it will catch up to her. Right now, I need to figure out what to do."

"You know you can stay here as long as you like."

"I know, but I like my independence."

"You are independent; you just need a little help right now until you get on your feet."

"Thank you for understanding."

"That's what I'm here for, to help you through every situation. I promised you that as a little girl that I will always be there for you. I have children, but you, my dear, are my heart."

"That means a lot to me."

"And so do you to me. Come let me fill your belly so you can get a good night's rest." They went in the kitchen. Pebbles followed them and sat next to Erin looking to get her belly filled too.

"Oh, I have to go get Pebbles some food."

"I have something for her. You go and eat I'll take care of Pebbles." She fixed the dog a nice bowl of soup with chunks of steak in it. She put the bowl on the floor. Pebbles sniffed it and began lapping it up. Erin smiled; she was so glad Pebbled liked the food, so glad she had her dog and her grandmother. After everyone was finished eating, the people cleaned up the kitchen, while the dog sat and watched. Erin put her clothes in the dryer, kissed her nana goodnight and headed to bed.

Pebbles jumped up on the bed. Erin lay on her side, Pebbles snuggled up behind her against her back. Pebbles would always lie there; she felt like a sack of potatoes, but it was a comfort to Erin, knowing her best friend was near. Erin loved the king-sized bed. She was always cozy and comfortable when she had plenty of room. She had a king herself, but it would be in a garbage truck in the morning. It was an unhappy thought, but she didn't dwell on what she had lost; she would have those material things again. She rested without a care. In the morning, she would be going to the store, and her life would be changing for the better.

Lick, lick, lick. "Pebbles, ugh, not this early in the morning," Erin said. Pebbles would lick her in the face when she had to use the bathroom. "Move." Pebbles jumped off the bed. Every time Erin would say move, Pebbles knew she was getting out of the bed. She opened the door to let her out. Erin stood outside and watched her run up and down the street. It was almost eight o'clock in the morning. She had to get to the store and get her dog some food. After ten minutes of being out, she took Pebbles back in the house, got dressed and went to the store. On her way to the store, she got a text message from one of her ex co-workers.

"Good morning, Erin, just wanted to know if you heard the news?"

"No, what news?"

"Apparently there was a hidden camera in the room where you and Elaine were counting money. It showed you counting money while Elaine watched. After you signed off on it, you waited until the money was put in the safe. When you left, she went back in the safe and took some money. The camera showed she had been doing this for a while, as long as three months ago."

"Why did it take so long to catch her?"

"Well, apparently she was working with someone. The security guard hid the surveillance tape. She promised if he did that, she would cut him in on some of the money. She didn't keep her promise, and he turned in the tape with all the footage on it."

"Did they know how much was stolen?"

"Twenty thousand."

"So then why did they fire me?"

"Because of you two being roommates, with the same address, they thought you were in cahoots with her."

"I had no idea what she was doing."

"Well, we have her on tape."

"You think they'll let me have my job back.?"

"It's hard to say. Just see if you'll get a call on Monday. If not, then maybe it's best that way."

"I worked at that job for ten years before Elaine. My drawer never came up short."

"And that's being considered as well. You're a good employee, Erin. I'm sorry that this happened to you. Maybe something better will happen for you. You are not at fault for this; you just had to take the fall for it."

"Thank you for this information. I feel a little better."

"You're welcome, take care." Erin sat in the car for a minute. She didn't believe what she had just found out. Elaine had been acting funny the past three months, but she couldn't put her finger on what was going on. She went into the store, bought Pebbles some dog food, brought a few tickets and went home. When she got home, her grandmother was cooking breakfast. Pebbles was in the kitchen wagging her tail; she was hungry too.

"Hey, Nana."

"Good morning, Erin, how did you sleep?"

"I slept good. You wouldn't believe what I just found out!"

"I'm all ears."

"They have footage of Elaine stealing money out of my register and a couple of others."

"Are they going to give you your job back?"

"I don't know. They think I was involved because she was my roommate. I don't think I want that job back. I mean I loved working for the bank, but I think, they'd be watching me all the time, and I don't think I would like that. Besides, I was getting tired of banking anyway. Maybe this was meant to happen."

"It's only meant to happen when there is a back-up. Do you have one?"

"I have dreams."

"Tell me."

"I want my own production company."

"Producing what?"

"Movies, Nana. I'd like to direct a movie."

"You have any skills to do that?"

"Hidden ones."

"Well, maybe it's time for them to come out."

"I want to go to school and learn. I believe I will be good at it."

"Do you have a name for your production company if you ever get one?"

"Yes, it's called Sparkle Productions."

"Why Sparkle?"

"Someone told me I shine when I come into a room, that I change people's lives."

"Oh, and does this someone have a name?"

"What makes you think it's a man?"

"I didn't say man, I said name."

"The way you said it, Nana, it sounded like you were asking what his name is."

"Well is it a he?"

"His name is Darryl."

"Is it serious?"

"Not hardly."

"Well, my dear, if someone notices something like that about you, it's serious. Has anyone else said something like that to you before?"

"No, not really."

"Then he's paying attention to you."

"He seems so distant."

"That's what he wants you to think, but he is closer than you can imagine."

"I don't feel he is."

"Give it time, you'll see."

"Is breakfast almost done?"

"Oh, I like your switch mode, how you changed the subject."

"There was no more to talk about."

"I see, yes, breakfast is almost done." Erin fixed Pebbles some food, and she ate it almost in one gulp. Erin and Nana sat down and ate. Puppy- eyed Pebbles looked hungry, so Erin gave her some sausage.

"What are you going to do for the rest of the day?"

"I want to see if they are going to call me, but I will look for a job for the time being."

"Take your time. I'll pay your car payment until you get on your feet."

"That may take a year."

"I'm your grandmother, not your Sugar Daddy. You'll find something; I believe in you."

"I was just joking, Nana. I'm going to find something. I'm just getting tired of this state; I want to move."

"To where?"

"Salisbury, Maryland."

"What's out there?"

"This house I was looking at, absolutely beautiful."

"Because it's beautiful you want to move there."

"No, Nana, I want to move there because it's a brand-new start for me."

"You've been doing some researching?"

"For a year."

"Is your spirit there?"

"It moved there last year."

"Well, go where you can live and be free. If it's there, go."

"I feel it's my purpose, like it's destined for me to be there."

"If you feel that way, then go."

"Thank you, Nana."

"You are quite welcome, Erin."

"Let me go and take Pebbles for a walk."

"Okay. If I'm not here when you get back, I'm with my ladies playing Bingo."

"You still play that?"

"Bingo!" They laughed. Erin leashed up Pebbles and took her for a walk. On her walk, she thought about Darryl. She hadn't been on the media for a while. She took a break because she kept seeing the same thing—people complaining, drama, depression, oppression. She didn't want to be bogged down with all that negative energy. What made her smile was Darryl, but she hadn't heard from him, so she didn't bother to contact him. After their walk, she looked at her car. It needed to be washed. She wasn't in the mood for that. She went in the house and turned on the TV. The news was on, and she saw Elaine's face. She turned it up so she could hear it. They had arrested her for money laundering from three different banks over the past five years. One point five million dollars totaled what she laundered. She would appear in court the following week.

She had been on the run for years, using different identities. Erin couldn't believe this at first. She lost her job because of this, and then she found out her old roommate was criminally minded. This was too much for one day. She turned off the TV and lay in bed. Pebbles jumped and lay on Erin's stomach. She stroked her back until she fell asleep, and so did Erin. She didn't wake up until four hours later. It was evening: no calls or texts from her ex-coworker. She thought she might have gotten something since she saw Elaine on the news. That was behind Erin now; even if they offered her the job back, she wasn't taking it. She checked online, looking at the house she wanted. When she first saw the house, it was on the market. That had been a few months ago. She adored that home—her spirit was already in it. She flowed through that house, went in every room. When she looked at the house again, she saw that it had sold a week ago. Erin was disappointed. Although she had never inquired about it, she was still disappointed. She wanted that house, but at the time she wasn't ready to make the move.

Erin went in the living room where Nana was knitting.

She said, "How was Bingo?"

"It was fun. I won a couple of rounds. After that, the girls and I went out for lunch, sat around and talked, then I came on home. I have a quilt to finish, so that's what I'm doing now. I came in to check on you and Pebbles. You all were sleep so I didn't bother you."

"I saw Elaine's picture on TV. They arrested her for money laundering."

"I saw that earlier. So now what?"

"I move on from here. I don't want my job back. I think I'm burnt out from that. It's so funny, Nana."

"What is?"

"Things I was getting tired of, I lost."

"In life you are going to lose some things to gain others. Life is going to change from day to day. You may not like it, but it's going to bring on what is better for you. We hold onto items, people, jobs, homes when it's time to move on. Who's to say, if you didn't get fired, would you have looked for another job? If you didn't get evicted, would you have looked for another place to stay? We get so complacent that we settle. We are comfortable, but God has a way of moving us out of that space. Take, for instance, a frying pan. The pan is the space you are in. You're comfortable, laid back, you're enjoying how it feels. Suddenly, you feel heat on your bottom. You start to squirm around; you stand up. Now you feel the heat on your feet. The heat is turned up a little more; you can't sit down nor can you stand up. The only way you would find relief is if you jump out of the pan. When that happens, you've moved from your comfort zone into another place. At times, God has to turn up the heat in order for us to move. We hear him but don't have enough faith to move and obey. He turned the heat up on you, Erin; now it's time for you to move on to better things. There are better days ahead for you. This didn't just happen; it was destined."

"I never saw it that way."

"We live and learn. Life just never tells us what age we will be when we do learn. Take notes and learn from this."

"You're a great teacher."

"I thank life; it taught me a lot. Now, Sparkle?"

Erin smiled. "Yes."

"Tomorrow we'll go shopping so I can buy you some clothes."

"Oh, you don't have to do that."

"I know I don't have to. I want to."

"I brought me a couple of tickets, so if I win tonight, I could buy you what you want."

"Well, let me give you a list."

"Let me get some paper."

"Just joking, love. If you win, I want you to begin your life the way you want it to be. Live for you Erin, not for someone else, live for you."

"I will, but I will still take care of you."

"Oh, I know, but I still want the best for you. Think about everything you want before you make that move. You want to move to Maryland? Stay down there a couple of weeks before you write it in stone that that's where you want to be. Just because a house may look good doesn't mean that the surrounding areas may be good for you. Test drive the city, see how it makes you feel. If your spirit settles in like it did in that house, then I give you my blessing to make your move, but don't move because it looks good."

"The house that I was looking at was purchased a week ago."

"That doesn't mean there's not another one for you."

"But I really loved that one."

"Well, who's to say that you can't have it. Just because someone bought it, doesn't mean they're going to keep it. Money talks, my love.

"Well in that case, will you go, and test drive the city with me?"

"I already put my seatbelt on."

"You're the greatest, Nana."

"That's what they tell me. I just smile and nod my head in agreement. What time does this thing come on to check your numbers?"

"Ten forty-five."

"That's way past my bedtime. Well, tell me in the morning so I can pack my bag."

"I will."

"Are you hungry?"

"Not really. I've been snacking and it's already after eight, so I don't want to eat anything, but I know greedy Pebbles is. Let me fix her bowl."

"You do that. I'm heading to bed. You have a good night."

"You as well." Erin fixed the dog's bowl and took it out on the patio by the pool. She sat the bowl next to the pool and put her feet in the water while Pebbles ate. It was beginning to get dark, but the breeze felt good. She thought about Darryl some more. She went on the media to see if he had reached out to her. He hadn't. She decided to shut it down. If he missed her, he would reach out to her, but it had been a month since she heard from him. It was nothing serious; she just liked him and the conversations they were having.

Pebbles finished her food. Erin walked her outside so she could go potty, and after that, they went in the house. Erin didn't want to go sleep, so she lay across the bed and watched TV. An hour later she was snoring along with Pebbles, Pebbles lying on her back like she was getting a tan. Minutes later, she barked, and Erin woke up. It was 11:45 pm; she had missed the numbers. No big deal, she'd check them in the morning. She walked Pebbles to the door and let her out. She walked into the kitchen to get some water. On the island was a paper with some numbers on it; Nana had written down the lottery numbers. Erin went to grab her ticket and looked at the numbers. She got all six numbers! She'd done a power play. She let Pebbles in and drove to the store to check the numbers.

She had some other tickets in her car that she hadn't checked so she grabbed them as well, walked into the store and checked the numbers. With six winning numbers, it came up winner two hundred fifty-four million. She slid the numbers under the checker again, and the numbers didn't change, and neither did the amount. She couldn't believe it. She drove back home and sat in the car. She thought all this had happened in a matter of one day. She would have to disappear for a while.

Two hundred and fifty-four million dollars. She still couldn't believe it. There was only one winner and she was it. She already had a vision she was going to be putting it to good use. It came at the right time. She went in the house and looked in on her nana. She was asleep, so she didn't bother her, but the conversation in the morning would be one she would never forget. Erin was too excited to go to bed. She looked online at the house again, wrote down the real estate agent's phone number; she was giving her a call very soon. She was glad she got off the media. Although her name wouldn't be mentioned in connection with her winnings, she was off to a good start by not being on there.

She went and sat on the patio. Pebbles jumped on her lap. She started to think what she would do first once she claimed her winnings. She was going to set up a trust fund. She didn't need that kind of money under her name. She didn't owe anyone, but she still needed to protect herself, pay off Nana's house, set her up comfortably. She was headed to Maryland afterward. Nothing was keeping her in Kansas City, Missouri. She had seen enough, and life was boring here. She thought about life after Kansas City for a while until she fell asleep on the patio. She slept until morning. When she woke up, she was covered with a blanket. She stretched, got up and went in the kitchen. Nana was having a cup of coffee.

"Good morning, Nana, how are you?"

"Good, Sugar, and you? Did you see the numbers I left on the table?"

"Yes, ma'am, I did."

"When I woke up last night and did a bed check, you were sleep, so when I turned on the TV, I saw the numbers. I wrote them down just in case you missed them."

"I appreciated that."

"Did you win anything? Are we going for that test drive in Maryland?"

"Nana, I believe we are going for more than a test drive."

"You don't say."

"I do say."

"So, how much did you win?"

"You ready for this?"

"Yes, ma'am."

"Two hundred fifty-four million dollars."

"In pesos, or American dollars?"

Erin laughed. "In American dollars, Nana."

"OMG, Erin, so does this mean you are leaving me?"

"See, I knew you were going to say that. Do you want me to stay here?"

"I want you to follow your dreams."

"I don't want you to worry about me."

"I'll tell you what. I'll go and be with you in Maryland for a little while, and see you settle in. If I'm comfortable with you staying there, then I'll be satisfied knowing that you are safe. You don't know anyone there, but I'll pray a prayer of protection over you. After I come back home, I pray I will have peace with you being there and me separated from you."

"You're making it hard for me to leave."

"Live for you, Erin, not for me, for you."

"How long will you stay with me?"

"Until I have peace to leave you."

"Will you come back and visit me?"

"I was going to ask you the same thing."

"You know we are inseparable."

"From the first time I held you in my arms. I knew then."

"You knew a lot of things."

"And that's why I keep you close to my heart. So, what will you do now?"

"Well, first let me sign my ticket, and then I can find out where I need to go to collect my winnings."

"You need to first set up a trust fund."

"I already thought about that."

"Smart girl."

"You taught me well."

"And you listened."

"To every word."

"When you find out where to go, when are you going to make that trip to Maryland?"

"ASAP, Nana. I want that house."

"You said it was sold."

"Money talks."

"Why don't you build a house?"

"Everything I wanted is already in that house, plus I don't want to wait forever for a house to be built. If I want one built, I can live in that house in the meantime, but for now, I want to begin the process. First I have to find an attorney."

"I know of one."

"Nana, who don't you know?"

"I traveled down many roads, made a few detours, took a couple of short cuts, and cut a few corners. In my traveling, I picked up a few strangers along the way. I've clothed and fed them, nurtured and ministered to them. They went on their way, but never forgot where they started. when I needed them, they were right there; they never forgot about me. I know doctors and lawyers, governors and mayors. I don't tell everyone who I know, but when I need them, I know where to go.

"When I am sick, I am nursed back to health, no charge. When

I need legal advice, I get it, no charge. I've been a mother to the motherless, and to this day, they call me Mother, and I call them my sons and daughters. Always sow a good seed, Erin, you never know when you may need to see that harvest. It may be in a year or ten years down the road. Make sure it's a good seed you sow, in fertile ground, and watch it grow.

"I sow with a pure heart, not because of the amount the harvest will be. The heart is pure because I want the harvest to be the same way. Be careful of the attitude you have when you put a seed in the ground."

"What kind of seed, Nana?"

"Time, money, and attitude. Whatever you sow into someone is a seed. You will reap a good harvest when you do it with the right attitude, not looking for anything in return. Just do it from your heart and watch the return."

"I love how you talk. You talk with so much wisdom."

"And I pass it down from generation to generation."

"I'm blessed to have you in my life."

"And you are a blessing to me. Shall I call my attorney?"

"Yes, Nana, you can call him." While she was calling, Erin was looking at her tickets, still in shock. She walked away from Nana for a minute, went in her room and began to pray. "God, I know I don't talk to you much, but I know I need to say thank you. I don't know why this happened to me, but I know it's for me because I'm holding the tickets in my hand. I ask that you give me wisdom, so I am not foolish with it. I do want to be a blessing to those in need. Show me what to do with this blessing. I hear my nana say this when she ends her prayer. She says in Jesus' name, so I'll end my prayer as she does, in Jesus' name, I pray, Amen."

There was a knock on the door. It was Nana. "Beautiful prayer, Erin."

"Thank you. I don't know how to pray, but I felt it in my heart to pray like that."

"It was sincere, and I know he heard it. Brian is not busy today, so we can go down to his office around 2:00 pm."

"That will be fine."

"It's eleven something now. You want to go and grab a bite to eat?"

"Sure, let me slip something on right quick and feed Pebbles."

"Let me get ready also. It wouldn't look right with me going to lunch in my bathrobe."

"Nana, you are so funny."

"I know. I should have been a stand-up comedienne, but my calling was to care for others when they needed me, and they needed my full attention, but I still make them laugh, so I still did my part."

"Yes, that part."

"Yes, all those parts."

"Look at Nana being hip."

"You, young ones keep me up to date with your language."

"You're doing good."

"Bet." She gave Erin some dap; she laughed and so did Nana. They got ready to go out to lunch. Nana got a call from Brian.

"Hey, Mommy, how's it going?"

"Good, Brian, what's up?"

"My client rescheduled their appointment so I'm free now if you would like to come now."

"Erin and I were just about to go to lunch."

"Well, I'm free for the rest of the day. Why don't I meet you guys for lunch?"

"That will be perfect." Nana gave Brian the address, and they met up within a half hour. Brian saw Nana sitting at the table. She waved to him. He came over and gave her a hug.

"You still are handsome as ever."

"Thanks, Mom, you're beautiful as always."

"Don't make me blush. Brian, I would like for you to meet my granddaughter, Erin. Erin, this is adopted son, Brian."

"Pleased to meet you, Erin."

"Likewise, Brian."

"So, what did you need to talk about, Mom?"

"What we have to say I don't want to say around people, so if you don't mind, after lunch we can go back to my house and talk about it?"

"That would be fine. Lunch is on me; order what you want." They ordered lunch and after an hour, they headed back to Nana's house. As they walked into the house, Pebbles began barking.

Erin said, "Girl, go outside with all that noise." She let her out, and they sat at the table.

"What's going on."

"Erin, you want to talk with him?"

"Yes, ma'am. I have a lottery ticket that's worth a lot of money and I want to set up a trust fund before I collect the money."

"Can I ask you how much for?" Erin looked at her Nana like can I trust him. Nana nodded.

"Two hundred fifty-four million dollars."

"In American dollars?"

Nana smiled and said, "I said the same thing."

"Yes, American dollars."

"Okay, so you are going to need to set up a revocable trust fund, where you can name yourself as the trustee and have full control over the trust. You can name a beneficiary in case you pass away; then the trust would go to the person you appointed. Are you collecting the winnings at one time?"

"I think that would be best."

"Then you definitely want to designate someone on the trust if anything should happen to you. You will need a tax attorney and financial advisor. I know them so I will get in contact with them."

"Is there a fee for doing all this?"

"No, ma'am. Your nana paved the way for you so there will be no charge for this."

"I just want to do what's right."

"She did it for you. Let's go to my office and type up the paperwork. Do you have a name for the trust fund?"

"Yes, I do."

"Great Let's get the process started and send you on your way." Erin, Brian, and Nana went down to the office. He typed up the paperwork, and Erin gave Brian the name of the trust fund she wanted it in. He typed up the papers, and she signed them as the trustee. He called the tax lawyer and financial advisor; they did a conference call. They faxed over paperwork, and she signed it. Brian got in touch with the bank she wanted her money deposited into under the trust's name. She had to go down to the bank to sign those papers. She thanked Brian for everything, headed to the bank and signed the papers. Erin was all set to collect her winnings.

On the way home, she said to Nana, "Are you ready to go to Maryland?"

"What's your hurry?"

"The house, Nana. I want that house."

"When do you want to leave?"

"Monday."

"That's three days away."

"Yes, ma'am."

"You really want that house?"

"Like a fish needs water."

"Okay, let me start packing." Erin looked online to see where she could pick up her winnings. She then booked two tickets to Maryland, leaving from the city where she would be on Monday. The drive from Kansas City to Jefferson City was two hours and some minutes, so the ride wouldn't be long. Brian had already submitted the information to the lottery officials with Erin's name and the trust fund name it would be under, so all Erin would have to do is walk in, claim her winnings and leave. In Missouri, she could claim her winnings anonymously.

Erin bought Pebbles a kennel for the car and plane ride. She wasn't leaving her puppy in anyone's care. She had already been through enough. Erin packed a backpack. She didn't have a lot of clothes, but she would buy some later. Nana packed her suitcase; everything was sitting by the door. Saturday morning, Erin washed her car, got in touch with the realtor again to let her know she would be in town and looked forward to meeting her on Tuesday.

Nana found Erin in the driveway and said, "Do you want to leave Monday morning, or leave today and we can relax today and tomorrow, and be there first thing in the morning Monday?"

"If we left today, we won't feel rushed. If we leave early Monday morning, we'll run into traffic. Yes, let's leave today."

"Good because I already made reservations. Check in is at 3:00 pm."

"It's 11:00 am now. If we leave in an hour, we will get there in enough time. Do they allow pets?"

"I looked into that. We're good."

"You know what? There's nothing slow about you; you are so on point."

"I do my best." Erin finished washing her car, and they packed up the car. She put Pebbles in the kennel, and by 12:30 pm they were on the road. During the drive, Erin thought about the house and Darryl. She wanted them both. She put Darryl on the back burner, and the house on the front one like it was the main meal, and she was keeping her eye on it. She was craving it. Her thoughts took her right into Jefferson City. She didn't realize she had been driving that long. They checked in. It was still a little early, so they got something to eat in a nearby restaurant. They sat on the patio. She didn't want to leave Pebbles in the car, but she left her in the kennel.

"Penny for your thoughts."

"Just thinking."

"You've been doing that the whole time on the road. What's on your mind, Sugar?"

"You ever want someone who didn't want you?"

"There were times in my life when that happened. Heartaches and heartbreaks were my partners, and I've danced with them many nights. Don't never be no one's fool, Erin. Don't let no one fool you into thinking you are loving them while they are loving someone else. Then your heart is aching because they are not returning to you what you are giving them. Take your time; don't rush love. If he wants you, he'll find you by any means necessary."

"I know, but I'm moving away from here."

"Erin, if he wants you, he will travel the highways, the sky, and the sea, just to be with you. Love will make him go the distance. He will travel just to be close to you. Establish yourself first. The type of man that you want must be the same way. Make sure he has a foundation that you can build on or stand on. The foundation isn't land; the foundation is the man, his integrity. He has to know his worth, and yours as well. Make him want you. Stand out. Make him look over everyone else and pick you. Be someone that he's never had, and he'll always want."

"Time will tell."

"No rush. He'll come at the perfect time."

"He's just in my thoughts."

"The way you've been thinking, he's in more than your thoughts. Eat up, my dear, so we can go to our room and rest your mind."

"Yes, Nana." Erin paid for their meal and they checked into their room. She let Pebbles out of her kennel and the dog jumped up on the bed and stretched like she'd been cramped in the kennel for days. Erin picked her up, and she licked her in the face. Erin smiled. She'd had Pebbles since she was a tiny puppy; she was like a child to her. Every time she thought about Pebbles being on that couch in the rain it angered her. She was not going to let that happen anymore, not to her dog or herself. No one was going to evict them again.

The rest of the night was quiet. Nana brought some knitting with her to keep her busy; Erin went out and walked Pebbles for about an hour. When she came back, Nana was sleep. Pebbles jumped up on the bed. Erin got in the bed and slept. In the middle of the night, she signed into her account on the media to see if there were any messages. There were none. In disappointment, she sighed and logged off. She wanted to deactivate it but had too many friends who wouldn't like that, so she logged out. Pebbles looked at the phone to see what Erin was watching.

Erin said to Pebbles, "He doesn't miss me; he doesn't even know I'm alive." Pebbles came over to Erin and licked her nose. Their noses connected, and Erin closed her eyes. Tears dropped. Pebbles licked her tears. She grabbed Pebbles and hugged her. "You and Nana are all I have." She lay there and fell asleep. In the morning they went down for breakfast, leaving Pebbles in the room in the kennel.

Nana said, "How did you sleep last night?"

"I did well; how about you?"

"If I could take this bed home with me, I would. That bed was the best thing I've slept on in years."

"We can find out who makes the bed and order you one.

There's nothing like a good night's sleep on a good mattress."

"You'd do that for me?"

"Nana, I would give you the world."

"Well, in that case, give me the world and have it delivered to my house. I'd like to make some changes to it."

"I know, right? There is so much going on in it. If I had the power, I'd make some changes myself."

"Tomorrow is the day."

"I know. I hope they don't have the press there. I don't want cameras in my face."

"Well, the lottery is in a trust fund name, so you won't have to worry about that."

"Yes, but still I don't want my face to be known."

"Disguise yourself then. Buy a wig and wear sunglasses or buy a mask and wear it."

"That's a good idea. After breakfast we can go and look for something." They finished up breakfast, went upstairs to get Pebbles, and went shopping. Erin left Pebbles in the car but cracked the window. They checked out a few stores, picked up some items, then rode by the Missouri Lottery Headquarters. It was a thirty-minute drive from the hotel.

Nana said, "Are you nervous?"

"Yes, ma'am, I am."

"With that kind of winnings, I would be too. You will be okay. Walk in there like it's a normal thing, claim it and start living your life.

"I know. I just don't want the money to change me."

"I know you, Erin, and it won't the only thing you will change is your location. That's it. I don't believe you will let the money run or ruin your life."

"I pray it won't."

"It won't." They headed back to the hotel and ordered room service for lunch/dinner. Erin got her outfit ready for Monday, walked Pebbles and then rested up for her new adventure in the morning. Check-out time was 11:00 am. They were up by 8:00 am and left by nine. Erin put their luggage in the car and put Pebbles in the back seat. They got in, and Erin took a deep breath.

Nana said, "Relax, it's almost over."

"I know, Nana, I know. They arrived there in forty-five minutes because of the work traffic. Erin cracked the window for Pebbles, and they proceeded into the building. Heads turned with smiles as Erin and Nana walked in. They went up to the welcoming center counter. Erin said, "I'm here to collect my lottery winnings."

"Ok, Minnie—I mean, what is your name?" Erin came in wearing a Minnie Mouse costume. She had a mask on, a mini skirt, with black thigh-high suede boots.

"My name is on the trust fund I will be claiming it under."

"Can I see your ticket and ID." She showed the lady the information. "Follow me." They went into a room and waited for about thirty minutes, then the lottery officials came in with the big check written out to the trust fund name she gave them. They took pictures. Nana didn't want to be in them, so it was Erin with her mask and the officials. After that was done, she went with one of the officials to have the money wired to the account it was going into. Erin already had a temporary bank card for that account. She got a confirmation that the funds were there, shook his hand, and she and Nana left the building.

"We did it, Nana, we did it, we did it."

"Yes, I'm so proud of you, and that outfit of yours! I've never seen a sexy Minnie Mouse before."

"I know, neither have they." They laughed. They drove to the airport and boarded the plane. The flight was an hour and forty-five minutes, better than driving for nineteen hours. Pebbles was on the floor between Erin and Nana, but if no one was sitting in a seat by take-off, she was putting her in a seat. While the plane was on the ground, she transferred money from her trust fund account to her regular account—not too much but just enough so she wouldn't have to pull out ID for her bank card with the trust fund. The plane was ready to leave. The seat next to them was empty, and Pebbles was secured with the seatbelt.

As quickly as the plane went up, it touched down. They were in Maryland in no time. Erin unfastened Pebbles, they deplaned and went to pick up the rental car. Before they went to the hotel, she wanted to take Nana by the house she wanted to buy. The forty-minute ride brought them to the house, which sat on an acre of land. Erin noticed a moving truck pulling up to the house as they were passing by.

Erin parked her car. Nana said, "What are you doing?"

"I'm going to claim my house."

"You can't just go up there and claim it."

"Watch me." Erin walked up to the house and saw a woman sitting on the steps. She was there alone. She didn't have any movers; she was just sitting there.

Erin walked to her and said, "This is a beautiful house. Did you just purchase this?"

"I did."

"Are you moving in today?"

"I am."

"I was looking at this house some months ago. I thought it was the most beautiful house I ever saw. Oh, where are my manners. My name is Erin."

"Please to meet you, Erin. My name is Pamela." They shook hands.

"As I was saying, I saw this house and fell in love with it."

"We did too."

"If you don't mind me asking, who is we?"

"My husband and I. Well, soon to be ex-husband."

"Oh, I'm sorry. I didn't mean to pry."

"You're fine. Maybe it was a good thing you came here."

"Why are you not moving in, and just sitting on the steps?"

"For one, I'm tired. I moved everything myself last night, and I don't even know if I want this house anymore. I wanted to share it with my husband, but now that we are not together, I don't think I want it. The mortgage is already high, and I don't know if I'll be able to pay for it by myself."

As they were talking, Nana and Pebbles were walking up to them. Nana said, "I have to use the restroom."

"Oh, you can use mine." Pamela opened the door and showed Nana where the restroom was.

"This house is beautiful."

"I can take you for a tour if you'd like."

"Oh, please can you?" Pamela took Erin on a tour, showed her the kitchen that had all brand-new stainless-steel appliances, showed her all six bedrooms, plus the bedroom in the attic that could be a man cave. From there, she showed her the indoor swimming pool, the den and sitting room, and then the spacious backyard. From the front of the driveway to the back yard, the house was just what Erin had seen online.

"Let's cut to the chase. I want to make you an offer for this house."

"I was hoping someone would. I don't want to live here alone."

"I'll give you a hundred grand over what you paid for this house."

"I would've just taken what I paid for it. I'm not looking for the highest bidder. I just want to be happy where-ever I'm at, and I know I wouldn't be happy here, not without him."

Nana came out of the restroom and said, "I see why your spirit is in this house; mine is too, and I am at peace that you will be fine here."

"We don't have to test drive the city?"

"No. I am at peace."

"Pamela, this is my Nana Georgina. Nana, this is Pamela."

"Please to meet you, Pamela."

"Likewise, Ms. Georgina."

"I had called the realtor to meet with her tomorrow about this property. I guess I can call her and tell her that I want to put in an offer."

"I would like that very much, and to show how much I appreciate you I'll decorate for free. I'm an interior decorator."

"Oh, I would pay you for it."

"You already have." Erin called the realtor. She drove Pamela over to the office while Nana and Pebbles stayed at the house. Erin didn't need to do a credit check; she bought the house cash money, no mortgage. She gave Pamela what she put down on the house, money for closing fees, inspections, every penny Pamela spent regarding purchasing the house, Erin gave back to her. Although Erin had to pay closing costs and title transfer, it didn't matter to her; she wanted to make sure everyone was happy.

Pamela moved into a condo that she loved, and as promised she helped Erin decorate the house. Nana stayed with Erin for a month and then she went back to Missouri. Erin and Pamela became good friends; they spent a lot of time together. Pamela needed Erin. She made Erin's move to the new state much easier. She stayed busy with the house and hanging out with Pamela. She didn't often think of Darryl; it was better that way. Erin took pictures of the outside of the house, and Pamela took a picture of Erin sitting on the step, in front of the Red door.

Three months went by. Erin hadn't been on social media; she was too busy to think about it. One night, she decided to get on and post an updated picture, so she posted the one sitting in front of her door. Three minutes after posting it, her friends swarmed in on her post. They had missed her and asked where she had been. Did she move? She felt like her friends were news reporters. She answered all their questions. It was good interacting with them. She did her regular post like she did before; everything was back to normal.

A week later, on a Saturday, Pamela picked Erin up, and they did some art shopping. Erin was looking for furniture. She was fixing up guest bedrooms. After that, they went to dinner and to a jazz club. She was enjoying Maryland. She knew she had picked the right area to move to. After a night of fun, Pamela dropped Erin off. It began to rain, and Erin hurried up to the house. Pamela beeped the horn and drove away. Pebbles came running to her. She picked her up and kissed her, then went and took a shower and cozied up in her bedroom.

An hour later, her doorbell rang. It kind of startled Erin because she didn't know anyone else in Maryland but Pamela, so who was ringing her doorbell? She looked outside. She didn't notice a car. It was 1:00 am; who could be at her house that time of the morning? She didn't do anything different to bring attention to herself. Was someone watching her? The doorbell rang again, and Pebbles started barking. Erin went downstairs. She didn't turn on any lights; she didn't want the person to know she was home. She peeked through the peephole. She couldn't really see the person. They rang the bell again. Whoever this person was, they were persistent.

When Erin didn't answer, the person left the step, walking to the car. Erin looked through her window and saw the face. She ran to the door and opened it. Before he could get in his car, he looked and saw her standing there.

He closed the car door, walked to her doorstep and said, "Hello, Sparkle."

"Hello, Darryl, how did you find me?"

"The Red Door."

"What red door?"

"This one."

"My front door?"

"Yes."

"That doesn't make sense."

"Are you going to invite me in?"

"I don't know you like that."

"I understand, but trust me, the way I feel about you, you will definitely want to get to know me." Erin knew exactly what he was talking about.

"Let's go somewhere and have coffee. You can follow me." Erin got in her car and he followed her. They drove to the closest diner, went inside and sat down. They ordered coffee, and Erin looked at his eyes. She was quickly drawn into them.

"How did you say you found me again?"

"The Red Door."

"How could that be? I didn't post my address; it's just me sitting in front of the door."

"You don't remember?"

"Apparently I don't."

"Some time ago, we were talking, and you said if we were to build a house, what would it look like."

"Oh, yeah I remember that. That was a while ago."

"The house we were building sounded like a dream home to me. I was enjoying how you put it together, then one day you sent me a link to a house and said this is exactly what we built. I loved what I saw. I could live there and enjoy life. I know we haven't been talking for a while, but I have been following you. I watched your posts; I studied your every move. Yes, call me the night stalker. At night when you are sleep, I'd read your posts. I love how people interact with you; you're witty at times and serious other times. I love how you respond to them. People love you, Erin'; that's why I call you Sparkle. You shine your light on everyone; you give good exposure. You encourage, you care. I believe that's why people are drawn to you."

"Thank you."

"Oh, you are most welcome."

"You never say anything to me; I never hear from you. Not in weeks. Why now?"

"I don't say much. I just watch you. Just because I don't say anything doesn't mean I'm not around. I'm discreet. I watched you through your posts. I studied you like that."

"I see. When did you get into town?"

"I just arrived when I rung your doorbell."

"No, you didn't."

"I promise you I did. When I hadn't seen you post in a while, I started to worry about you, but I didn't want to get all in my feelings. I was missing you so when you finally posted a week ago, and I saw that red door, I immediately went to that link you sent me. It was the same door, the same red door, with a glass screen door, and red brick steps. 'She moved away from me,' I said in my thoughts. My heart said, go to her. I started to crave you. Nothing else could satisfy that; you were my butter pecan ice cream. I don't like no other ice cream but that one. Driving here, I was hoping you would be at home, be alone, hoping you were single. You were worth every toll I paid, every fill up at the gas station, every horn-honking road-rage person on the highway. You were worth everything for me to get here."

"Wow, that is so beautiful. So where are you staying?"

"I got a hotel not far from here."

"How long are you staying?"

"As long as you will."

"I just bought a house, so I'll be here for a while."

"No problem. I am a man of wealth. I can find a place to stay."

"Why do you want me?"

"Because every other woman is not my flavor. You are my butter pecan."

"I missed you, Darryl."

"I know and that's why I'm here because I missed you too. Let me be a part of your life. I want to see where this goes. I like how I'm feeling, and I know if I'm feeling this way, nothing but good can come out of it."

"I like the way it sounds. In the morning come over for breakfast, and we can talk some more."

"I would love that."

As they ended their conversation, her phone rang. Erin answered. "Hey, Nana, it's kind of late for you to call. What do you mean warrant, for who? Me, for what? WHAT? OMG! There's got to be a mistake! I'll come home as soon as possible. Don't get all worked up. I'll be home. Bye, Nana."

"Erin, what's wrong?" She was quiet, shaking her head. "Please tell me what's wrong."

"I have to go back home."

"Why?"

"There's a warrant for my arrest."

"Warrant! Arrest! For what?"

"Money laundering."

TBC IN VOL. III

A NEW HORIZON

"Can I come over?"

"No, I'm busy."

"When will I see you?"

"We'll make plans."

"I'll be in the neighborhood."

"I'll be out of town."

Excuses, excuses, excuses. Shayla was getting tired of them. The more she wanted to see him, the more excuses she got that he couldn't. What was really going on? She was going to find out soon. She got in her car and took a trip over to his house. Whatever he couldn't tell her on the phone, he was going to tell her face to face. When she pulled up to his driveway, she saw the taillights of his car blink off. She got out of her car and he got out of his— and so did the passenger, a lady asking questions about who Shayla was.

He replied, "She's nobody."

Shayla got the answer she was looking for. She said, "And nobody to you I will remain."

She got back in her car and left. She got on the highway to go back home. As she drove, she threw her phone out the window. In her rear-view mirror, she saw her phone crushed under the tires of a tractor-trailer. She smiled and cried, not knowing that in two weeks, thirty-one thousand feet in the air, her life would change forever.

Shayla worked in an activation center for a cell phone company, so she was always talking with someone new every day. She built a relationship with some customers on the phone. At times they were good calls; others were call it a day; she was going home. She took the good with the bad. She loved her job, so she could take them as they came.

One day she got a call from a customer who wanted to activate her phone. The call was about forty-five minutes, but the entire call was pleasant. The customer remarked on how nice she was during the conversation. Although the process took a little longer than normal, the conversation made the process easier. After the phone was activated, the lady thanked Shayla again for great customer service, and said if there was a survey for her to take, she would give good feedback. She ended the call and went on about her day. She thought about the lady often and wished she had kept her number to continue the conversation. Two days later, she got an email from her supervisor, stating how much the lady had enjoyed the conversation and service, and that she had left her number to call. Shayla was excited about that, and after work, she gave her a call.

"Hello, can I speak to Ms. Bobbie?"

"This is she. Is this Shayla?"

"Yes, ma'am, it is."

"I have tried to track you down for the past two days. It was kind of hard because I didn't know your last name."

"Yes, ma'am, I can see that. I'm off on the weekend, but I saw your email when I came in."

"I just wanted to say, you are such a sweetheart. You made the process very easy. Your personality is very outgoing; you're going somewhere, young lady. I don't know exactly where, but I felt led to tell you that with the type of personality you have, it's going to take you farther than what you're doing now. I wanted to tell you that."

"Ms. Bobbie, I do thank you for those words. I needed to hear them, I am a published author, so maybe the success will happen through my book."

"Oh, you're an author?"

"Yes, ma'am, a first-time author."

"I'd like to read it. Send me a copy."

"Yes, ma'am, I will do just that." Shayla got her address and sent the book the next day. A week went by; she didn't hear from Ms. Bobbie, but it was confirmed that she did receive the book. Every day at work, there was a different kind of activation, some long, some short. Working in the activation department made the day go by fast and the week followed in the same flow. She was without a phone for a week; she just didn't feel like having one. That weekend she was going to get a new one, with a new number. Not many people were calling her now, but within two weeks her phone would be ringing more in a month than it had in the previous year.

She thought about Desmond. He dogged and dodged her from the very beginning. He knew how to play it, and when to say it. She called him the smooth operator, a charmer; he was out to harm her. He knew how she felt. He couldn't be honest, so when she pried, he lied. It would've been better to say, I'm not ready for this, or anything, but string her into a place of emptiness. She allowed him into her world, but he was closed-up with his. He led a secretive life, allowing no access to his whereabouts. Before she saw him at his house, she was slowly letting him go. That day in the driveway was closure. She was moving on, finally.

A week after her new phone, she needed to set up her email. When she did, she had five emails from Ms. Bobbie and one from someone named Joshua Taylor. She didn't know him, so she was going to erase it, but she checked Ms. Bobbie's email first. Her email said call me ASAP. She found her number and called her. "Ms. Bobbie, hey, it's Shayla. I got your message. Are you okay?"

"Yes, I'm fine. I've been trying to get in touch with you for the past week. I have some good news and some better news for you, which one do you want first?"

"I'll take the good news for two hundred, Ms. Bobbie."

"It's funny that you should say two hundred. Ok, so the good news is that your book is awesome. The better news is, I sold your book."

"What's better about that?"

"The gentleman I sold it to is a director."

"How did you manage to run into him?"

"I was on a flight going to California and decided to read your book on the flight. He noticed the book and asked questions about it. I told him that you were a new author. I just got the book in the mail and started reading it. He loved your cover and your picture. He asked where he could get the book. I told him, but he said he wanted my book. I asked him why he couldn't order his own, and he said that he was already in love with the author and he didn't want to wait in the mail to get one. Guess how much he offered me for my book?"

"How much?"

"Two hundred dollars."

"You're kidding me?"

"No, ma'am, I'm not. Although you wrote my name in it, he still wanted the book as is."

"That's so awesome! What is this gentleman's name?""

"Joshua Taylor."

"Are you serious? I got an email from him."

"I gave him that, not your phone number. As a matter of fact, what happened with your number? I called and it kept going to voicemail."

"Long story. I'll share it with you one day."

"Okay, looking forward to that one. Are you going to check your emails?"

"As soon as I get off the phone with you."

"Well, call me back and let me know what they say."

"I sure will." She hung up the phone and checked the email. He introduced himself, told her about how he got her book and asked her to call him. She called Ms. Bobbie back.

"What did the email say?"

"He wants me to call him."

"Are you?"

"I don't know. This is so unexpected. I just wrote a book and that was that. I thought bigger things, but not this quick."

"Shayla, if you don't call him, I'm going to put you over my lap and whoop you. He's a very nice-looking young man, very, very easy on the eyes."

"You sound like you're blushing."

"I probably was, but he wasn't looking at me, he was looking at your picture. Call him, I want to know what he has to say."

"Yes, Mama, I'll call him."

"Aww, you called me Mama."

"After you said you were going to put me over your lap and beat me, yes, ma'am, I can call you that."

"Call him and then call me back."

"Yes, Mother." She took a deep breath, looked at the phone number for a minute, wondering if calling this number was going to be good or better. She dialed the number. Ring, ring, ring.

"Hello." Just at the sound of his voice she started to melt.

"Hello, may I speak to Joshua?"

"This is he. And who do I have the pleasure of speaking to?"

"This is Shayla."

"The author of the book that I have been reading for the past week, Shayla?"

"Yes, I believe so. I don't know if there's another author out there with that name, but yes this is me. You sound like you're just waking up."

"It's been a long night, working on some locations for different projects. Let me get up and get some coffee so I can be wide awake to talk. I don't want to snore on you." They laughed. In a soft, tender voice, he said, "I've been waiting on you."

"That sounds promising."

"It may come to that. You may already know how I got hold of your book. I felt like I was at an auction. Ms. Bobbie would not release that book to me; I had to bid to get it."

"Was it worth the two hundred?"

"I would've paid two thousand for it."

"Whew, I didn't make that much in book sales."

"You will make that and more."

"I'm listening." She heard him stirring his cup of coffee.

"How long have you been writing?"

"I just started."

"You never wrote before?"

"Never."

"Did you go to school for it?"

"No."

"Well, somebody taught you. Who was your teacher?"

"Pain."

"I see. I can hear your voice as I read. Your stories are so profound and very visual. Your voice puts me there in the story, and I would like you to be here to be a part of mine. I am a first-time director, looking for some new ideas. I found them in your book. I'm putting together some projects. I would like to sit down and talk with you about being a part of what I'm doing. I believe meeting Ms. Bobbie on that plane was perfect timing; what I was looking for she had in her hands. I would like to come and have lunch with you next week so we can talk about this some more. I want to pick your brain."

"Not much to pick out of it."

"For what I've read, I need to."

"I don't know you. Can I bring along someone?"

"I hope it's Ms. Bobbie. I like her; she reminds me of my mother."

"That's who I was thinking about."

"Sure, you can bring her. I'd like to see her again. Pick out a place to meet. I will be in your town next week, so we can do a meet and greet."

"Oh, you sound so poetic."

"And it's in motion! I'll see you next week." After they ended the call, Shayla called Ms. Bobbie.

"Okay, tell me what happened."

"I think he's in love with me."

"I knew that but tell me what happened."

"He wants to meet me next week to what he calls pick my brain."

"Are you going to let him?"

"Ms. Bobbie, what does that mean?"

"He wants to know what you're thinking. Obviously, you said something in your book that got his attention. You've awakened something in him, and he wants to go deeper into your thoughts."

"My pain helped me to write."

"That's all it takes—the thought, and now the results."

"The results of what?"

"The results are what's going to happen after you meet him."

"You mean us three?"

"Oh, is he bringing someone?"

"No, I am."

"Who?"

"You, Ms. Bobbie. I would love for you to join us. I don't know him, but you've met him, and I don't want to go by myself. Besides, he would like to see you again."

"Oh, Shayla, I would love to join you guys. When are you meeting?"

"Next Saturday."

"Let me clear my calendar, and I will drive up that Friday. I'll book my hotel and meet up with you Saturday."

"Ms. Bobbie, please come stay with me. I would love to meet you before Saturday; that will be our bonding time."

"I feel we've already bonded, but I would love to put a face to this voice. I will let you know when I'm leaving. I have your address, and I look forward to seeing you next Friday."

"Perfect. I'm off for the week, so I shall see you then." Click. Shayla sat down and reclined in her chair, processing everything that had just happened. What might come out of this? She thought big as far as writing books…but could this go further? What was in her book that he saw? She was going to find out. While on vacation, she decided to do some spring cleaning. First, she started with pictures. She deleted her backed-up photos, she didn't want to be reminded of pain anymore, so any photos she had with Desmond, she deleted. It was easy. She felt a connection with Joshua, something she didn't feel with Desmond, but her heart was still guarded. She released her pain on paper; she vented on a blank canvas for the world to see. She cleaned up the guest room, worked on her new book, picked up some items from the store to fill the refrigerator for her guest. Ms. Bobbie and Shayla talked on and off until Friday. Ms. Bobbie called her Friday morning to let her know she was leaving by twelve and would be there around two. Shayla went to the nail salon, then ran a few more errands. She was back at her house at one-thirty. Ten minutes later a car pulled up in her driveway. She looked out the window. A lady walking up to her door—it had to be Ms. Bobbie.

She opened the door and said, "Ms. Bobbie?"

"Shayla?" They hugged each other like friends who haven't

seen each other in years.

"OMG, you are too cute."

"Thank you, Ms. Bobbie. Let me take your bag, come on in." They went into the living room and sat down.

"Would you like something to eat or drink?"

"No, I'm fine. Your voice does match your face; you are just too cute."

"Well thank you. I pictured you the same way. A pretty voice like that has to have a face that matches." They laughed.

"Tell me about yourself."

"What's there to tell? I'm a single mom of a grown lady now; I work to make ends meet, and I wrote a book."

"That's enough for now. You will fill me in later."

"What about you, what's your life like?"

"I'm a retired teacher, married to a wonderful man. I have two children, and I think I may go into management."

"Managing what?"

"Your New Horizon."

"Am I stepping into something new?"

"You are. Look at what has happened thus far. You wrote a book, and now it's in the hands of a director who is coming to see you tomorrow. It can't get any better than that. Don't question why, although you've probably already done that through the week. Timing has everything to do with what's going on now; don't over-think anything. When we first talked on the phone, you didn't know all of this was going to happen. Sending your book was you sharing your vision with me. You didn't know I was going to California, and I didn't know I was going to meet Joshua on the plane. Everything happened at an appointed time. You wrote your book at the appointed time for all this to take place.

"I don't know what Joshua saw in your book. He only saw the cover. Not knowing what the contents were, he saw the beauty on the outside. Now he wants to know the beauty of the author. Be the match he saw in your book. What I've read and seen in your book is totally different from what he saw; we all got something different from it. Well, I didn't get to finish it, so I am going to need another one, but he was persistent about getting it, so I let him purchase it. I believe your life is about to change, and I want to be there with you when it does."

"Ms. Bobbie, my life changed when I talked to you on the phone."

"Oh, sweetie, I know. We all connect with people every day, but our connection was ordained."

"It sounds special."

"For certain people it is, and you are one of them."

"Thank you."

"You're welcome."

"What does Joshua look like?"

"He's a man who makes you smile."

"What does that mean?"

"I'll let you decide that for yourself. You're meeting him about your book, not about his looks."

"I know, it's not a blind date, but he knows what I look like. Why can't I know what he looks like?"

"I already gave you a description of him. He's a man who will make you smile. Just be yourself, don't do anything extra."

"I've always been that way."

"I'll tell you this much; he stared at your picture for a while. I never saw him open up the book."

"That was a selfie picture I took, no make-up, just a regular picture."

"Well, he saw something. Let him tell you what it is. Don't ask questions, answer his. Then when the time is right, ask yours."

"I will do that. Are you hungry?"

"I sure am."

"I made spaghetti. Let's eat and then I'll show you to your room." They ate, laughed, and shared special moments. They bonded quickly, and for the rest of the evening they relaxed. In the morning, Ms. Bobbie got up to cook breakfast. Shayla came in minutes later to make coffee.

"Good morning, Sunshine."

"Good morning, Ms. Bobbie, how did you sleep?"

"If I could take your mattress home, that would be awesome. I slept so well, I thought I was home."

"You are home."

"I feel like it." They smiled. "Tell me more about this Desmond; he sounds like he's going to be lonely when he gets older."

"To heal, I'll talk about him."

"The way you sounded last night, that's all I want you to do." Shayla fixed her coffee. Ms. Bobbie fixed their plates and joined her at the table.

"Desmond is what you call stuck on himself. Ladies love him and he knows it. He likes the attention he gets. He is like someone drenched in honey and a swarm of bees surround him. Well, that's how the ladies are with him. He can pick and choose who he wants. He isn't the committed type and I knew that. When I started writing, he sounded interested, said he would help. That didn't happen. I didn't ask anyone to help me; it was my project. I liked him, but his arrogance rubbed me the wrong way. It was time to end it, but he already did that. I just had to follow suit and leave him alone." Ms. Bobbie got up and went in her purse to get something. She came back with a compact mirror, opened it and gave it to Shayla.

She said, "When you look in that mirror, what do you see?"

"I see me."

Ms. Bobbie got up and tried to see herself in the mirror, but she couldn't. "What I tried to do was see if I could see myself along with you in that compact mirror. I couldn't because there was only room enough for one person. That's how an arrogant person is; they only see themselves and no one else. There's no room for you; they are selfish. Come with me." They walked into the hallway where there was a mirror where they could see each other together. "That's what you want, Shayla. Be with someone that you can see yourself together with. Never let someone put you in a compact situation, where you feel alone.

"He knew how you felt; he loved the attention you were giving him. You weren't the only one, but you don't have to feed that ego anymore. Let him starve; there's someone better waiting on you."

"You think so, Ms. Bobbie?"

"I know so, Sugar. Let's finish up breakfast and then get ready for our lunch later." As they were finishing up, Shayla got a text from Joshua, saying if she didn't mind could they cancel lunch and meet for dinner. She said that would be perfect. He sent a smiley face and texted her where to meet him. She told Ms. Bobbie the change of plans.

She said, "Dinner will be better than lunch. The mood is different at night than in the afternoon."

"What type of mood?"

"You'll see. So, what are you going to wear for Mr. Joshua?"

"I am going to wear a casual outfit, nothing revealing."

"Casual is cute. I'll do casual too."

"Besides, I don't know what the meeting is about. I want to be relaxed while we're having it."

"Are you nervous?"

"Do I look it?"

"Well, you've been tapping on the counter for the last two minutes.

I thought you were typing something."

"It's a habit."

"Calm your nerves, you're going to do just fine. Look at it as an interview. Stay focused, answer the questions. Eye contact is good. Let him know you are paying attention. Don't yawn no matter how boring the conversation may get. He's interested in your book; make it worth his while to come see you."

"Yes, Ms. Bobbie, I will do just that."

"Also, minty breath is good. Have some gum or a mint while talking to him."

"Yes, Mother."

"Good girl. Let's go pick out your casual outfit." While looking for an outfit, Ms. Bobbie said, "Shayla and Joshua."

"What about me and Joshua?"

"I like the way it sounds. It sounds way better than Shayla and Desmond."

"What are you saying?"

"I'm not saying anything. I just like the way those two names go together."

"He may not even be my type. This is a meeting, not a date."

"Why can't it be both?"

"Because you are coming with me."

"I can always move to another table."

"I'd rather you stay. Whatever he has to say, I want you to be there to hear it all."

"I would never leave you, Sugar. I'll be right there."

"That's comforting. I would love to hear my man say that to me."

"Say what?"

"I'll never leave you."

"Maybe Joshua will. I mean maybe he will."

"Why do you keep saying Joshua?"

"Because I have a good feeling about this meeting."

"Well, at least you feel something. I've been so numb about everything I've been going through I don't know what to feel anymore."

"A new horizon, new attitude. We have an hour before we meet him. Are you going to wear any makeup?"

"No, I like my natural beauty. I'll show the natural side of me first. I have nothing to hide."

"That's good. You have pretty skin, don't clog your pores with it. Let your skin breathe tonight. You ready to head out?"

"Yes, I am."

"Do you want to drive or should I?"

"I'll drive since you're visiting."

"Yes, you're driving Ms. Daisy, I love it."

"You want to sit in the back?"

"No, I want to see everything. Put me where I can see it. I call shotgun."

"You're the only one riding with me, Ms. Bobbie. You only call shotgun when it's more people riding in the car."

"Oh, okay, shall we ride?"

"We shall." They got in the car. Shayla put the address that he texted her in her GPS, and they headed to dinner. They drove up to the location, Lexi's Lounge. They got out and immediately heard music. They stepped inside. A live band was playing, people were laughing and dancing, and the smell of food filled the air. Shayla and Ms. Bobbie found a table and watched the people on the dance floor having a good time.

Ms. Bobbie was rocking to the beat, Shayla tapping her feet. The club was invigorating. They were clapping and dancing, swinging hips, dipping low, Ms. Bobbie bouncing up and down in her seat, looking like a little kid on a horse. She was having a good time. Shayla was too. She was looking around. It was a happy crowd. Then the lights went low, the music stopped, the dance floor cleared, and fingers started snapping. Ms. Bobbie and Shayla didn't know what was going on, but they were still having a good time.

Someone came through the door, fingers still snapping. A man came to their table, grabbed Shayla's hand, and whispered in her ear.

"Come dance with me." They walked to the dance floor. "Follow my lead, don't be afraid, flow with me, Shayla." They reached the dance floor. A light shined on them, and the music played. While the people in the audience were still snapping their fingers, he moved slowly. She did the same. The scent of his cologne drew her closer to him. He slowly pulled her in. He gripped her lower back, and she pressed into his. The drag was slow, but their energy was igniting. He swung her around, and when she came back to him, they both raised their arms, and their fingers locked. Her leg lifted around his waist; he dipped her backward. When she came up, their eyes locked, and they danced until the song ended. The lights went out, the fingers stopped snapping, and the hands started clapping.

He walked Shayla back to her seat and kissed Ms. Bobbie on the cheek.

Ms. Bobbie said, "Joshua, you are the man on the dance floor, how did you put this together?"

"This is an old spot of mine. I come here every time I'm in town. I told them I'd be in town this weekend, so I thought I invite you here, and have some fun. So, this is Ms. Shayla. I am Joshua. I hope you didn't mind my introduction to you on the dance floor; I wanted to do something different with you, instead of coming and say 'Hello, I'm Joshua,' like something boring. I wanted to do something you would remember." Shayla just looked at him and smiled. Ms. Bobbie was right;

he would put a smile on your face.

"That was the best introduction I ever had, thank you for that."

"It's my pleasure. Are you ladies ready to order something to eat? They have the best chicken and waffles here."

"I've never had it."

"Neither have I," Ms. Bobbie said.

"Okay, since you ladies have never had it, you'll can order something different. I'll order this for me and let you taste it off my plate." They both smiled and blushed. Joshua was so good-looking, there were no words to describe him. He just looked oh so good. His looks did make you smile, and that's what Shayla did the entire night. Their food came, with extra plates. Joshua cut Ms. Bobbie some and put it on her plate. With Shayla, he did something different. He cut some and fed it to her. She slowly chewed her food, looking at him.

He said, "How does it taste?"

"MMM, so so good. I want some more."

"What about your food?"

"I'll take it home." They shared his plate. After dinner was over, they went out on the patio.

Ms. Bobbie said, "I'm going to call my husband and chat with him, so if you'll excuse me." Joshua stood up as Ms. Bobbie walked away.

He sat and said, "I read your story 'Swallowed Thoughts.' Very interesting. I'd like to know how you came up with that title?"

"It's a sensual story."

"I've noticed that. How did you come up with it?"

"It happened to me. I was in a long-distance relationship. We talked on the phone a lot because we couldn't be intimate. Because of the distance, we'd have a conversation about what we would do to each other. I would get excited about what he would do to me. Every time I thought about it, I'd swallow. I think it happened to him too. I held onto everything he said he would do to me."

"What happened to that relationship?"

"It fizzled after a while. The conversation began to get boring. I was snoring ten minutes into the conversation, but I kept the title as swallowed thoughts because an intimate or sensual conversation will have you doing just that. The relationship doesn't have to be long distance. You and I could have that same conversation sitting face to face and it could happen."

He swallowed.

"See, just like that, the thought aroused you."

"Can I tell you why I made this trip to come see you?"

"Yes, please."

"As I read your stories, they became very visual to me. I felt I was a part of the story. I felt connected to the character. I felt you were talking to me. I swallowed so many times, I couldn't count. Shayla, your stories are like medicine to the soul. I'm reading the stories as if you're reading them to me. You're gifted. You talk on different levels like you want people to hear you, clearly loudly.

"It was the pain I had gone through. It was my fuel, and with my imagination, I picked up my pen, and I became an author."

"Your pain turns into pleasure. It created something deep, and I want to help you create something bigger."

"Like what?"

"You ever write a screenplay?"

"Never."

"I'm going to show you. You have a vision. It started on a piece of paper, but I want to help you put it on a screen."

"Like television?"

"No, like a movie. It's time for a new face to be seen. As you know, movies fizzle because it's the same thing, over again. You have new ideas, and I want you to get all the credit. I will teach you how to be a director and a producer. You're already a writer, there's talent in you that I want to see come forth. I will guide you if you let me lead."

"Like you did on the dance floor?"

"Just like that. If you don't mind, we'll start by doing some radio interviews so the people can get a feel of what's to come. I want to introduce you to the world. You're going to go from local to worldwide; people need to hear what you have to say, share your vision, so they can see what you are all about.

"What do you say, Shayla?"

"I love that you see all this in me. I have to start believing what my purpose is, and you just opened it up for me."

"I have certain keys to unlock certain doors. I want to unlock all of yours."

"Are you married?"

"Not yet."

"Why?"

"Because I wanted a certain woman who had a passion unknown. She didn't have to speak; she didn't have to showcase it; it was a quiet kept secret. I glimpsed it when I saw your picture. What were you thinking when you took it?"

"Rescue me?"

"A soft cry, and only I heard it. A soft cry for what?"

"Here I am with all this love to give and no one wants it. An innocent love so pure, it's just building up ready to be released, but I don't want to give it to anybody; it's a river so deep."

"That's what I saw. Your eyes, so soulful. Let me help you birth your vision, and then we can work on something else. Right now, you need to be introduced to the world. I'm going to set up an interview at the radio station. I want them to hear your voice, your laugh, how you breathe. I want you to saturate the airwaves. A star is about to be born, and I want to be there when you are birthed. Let's build your empire. After the interview, we will work on your screenplay. You have so much potential, and I want to see you use it in the right way."

"Is there a contract involved?"

"Only if you write one up. You're going to be your own boss."

"What about financing this project."

"I got you, Shayla. If I didn't think this was worth my backing, I'd move onto something else. I can co-produce, but you are the producer."

"I never expected to hear all this."

"Isn't it about time you did?"

"I believe so." Just as the conversation was getting ready to end, Ms. Bobbie came back to the table.

"So, what did I miss?"

"I'll fill you in on the way home."

"I have a couple of meetings in the morning. I will be in touch." He got up and kissed Ms. Bobbie on the cheek and kissed Shayla on her hand. They watched as he exited the door.

"So, what happened? Did I stay away long enough?"

"You set that up. You said you weren't going to leave me by myself with him."

"The way I saw you two on the dance floor, I think you were fine by yourself. What did he say?"

"He wants to put my book on the big screen."

"Television or movies?"

"It could be both."

"I told you, Shayla, you have extraordinary talent. You're going places."

"He wants to set up an interview on the radio in two weeks."

"That's a great start."

"I know, but every step of the way, I want you with me."

"I told you I would. I never go back on my promise."

"That's good to hear." Shayla grabbed her food to go, and they headed home. Sunday came, and Ms. Bobbie headed back home. Two weeks later, Shayla was on the radio. Joshua introduced her as a debut author and soon-to- be producer. She talked about her book, gave a snippet of what was in it. Her sales had escalated; the world was seeing a new name and face. Joshua scheduled her book signings, and she took pictures with people who bought her book. She was posted on all the media channels, and her name was spreading before the screenplay was written. She and Joshua took a lot of pictures together; they were looking more like a couple than business partners. Ms. Bobbie went to all her book signings. She looked like a proud mother with Shayla. After the book signings, Joshua said that they would work on the screenplay in a month. Shayla loved the relationship they were building, and so did Ms. Bobbie. She would talk to them like children, and they respected her for it; she adored them both. Shayla's book went to bestseller in a week. She was excited. Joshua said he would be in town to take her out to celebrate. She gave her two-week-notice at her job. The money she made from her books she was putting towards her production.

Saturday evening, Joshua texted her to let her know he was on his way to pick her up. The doorbell rang. She thought it was him. She opened the door and it was Desmond.

"Well, this is a surprise. I haven't seen you in forever. What brings you in this neighborhood?"

"I saw your book. Congratulations."

"Well, thank you, but you've seen my book? Don't you have it, didn't you buy it?"

"Yes, I have it, but I wanted to congratulate you on your success. I would like to take you out so we can celebrate."

"Oh, so we can celebrate?"

"Well, I tried calling you, but your number is disconnected, so I thought I'd come over and take you out."

"Oh, okay, let me grab my jacket and purse."

She came back and said, "It's funny; before all this happened, I used to call you and want to spend time with you. You always had excuses. Never once did you call me as I was writing my book. You never came through for me when you said you would. Now that I am successful, you have time for me. You want to spend time with me now. What about the days and nights I was lonely, and my heart was breaking? I needed you to be there then, but now you have time for me. You didn't help promote my book; you did nothing, and now you have time for me. This is one harvest you will not reap, that you have not sown." She walked to the door, opened it, and said, "Excuse me, I have to let the dog out." She opened the screen door.

He said, "I didn't know you had a dog." He walked out the door.

She said, "I just let him out. Please don't come back." A car door shut; Joshua was walking up to her door.

Joshua said to Shayla, "Hey, baby, who is this?"

"Oh, he's nobody to me."

"Well, excuse me, nobody to her, I have to take this beautiful lady out to celebrate her success." They walked to the car. Joshua opened the door for Shayla, and she got in. He walked over to his side and smiled at Desmond. He got in the car and drove to the restaurant.

During the drive, he asked, "Was that him you were telling me about?"

"Yes."

"What did he want?"

"Your benefits."

"What do you mean by that"

"All the hard work you did for me, he thought he was going to reap the benefits while he did nothing."

"You deserve better than that."

"I know. That was then, this is now; I'm over that." He grabbed for her hand and held it until they got to the restaurant. They went to their reserved table, and he ordered some champagne.

He said, "There are so many great things ahead of you. A New Horizon. I want to start off by giving you this." He took out a blue velvet box and sat it on the table, then said, "You can't open this box until Ms. Bobbie gets here."

TBC IN VOL. III

RELIVING THE MOMENT

On the way to pick up Lela's parents for dinner, Lela said, "Let's make it a family dinner."

"Who do you have in mind?" Timothy asked.

"My cousin and her mom."

"Call them up and tell them the location, and we will meet them there." Lela called Jazz and told her where they were going for dinner. She said invite your mom also; Jazz said okay. Lela called the restaurant to make reservations. Minutes later they drove up to her parents' house. Timothy beeped the horn, and her parents came out. Lela got in the backseat with her mom. Her dad sat up front with Timothy.

Mom said, "How was service?"

"It was unexpected but beautiful."

"What happened?"

"The children that I used to watch at summer day camp brought me gifts. It was an unexpected appreciation. I was just going for service, and they served me with gifts and love."

"That sounds beautiful, Lela. I know you appreciated that."

"Mom, I absolutely loved it. I loved those children; they were very dear to me then, and it brought back memories of my youth."

"Are you going to keep in touch with them?"

"Yes, we exchanged phone numbers, so I will definitely be in touch with them." Dad looked at Timothy and nodded his head; Timothy did the same thing. Neither had anything to talk about as the ladies giggled in the back. They drove up to the restaurant. Timothy g0t out and opened the door for Lela. Dad opened the door for Mom. They proceeded into the restaurant and were escorted to their table. They were the first to be seated; the others had not shown up yet.

The waiter asked, "What would you like to drink?"

"We're waiting for a few more people. Can you give us a minute or two?" Lela said.

"Sure." The waiter left. And a few minutes later, in walked Jazz and her family. Everyone got up and greeted with hugs and kisses.

"Aunt Susie!" Jazz said to Lela's mom, hugging her.

"Auntie Janet!" Lela said to Jazz's mom and hugged her. The men shook and hugged.

The waiter came back and said, "Now that the gang's all here, can I take your drink orders?" They all gave their orders, and he went to get what they requested.

"Lela, I'm so glad you called me. We were trying to decide where to go for dinner. I was at my mom's house when you called, so we were already together."

"I thought about it on the way to pick my parents up. I thought it would be nice to get together with family."

"Well, you were spot on, girl."

The waiter came with their drinks and said, "I'll give you a few minutes to look over the menu." He left and they all went back to talking.

Lela said to her Auntie Janet, "I heard your house is immaculate. I'm sorry we didn't make the house-warming party; we were out of town."

"It's okay. You guys have to come over and see it."

"Well, if no one has plans, maybe we can go after dinner," Lela said. They all agreed.

"I never did ask you, Derrick, how is the four-minute drive to my mom's house?"

"Well, it's not a four-minute drive anymore. Since I proposed to your mom, it's more like a ten-minute walk. I must get into shape for our wedding." They all laughed.

"Oh yes, I did hear about that proposal. Can I see the ring?" Susie said. Janet showed her the ring.

"It's so beautiful. Did you all set a date yet?"

"We're working on it. Right now, we are thinking do we want to put his house on the market or rent it out? Since mine has just been built, we don't need two houses."

"I say rent it out for a year and see how that goes. If you have good renters, then that could help pay for Janet's mortgage," Lela's dad said.

"Eddie, who said I had a mortgage?"

"Well, excuse me, baller." They all laughed.

"I'm very independent. Whatever Derrick does with his home, I will leave that up to him, including the financial part of it."

Derrick said, "We are in this together. Whatever I do, I include you, nothing hidden."

"I appreciate that." She smiled.

The waiter came back and said, "Have you guys had a chance to look at the menu?"

"Not really. Let's order our food, and then we can talk," Jazz said. They looked at the menu, and within ten minutes they ordered their food and went back to conversing.

Susie said to Jazz, "Lela is just loving working with you. I hear your construction company is off to a good start."

"I'm loving it, Aunt Susie. Since I built my mom's home, my phone hasn't stopped ringing. I have projects in Deland, Deltona, and the Kissimmee area, so I have been quite busy since the grand opening of our business, thanks to Lela. She has been such a big help. Eventually, our business will be growing, and I may need another location. I may have you run that one, Lela."

"That's right. Keep it in the family, I would love to do that."

"Let's see where this year takes us, and we can definitely spread our wings in a different area."

"I believe we will."

"I believe so too, Lela." The waiter brought their food, and they ate and conversed. They had so much to talk about since some hadn't seen each other for a while. And there was a new addition to the family who was enjoying the company too. Timothy and Lela weren't dating; they were old friends, but they enjoyed the feeling of love at the table, how the couples looked at each other, how they laughed and caressed, how one would finish the other's sentence, one wiped the other's mouth. They just loved how each couple showed a different type of love. They were into each other; they knew one another; they looked like they belonged together.

Two hours later they finished their dinner, but the conversation was just getting started. Mr. Daniels paid for the dinner, and everyone else contributed to the tip. They piled into their cars and followed Jazz to her mother's house. The neighborhood was inviting—manicured grass, every house looking brand-new. They weren't just built, but the owners kept their houses up to date with paint and renovations. It looked like a million-dollar block for the rich and famous, but people just knew how to take care of their investments. They all pulled up in the driveway. The men rushed in the house like they were trying to get in the barber chair first at the barber shop, but they were hurrying to see the football game.

The ladies laughed and let the men be entertained by the ball tossing, as Susie would say. She never could understand the sport. Lela, Janet, and Jazz knew that, so while they were watching football, Janet took the ladies on a tour. While they were busy, the men had a conversation during a commercial.

Mr. Daniels said, "Tony, how long have you been married to Jazz?"

"Five years, sir."

"Derrick, how long did you know Janet before you asked her to marry you?"

"One year, sir."

"Timothy, you ever plan to get married?"

"One day, Mr. Daniels."

"So, I'll leave this question to Derrick and Tony. Why did you ask these women to marry you?"

"Janet was like money in the wind. I saw her value and I ran after it. I knew the first time I saw her that she was mine. It took a little time for me to get to her level, but I knew the first time I saw her, I wanted her to be my wife."

"Jazz motivated me; she spoke to me. When she wasn't even talking to me, when she was having a conversation on the phone with someone, I was sitting behind her. I didn't know her, but by the time she got off the phone, I did. I was building my company at that time. She had the brains; I had the skills. She gave me what I needed, and we built the foundation, literally. We connected on everything. She sparked fuses in me I thought were dead. I loved her mind before anything else. I needed her in my life, so I asked her to be my wife."

Mr. Daniels said, "'When I first met my wife, she cooked me breakfast. She was working at a diner. She wasn't the waitress; she was the cook. I wanted steak and eggs that morning, and she had cooked it just the way I liked it, so for the next two weeks, that's all I ordered. One morning after eating, I told the waitress, hats off to the chef; he can really cook a good steak.

"The waitress said, 'She can cook a good steak.'

"'The cook is a woman?'

"'Yes.'

"'I must meet her.' The waitress went back to get her. It wasn't busy, so she came out. When I saw Susie, I fell in love with her freckles. It wasn't how she looked; it was her freckles. They were just so beautiful to me. She was this light-skinned black beauty with freckles and a dark mole by her lip. I'd never seen anyone like her before. I stared at her freckles before I saw her face. What she thought was imperfection was perfect to me. See, love doesn't have a face or shape; love just is. I saw something she didn't. My eyes were different from hers. She saw who she already was; I saw what I wanted her to be. She was my life. I already knew she could cook. We went out for a while, and every time I was with her, I was counting her freckles. She asked me how long, would I be doing that. I said, for the rest of my life if you let me. Thirty-five years later, I'm still counting them.

"I never lost interest in who I married. We always did something new; we grew together. The reason I'm talking to you men is because these women who you are married to or marrying. They are my family—by marriage, but they are still my family. Cherish these women; they are hard-working, independent women who are trusting you not to break them. Don't break their hearts; don't break their rhythm. Whatever they are working hard for, work with them. They already have foundations. Be a support system for them if they do fall. No matter how heavy the weight is, you will be strong enough to catch them and support them.

"Make them proud and compliment them with words and actions. Make her want you more. Give her something to smile about every day. She may get mad about something, but you make it your business to put a smile on her face before the day ends. Don't forget about your marriage when you get married. Getting married is the ceremony; marriage is the foundation you build that together. Know what marriage is before you have the ceremony."

The men were silent. The game came back on, but the men were more into the conversation than the game.

Meanwhile, after the tour, the ladies went out on the patio. Janet bought a pitcher of iced tea. They sat around by the pool. It was getting dark, so she turned on the pool lights and sat down. "Your house is beautiful, Janet. Jazz, you put this house together like I have never seen before."

"Thank you, Sue."

"Thank you, Auntie Susie."

"You both are welcome," Sue said.

"I see how Daddy was looking at you, Mommy," said Lela. "He

always looks at you the same."

"He was probably counting my freckles." The ladies laughed.

"What makes Daddy love you the way he does?"

"I let him be the man. I never disrespected him I never tore him down. I knew what my place was, and I stayed in it. I encouraged him. I anointed his head with oil and prayed for him. I let him love me the way he was conditioned to love me; he had a love that was made from scratch." She had their attention. "Edward's love was like macaroni and cheese made from scratch. He didn't have the mac and cheese boxed version where you have some ingredients in a box that you've never heard of, and it's imitation. The mac and cheese made from scratch has the right ingredients, the noodles, three or four kinds of cheese, eggs, milk, salt and pepper, butter, etc. You take your time making that because you want it to be right. You let it bake and brown at the top; it's gooey with all the cheeses. You taste it and it melts in your mouth; it tastes like real mac and cheese.

"That's what your Daddy had for me. Nothing about him was imitation. He was real with everything, down to his love for me. He didn't share that recipe of love with everyone, only with me. A man that truly loves you won't give you everything he gave someone else; he'll save the best for the best. To keep my marriage healthy, spicy, long-lasting, every day I'm Reliving the Moment, from the day I met him up until now. I think about how we met, the love that we grew into, the moments we shared. You never forget where you started. Never let anything interfere with what you have.

"Stay true to your vows. You have witnesses everywhere. Never take the position that he was appointed to have; share your wisdom and knowledge, but don't become the boss. Let the man be.

"Let him be brave."

"Let him be afraid."

"Let him flow."

"Let him grow."

"Let him teach."

"Let him learn."

"Let him work."

"Let him flirt."

"Let him yearn and crave for you."

"Let him praise you."

"Let him pray for you.

"Let him drive while you enjoy the ride."

"Let him lead as you follow."

"Let him buy the house, and you decorate it. Whatever memories you build together, relive each moment. Bring back to his remembrance why he chose you to be his wife. Be witty, be fun, be spontaneous, and be one. Remember you are working together as one, not against each other as enemies. In years of marriage, you learn each day who your husband is. There will be good days and bad ones. When it gets rough, don't run from him, run to him, grab him and pray with him. No matter how it looks, you are in it together."

"I hear you, Mommy."

"We all hear you. I take all that and more. Those are keepsakes, and I will use every one of them," Janet said.

"So, will I," Jazz said. The game was over, and the men joined the ladies on the patio. Eddie sat with Susie, Derrick with Janet, Tony with Jazz, and Timothy stood by Lela.

Edward said, "So, what are you ladies up to?"

"Just chatting, baby."

"Anything interesting?"

"Just a word of wisdom."

"Sounds like an earful."

"And they heard every bit of it."

"Auntie, you have a beautiful home. We should do a cook-out one weekend."

"Let's plan one soon."

"Sure thing. Mom and Dad, are you guys ready?"

"Yes, we are." Everyone got up and hugged, kissed, gave handshakes, daps, fist bumps. Janet walked them to the door. She waited for them to pull out of the driveway before closing the door. It was a quiet ride home. The music was playing; that was enough to drive home on. When they arrive at Lela's parents' home, Lela kissed her mother goodnight. As they got out, Lela hugged her daddy and kissed him on the cheek. Lela got in the front seat. Timothy didn't drive off until they were in the house.

While they were driving back to drop Lela off to her car, she said, "I want to apologize."

"For what?"

"I should have asked you if it was okay that I invite my family, instead of just doing it."

"It's okay. I didn't think nothing of it. It was good that we all met; I had a good time."

"I understand that, but I don't want to step over any boundaries."

"Are we setting any?"

"I look at my parents, and I want what they have. You can feel what they have. I want that."

"What are you saying, Lela?"

"I think I would like to have that with you."

"What if I don't want the same thing with you?"

TBC IN VOL. III

PERFECT COMBINATION

Time to clean out the phone. Lacey had upgraded her phone for the last three years, and every time there was an upgrade, her information was transferred over to the new phone. Numbers and pictures had piled up in her phone like dirty laundry. She needed more space on her phone, and since she hadn't talked to some people since her last upgrade, she was deleting them. A total of a hundred and fifty pictures and numbers she said goodbye to; no love lost there. She held onto one number like a memory; she wasn't ready to let it go. Beside the number was a heart. It had been a while since she heard his voice; last time she heard it he was getting married.

She still held onto the number. If he called, she'd know who it was. The last time they spoke was four years ago. What was she holding onto? Nothing. So, she reached out to say hello. She texted instead of calling. Twenty minutes later, a return text came back.

"I'm sorry. I am not him."

She texted back, "My apologies. It was an old number of a friend; I'll delete the number."

"Why would you do that?"

"Because the number doesn't belong to my friend."

"Maybe you need a new one."

"I don't know you."

"Maybe you should."

"Deleting the number, goodbye."

"Don't say goodbye."

"Goodnight." No response. She was glad that conversation was over. Quite psycho and weird. She didn't want to cook dinner, so she made herself a bowl of cereal and sat down to watch a movie. A text came in.

"What are you doing?" She remembered the number although she had deleted it. She didn't respond; she went back to looking at TV. Another text came in.

"Please talk to me."

She responded, "I don't know you; you might be a serial killer."

"Cereal, mmm, sounds good right about now, but a killer I am not."

"Well, you may not be one, but I still don't know you. It was just a random text that I sent to an old friend; I didn't know he didn't have this number any longer. Please don't text me again."

"I apologize. I won't bother you again." She was relieved at that. She turned off the TV and went to bed. The next morning, she got ready for work. No text from that number; she hoped he took her seriously. She headed to work. She liked to play music on her way to work; it was her coffee in the morning, how she was hyped to get the day started. As she pulled up to the red light, a car pulled up next to her. She glanced over; the man driving was nice-looking. He didn't look at her, he was more in tune with the conversation he was having on his phone. The light turned green, and she drove off.

She had a long day ahead of her. She had fittings to do for an upcoming fashion show in two weeks and her models would be coming in an hour. She did her layout, walked the runway, checked the lighting, made sure all chairs for important clients had their names on them. She was going to do a rehearsal with the models this weekend, and everything needed to be on point. After she checked everything she went back to her office. A text came in.

"Good morning." It was a text from that deleted number. She ignored it. The models started coming in. She got busy with them, alternating alternative she called it. If something didn't fit, she made something new out of the garment, let the hem out and stitched quickly. She was good at that; she was a seamstress at the age of ten and had been making clothes all her life. She was about to show the world what she was made of, and what she was making.

The fittings went perfectly. The models weren't eating carbs, and she wanted them to continue that diet until the day of the show. She told them to be back on Saturday morning for rehearsal and said goodnight to them. As she sat down at her desk, a text came in.

"I don't know why, but I can't get you out of my mind." The person from the deleted number texted her. She blocked the number. She locked up the warehouse and headed home. She stopped by the store to pick up groceries and while shopping she saw the man who had been at the traffic light. He was at the register when she walked in, on his phone. She thought he was quite handsome. She was walking, still looking at him, when she bumped into some cans and they all came crashing down. The commotion got his attention. He smiled at her and left. She was embarrassed. She picked up the cans, found what she was looking for and headed home. On the way home, she stopped by the gas station. While at the pump, she saw one of her models getting out of a car.

The model walked over to her and said, "Lacey, I was just getting ready to call you."

"What's up, Mandi?"

"Some of us are going to the jazz club tonight to hear my brother play the sax. It's his debut. I know you like jazz, so I wanted to know if you want to hang with us?"

"I'm not doing anything tonight. What time and where?"

"It starts at eight, I'll text you the address."

"Ok, that will be fine. It will give me time to get ready."

"I'll have seats reserved for us."

"Okay, I'll see you later." Lacey pumped her gas and went home and got ready for the event. It sounded casual, so that's how she dressed. She got a text from Mandi with the address and headed out. The drive was twenty minutes away, not far at all. Across the bridge and she reached her destination. She waited in the parking lot. She didn't want to be too early, so she waited to see when Mandi would show up. Then she got a text from her.

"Girl, where you at?"

"In the parking lot."

"Well, come inside. We are already here." Lacey headed into the club. Mandi met her at the door, and they walked to their reserved table.

"We have front row seats?"

"Yes, I want Jeffrey to know that I'm here."

"Oh, okay." The lights went low on the stage. T The event started out with a soloist, then a drummer came on stage, followed by a cellist, and last but not least, the saxophonist.

"That's my brother Jeffrey on the sax." Lacey couldn't believe her sore eyes. Yes, that sight to see was the man from the store. She was glued on him now. Each musician had a ten-minute solo. After their solos, they combined their sound into one. It was the perfect pitch, so mellow, smoother than butter on bread. It was the perfect combination. It was an aphrodisiac melody. The sound of the sax was an arousal for sex, but intimately; it was the beginning of foreplay. Mandi looked at Lacey. Lacey was star-struck; she looked at Jeffrey like she was a fan. After the performance was over, the crowd gave a standing ovation. This was the debut for each musician on stage. They all came to the front of the stage, took a bow and exited backstage.

Lacey said, "I loved the way he played that sax."

"I know. I saw how you looked at him."

"Oh, I didn't mean for it to be noticeable."

"It's okay. He gets that all the time, and he don't be playing his saxophone. He's just good looking. The ladies are always batting their eyes at him; he doesn't pay them any mind."

"You think he wouldn't mind playing at the show next Saturday?"

"I invited you so you could hear him play. I was going to ask you what the line-up for music was for the show."

"I had a playlist ready, but I think he can start off the show. That would give our audience a delightful sound before you ladies walk the runway." While they were talking, Jeffrey walked up to the table. Mandi stood up and hugged him and then introduced Lacey.

"Jeffrey, this is my boss Lacey. Lacey, my brother Jeffrey."

"Oh, yes, the lady that knocked down the cans in the store."

"Oh, this was the lady you were telling me about in the store."

Lacey smiled in embarrassment. "It's nice to meet you, Jeffrey."

"What were you looking at to walk into the cans?" Mandi said.

"There was something on sale and I was walking looking at it and I didn't see what was in front of me." Jeffrey smiled.

"So, can I buy you ladies a drink?" They nodded. He went and got drinks and sat down at the table with them.

"I enjoyed your sex." She turned away and sipped her drink, hoping he didn't catch what she said. She turned back around and said, "I enjoyed how you played the saxophone; you play with such a burning desire."

"Meaning?"

"Meaning, you play in a descriptive way, like an SOS. You send out signals, hoping that someone can detect them and come to your rescue."

"You picked that up from me playing?"

"Was I right?"

"I'm not sure if I want to answer that." Mandi saw the chemistry developing quickly.

She said, "Jeffrey, we have a proposition for you."

"I'm listening."

"Remember I told you about the show we have next week?" Jeffrey was nodding his head but couldn't take his eyes off Lacey. Mandi snapped her fingers.

"I'm listening, continue."

"Lacey would like to know if you would play for the event."

"I would like that, but I would rather hear it from her lips." Mandi smiled.

Lacey cleared her throat and sipped her drink. "You play with a hypnotic style that can't be duplicated."

"Interesting, tell me more."

"I know I'm stroking your ego right now."

"Amongst other things."

"Like?"

"No need to share that with you right now."

"Oh, you sound like there will be another time."

"It could be if you would like it to be."

"I heard the women are drooling over you. I don't want to be in competition with them."

"Can I tell you something?"

"Sure."

"A woman I want won't have to compete with anyone because I would never make her feel that way. I'm a one-woman man. I know what I want; I don't do taste tests—I mean, I do." Lacey swallowed. "What I mean is, I don't date a lot of women at the same time and then choose. I give myself time in between. I date and see if we have any chemistry because it is important to me. If I don't see the importance in dating her, then I move on, giving myself time and space to date again. I don't like baggage. I don't like residue."

"Residue?"

"Yes, lingering feelings and emotions. You may still have feelings for someone or pain that someone has caused you. My thing is, if you want to make it work with someone else, clean up before you mess up. Don't destroy a good thing because of someone else's mistake. Can I ask you something?"

"Go ahead."

"Do you know me?"

"Not really."

"Do I remind you of someone?"

"No, you don't."

"So, if you don't know me, and I don't remind you of someone, why would you treat me like them?"

"At times your behavior may trigger memories of certain things that they've done."

"But do you think I would intentionally do that?"

"I don't think you would; you wouldn't know anything about my past."

"Exactly. With the very intent of my heart I would do my best not to hurt, destroy, or remind someone of their past pain. I don't know what you've gone through, but I would never take you down that path of pain."

"Why are you telling me this?"

"Because you decoded my message; you saw my SOS, but I wasn't asking you to rescue me. I was asking you to come to me."

"Why me?"

"Because you and I are a Perfect Combination."

"How can you tell by looking at me?"

"The same way you felt my music. You just know. We are like ingredients mixed together, combining them together, and it tastes oh so good. You and me, baby, I mean Lacey."

"This is crazy."

"No, it's not. It's fate. You were looking at me when you walked into those cans. I already had my eye on you when I saw you at the stop light. I was just getting back into dating. I give myself six months to evaluate myself, find the error of my ways, and then start fresh again, so when I saw you, I thought, I'd like to pick her mind and see where it's at. I didn't rush into it. I always said anything that is for you, it will come to you, and you came to me."

"It was a spur-of-the-moment invitation."

"Whether it was or not, you still came to me. You're my energy, Lacey. I felt that when I first saw you; I couldn't get you out of my mind."

"This is a joke, right?"

"Does it look like I'm playing?"

"You could be. I don't know you."

"Don't ruin the moment, flow with me."

"Flow with you for how long?"

"Until our energy decreases."

"And when will that be?"

"There's only one way to find out. Let me take you out tomorrow and see if our energy is still as strong as it is tonight."

"Then what?"

"I can't tell you what until the when, so for now, we'll wait until then. Is it a date tomorrow then?"

"Yes, I would like that."

"Shall I call you tonight? Maybe we can have a conversation before you close your eyes and fall asleep?"

"I would like that." She gave him her card, and he put it in his pocket.

"I need to get going I have some work that needs to get done."

"I'll walk you to your car. Mandi, I'll be right back. They walked to her car. He said, "I look forward to reading you a bedtime story."

"Looking forward to that." He kissed her on her hand. She got in her car, and he closed the door. He pulled out her card and phone and texted her something. As she was backing up, getting ready to pull off, he waved her down. She stopped and rolled down the window.

He said, "I can't call you."

"Why not?"

"Because you blocked my number."

TBC IN VOL. III

AN EROTIC RENDEZVOUS

She's in town, she's in town. He sighed and slumped down in his chair, in his thoughts. She wouldn't want to be bothered with me. He never supported her in her dreams, never promoted her demo; he would be the last person she would want to see. Calvin was looking at the commercial. Keisha was in town on tour. Last year she released her debut album "Once in a Lifetime." It went platinum the first week it was released. She had been touring for the last six months. The week it came out, he bought the CD. She expressed her life on it. Some things sounded familiar to him as if she was talking about him and to him.

Calvin would've loved to go to her concert. But the tickets started at two hundred dollars, and he couldn't afford it. His house was about to go into foreclosure; he was behind in his bills; the sales weren't coming as they used to. The concert was sold out, so even if he had the money, he wouldn't be able to go. Some time ago, he had tried calling her. She had changed her number. He had no way of contacting her to say Congratulations on your success. Keisha had a unique voice. When she sang, it was so melodic, she would lull Calvin to sleep. He enjoyed hearing her sing. Friends encouraged her to do a demo. She didn't think she was that good, but she did it because she trusted her friends.

Keisha was already writing music. At that time, she didn't think she could sing what she was writing; she didn't have faith in the voice other people were hearing, Calvin knew she would be a star with the voice she possessed, but he never pushed her. He dreamt of her on stage one night in front of a sold-out audience. He knew then what she was going to become but didn't share that with her.

The concert was for two nights; this was the last night she'd be in town. He would love to see her, but for now, it was impossible. The commercial went off. He sighed again. He went to the mailbox to get his mail, past due notices, robbing Peter to pay Paul. It was all coming to a dead end.

He got dressed for work and hoped he could get some sales to at least pay for his mortgage. As soon as he was about to step outside, it started to rain. He shut the door, slumped down on the floor and released anger and frustrati0n into his hands. He thought, I can't lose my house. He had it built five years ago; everything he had, he put in this home. He couldn't lose it now. There was a knock at the door. In a frustrated voice, he asked, "Who is it?"

"Fed Ex."

Calvin didn't want any more bad news. "Leave it at the door."

"It requires a signature." Exhaling the frustration, he wiped his face and swung open the door like an irritated non-believer who wants to tell a witness to go knock on someone else's door. The Fed Ex man was getting drenched in the rain. He handed him the envelope and the device for his signature, then ran back to his truck and pulled out. Calvin closed the door and lay the brown envelope on the counter. It started thundering and there was lightning; the lights flickered and went out. He thought the lightning must have hit a transformer. He looked out his window. Everyone else's lights were on. He thought, my lights can't be off! He hit the switch for the lights; they didn't come on. They cut my lights off, he said in anger, looking around for candles.

He lit some candles and sat on the floor in disgust because he let it get this far. He was glad he didn't have anyone in his life; they would probably look at him as less of a man. He knew who he was as a man; he didn't need anyone judging him at this critical time in his life. After beating himself up without a TKO, he got up and took a shower in his candlelit bathroom. It looked romantic, but that wasn't his mood. He just wanted to shower and go to bed. After the shower, he lay across his bed. He was hungry, but he couldn't cook anything. He went into the kitchen and made a cold cut sandwich. He knew he needed to eat up the cold food before it went bad. He grabbed a bottle of water, grabbed the envelope and sat at the table in the living room.

Eating his sandwich to quiet the voices in his stomach, he looked at the envelope. Only his name was on it, no name or return address. He thought that quite odd. If he wasn't home, how would it be returned to sender? He finished his sandwich, drank his water, grabbed the envelope and opened it. It contained an elegant, black lace envelope, saturated with a perfume that smelled expensive. He opened the envelope. Inside it was an RSVP by 8:00 pm tonight; there was a number to text to respond. He thought—what kind of joke was this? There was no address to go to, just a number to text. He looked at the clock; it was 7:55 pm. He liked the envelope and the fragrance. He thought whoever sent this must really think something of him. It was 7:58 pm. He thought what the heck, text the number and see what happens. He texted the number at 8:00 pm. A text message came back, "Thank you for your response to the RSVP." Then another text came, "TONIGHT AT MIDNIGHT, you are invited to this address."

He looked the address up. It was a mansion. He didn't know anyone who had one. He didn't know anyone in that neighborhood, plus it was an hour-and-a-half drive. What kind of joke was this? He wasn't in the mood for one. He had enough going on. Just when he was getting ready to erase the text, another one came in.

"Don't be late." He thought how could he be, late to something he wasn't going to? He laughed and lay across his bed, thinking about Keisha and the concert. He knew that she would give them their money's worth. Not only could she sing but she could dance as well. He wanted front-row seats, just to see her up close. He knew that would be as close as he would get to her, but it would be worth it. For someone that wasn't going anywhere, he was watching the clock like he didn't want to be late to an interview. What could possibly go wrong? He didn't have any enemies—well, as far as he knew he didn't. It was Saturday; he didn't have any plans to go anywhere other than the RSVP. He didn't have anything else to do. He thought what the heck, he'd go. He was a timely person anyway, and he didn't want to disappoint this mysterious person.

He grabbed a candle and looked in his closet for something to wear. Since the invitation was elegant, he wanted to dress for the occasion. Were there going to be others there? He dressed and smelled the part; whatever was waiting for him there, he wanted to be on point. He had just gotten a haircut earlier that day. He did a little trimming of his beard and mustache with the razor. It was 9:45 pm. He wanted to leave early so he could gas up the car. He blew out the candles, went in the garage to get in his car, and pressed the garage door opener. He was stuck. His lights were off, and he needed the electricity for the door to open. Knowing he had to manually open the garage door frustrated him more. He got out of his car and slammed the door. As soon as it slammed, the lights came on. He hurried and got in his car, pressed the button, and the door opened. It was still raining, but the rain wasn't going to stop him from going. He pulled out of the garage and hit the remote for the door to close. He didn't leave the driveway until it closed all the way.

He went by the gas station to fill up. He spent the last twenty dollars he had to his name. He couldn't use his debit card; his account was already negative. There were more negatives in his account than in an old-time photography shop. He gassed up and headed to his destination. During the drive, there was no traffic anywhere; the ride was going to be smooth. Although it was raining, it was just him and the road, with thoughts of what would be waiting when he arrived. His arrival time was 11:45 pm. He was early and didn't know if he should go in now or wait. He received a text, "Timing is everything. Thank you for being on time. Please come in."

Calvin looked around to see who was looking at him. He didn't see any other cars. He got out of his car and stood there. The mansion was immaculate. He didn't think anyone would harm him, not in this place. He got another text.

"I'm waiting for you. Please come to me." Who wants me? he thought. He locked his car and walked up the steps to the unlocked door. When he opened the door, the house was filled with candles, with rose petals making the shape of an arrow leading to the stairs. He walked up the stairs, followed the petals to the bedroom door. He opened the door and there was a luxurious room decorated for seduction. The fireplace on the wall had a fire in it burning with intense flames; smooth jazz filled the air. He saw the arrow of petals pointing to the bed. He walked up the steps to the bed. A few feet from the bed there was a jacuzzi. On the bed, there was a blindfold and note beside it.

The note said, "Welcome, Calvin, to An Erotic Rendezvous. Put the blindfold on, sit on the bed and wait for me." He thought, who knows me to go out of their way and do this? Was it an ex-girlfriend getting ready to punk him? He wasn't quick to put the blindfold on. He did sit on the bed, but he didn't put the blindfold on. He got a text,

"Time is of the essence. Trust me and put the blindfold on." He was enjoying the playlist, and the room didn't look like the work of someone who would do him no harm, so he relaxed and put the blindfold on. Two minutes later the door opened. He sat up and started moving his head like he wanted to ask who's there, but he said nothing. Music was playing. He heard ice cubes drop in a glass, something being poured in the glass, and footsteps walking up the stairs. An ice cube was placed on his lips. He jumped as if he was scared, but then enjoyed the ice rub. Someone grabbed his hand and placed the drink in it. He sipped it slowly and licked his lips with a smile. He enjoyed it until was gone.

"Who is this?"

"Shhh," the person whispered.

"I'm going to take this blindfold off if you don't tell me who you are." She held his hands to stop him trying to take it off.

"Please don't," she whispered. She caressed his face, and this calmed his fear. His movement of relaxation showed that he could trust this person who was in control.

"Your caress reminds me of a touch I once felt before. I trusted that touch then. It feels very familiar, so I trust you. Please continue." She got up and walked away, then came back to him. She placed a chunk of pineapple on his lip. He bit it, juice squirted out of his mouth, and she giggled. He smiled. She took a cloth, wiped his mouth and fed him another one.

"Open your mouth." He opened it, and she placed a strawberry in it.

"Do you like it?" she whispered.

"I love this."

"This what?"

"What you're doing to me." She moaned mmm. She fixed him another drink, put it in his hand and grabbed the jar of honey. She waited for him to finish his drink. She saw the drops of sweat sliding down his neck. After he finished his drink, she unbuttoned his black silk shirt. He grabbed her hips as she unbuttoned it. He rubbed the lace material of her nightie against her thighs. After she was done, he took his shirt off.

He said, "Is that all you want me to take off?"

"For now," she whispered. She took an ice cube and rubbed it down his throat. He jumped from the cool feeling. She then rubbed the ice cube down his chest, against his nipples. He moaned. She rubbed it down his back and seductively blew on his back to dry the area. She grabbed a cold rag and wiped down his chest and back to dry every wet area. She took her finger and dipped it into the honey jar, then placed it on his lips. He licked his lips.

"Oh, that tastes so good." She dipped it in the jar again and placed it on his lips, licking it again. She took her finger and dipped it in a different jar of honey.

She whispered, "With your permission, can I have your tongue?" He opened his mouth and gave her what she asked for. She placed her finger on it. He closed his mouth with her finger still in it, and he tasted it.

"What is this?"

"Do you like it?"

"I need to taste it again."

She dipped her finger again and let him taste it.

"OMG, Keisha?"

"Do you want to taste it again?"

"Yes, yes," he begged her.

"Lie down," she whispered. He lay down on the king-sized bed. She placed her body over his face just enough for him to reach up. He licked the honey from her hive, softly, slowly. She grabbed the headboard and moaned. He grabbed her thighs and started to lick her harder, but in a seductive way.

She whispered, "I missed this." She stopped him.

"Why did you stop me?" She reached back and felt his nature on the rise, throbbing like a heartbeat.

"I can't be greedy and enjoy all this pleasure and not share some with you." She got up and unbuttoned his pants, his nature looking like a soldier saluting, standing in the rain. It had her attention. He was dripping like the ice was running down his back. She licked him from the base and came up and licked the top of his cock, which was dripping like a waterfall.

"OMG." She opened her mouth and covered every bit of him, then seductively, slowly, went up and down like a yo-yo, saturating every area with her saliva. No dry spots, she made sure of that.

"Are you enjoying this?"

"More than you know." He reached for her and lay her down on the bed. He slid his cock up and down and hit her clit. She moaned, then he penetrated her pool of silk.

"You're so wet."

"You're the only one that gets me this way." He kissed her passionately. They moaned with ecstasy. She wrapped her legs around his back, and they moved simultaneously, like the beat of the drum. She grabbed the sheets, then his back.

"Calvin."

"Keisha."

"Omg, Calvin."

"Omg, Omg, Shh, Keisha." They climaxed at the same time, panting and sweating. He interlocked his hands with hers and kissed her liked he missed her, like it was his first time kissing someone he loved. He kissed on down her neck and licked, sucked and licked her nipples. He wanted to lick every area of her body. He kissed her softly again. She took the blindfold off, and their eyes connected. He looked at her like it was his first time seeing someone.

"You're so beautiful, Keisha." He kissed her again.

"You haven't changed one bit, still handsome as ever, still can dress, smelling good, and you taste so delicious."

"I tasted good?"

"OMG, I knew it was you when you put your finger in my mouth. No one tastes like you, Keisha. I see you're still eating those pineapples."

"Yes, what you eat and how you take care of your body will determine how you taste. Plus, I drink a lot of water."

"It felt like a faucet, still juicy as ever."

"I know, right?"

"Can I ask you something?"

"Sure."

"Why did you pick me? You could've done this with someone else. Why me?"

"Because you're not someone else. You're special to me, Calvin."

"But you're a multi-platinum star. You could have anyone you want. I wasn't going to come; there was no name on your invitation, just a phone number. You know I don't like mysteries. I need to know who it is before I go anywhere."

"Well, I'm glad you came, and you did, and so did I. I thank you for that. Just because I'm famous, Calvin, doesn't mean anything. I tour; I hang-out; I do radio and talk shows, but that doesn't mean anything when your heart is at home. Yes, I could have anyone, but I don't want them. I get hit on a lot. Why? Because I'm famous. They don't know me, but you do."

"Why won't you let them get to know you?"

"Why can't I have what I want?"

"What do you want?"

"You, Calvin, I want you."

"What can I possibly give you?"

"Your heart."

"I always gave you that."

"And I came back to reclaim it. You were always real with me; you took care of me. Anything I ever wanted you gave me."

"Back then I could take care of you. I was making money to take care of us."

"I know. You gave to me when I didn't have anything. You were my support system. Although you didn't push me with my career, you were still there for me."

"I didn't want to lose you. I thought you would forget about me once you became famous."

"A real person never forgets where they came from. I know I haven't been in contact with you much, but my heart was thinking about you all the time."

"Whose house are we in?"

"It's mine. I bought it some months ago. I didn't want to leave the state, so when I'm not touring, I'm home."

"So, what do we do now?"

"Well, I have a plane to catch in four hours. Maybe we can talk later."

"I would like that."

"Come take a shower with me; I have to get ready." They took a quick shower and got dressed. "Walk me to my car."

"I sure will." They walk down to the awaiting limo.

She said, "I hope to talk to you soon."

"Let me know when you get back."

"Oh, it will be sooner than that." She kissed him and softly caressed his face, then she got in the car and left. He walked to his car and saw an envelope on his windshield. He opened it. There was a check for two million dollars and a note.

"I have a proposition for you. I am doing a project in Haiku Mill in Maui, Hawaii. If you would like to revisit what we did tonight, meet me at the airport in four hours. I hope I see you there." He couldn't believe she wrote him a check for that amount. He could pay off his mortgage, maybe even quit his job, depending on what kind of project she was doing. He got in his car and drove home, packed his bag, grabbed his passport, and changed into some comfortable gear. He had two hours to go. It would take him forty-five minutes to drive to the airport. He rebooted his alarm system and made sure the cameras were working so he could view his house on his phone.

He secured his home, got in his car and headed to the airport. On his way there, he stopped by the bank and deposited the check in his account. When it cleared, he was paying off his mortgage. He deposited it, got his receipt, and headed to the airport. Keisha always made him feel special because he made her feel the same way. He was still shocked that she thought about him. Then again, she didn't let fame and fortune change her feelings. She was always humble, and she kept that same attitude. He was glad about that. Arriving at the airport, he saw one red jet. It looked like a private one. He parked his car and got out, looked at his watch. Tt was one hour until take-off. He leaned against his car and waited.

Minutes later a limo pulled up next to the jet. He saw Keisha exiting the car. The trunk popped open, and the chauffeur took her bags out and put them on the jet. Keisha looked at Calvin and smiled. He grabbed his bag and walked over to her.

She said, "I'm glad you decided to join me. Shall we get on the plane?"

"Yes, but first I want to say thank you."

"For what?"

"For the check you wrote me. It came at the right time; I was in a dire situation."

"That's your fun money."

"Fun money? I have bills that need to be paid."

"You mean your mortgage?"

"Yes, amongst other things."

"I paid your mortgage off yesterday."

"What do you mean you paid it off?"

"Meaning I paid it off. Remember when we went to the bank when you first got your house built? I introduced you to the banker for your loan."

"Um, yeah."

"I've been in touch with him. I've been meaning to pay that off, just been so busy, but as soon as I settled down yesterday, I did a money transfer and paid off the mortgage. Your lights, did they come back on?"

"What the—?"

"Did they come back on, Calvin, yes or no?"

"Yes, they came back on. How did you know they were off?"

"Because I care about you, and I care about your needs as well, so I made sure that I would be there for you in any situation. Shall we get on the plane now?"

"Why? It doesn't leave for another hour."

"I only said that to give you enough time to get your things together. We are leaving as soon as we get on the plane, so shall we?"

"We shall." They got on the plane, she poured him a glass of champagne and handed it to him. "So, what's your proposition?"

"We'll talk about that when we land. Are you ready to fly?"

"Like an eagle, baby."

"Let's get lifted then. Pilot, we are ready for take-off."

"I'm glad you never changed. Glad you stayed the same."

"There's only one thing I want to change."

"What's that?"

"My last name."

"What do you want to change it to?"

"Yours."

"That sounds like a proposal, not a proposition."

"The proposition is my project in Dubai. The proposal is my position that I want to be in with you."

"You want to marry me?"

"The question is do you want to marry me?"

"Answering a question with a question is not the answer I was looking for."

"Keisha?"

"Yes?"

"I'm not in a position to ask you to marry me. I don't want you taking care of me; I want to take care of you."

"You've already taken care of me, now we are taking care of each other. Please don't look at my fame as me taking care of you. You made it comfortable for me, let me be that for you." Calvin pulled a ring out of his pocket.

"What's this, were you going to ask me?"

"Not that I was going to ask you, but I bought this ring for you years ago. I was going to get rid of it when you became famous. I thought she'll never marry me now; she would never think of me anymore, but I kept it. The only reason I bought it with me was to show you that I was going to propose to you back then. I just couldn't find the right time."

"This is the perfect time, Calvin."

"So, Keisha?"

"Yes Calvin?"

"Will you marry me?"

"Yes, Calvin, I will marry you." He put the ring on her finger and kissed her. The plane took off down the runway.

"How long will we be in Dubai?"

"Forever."

TBC IN VOL. III

MY NAME IS KEILANI

Flights scheduled for the next two weeks, car and hotel booked, suitcase almost packed for tomorrow's trip, Dionte was all ready to take flight. Although the plane ride from New York to Massachusetts was thirty-six-minutes, he'd rather do it that way than take the three-hour train ride. His trips were paid for by the company, so cost didn't matter to him, but the sooner he could get there the better. Walking in from a long day's work, he needed to wind down. He looked at the bottle of Peach Cîroc that used to be his sedative for the night, but he needed something different. He needed something to numb his loneliness. He had chosen this lifestyle, but it was getting old and tattered.

His life was wonderful, and anyone who shared it with him would reap the benefits. He had so much to give, but it was always to unappreciative recipients. So, to keep his emotions intact, he chose to stay busy with work without enough time to play. He would work so much until it tired him out. Walking into the kitchen, he grabbed a glass, added some cubes, poured a drink. He saw the blinking light on the machine. There were messages; he wasn't in a hurry to listen to them. He sat down on the couch, propped his feet up on the ottoman, and turned some music on. He iced his forehead with the glass like he was cooling a fever, took a deep breath, picked up the remote, turned the volume down on the stereo, and then hit the button for the voicemail.

Message one. "Hey, man this is Khalif. Hit me up when you got a minute." Message two. "This is the shuttle bus service confirming your pick-up time for tomorrow at 7:00 am." Message three. "Hey there, old friend, this is Janay wanting to know if you wanted some company tonight." Dionte hit the delete button for that message. Message erased. He got up to use the restroom, turned the volume up on the machine so he could hear it. Message four. "Man, answer your phone this is Khalif again." Message five. "This message is for Dionte Sinclair, this is Keilani. I'm calling regarding your online order you made. We regret to inform you that the item is no longer in stock, but we have it on back order. If you have any questions, you can call us at

1-800-xxx-xxxx, using this reference number. Thank you for shopping with us, you have a good evening."

He slowly walked to the answering machine, caressed it like he was wiping the dust off it, and erased all the messages except for the last one. He sat in his recliner, propped his feet up, laid his head back, grabbed the remote, and hit it for voicemail again. This time he put it on surround sound. He played that message repeatedly. After the tenth time listening to it, he got a pen and wrote down the number she left. It was too late to call; it was after office hours, so he listened to that message five more times before he went to bed. The alarm went off promptly at 5:00 am. Not much sleep for him; he'd just gone to bed two hours ago, but he got up like he'd had eight. He jumped in the shower, shaved, and got dressed. He tucked the phone number away in his pocket. If he was going to leave anything, that number wasn't going to be it.

He finished packing and headed downstairs. As soon as his feet hit the pavement, the shuttle bus pulled up. He got in, took the phone number out, and saved it in his phone. He texted Khalif and told him he'd be in town around 9:45 am.

Khalif texted back, "It's about time you got back with me, bet, see you at the meeting."

The ride to the airport was thirty minutes. He had never been anxious about anything, but this phone call he was about to make triggered that emotion. He was on countdown for that business to open so he could justify why he listened to that message sixteen times. He arrived at the airport and checked his bag. His flight left at 8:20 am. The business didn't open until 9:00 am; he'd wait until his flight landed. While he was waiting, Khalif texted him.

"If you're not in a hurry to get back to New York on Friday, check out this club with me; I have to show you something."

"You know I don't do clubs, haven't in years."

"Well, you don't want to miss this. I promise you you'll thank me later."

"Every club has the same thing. I'm not interested."

"Have I ever told you anything wrong?"

"Hmm, where do I start?"

"Aw, man, I know you not still tripping over my sister cutting your hair." Dionte rubbed his head. "That bald spot grew back, didn't it?"

"Yeah, I had to wear a hat in the summer for a week."

"Well, I told you she went to school for hair. She said she knew how to. I believed her."

"Two weeks of going to school does not make you a barber. I'd never sit in her chair again."

"Man, that was twenty years ago. She's a professional now."

"Yeah, a professional bald spot cutter. Just joking. I trust her now; she's cut my hair since then. She's the only barber I go to now."

"Trust me about the club."

"I'll think about it." It was time to board the plane. He got on the plane for the short flight, hoping it was twenty minutes instead of thirty-six. He knew as soon as he touched down, he would be dialing that number. He went to sleep; he needed to. His meeting was at 12:00 pm, and he would be touching down by 9:05 am. He still had to get his rental and check-in. He had a thirty-minute ride to his hotel, so he had a total of three hours before his meeting to settle in.

While asleep, he played the message repeatedly in his mind. Her name was beautiful, and he wondered if she was just as beautiful as her name. He felt a jolt; the plane had touched down. He quickly unfastened his seat belt. The plane came to a stop. He got off, picked up his car and headed to his hotel. By the time he got there, it would be about 10:15 am. The meeting was downstairs in the lobby, so he didn't have to get on the road again.

He arrived at the hotel, checked in, got his key, and took the elevator up to his room. He put his suitcase on the bed, pulled the number out of his pocket and started dialing. The phone rang, and a voice answered.

"Thank you for calling Design It Your Way, this is Dana, how may I assist you?" He knew that wasn't the voice that left the message on his phone, so he went into detective mode.

"Yes, hello, Dana, my name is Dionte. I received a call last night from one of your salespeople. Her name is Keilani. If it's possible, can I speak with her?"

"Sir, is there anything I could help you with?"

"I would like to speak with her."

"This is a call center, sir. We have over five hundred people in two call centers that make phone calls. Although you've given me her name, I don't know who she is. Some of us work from home, so we don't have direct contact with other representatives. Is there something I can assist you with?

"She left me a reference number. Maybe you can pull her name from that?"

"What's the reference number?"

"LMCYWFD." He heard the lady typing.

She said, "We don't have a reference number like that, sir. Can I have a phone number in reference to your order?" He gave her the number. "It looks like your order is on back order; is that the reason you're calling?"

"No, it's about the lady who left the message."

"What about her?"

"Oh, never mind. I guess you can't help me."

"Is there anything else I can assist you with?"

"Sigh, no, I guess not."

"Thank you for calling Design It Your Way, you have a good day, sir."

"Thank you, you as well." Click.

Dana turned around and said, "He called in. Now what?

"If it's him, I will know soon," the voice said.

Dionte sat on the bed in disappointment and stared at the number. He was tempted to throw it away but held onto it. He wanted to call back, but he knew he probably wouldn't get the right person on the phone. He got up, put the number on the dresser, and looked at his watch. It was 11:15 am, and he had a couple of minutes to get some sleep, so he lay on the bed and stared at the ceiling. That voice he heard on his machine—he had heard it before, years ago. It was a voice of therapy, melodic and smooth, like jazz, like a glass of brandy straight. He had heard it over the radio one night.

He was out of town. He had just gotten in from a stressful meeting, and he needed to wind down. He turned on the radio. A midnight show was just coming on, called Essence of Intimacy. The host, Desire, was sharing her love and experience with her story, Can I touch you there. He was so into the story that he was hoping one day he would meet someone like that. She did say she would be out of town, so he didn't know if the show was going to air the next night.

He tuned in the next night, and the show continued but with another host, Keilani. When Dionte heard her voice, he melted like snow. Her voice was hypnotic. She talked about her experience of a Midnight Drive. He was more interested in her voice than what she was saying. He crept closer to the radio, took out his earphones, plugged it into the jack, closed his eyes and listened to her voice. He lay on the floor and imagined her next to him. He listened to the music and her voice; he loved the collaboration.

He was floating on her thoughts, coasting down a tranquil lake on a moonlit path shadowing the water. Saliva began to fill his mouth. He swallowed as her voice deepened into words of her interlude. He stretched out his arms and gripped the carpet as if he was reaching a climax. The climatic part she reached was in his mind; she reached that point, and he exhaled as if he was smoking a cigarette after sex. She had just satisfied him, he thought. What did she just do to him? Did she know? Was this something she did on purpose with every man? Did she do this to every man, or was it just for a destined one who was listening that night? But how many were listening? Did they feel the same thing he did?

The music ended, as did the interlude. Her voice again erected his mind. He smiled; she satisfied every part of him. She ended the show, saying, "The next time will be the right time. I'm your host, K. Thank you for listening to Essence of Intimacy." She went off the air and he lay there thinking, where is she? I want her. That woman made love to my mind; she took control of my whole being. She took him by force, and he wanted to thank her. One more night in town. He tuned in the next night, and there was another host. He was disappointed. It was a man. Every night had a different host. He wouldn't know who would be on tomorrow; he was going back home in the morning.

He told Khalif about it. Khalif told him to check out the website online to find out anything. He did, and it only showed the owner's face and name. The show was new, so whoever was standing in for her wasn't listed. They only had taped shows. He ordered the CD of the night. He followed the show online, but never did he hear her voice again until that night at his apartment. He wondered how she got his number. What did he do so right for her to call him? Dionte woke up. He had ten minutes to make it to the meeting. He brushed his teeth and jumped on the elevator.

He saw Khalif going into the meeting. He sat down next to him. They shook hands. Board of Directors meetings usually last an hour or so, and if people are not bored, meetings can last up to two hours with a lot of Q&A and positive feedback. This meeting lasted two and a half hours. Trustees were appointed, paperwork signed and notarized. A local organization started years ago for a youth group called Empowering their Lives was beginning another organization in another state, and the board was appointing people in positions to oversee it.

Dionte had functions for fundraisers for the organization in the

New York area for three locations, along with ordering t-shirts and other products. Design it Your Way was a company that he was using to fulfill those orders. He was doing a fundraiser one year and saw their shirts and inquired about them. What he ordered was on back order.

After the meeting, Khalif said, "You are a hard man to get hold of these days. What's going on with you?"

"Work, work, and work. My job can be tedious and stressful at times. No time for fun."

"Well, we don't have any meetings tomorrow, and I know you're heading back in the morning, so hang out with me tonight."

"Oh, that club thing you were telling me about. Man, I told you I'm not into that."

"I promise you, Tay, if you come with me tonight, I won't ask you to go to another one with me." Dionte heard the sincerity in his voice, something he hadn't heard before in all the years knowing him.

"Okay, I'll come with you tonight."

"Cool, I'll pick you up at 7:00 pm."

"What kind of club opens at that time?"

"The main event is at 7:30 pm. Be ready at seven."

"Main event? Is this a wrestling match you're taking me to?" Khalif was getting ready to walk away. He walked back to Dionte and put his hand on his shoulder.

"Tay, what you will see tonight you will never, ever want to wrestle with. See you at seven, my man." Khalif got in his car and drove off. Dionte stood there with a puzzled face. He wondered what Khalif could be up to. He went back to his room, sat on the bed, and looked at the number on the desk. He thought about calling it and decided not to. He walked to the desk, picked up the paper and threw it in the trash. He already had the card to the business; if he needed to contact the company, he had that on speed dial, so no need to keep the other number. He looked in his bag to pull out something for tonight. He always had a spare fit in case he might have one of those nights like tonight and wanted to go out.

He got back in the bed to catch up on the sleep he didn't get at home. He had almost fallen asleep at the meeting, but Khalif kept nudging him to stay awake so off to sleep he went. He dreamed he saw a face with shades on at night, driving in a car. The streetlight hit her glasses like a strobe light. Lips red, hair slicked in a knot, she drove. He woke up, looked at the clock. It was 5:30 pm. He wanted to go back to sleep and see how this dream ended, but he knew he had to get ready.

He jumped in the shower, thinking whose face was that in the dream, and where was she going. Was he in the car during the drive with her? He would love to be the one she was on her way to see. Drying himself with a towel, then wrapping it around his waist, he began to shave. The five o' clock shadow showed up early. He heard his phone beep; it was Khalif saying he was on his way. He slipped on his clothes, sprayed on his best, and took the elevator down. By the time he got outside, Khalif was pulling up.

"Well look at Dapper Dan."

"Don't start with me. You know I don't go anywhere looking any kind of way."

"Oh, I know, I'm just messing with you. For someone that don't know what's going on, you sure did dress for the occasion."

"You still at it."

"Come on, man, I'm just messing."

"So, what is tonight all about?"

"Okay, Tay, you ready for me to tell you?"

"Yeah, I wish you would."

"Okay, I'll tell you as soon as we get to the club." Dionte looked at him like he wanted to go upside his head. Khalif looked at him, like what are you going to do? Dionte looked straight ahead and didn't say anything else until they got to the club. They pull up behind a Porsche Cayenne SUV, with a K as the license plate. Not a soul was in sight. The club was lit up on the outside, but it didn't look like there was any activity going on.

"Man, what's happening?"

"Just chill, Tay, and come on inside." They got out and went inside. Khalif said hi to Steve the bouncer. He nodded his head, watched them go by, then went to the door and locked it.

Dionte turned around and asked, "Why did he lock the door?"

"Do you trust me, Tay?"

"Yeah, man, I trust you."

"Then chill, man, I got you." They walked to the club's dance floor and up to the bar. The bartender was there waiting on them.

He asked, "What are you drinking?" They gave their orders. They saw two ladies and a gentleman approach the bar.

Khalif said, "Dionte, I'd like for you to meet the owner of this club. His name is Damian, and this is his twin sister, Dana. This is the DJ of the club and his lady, Naomi." Dionte shook their hands. The bartender gave them their drinks.

Damian said, "Their tab is on me tonight." The bartender nodded his head. Damian said to Naomi, "Is she ready?"

"Yes, she's ready." Dionte was thinking is who ready?

Khalif said to Dionte, "Turn your seat around."

"Why?"

"Would you just do it and stop asking questions you won't get answers to." He turned his chair around, as did the others. Damian went to put a chair in the middle of the dance floor, then he walked back to the others. Naomi hit the remote. The light in the middle of the dance floor came on, shining on the seat. She hit the button for music. When it began to play, Dionte's face looked as if he knew the music. He stood up.

Khalif put his hand on his shoulder and said, "Relax, man, enjoy the show." Suddenly but stealthily, a silhouette crept on the floor. She walked around the chair, sat on it, and crossed her legs, then she opened them wide. She began to dance, a burlesque sensual dance. Her body moved on that seat like a slow grind on a man's lap. Dionte sat there mesmerized. He swallowed more times than he could count. Her hips swayed in a motion that would hypnotize a man in seconds. Who was this woman? Everyone just sat there and watched her dance. Damian and Naomi looked at Dionte. He looked like a kid opening his presents on Christmas. Khalif just smiled. Dana did as well. The lady danced seductively. Dionte never took his eyes off her. As the song started to finish, she pointed her finger to Dionte, gesturing for him to come to her. He sat still.

Khalif said, "Man, you better go and see what she wants."

"I don't know her, but I feel I do."

"There's only one way to find out." Dionte stood up and followed her upstairs to an office. She opened the door.

When Dionte came in, she whispered, "Close the door." He closed the door and walked to the desk. She sat down in this big leather seat. "Do you know who I am?"

"No, who are you?"

"My name is Keilani."

To be Continued.

"Keilani? From the radio show, Keilani?"

"Yes, Dionte."

"I'm your biggest fan."

"So, I hear, but I'm not a star."

"You are to me."

"Thank you for the compliment. I'm glad to hear that, but I am very humble. Gifted but humble." Dionte sat down like his knees were getting ready to buckle. "Are you okay? Do you need a glass of water or something?"

"No, I'm fine." He just stared at her.

"What's wrong?"

"I can't believe you're sitting in front of me."

"Would it help if I told you the same thing?"

"Why would you be interested in me?"

"I used to think the same thing—why would someone be interested in me until I found me."

"What do you mean?"

"Dionte, when you look at me, what do you see?"

"A fine woman of elegance."

"I thank you for being modest, but what do you actually see?"

"Well, I'm a man so—"

"Well, I hope you are because I'm not gay. What I want from you is your honesty."

"In my younger days, I would have said, your booty is plump like a tomato. I respect you, and I would use words with wisdom and tell you, as I said earlier, you are a fine woman of elegance."

"Most of my life that's what I heard. Oh, she fine. Look at her body, oh her waist is so small; oh, I would love to have her shape; look at her booty. I heard that all my life. Not one time did someone say I like who you are. It was always about how I looked, so I always went by how I looked, instead of becoming the person I am now. Oh, you look good in short shorts, so I wore them. Wear half shirts, I wore that. Wear thigh-high boots; I walked in them. But everything someone told me to wear, although I had the body to wear it, and I must say I looked good in it, it wasn't me. I had a voice but was listening to everyone else's.

"The day of graduation from high school, I found myself. I created me. I found my strengths, and they overpowered my weaknesses. My weakness was my silence; my strength was my voice. My weakness was I sat down; my strength was when I stood up. My weakness was I was afraid; my strength was courage. I wasn't afraid to be me any longer. I spoke when they told me to be quiet; I stood up when they told me to sit down; I ran when they told me I could only walk. I told myself I was beautiful when they called me ugly. What you see now, Dionte, took time to become. I spent many nights alone from heartbreak and pain. I had to be broken to become stronger. I have scars, but I'm not wounded. The reason why I'm here, Dionte, is because you heard my voice without seeing my face."

"Well, anyone that was listening that night heard your voice."

"No, Dionte, you heard me. It wasn't about how I sounded; it was the volume."

"I don't understand what you mean."

"You heard the depth of my emotions. You heard something different than anyone else. You felt something no one else felt that night."

"How do you know that?"

"Because when the music started playing, you stood up. I connect with you through the music I played. My music collaborates with how I'm feeling."

"I said that the night I heard you on the radio. I loved the collaboration. The music was a definition of your interlude. It didn't clash; it gave it a splash of color."

"What happened that night you heard me?"

"Seriously, I felt like you made love to me."

"You were the only one that felt that, that night."

"How do you know?"

"Because it was only for one person that night. That's how I am with my mind, body and soul. I only share myself with one person. When I speak, I have a targeted person in mind. I am not promiscuous. I don't want every man to feel what I'm saying, just one."

"How do you know when you found him?"

"The way he responds to me, like you did."

"But what if you're not compatible?"

"I don't think the worse. I just flow and see where it goes."

"Before we go any further, can we back this conversation up?"

"How far do you want to go back?"

"Back to you leaving the message on my voicemail."

"I'm listening, but before we start there, I think we need to go back a little further."

"How far?"

"The night you heard me on the radio."

"Okay, I'm listening."

"A couple of days after the show, I got a call from my uncle saying how someone was touched in a special way by my voice. I said oh, okay. Then he went into detail about how the person reacted to my voice, not what I said but my voice. It piqued my interest, so I asked what else happened. I liked the reaction. I wanted to see a picture of you. I got it, and I liked what I saw. Ironically, you were using my company for your t-shirts, so when your order was on back order, I wanted to leave you the message."

"You know I played that message fifteen times."

"Did you really?"

"I sure did."

"I'm glad to make a good impression on you."

"I had missed that voice. When I heard it, it was like a soothing drink. Your voice melts me, Keilani."

"I'm glad to have that effect on you."

"So how did I get here?"

"Hopefully. by a car."

"This club, your dancing, was this planned?"

"Like a well laid one."

"Who planned it?"

"Khalif did."

"How do you know him?"

"He's my uncle. Damian and Dana are my cousins. Years ago, we started businesses. Damian came into some money and opened a couple of clubs. He has another one in Miami. Since we are so close, he asked a few of us if we wanted to open businesses. What would we want to do? I'm very good with art, I like to draw a lot, so Dana and I went in together as partners to do the t-shirt company, and it's off to a good start."

"Yeah, I got that information from Khalif about ordering t-shirts through that company."

"Yes, it is very ironic, isn't it?"

"How were you able to be on the radio that night?"

"Kendrick is my brother. He is married to Desire. They were

going on their honeymoon, and she didn't have anyone to cover for her. She was going to re-run some earlier shows, and I told her you don't want to sound like a broken record. I told her about some stories that happened to me, and she said that was perfect. So, on Friday and Saturday, I did the show, and then she had someone else fill in the days I wasn't there."

"Tell me about this well-laid plan."

"I wanted to meet you. I wanted to see if I had the same effect on you in person that I did over the radio."

"Keilani, your body moves like the waves in the ocean."

"That's funny."

"What is?"

"How you say my body moves like the waves in the ocean."

"Why is that funny?"

"Because when I swim, I don't use my arms, just my body. It looks like the waves. I stay in the water mostly. You would think I was a mermaid. I love the way water feels on my skin. I swim twice a day. I exercise and dance in it as well; it keeps my body toned."

"Toned is an understatement. You're very sensual when you dance."

"I'm very sensual in a lot of ways. The way I think, walk, talk and dance is my energy. I'm confident in how I feel, and I show it in my movements. My body speaks before I open my mouth."

"I noticed that. Okay, back to the plan."

"So yes, I wanted to meet you so I asked my cousin if I could use his club before it opened. I knew you would be in town. I wanted to introduce myself to you with a performance. I would have given you a lap dance, but I didn't want to come off as easy, especially since we didn't know each other."

"I would've loved that."

"I know, but I wanted to get to know you in a different way. I don't want you to lose respect for me."

"You just don't know how much I wanted to be in that chair."

"I wanted you there. I felt your energy. But I want to get to know you without being sexual. In due time we may be that way, but I just want you to know me. I believe that's what you want too."

"Your body is full of seduction. I know that's something you can't turn off. It sends the right signals, Keilani; I can't help but be drawn to that."

"I could turn it off if I wanted to, but then I wouldn't be me. My seducing way of walking is not to draw men to me; it's to draw the man to me. My body has a way of moving that I have no control over, so when someone asks me why I walk this way, I tell them because I'm built to walk like that. It's like a car, the engine is built to run a certain way. I am built to walk and love a certain way."

"I've seen the way you walk. I love it, oh I so love it. What is it like loving Keilani?"

"Would you like to know?"

"Would you allow me to?" Keilani walked over to Dionte and touched his face.

He closed his eyes, and she asked, "You ever hear the story Can I Touch You There?"

"I don't think I have. Is it your story?"

"No, it's my brother's wife's story. It's about how they met."

"Do I need to listen to it?"

"It's about an unusual encounter, but they found love."

"Do you think our encounter is unusual?"

"It depends."

"On what?"

"On how you're feeling now."

"I felt the pulse of your heartbeat when you walked on the dance floor. I stood up and was ready to walk to you. I felt like this raging animal and you lassoed me in to tame me. The way I felt tonight is how I felt the night I heard you on the radio. I felt so relaxed, like a night of a Quiet Storm."

"What is a Quiet Storm?"

"You, Keilani, you are my Quiet Storm."

"Explain to me what that is."

"A quiet storm, you're like lightning. You see how it lights up the sky. That's how I felt when you entered the room. You lit it up with your aura. You ever hear the trickling of rain? It's soothing. The cracking of thunder, although it's loud, and it may scare you sometimes, still sounds good. I enjoy the storm, the sound of the thunder and rain. I lie in bed and hear the rain and it soothes me. The thunder awakens me, and then the rain settles me. You've awakened me, Keilani; you are my thunder and rain, my Quiet Storm. You caressed me with your voice, and you entertained me with your dance. I sat there quietly, but excited; you calmed the raging seas in me."

"Rain, hmm. Can I rain down on you?"

"Drench me, Keilani. I need it, I open my mouth. I want to taste every part of you. I don't want to miss anything."

"What's going on with us, Dionte?"

"I don't know, but I don't want to stop whatever it is."

"It feels so good, so, so good." There was a knock on the door. Keilani walked back to the chair and said, "Come in."

It was Damian. He said, "Well, I haven't seen you in like two hours. I wanted to make sure you were okay."

"Oh, we're doing fine. We were getting acquainted."

"Well, the club is going to open up in a couple of hours. Take all the time you need."

"Thank you, D. We will be down in a few." Damian left and closed the door.

"If you'll excuse me, I need to change my clothes."

"What's wrong with what you have on. I love it."

"Not my outfit but what's under it."

"Oh, you had a silky rainstorm?"

"Yes, I think my dam broke."

"Dang, it's like that."

"It is."

"I want to touch it. I'm being mannish, but I do."

"In due time. Let me go freshen up." Keilani walked in the bathroom. Dionte looked at her like a dog in heat; he wanted her badly, but at the same time he wanted to get to know this person who was making his temperature, amongst other things, rise. She came out of the bathroom with a bag.

She said, "Are you ready to go downstairs and join the others?"

"I would like to get to know more about you."

"Let me give you my number and then we can talk some more."

"I would like that."

"Me too." They walked downstairs to join the rest of the gang. As they walked towards them, they were smiling at Keilani and Dionte.

Keilani said, "What are you guys smiling about?"

"We were getting ready to get you a room at a hotel. You all were taking too long up there."

"Oh, we were just talking."

"You all could've done that down here," Khalif said.

"We wanted some privacy."

"I respect that," Khalif said.

"So, what's up for the rest of the night?" Keilani said to Dionte.

"I'm leaving tomorrow morning. I have a flight back to New York."

"I know. I have a busy schedule for tonight. I have deadlines that need to be done, so I'm going to say goodnight to you guys for now. Can you walk me to my car, Dionte?" She kissed her family goodbye, grabbed Dionte's hand, and they walked out to her car. It was the Porsche with the K on the license plate. She unlocked the door and told Dionte to get in. They got in the car, and she said, "I enjoyed tonight in so many ways. I never thought I would feel the way I do now. I don't want to lose how I'm feeling. The reason I'm leaving now is not only because of the deadline, but I don't want to cross boundaries that I set for myself. I promised myself I wouldn't sleep with a man until I know for sure he is serious about me. But at the same time, I've never had an encounter like this with a man before either. I don't want to ruin what could very well be good."

"I totally understand you. Having been hurt before, I really want to take my time with you. I think you're very special and I don't want to lose what I'm feeling."

"So, let's talk and see where this leads us to."

"I would like that very much."

"Can I kiss you, goodnight, Dionte?"

"I've been wanting to taste those lips all night." She leaned over and kissed him, her tongue tasting like peppermint, breath cool as the winter storm. After the kiss, Dionte touched his lips.

"Dang, girl, if your kiss feels like that, I can imagine what the rest of you can do."

"In due time you will find out. Good night, Dionte."

"Goodnight, Keilani." He was getting ready to open the door.

Keilani said, "Oh, I forgot to ask you, when you called did you get a reference number?

"Yes, I got one."

"Do you remember what it was?"

"Yes, it was LMCYLFD."

"Do you want to know what that means?"

"Yes."

"It means let me change your life forever, Dionte."

"I think you already did."

"Before you go, I have a gift for you. She took her underwear out of the bag and ran it across his nose. "You can sniff on these until I see you again."

Dionte took them and caressed the center that was still moist, he was aroused. He closed his eyes, inhaled slowly, and whispered, "OMG, Keilani."

TBC IN VOL. III

CHECKMATE - GAME OVER

Brown, red and orange leaves, along with others of various colors began falling on the ground; it was beginning to look and feel like fall. Summer had ended, and the fall was off to a great start. The weather began to change and so did clothing. Cleo packed away her summer gear and started pulling out the cold-weather wear. While around the house she'd have on her half shirt and boy shorts; she liked to be comfortable inside. She worked from home, so she barely went out; she'd go visit her friends and chill at the Karaoke bar on Friday nights, but when she wasn't doing any of that, she'd be at home.

Although she had lived in the area for some time, she was very discreet. She didn't want to be known; that was her life, and that's how she liked it. She had a lot on her plate in months to come. Besides working, she had a bridal shower and wedding to plan. Her best friend Desire's sister Simone was getting married in six months, and she'd asked Cleo to help her plan it. So, while she was working on her regular job, she was also coordinating the plans for the wedding and shower.

It was Friday evening. She'd clock off in ten more minutes, deciding then if she wanted to go to Karaoke night. She didn't perform; she just liked to see the entertainment. She wanted to see who got booed, and who the audience liked. Cleo could sing; she just didn't show that side of her. Hidden talent was what she had, and that's how she liked it. She checked the weather: fifty-one degrees, perfect for fall. She clocked off, found something to wear, took a shower, lip-glossed her kisser, dressed, and headed out for the night.

She asked Desire if she wanted to join her. Desire said she'd love to; she'd text Simone to see if she wanted to as well. Cleo told her what time to meet her there. Desire texted back, "Okay see you soon." Driving to her destination, Cleo hummed a song she'd heard on the radio at home. As she came to a red light, the song comes on. She smiled and bit her lip. She closed her eyes as she listened to it. She would love to sing this song with someone that she was serious with, no boy toy, no one-night-stand man. She'd want that serious kind of guy, the one who reads her like a newspaper, knows all the details about her, has the facts, that take-your-time-to-get-to-know-me kind of guy, yeah, that one right there, the one that's not afraid of her intellect.

The light turned green, the car behind her honked its horn, and she opened her eyes. She'd gotten lost in the moment. She started driving, the song ended, and she smiled again. It made her feel warm and cozy, so snug, like a romantic night in the winter in front of a fireplace. She arrived at the spot, parked her car, texted Desire and told her she'd be at the bar. Cleo grabbed a seat and ordered a drink.

"Desire joining you tonight?" the bartender asked.

"Yes, she is."

"I'll make sure to save her a seat."

"Thank you, David. Save two; her sister may be joining us." David sat two glasses on top of napkins and put out a reserved folded card in front of them next to Cleo so one would sit there.

"So, are you performing tonight?" David asked.

"Don't do me."

"I heard you. I know you, so don't act."

"You don't know squat."

"Don't make me call Mommy on you."

"And tell her what?"

"You're disrespecting your elders."

"Boy, bye, you are a year older than I am, and I don't consider you an elder. You're older than me; that's it." They laughed. David was the oldest out of five children. Cleo was the middle baby, and the other three lived out of town. Cleo and David were close. The crowd started to come in. The bar filled up quickly on Fridays. It was everyone's home away from home; they all knew each other and were pretty much family. Most of them had grown up together, raised families, still lived in the same neighborhood they had as children.

They all spoke to Cleo and David and found seats.

Desire and Simone came in and David gestured to their seats. "Hey, girl," Desire said to Cleo.

"Hey, boo, glad you can make it. Hey, Simone."

"Hey, Cleo." Simone came over and hugged her. "So, Simone, are you excited about getting married?"

"Super excited. I knew it was going to happen but not that soon."

"So how did he propose to you?"

"Well, a couple of months ago we were all out to dinner, and he realized how much I meant to him, but he had to go back home. He lived out of state, his business was there, so we communicated as distant lovers. It worked for a while, but I was missing him. I told him and he agreed, so one night on Skype he asked me what I was doing. I told him nothing. He said come outside. I jumped so quick and ran outside and there he was. I ran into his arms, and they felt so good. He said he needed to be closer to me, so he moved his business here. As we were going in the house, he said oh and I'd like to marry you. Kendrick and Desire knew. He pretty much proposed to me the night we had dinner, but we had to give each other time to make sure our hearts were ready to receive one another."

"So, where's the ring?" She showed her. "Oh, that's a sparkler; he's got good taste."

"Before he gave me the ring, I told him he didn't have to spend a lot on it. He already had it, so what I said wouldn't have mattered."

"Well, I'm happy for you, Simone. You deserve the best; we all do. And Desire, you are glowing, girl, what are you using on your skin?"

"Just the regular skin cleanser and moisturizer, nothing new."

"Well, whatever it is, keep using it. Your skin looks pretty."

"Thank you, girl. So, when are you going to hook up with someone, Cleo?" Desire asked.'

"We could've gone all night without you asking me that. I'm very particular. I want a certain kind of guy, and I'm ending this conversation."

"Good because I must use the restroom anyway," Desire said. She excused herself while the emcee introduced the acts.

"We have a few, not many, singing tonight. First we have Kay to do her song." She walked up to the mic. The music began. She started singing and was quickly booed off the stage. She flagged her hand and said, "Haters." The emcee said, "Next, we have Tiny and Ray doing a duet, let's welcome them." The audience clapped their hands. The music started. It got Cleo's attention and she turned around to see how this was going to turn out.

Tiny started to sing, and her voice sounded like nails on a chalkboard, screeching and irritating. They were booed off the stage before the second verse. Cleo was disappointed; she loved that song. It was almost like they desecrated it. At that moment, Desire came back from the ladies' room.

Simone asked Desire, "Girl, I thought you fell in the toilet and I had to plunge you out. Are you ok?"

"I think I might be pregnant."

"Are you serious, Desire? Omg, does Kendrick know?"

"Well, I just started feeling like this a couple of weeks ago. He and I talked about kids. We had put it off for a while so we could enjoy one another, but I may be."

Cleo said, "After we leave here we can go by the store and pick up a test and see, but first, let me correct something here before we go." Cleo got up to go to the stage. Desire and Simone turned around to see what she was going to correct. Cleo whispered something in the emcee's ear, and the emcee introduced Cleo. David smiled as he saw his sister getting ready to unleash her talent to the audience. He stopped cleaning glasses to see her debut.

Cleo said, "This song means a lot to me. I don't have a guy to sing the male part, but if you know the song, you can come up and help me sing it." The music started playing, and the audience started to boo. Cleo said, "Cut the music." The emcee did. She continued, "Just because the music is the same does not mean the voice is. Don't come for me until you heard me. Music please." She began humming into the intro of the song.

"You don't know, babe
When you hold me
And kiss me slowly
It's the sweetest thing
And it don't change
If I had it my way
You would know that you are

You're the coffee that I need in the morning
You're my sunshine in the rain when it's pouring
Won't you give yourself to me
Give it all, oh

I just wanna see
I just wanna see how beautiful you are
You know that I see it
I know you're a star
Where you go I follow
No matter how far
If life is a movie
Oh you're the best part, oh oh oh
You're the best part, oh oh oh
Best part

The audience was still and seductively swaying to her hypnotic voice. When the male part came, a gentleman from the audience sang as he walked up to the stage and sang.

It's the sunrise
And those brown eyes, yes
You're the one that I desire
When we wake up

And then we make love
It makes me feel so nice

You're my water when I'm stuck in the desert
You're the Tylenol I take when my head hurts
You're the sunshine on my life

I just wanna see how beautiful you are
You know that I see it
I know you're a star
Where you go I follow
No matter how far
If life is a movie
Then you're the best part, oh oh oh
You're the best part, oh oh oh
Best part

If you love me won't you say something
If you love me won't you
Won't you
If you love me won't you say something
If you love me won't you
Love me, won't you
If you love me won't you say something
If you love me won't you
If you love me won't you say something
If you love me won't you
Love me, won't you
If you love me won't you say something
If you love me won't you
If you love me won't you say something
If you love me won't you
Love me, won't you

The audience stood up and screamed. They loved it. The emcee said, "That's 'The Best Part' by Daniel Caesar and H.E.R and Cleo and, what's your name, sir?"

"My name is Lamar."

"Cleo and Lamar nailed it. They sang that thing. Let's hear it for Cleo and Lamar. That sounds like a cute couple name, are you both single? Let me stop, I'm an emcee, not Cupid, let's hear it for them again." The audience clapped. Cleo and Lamar left the stage. Lamar asked Cleo if he could buy her a drink.

She said, "I really have to go, but I thank you for filling in that spot for me; you have a nice voice."

"So, do you. Will I see you again?"

"Maybe not." Cleo walked fast to Simone and Desire and told them, "Let's go." Cleo kissed David goodbye and they left the bar. Cleo almost ran to her car.

Simone said, "Speed racer, hold up, what's your hurry?"

"We have to get to the store to get a test for Desire."

"Ok, Cinderella, it's not close to midnight yet, so I know your car is not going to turn into a pumpkin, and you didn't leave a glass slipper because I can see you still have on your shoes. What's spooking you?"

"Get in the car."

"But we drove here."

"Get in the car; I'll bring you back to it." They all got in the car. Cleo started driving.

Desire asked, "What's wrong, Cleo?"

"That song. That song means so much to me, and I sang it not knowing someone was going to help me sing it."

"But you did invite someone to help you sing it if they knew it."

"I know, I know, I know, but the way he sang it put me in a climaxing situation."

Desire and Simone said, "Ooh."

"How do you feel now?" Simone asked. Cleo looked at her and rolled her eyes.

"Oh, she needs to finish what she is feeling." Simone and Desire laughed. Cleo didn't find any humor in it.

"Cleo, what's the problem?"

"Nobody has made me feel like that before."

"Ok, I can totally understand that. Kendrick did that to me when I first met him, so I know that feeling," Desire said.

"Are you scared?"

"Hell, yeah."

"Of what?" Desire asked.

"That's the thing, I don't know."

"You're afraid of the unknown."

"Yes, something like that."

"The mystery of certain things that pull you out your comfort zone, that are not known to you can make you fearful, but don't be afraid of it. It may be a good thing," Simone said.

"Drop it. I don't want to talk about it anymore."

"Okay, we'll drop it for now, but you'll be thinking about it tonight." They pulled up to the drugstore and walked in to look for the test. Meanwhile, back at the bar, Kendrick and Jesse arrived. They greeted David and sat down to have a drink.

"Where are our ladies? They said they'd be here," Kendrick asked.

David said, "They stepped out for a minute with Cleo, they should be right back."

"Oh, if they're with Cleo, this could take a minute," Kendrick said. Lamar came up to the bar and ordered a drink. Kendrick noticed him. "Lamar is that you?"

Lamar turned around and noticed Kendrick. Lamar said, "Kendrick, what's going on?" Lamar got up and greeted him.

"Player, player. Listen, folks, this dude here played so many women, they set him up one time. He did a midnight run to one he was creeping with. When he got to the house, all ten women he was dating were there. They grabbed him, tied him up and college paddled his behind. He couldn't sit for a month, the booty still tender." They all laughed.

"Man, they whooped me worse than my own mama. I still got paddle scars; they look like stretch marks."

"So, what's going on, Lamar? Oh, let me introduce you to my best friend, Jesse. This is Lamar, Lamar, Jesse." They shook hands. "So, what brings you to this neck of the woods?"

"You know I'm over the JDRF, that basketball court we use to play hoops on back in the day? We're trying to get the neighborhood kids involved in some after-school activities, keep them off the video games. Get them into some activities where they can move their bodies like we did back then, so they won't end up obese and diabetic."

"That sounds like a good plan. Let me know what I can do to help. You know I'm all about the kids."

"You have any yet, Kendrick?" Lamar asked him.

"No, not yet. My wife and I, we're getting up there in age, but if we have one, I believe we'll be good parents."

"You have any?"

"I have nieces and nephews, that's all I need."

"I hear you on that one. So, did you see the performances tonight?"

"Man, did I. I was part of one."

"What, you, up there singing? Black man can jump but sing? Nope, you have to show me that one."

"Oh, he did quite well, I must say," David said.

"By yourself?"

"No, with Cleo."

"Ooh," Kendrick.

Jesse said, "What's that ooh about?"

"Cleo is not your average kind of girl; she's like an aphrodisiac. She makes you feel a certain kind of way that's not normal. She doesn't do it on purpose; it's just in her."

"Oh, that's why I was feeling like that. Man, parts of me were moving like she was playing the flute and a snake was coming out of the basket." They laughed. Lamar didn't.

Kendrick said, "Oh, so anyways, did you get her number or something?"

"No, she hurried out with the two ladies she was with."

"That must've been Simone and Desire. Let me text them and let them know we are here," Jesse said.

"So, Lamar, you still playing the field?"

"Not really."

"What does not really mean?"

"I'm not ready for commitment."

"Oh, I see."

"What does that mean?"

"It means, don't try Cleo. She's all about that loyalty. You see, Lamar, she's the type of woman that you get when you come out of the game, not the one to get when you're in it. You've probably had some good women who wanted to love and take care of you. The hearts that you played with should've been the one you stayed with. There's no upgrade once you've had a good woman. Yeah, women, they come a dime a dozen, but Cleo has a carton of her own. She's in a class of her own."

"Why didn't you get with her?"

"Because she's my niece, fool. I do my family, but not like that. I protect them, so before you think about messing over her, don't."

Jesse came back and said, "Simone and the ladies are at the store. They'll be back shortly."

Kendrick looked at Lamar and said, "Do we have an understanding?"

"Yes, we have one."

"Good. David, give the man what he wants, put it on my tab."

At the store, Cleo was looking for a pregnancy test, Simone was texting Jesse, and Desire was in the restroom. Cleo found one, paid for it, and took it to Desire.

"Do you want to take the test here or wait until you get home?"

"I can wait; I'm liquid out. I don't have any more to share on a stick."

"How do you feel?"

"I feel fine, just queasy, but I feel ok."

"Good. Well, finish up in there so I can get you back to your husband." Desire washed her hands and came out. Cleo noticed a certain look on her face.

"What's wrong?"

"I was thinking if I am pregnant, am I going to be a good mother."

"Desire, baby look at me. You are the best at everything you do. That's the last thing you need to worry about. You take good care of your husband; you've taken care of your family. It will all come naturally. If you want to practice, get a puppy before your child is born. See how you interact and take care of it; that will help you along the way."

"A puppy, really, Cleo?"

"Well, girl, get a fish. Let's go." They got in the car and headed back to the bar.

On the way back, Desire asked Cleo, "Do you still have that feeling going on?"

"I'm okay now. Looking for that test took my mind off what I was feeling, so yes, I'm good."

"Do you want that feeling again?"

"Good question."

"Do you have an answer?"

"Apparently not if I didn't give you one."

"Still a sassy mouth."

"You know me well."

"Well answer me this, do you think he felt the same way as you?"

"It was just a song. It was soul-drenching the way he sang it to me. He was speaking directly to me. I don't know if he sung it that way because he was feeling the song, or he was feeling me. He doesn't know me, so I doubt he was singing directly to me. Whatever he was doing, it got to me, and I'm a hard nut to crack."

"If you had a chance, would you ask him how he felt tonight?"

"I'm not interested in him, so I wouldn't ask him anything."

"Okay, so you summed up the conversation. I won't ask you anything else about it." The ten-minute drive back to the bar passed in complete silence. When they arrived, Desire and Simone got out, but Cleo stayed in the car with it still running.

Desire said, "You're not getting out?"

"I think I'm going to head home."

"I have to use the restroom again. I'm going to take the test here. I would like you to be here when I take it."

"Okay, let me park, and I'll be right in." Desire waited for Cleo to park. She found a spot and they all headed in. Simone saw Jesse first. She walked up to him and kissed him. Desire saw Kendrick and went over to him. Cleo saw Lamar and frowned. Lamar saw Cleo and smiled. The only empty seat was next to Lamar. As Cleo walked over to sit next to him, she felt that feeling again. As she got closer, the pulsation of it was faster and faster. When she sat down next to him, she grabbed her stomach and closed her eyes.

Lamar and Cleo both said OMG. They looked at each other and said, "You felt it too." Kendrick, Desire, Jesse, and Simone looked at Cleo and Lamar. Cleo closed her eyes again, still holding her stomach. Lamar looked at her and whispered in her ear, "What are you feeling?"

Cleo took Lamar's hand and placed it on her heart; he felt the rapid pulse beating. He said, "What do you feel, Cleo?

She opened her eyes and whispered, "You're making orgasmic intercourse to my soul. I'm heightened in places unknown to me, but it feels so good. Lamar, it feels so, so good. I'm in a place I've never been before, and I don't want to leave. My whole body feels your touch. Every place you touch me, I climax. You're just into me so deep."

Cleo inhaled and let out a seductive exhale. "What did you feel?" she asked Lamar.

"Nothing, absolutely nothing."

"Oh, I see." Cleo got up and grabbed Desire and went in the bathroom; Kendrick looked at Lamar like he wanted to punch him.

Kendrick got up, went over to Lamar and said, "I think it's best you go. By the time she comes out, please be gone. If she's hurt, please, I beg you, please don't be here. Better yet, let me escort you to the door because obviously, you still haven't matured yet."

"You can't put me out. This isn't your bar."

David said, "But it is mine, and that's my sister. I think its best you go now."

"So, it's like that now?"

"Don't make this harder than what it is."

"I didn't think a woman could make me feel the way she did."

"So why didn't you tell her that?"

"Because I'm scared. I'm scared that she could actually pull me out of my game status."

"You want to be like that all your life, just playing with women's hearts and emotions. Why don't you just stay single?"

"I like companionship."

"Okay, so tell me this, do you let them know that this is only temporary, you don't plan on being with them, you just want a beneficial relationship with no commitment?"

"That works for me."

"This fool. What were your plans with Cleo again? Oh, that's right, there are none. Have a good night, Lamar." Lamar got up and left.

Cleo said to Desire in the ladies' room, "I thought you had to go to the bathroom. I came in here so you can take the test. I poured out my soul to that man and he told me he felt nothing. I feel like such a fool." Desire flushed the toilet, came out and handed Cleo the test wrapped in tissue.

Desire said, "What does it say?"

Cleo looked and said excitedly, "I'm going to be an auntie! I'm so happy for you and Kendrick; you guys are going to be so good at this."

"Yes, this is a lot to take in."

"When are you going to tell him?"

"You think I should do it now in front of family and friends?"

"I couldn't think of a better time." They freshened up and walked back to the bar. Everyone was there except Lamar. Cleo was okay with that. Desire went to Kendrick and asked, "How good are you on test results?"

Kendrick looked confused. He said, "Depending on what kind of results you're looking for on a test?"

"I figured you would say that. I took this test, and I'm having a hard time reading the results."

"What kind of test did you take?" She handed him the pregnancy test. He said, "In college, they never told us how to read one of these, and I never had to read one before, so in my debut of reading this, it looks like I'm going to be a daddy. Did I pass the test?"

"With flying colors, baby, with flying colors." Kendrick hugged Desire and then kissed her. Simone screamed.

"I'm going to be an auntie! OMG, I'm so happy for you guys."

Kendrick said, "This calls for a drink. David, give Desire lemon water; the rest order what you want." David fixed their drinks. Kendrick made a toast. "Raise your glasses. Here's to us being new parents! May we be the best ones. Cheers."

Everyone said, "Cheers." Simone hugged Desire, and so did Cleo. Jesse went and shook Kendrick's hand and hugged him.

Jesse said, "Man, I'm so happy for you guys. You're going to be awesome parents."

"Yeah, we said that we would wait, but no better time than the present." They celebrated for the rest of the evening, and in the wee hours of the morning, they all ventured home. In the morning, Cleo got up. She needed to run to the store to pick up items for dinner. She threw on something quick to run to the store. She put her buds in her ears and turned on her favorite song. She grabbed a cart and strolled through the aisle humming. Her body swayed with the music; she was in her own world and she loved it.

She turned the corner of the aisle. Lamar came down the aisle she just turned from. He walked and hummed, she strolled and hummed. Both had buds in their ears so neither one heard each other. She turned the corner, and he came down the aisle she was leaving. She backed up to go down the aisle she just left; he backed up and went to the opposite aisle. They still didn't see or hear each other.

She found what she was looking for and so did he. They started walking down the aisle together on opposite sides. She started singing more loudly and so did Lamar. By the time they got to the end of the aisle, they saw a crowd of people looking at them. They took out their earbuds, still singing, and heard each other. They fully came out of the aisle and saw each other. Lamar smiled. Cleo didn't. People started clapping. One said, "You all sound so good, you gave the store a concert." Cleo went to the register to buy her items; Lamar went to another one to purchase his. She left the store first and went to her car. Lamar came out and approached Cleo.

She said, "What do you want?"

"I deserve that. Last night I should've been more honest with you. Can I make it up to you?"

"What's there to make up? You said you didn't feel anything; there's nothing else to say."

"I lied to you. Let me cook dinner for you tonight. I can explain myself."

"I don't even like you, Lamar."

"After I talk to you tonight, you may like me, maybe even love me."

"I'm not in the mood for that either."

"Somethings you don't prepare for. They just happen."

"Well, I'm not looking for anything to happen."

"Oh, but it did last night. Here's my address and phone

number. I expect you around seven." Lamar left Cleo, got in his car and drove away. Cleo watched him leave. She thought is this some type of game. Would he do to her tonight what he did last night? Was this a waste of her time? She had enough time to think about it. Cleo got home and texted Desire about what just happened at the store. Desire texted back.

"Are you going tonight?"

"He shot me down last night like target practice. I don't know if I want to relive that again."

"Maybe what he wanted to say, he didn't want to say in front of company. Go tonight, Cleo, at least give him a minute to explain himself. I won't call it all lost just yet."

"He is kind of cute."

"Listen to his heart. This is not about how he looks; it's about how he feels."

"Yes, dear, I will, so is Kendrick ecstatic about being a daddy?"

"That's all he talked about on the way home."

"Well, I'm happy for the both of you. He's going to be a good daddy. He does a good job being an uncle, so the daddy part shouldn't be a problem for him. And you will do an awesome job, don't worry yourself. Ok, let me find something to wear tonight. I'll give him one more chance. I'll let you know how it goes tonight."

"Yes, please keep me posted."

"From the minute I step in the door. Chat later."

"Ok, talk to you later." Cleo went back to bed. Since she didn't have to cook, she wanted to get rested up for tonight.

Meanwhile, at Kendrick's house, Desire said to her husband, "Cleo ran into Lamar at the store. He invited her for dinner tonight. I told her she should give him another chance."

"If he knows what's good for him, he'd better do right by her. I don't play when it comes to my family, Desire, you know that."

"I do, baby. What do you want for breakfast?"

"Nothing right now. I just want you to lie in my arms so I can stroke your belly." Desire got back in the bed and lay in his arms. He started stroking her belly.

He said, "We waited so long for this. I'm so happy. I hope the baby comes out looking like me."

"He or she will; you have strong genes in your family."

He kissed her on her forehead, and said, "I sure hope he does." Desire smiled; she didn't notice that Kendrick didn't. Later that afternoon, Cleo got up and went online to check out ideas for Simone's bridal shower. While doing that she texted Lamar to say that she would be coming over for dinner tonight. He texted back, "I'm looking forward to seeing you." She had two hours until dinner. She picked up her guitar, sat by the bay window, looking at the leaves falling, and strummed a few strings.

The wind blew leaves in front of the house. She saw them swirling. Some brushed against her window. It was a perfect day in October, and it was beautiful. She played about ten minutes and then watched the children play in the leaves. She remembered her youthful days when she did the same thing. Time had passed so quickly. She still felt youthful but not as energetic. She checked the clock. She had an hour and some minutes. She showered and got dressed, headed out early so she could get some gas. That would give her twenty-five minutes to get to his house at seven even.

After gassing up the car, she headed to Lamar's, thinking of what kind of night this was going to be. Was she going to be disappointed? She couldn't shake how he made her feel last night, but she was going to his house anyway. She would have to wait and see how this turned out. She pulled up to his house and sat there. It was six fifty-five; she turned off her car and sat there. She took a deep breath and didn't budge.

She saw his front door open. He walked to her car, gestured her to roll down the window.

He said, "Dinner is ready, but I'd prefer you come in and eat it. This is not a curbside dinner date order to go kind of night." Cleo smiled. She rolled her window up. He opened her door and then closed it, and he grabbed her hand and walked her into his home. It was so warm and cozy, just how she felt last night. It looked like the night was off to a great start. Lamar poured her a glass of wine and then asked, "Are you ready to eat?"

"Not really. I'm more interested in what you have to say."

"Okay, then let's talk, and maybe your appetite will come later. Let me put the food in the oven to keep it warm." She agreed. Lamar went into the kitchen to put the food up and returned. "I first want to apologize about last night, I should've been truthful, but I haven't been that way to a woman in years.

"That song we sang last night that was my song to sing to the woman I'd fall in love with. I was saving that song. I said I wouldn't sing it until I knew she was the one, the only one."

"Okay, I'm listening."

"I'm really hoping that you are.

"As many times as I've heard that song, it sounded so different when it started playing, when you started to sing it. I was smitten by the sound of that poetic whisper out of those beautiful lips. Parts of me were awakened that did not need to be touched. I sat there and was not going to say a word. The more you sang, I kept hearing 'go to her, she needs you, not just to sing that song, she needs you, she is your best part.'"

"Why didn't you say this to me last night?"

"I wasn't ready for commitment. I come from a family of men who played the field their whole life. I grew up around that. That's what they taught me, and that's what I did. I was so good at it, I got bored with it. It didn't mean anything to me. I had to go back and apologize to the women I hurt. Cleo, I don't want to do that anymore.

Check-mate game over. You got me in a position where I can't move in that direction, no matter how I try. I was supposed to be with someone last night. I didn't have the desire to go, so I came home and thought about you all night.

"I want to do something different with you that I've never done with any woman before. I want you to be my friend. I don't want to be intimate with you. We were that last night. I just want you to be my friend; I need you to be that for me, please. I don't want to jeopardize anything that's so special, and that you are, Cleo. So, what do you say, my friend, will you be mine?"

Cleo stood up and said, "No. Can I go now?"

"After all that, you're going to shoot me down?"

She smiled and said, "How does it feel to get shot down off of that high?"

"I deserved that. I should've been more considerate of your feelings last night, but I am now."

"That's good to know. Yes, Lamar, I'll be your friend. We will grow as we go."

"I'm glad to know that. Now shall we eat?"

"I'm starving." Lamar fixed their plates and they talked for the rest of evening.

Thanksgiving, they had dinner over at Kendrick's and Desire's house. Simone, Jesse, Cleo, and Lamar filled the seats at the table. Kendrick was glad that everything worked out with Lamar and Cleo; she looked happy. He glanced around the table to see everyone happy. He looked at his beautiful wife, with her pregnancy glow. He just stared at her, but not with a look of love.

After dinner was over, they all packed a plate of leftovers; they hugged and kissed each other goodnight and went home to get ready for Black Friday shopping in the morning. Kendrick and Desire cleaned up the kitchen and then headed to bed.

When they got into bed, Kendrick said to Desire, "Baby."

"Yes."

"Remember last month when I said that I hope the baby looks like me?"

"Yes, I remember you saying that."

"You want to know why I said that."

"Why?"

"Because I can't have any children, Desire."

TBC IN VOL. III

ABOUT THE AUTHOR

Author Erica C Thomas was born and raised in the City of Brotherly Love (Philadelphia). From a family of five, she is the mother of three beautiful children and the grandmother of two girls. With a wit of comedy and sarcasm, as a young girl, she always found herself listening to music of all kinds, loving music so much she began to write songs. With a themed notebook, she would write songs. Lyrics were the easy part; writing the music was complicated, but the sound of music was in her soul. She didn't go far with her talent in that field, but years later her talent would arise again. What was dormant became a format on paper. With a pen and her imagination, she debuted as an author, writing her first book, Short & Sassy in 2018. She found her purpose again. She loves to write how she feels, and she is sharing it by releasing her thoughts to the world on paper. She comes from a family of talent. She also loves to minister. She cares for others, lending an ear to hear and a mouth to speak in the time of need.

VOL III COMING SOON!